VICTORIES

ALSO BY GEORGE V. HIGGINS

V·I·C·T·O·R·I·E·S

George V. Higgins

ANDRE DEUTSCH

First published in Great Britain in 1991 by
André Deutsch Limited
105-106 Great Russell Street, London WC1B 3LJ

Published in U.S. in 1990 by
Henry Holt and Company, Inc.

British Library Cataloguing in Publication Data
Higgins, George V. (George Vincent) *1939-*
Victories.
I. Title
813 54 [F]

ISBN 0 233 98670 7

Printed and bound in Great Britain by
St Edmundsbury Press, Bury St Edmunds, Suffolk

283445

VICTORIES

1

In the winter of 1947, Joseph W. Martin, Jr., a portly man of Republican affiliations, dour appearance, and publicly phlegmatic disposition from southeastern Massachusetts, at the age of sixty-two commenced his eleventh term of membership in the House of Representatives of the Congress of the United States. He ascended notably in rank as he did so, succeeding Sam Rayburn, sixty-five, a Texan as well as a man of formidable bulk, magnetic personality, and entering his eighteenth term; the previous three he had spent majestically—some said tyrannically—as Speaker elected by the Houses controlled by his fellow Democrats. President Harry S Truman was reported little soothed by reminders that his fellow Americans had proven no more ungrateful for their successful wartime leadership than had the British voters who had seemed to repudiate the party coalition under Churchill that had inspired their nation to persevere to victory over Germany; the President, rumored to express himself privately in language even stronger than the blunt words he favored in his public utterances (he had not yet issued public reactions to newspaper music critics displeased by his daughter Margaret's art at the piano), was reported plainly unappeased.

Speaker Martin seemed to move as cautiously in his new position as he had argued, as a minority member, in his unsuccessful efforts to urge fiscal restraint upon preceding Democratic majorities. But his

1

caution implied no stupidity or shortsightedness to his Republican colleagues who had come to know him well over the years; they found him, as they had hoped, fully cognizant of the vicissitudes of power, and as mindful of the necessity to seize the days that favored them as avidly as their Democratic colleagues had during their own.

Among those loyalists had been Robert D. Wainwright, a spare man about five eight, whose approaching sixtieth birthday would coincide with his fifth term representing the voters of the Second District of Vermont. He knew every one of them by name, those he distrusted and disliked, the many whom he had found to be passable, and the few he actually respected as well (Bob Wainwright did not squander time acquiring or considering information that would have enabled him to make careful judgments upon whether he liked people that he met, or they liked him; he had a wife—both her parents and his were dead—and he liked her well enough, so as far as he could see he'd gotten along all right with that approach for over fifty years, and it was adequate).

His knowledge was not the superficial kind that came from listening attentively to inquiries and complaints that voters had addressed to him in 1938 when he had first run for office. It was the kind he had acquired in the course of his employment over his previous thirty years, starting in 1908, as treasurer of the Canterbury Trust Company. In his mature years he would say if pressed very hard that at twenty, two years out of business school in Burlington, he had not been qualified of course to take on even the job as assistant treasurer, job that size, "even in a bank that small, less'n thirty years old," omitting the fact that his father, Robert Sr., had remained in place as treasurer and his overseer until 1931, when Robert was forty-three and his father had moved up to president of the board of directors, still in the office every day. That allowed Wainwright to permit his listeners to assume he must have been qualified at twenty, knowing that they lacked the facts and would therefore be mistaken. A Wainwright always knew everything about his constituents, things they didn't know themselves. And they knew nothing about him, though they believed they knew a lot.

His grandfather had believed that was the right mixture of things. Thomas Wainwright had inherited the family farm in Canterbury, south and west of Addison, two miles from the eastern shore of Lake

Champlain and "across the other side" from Port Henry, NY. Joseph, Thomas's father, was the first known native-born of his branch of the Vermont Wainwrights; in 1849, when he died, Thomas had just turned sixteen years old. He had immediately and quietly, with no fanfare whatever nor any family discussion, pledged the entire value of the property to the hilt, investing the proceeds equally in sheep and railroad stock. Twelve years later he had paid off the loans entirely with profits made from production of wool for Union Army uniforms needed for the Civil War, leaving him with the farmland and the railroad equities.

He held on to the Vermont Central, and the Connecticut and Champlain (renamed the Rutland and Burlington in 1847), holding his tongue when wiser men told him the lake traffic north and south would carry all the freight there'd ever be. It didn't. In 1877, he began to see the first carpetbaggers fleeing by-then worthless sheep farms and climbing onto trains at Montpelier, leaving for free, fertile lands on the plains of Kansas, and what they thought were riches in promised lands of New Mexico and Colorado; he considered his son Robert, then but three years away from his twenty-seventh birthday, unmarried, but still settled and farming, and he consulted his moneyed friends. He determined that the time had come to embark on something new.

"What we need, gentlemen," he had told his friends, and told his son less formally, "is an enterprise that will enable us to combine the best resource that we own with the best resource the state has left. The railroads are the one we own. The one we don't is timber, and as this country grows westward, at least for the next two decades, this country will need lumber desperately. Therefore I think the thing for us to do is to form new local small banks. Banks that will lend money to strapped farmers much more readily than the big banks in the cities. Banks that will begin small and stay small, but take risks. That farmers who are now in trouble will be glad for our kind help."

Thomas's rich friends had jeered him. They called him a damned fool, and said that while he might lose all his money if he wished, they would not risk theirs with him. They said if he loaned money to those farmers he would lose it, because he'd find out in short order that they couldn't pay it back. They said he'd lost his mind.

3

"Hear me out," he said. "You didn't see me hollering in the Reverend Burchard's meetings in the tents along the line. You didn't hear me there, talking in tongues, or casting devils out. Of course they will not meet those loans we give. And then what do you think will happen? We will have their land. Their land with trees that they don't like. Good Vermont hardwood. Timber to cut and load on trains, trains that belong to us. To take to sawmills that we own, and then to markets elsewhere. Markets more accessible to us than they will ever be to Maine or New Hampshire. And this in a state in which many men are out of work. Who will stay if we can give them honest day's work for an honest wage." Thomas Wainwright's friends had grasped his point.

His son, Robert, had required even less argument, and no reminder that he did his farming on land that his father owned, lived in a house his father owned, depended on his father for his food and pocket money, and had no prospect whatsoever of ever owning anything, except the right to work for wages for someone else when his father died, unless he at once devoted his attentions to mastering bookkeeping and took immediate steps to acquire a wife who would give him a family in the house that his father would provide for him in Canterbury.

The bank opened in 1882. It had functioned precisely as Thomas Wainwright had predicted and demanded that it should, maintaining farmers stretched to their limits until, financially unable to let their land lie fallow, they had at last exhausted their arable fields by over-tillage. Robert foreclosed with tight-lipped displays of reluctance. Thomas had warned him never to betray any other emotion on such sad occasions, showing neither his gratification at the bank's acquisition of two or three hundred acres of ruined real estate (it would be valuable timberland in twenty years) nor his satisfaction in the bank's immediate sure profit from a couple hundred acres of virgin maple and oak that the farmer and his predecessors had never gotten around to cutting. He hid as well his glee that things were working as planned, and at the sheriff's auctions he invariably found, just as Thomas had predicted, the bank was the only bidder for the amount of the unpaid mortgage.

Robert had been systematically engaged in his sixth year of that quiet process of acquisition when Robert Jr. was born in August of 1888. The new baby's father by then was no farmer anymore. Robert Sr. was an experienced professional, thirty-five and most solemn, able to handle calmly the inevitable disruption of a small child in the home. He ignored it. He had by then become quite accustomed to his work as well, reassuring depositors made nervous that the assets put up by the stockholders of the Canterbury Trust were "more than ample to cover" the mortgage defaults that they saw exploding around them each day.

"I hope you'll think of that," Robert would say, as Thomas had instructed him, "if the day should ever come when someone shall come up to you and say that you should shift all of your deposits to one of those savings banks, or some fool newfangled cooperative, that has little more to lend than the deposits that it gets, because none of them is insured if those loans are not repaid. This bank is named because of what it is: a trust. It is a trust of the monies that our depositors give us, but it is also a trust declared by our stockholders, who have pledged their private assets to make sure the bank stays solvent. As solid as a rock. They have their faith in this county, and this country, and its people, and they have backed it up with their own hard cash, and you should remember that."

In 1927, Thomas Wainwright died at the age of ninety-four in his sleep, in his bed, on the farm in Canterbury where he had lived all his life, the stockholders surviving and succeeding by inheritance those who had died since 1882, through the bank he had envisioned jointly owned more than 100,000 acres of mixed fallow-farm and woodland, extending through the western area of the state south of Burlington all the way to Rutland, from the western slopes of the Green Mountains over the crests to the foothills on the other side. By shrewd expenditure of capital, Robert Sr. added another 40,000 acres during the Depression.

On the May morning in 1947 when Speaker Joe Martin called upon "Young Bob Wainwright," as he always called him (Robert Jr. was then fifty-nine), in his basement office in the Longworth Building— the Speaker did not stand on ceremony, and Bob Wainwright had no wish to leave the dark, small, and cramped space he'd had since 1938, even temporarily—to propose a matter to him, that land his grandfather and father had spied was at the back of his mind, as indeed it often was.

The Speaker's purpose was to carry out a promise he had made in

5

caucus to his party five weeks before, when they had met to plan their tactics after Easter recess. He had made the point then that as a minority for so many years, they had been thwarted at every turn by the Democratic majority in their own chamber, and frustrated as well at every other turn. "The Senate's been Democratic. The Supreme Court has been, too. The President . . ." There had been a few sour grins. No matter what they wished to do for their party or their districts, unless they had first kowtowed to Democrats, most of them had not prevailed. The Depression had hit them first, then all those public works that you couldn't vote against if you had to run again, and unlike two-thirds of the senators, who didn't run each time, they always had to run. And then the war had come along, and yes, the man had led the country, but doing just as damned little as he could to help them out.

Therefore, the Speaker had suggested, it was time for putting on their thinking caps. For a while they had the House. That "while" might not last. They'd have to bargain with the Senate still, of course, and Truman in the White House was no easy mark. But still they had some power, the first time in many years, and after all those TVAs, and REAs, and so forth, wasn't it about time they got something for themselves? Something solid, to help people, but still, to help themselves. After all, that was how the Democrats had prospered, was it not? By taking care, when helping people, always to help themselves. Using other people's money.

Bob Wainwright had gone home for Easter thinking about Lancaster Notch, and he had come back again, thinking the same thing. He did not tire the Speaker with all the facts as he knew them; the Speaker, after all, was a swamp Yankee from Massachusetts, and he was a Yankee from Vermont, and there wasn't any need for him to waste the Speaker's time with a lot of history that wouldn't interest him. "I have thought about it, Joe," Wainwright said. "I've thought about it a good deal.

"I came in here in thirty-nine, and it's been just as you said, every year since the first day I came through that door. All I ever heard was 'help the people, help the people,' but damned if I could ever see how we were helping mine. And a lot of mine needed help.

"Now," he said, pronouncing it *naiow*, "it's not as though a man who

6

looked real close up at my district, all these years since the Big Crash, it's not as though a man like that would not find people needing help. But could I get it for 'em? No. I could not do it. 'Next year,' and then after, it was: 'Year after next, for sure.' But somehow it never come.

"All right," he said, and he leaned forward, "well, you've got my hopes up now. I've got this place, Lancaster Notch, poor as poor can be. It's been damned poor since 'fore the Crash, and all it's done's get worse. There's people livin' up there, Joe, and they could use some help. And if we help those people, why, no tellin' what she'll do. Might bring some jobs in, make some money, put our veterans to work. And I say that that's what we do. Lancaster needs our help, and if you want the history of it, well, I'll give it to you. But otherwise I think all I need's to say: a road. Just give me a goddamned road."

The road Young Bob Wainwright asked for was rammed through in a compromise of public works appropriations passed and signed in January of 1948. Construction began the following spring. It was nine miles of two-lane, east-west, uphill, downhill, curving blacktop, sheer hell in the winter and no picnic on summer nights either, when night ground fog comes in and lies down in the valleys. But it connected Lancaster Notch to Occident, Vermont, and it opened in the summer of 1949. It remains in fairly good repair today; it should, because after all, it is a federal road.

The road descends steeply through what remains of the dense hardwood forest, woodland silent with the history that Wainwright saw no reason to impose upon the Speaker back in 1947.

The forest attracted the interest of the Stapleton Lumber Company in the early 1920s. The company acquired logging rights to more than three thousand acres, and rights-of-way to construct a narrow-gauge railroad spur that snaked laden with tall logs through the deep snow down the mountainside and crawled back up again, empty except for provisions for the loggers and hands. At the lower end of the spur, west of Charlotte, near the Connecticut River, the spur connected at a junction of the normal-gauge railroad purchased over forty years before by Thomas Wainwright and his friends, and handy as well to the mills they built there at the end of the spur. The big train carried the finished lumber south and west to the big cities devouring wood, as long as the mills could produce it. The men could cut, and the small railroad could carry, enough logs in winter to stockpile the mills in the flatlands until harvest-time in the fall, so the mill workers came and remained. But when mudtime came in the spring every year, and it was no longer possible for horses to pull the logs out of the high woods to the platform near the small train, the workers on the mountain dispersed to their homes in Canada and Maine, and the high operation shut down until the first frost came. Still, from the first, a few of the highlanders stayed.

The Depression halted the building industry in 1930, gradually forcing Stapleton to close its tracts and its mill, abandoning the railroad that connected them along with the acreage it had optioned and its railroad right-of-way to reconquest by forest and weeds. An estimated ninety men lost their jobs, loading their duffel on the logging flatcars for the train's last run down the mountain, through the center of the village of Occident, then farther west through the flat meadows between Occident and Charlotte, ignoring cows out to pasture who raised their heads and looked sleepily and puzzled at the same train they had seen the day before, not remembering it the next day, or the other after that, when they would not see it again, nor miss it when they did not. Most of the men took the passenger train north to Burlington, changing for trains heading farther north to their homes in Canada, and they did not return.

The seven or so families that had settled in the Notch and built homes on land they did not own, having nowhere else to go when they arrived, and nowhere else since then, scavenged ferally in what remained of the Stapleton occupation. The managers had ferried a few cows up the mountain on the train, to provide milk for cooking food for the lumberjacks and crews, and had not bothered to retrieve them. The stragglers took them in. There was one old bull, kept to freshen the cows, and they bred him to exhaustion. When a new female was born, they were delighted, but when a new male arrived, they were overjoyed. They raised four males to adulthood and then castrated them, avoiding interbreeding—they were poor, not stupid—and making good use of them as oxen to take over the plowing, as the old lumber dray horses grew feeble and died. They grew corn in the stripped earth where the trees had been, feeding it to pigs raised for market and meat, and with fair success cultivated fields of clover and grass that kept the cows and a couple small sheepfolds. In the spring and the summer they caught trout from the rapid white streams that rolled over the rocks down the mountain, and they hunted deer, squirrel, birds, and wood-chucks, without license or care for the season. They ate everything that they shot. They did not go down from the highland; when their children reached puberty, they selected mates from among others there.

The train engine, tender, and rolling stock rusted in the yard west of Charlotte, its landlords frustrated in their efforts to force removal by Stapleton, long gone into bankruptcy. When Lend-Lease first restored and then multiplied the value of scrap iron, the station landlord hired men who used welding torches to cut up the stock and load it onto trains heading south toward resmelterers.

The population of the Notch reached its peak of about 225 in the years immediately after World War Two, when the GI Bill guaranteed all returning veterans cheap home financing, and the lumber industry returned to vigorous life. Court proceedings instituted by the heirs of the owners of the bankrupt Stapleton company established that while its receivers had not placed any value on the timber rights acquired after World War One, finding them worthless at the time, the creditors whose monetary rights had been secured by that collateral had elected to accept the then-valueless rights in lieu of further payment. Therefore, the courts ruled, those rights had not reverted to the Stapleton stockholders but remained, whatever their current and presumably increased value, including all timber grown up on the property since its closure years before, the property of the defaulted creditors. Those were the heirs of Thomas Wainwright and his associates.

Ably assisted by the support of his colleagues in the Eightieth Congress (none of whom knew any of this history, any more than he knew any of the background of the projects he voted for in their behalf; there were small similarities, but all were tactful gentlemen, mindful of one another's time), Robert D. Wainwright, R., Vt., therefore on that occasion at least effectively demonstrated his close attention to the needs of his district by securing passage of federal funding for the construction of the mountain road in 1948, "to serve the vital economic interests of the region."

9

Wainwright, who had briefly succeeded his father as treasurer of the Board of Directors of the Canterbury Trust before his campaign for Congress, at once undertook arrangements to finance complementary private undertakings by reputable local businessmen who similarly wished to advance the economic interests of the region. Most of those businessmen served on the board of directors of the bank. Congressman Wainwright and his wife also invested in logging rights, "to show our faith in the community." The consortium of investors formed Lancaster Notch Lumbering Corporation, with headquarters of record in Wilmington, Delaware.

The War Department's officers for the disposal of surplus matériel turned over two large bulldozers; one grader; two small bulldozers; four tractors; eighteen flatbed trailers; twenty Jeeps; nine two-and-one-half-ton trucks, four equipped with heavy-duty diesel electric generators; and several automobiles that in the judgment of supply officers were no longer necessary to ensure American preparedness. The price of the equipment was never publicly disclosed, nor ever publicly sought.

When the seven or so highland families, by then including somewhere in the neighborhood of eighty people, caught wind of the construction coming up the mountain, they selected male members between eighteen and sixty to descend through the woods each morning to the nearest point of construction and display their rifles and shotguns. Whenever surveyors or construction men scanned the woods around them, they saw three or four silent, armed men; sometimes they heard shots off the road. When the highway builders reached the top of the Notch, Congressman Wainwright and two fellow investors rode to the end of the pavement, about four hundred yards from the top, then got out and walked the rest of the way. It was a flat, hot day in August '48, and it took them awhile. When they arrived at the enormous dilapidated bunkhouse and cookshack in the middle of the camp, over forty people were waiting. Some of them carried guns.

"My friends," the congressman said, "we mean you no harm. We will not disturb your farms, or your way of life. The men who come to work here, cutting trees for timber, will have orders not to bother you. Or your fields and crops. If you will welcome them, perhaps sell them food, let them sleep in your barns until we have housing for them, they will give you money. When all this is over, you will have more land cleared, for whatever use you choose. We will not try to take it from you. All that we want's the trees."

Lancaster Notch Lumbering clearcut approximately 60 percent of its acreage between 1947 and 1962, concentrating first on the growth that had arisen around the old lumber camp in the years since its closure, to get a purchase on the land, then bulldozing access to the flatter parts of the terrain around it, clearcutting and leaving the bare earth to reforestation, over the years gradually winding down an operation that was becoming more and more vulnerable to competition from Canadian and Maine camps getting cheaper trucking service from outfits bordering upon new Interstate highways, while being plagued by a shortage of local workers, and becoming less and less able to maintain or replace the old war-surplus equipment.

During those fifteen years, at least eighteen loggers and drivers, most of them combat veterans, joined the seven families, and remained when the company closed.

On the night of the last day in July, Henry Briggs in full dark-green uniform—Stetson hat; shirt and tie with clip, badge; trousers with one-inch black stripe down the outseam; black leather belt with holster, two ammunition pouches, handcuffs; Smith & Wesson .357 revolver—left his home in Occident in the green Jeep half-ton pickup assigned to him by the Vermont Forest Service. He drove southwest down the hill from his house and took the oblique left up the Notch Road to the northeast at Whipple's IGA Store in the village. About six miles up the mountain he stopped and backed into what was left of an old logging road, banging the trailing edge of the rear gate as the wheels first dropped into the ditch eroded off the shoulder pavement and then clattered up the steep gravel grade. There was a moon. He shut off the headlights. He took his six-cell flashlight from its holder under the dashboard, got out of the truck, and closed the door as silently as he could.

He climbed about a mile up the hill until he came to another logging road. Just beyond it, its right wheels in the ditch, there was a car that shone blue in the moonlight. Its trunk was open. He went to the car and rubbed his right hand down its left rear fender. He felt three metal ridges, and at the top of the fender, a fin and cylindrical light. He loosened his revolver in the holster and took a breath. He walked on the edge of the gravel, on grass and leaves long dead, trying not to make any noise. At the top of the upgrade there was a clearing. He paused for a moment. He made out the shapes of two men sitting on a low rock wall, and a faint illumination not caused by the moon. The men were bending over. He patted the front of his shirt, felt the badge, took the gun from its holster, and turned on the light, at the same time saying: "State warden. Fish and Game. Sit tight." He cocked the revolver as loudly as he could and started into the clearing.

One of the men said: "That you, Henry?"

"Sure is, Bunny," Briggs said. "Your friend someone I know?"

"Don't think so," Bunny said. "I just met him myself."

"Likely story," Briggs said. He stood in front of the two men. He deliberately blinded the man to Bunny's left with the flashlight. Then he played the light around them. There was a doe on the ground, freshly throat-slit and gutted, a small entrance wound at her throat. Resting on a rock next to Bunny was the source of the faint light: a flashlight taped to the bottom of the barrel of an old wooden-stocked .30–.30 Savage. On the grass next to the deer's throat was a six-inch Kroningen knife with blood on the birch handle and Swedish-steel blade.

Briggs put the light on the man next to Bunny. He was about twenty-two, a hundred and eighty pounds, dressed in a tan chino shirt and work pants. He wore a Mack Truck hat, and he had not shaved in some days. "You," he said, "what's your name?"

"Ah, Henry," Bunny said, "lemme talk, all right? This here is one of my friends, the Garners. Garners from up in the Notch. You know the Garners. This one happens, be Eddie. He's a little shy, okay? Never been to school."

"Oh, well, how's he at shooting, then?" Briggs said. "How's he at jacklighting deer? Freezing the damn things in their tracks with the fucking light, out of season of course, and never mind if it's a buck, and then shooting them through the gullet before they can move."

Bunny cleared his throat. "Henry," he said, "there's only one gun here."

"Which is generally all it takes to shoot a paralyzed deer," Briggs said. "And which I think I recognize. Right now it seems to me to be in the possession and control of the man who had it the last time that I saw it after dark last April in that little thicket at the west corner of Bill Cook's south pasture, just this side Charlotte. And damned if there hadn't been a spikehorn in that neighborhood that night—saw him jump right out that thicket when I put the spotlight on him just as you're takin' aim."

"Yeah," Bunny said, "well, I wouldn't be surprised. But just listen me a minute."

"I've done that before," Briggs said. "What I should've done before is take that damned rifle away from you, because if I'd done that then it'd be up there in the lab, Roxbury now, 'stead of lying on the ground here next to that dead doe."

"But you didn't get in trouble, did you," Bunny said. "For not doing that, I mean."

"Not so far," Briggs said, "but I learned a long time ago, you push your luck far enough, long enough, sooner or later it'll happen: shit up to your ears. Your habits aren't exactly a big secret in this region, case that hasn't crossed your mind. You keep gettin' 'way with this, pretty soon every time I grab a fella doin' this, he'll take his jacket off, show a collar under it, and 'spect me to let him go. 'Privilege of clergy, Warden Briggs,' he'll say to me. 'You know what that is, Henry, don't you, all that that includes? I get into ball games free, and those pesky Fish and Game laws don't apply to men of God like us.' Then I'll arrest him anyway, and I will take him in, and *that's* when all hell will break loose, because I didn't bring you in, all the times that I caught you."

"Okay, okay, now calm down, Henry," Bunny said. He patted the carcass. "Now this is a road kill, all right? You see that wound that she's got in her throat there? That's got to be an antenna. Poor thing must've tried, jump over the road, just as a car's coming by. And the darned thing went right through her throat.

"Now," he said, "Henry, you know how I am, I've got a parishioner, the Notch. And I know it's late, but she's very sick, and if I go home, I won't see her. I'm getting along myself. I'll be sixty-four next November. So if I go home, well, I'll have a drink, and then I will fall right asleep. And she's got no phone, so what do I do? I know she can't get to me. Or her family can't, at least. So on my way home, I said: 'I'll go there. Make sure that she isn't failing. And, if she is, well, I will anoint her, and this will comfort her mind. The sacrament 'most always does.'"

"Well, you must be running really late now, then," Briggs said, keeping the light on Garner. "Stop on your way up to pick up a road kill, butcher it, and sit with this kid. Old woman's probably dead by now, on her way straight down to hell."

"Henry," Bunny said, touching his left arm, "why let this meat go to waste? Why let it go to the pound in the city? Why give this good meat to dogs?"

"Bunny," Briggs said, "because you're not supposed to jacklight deer, or hunt them any other way when they're out of season. And you're not supposed to kill young does. Let them have a chance to breed. Because it's against the damned law, Father. It's against the fucking law."

"I don't like your language, Henry," Bunny said.

"Father Morrissette," Briggs said, "let me remind you, I'm a Protestant. I'm not in your jurisdiction. But I am an officer of the law, and you are therefore in mine. What the hell were you doing? Teaching this dummy your tricks? So I can go up against him?"

"Henry," Morrissette said, "Eddie's afraid of guns. He heard a gun go off recently, quite recently in fact. I was training him to shoot. Not tonight, of course. And he put his hands over his ears. So I guess I know why all the Garners I know, many of whom certainly shoot, why it is that this boy can't. So that is that. You don't need to worry about him."

"Well," Briggs said, "I really haven't been, you know, 'til I saw him with you. That was when I started."

Morrissette patted Briggs again. "God compensates each of us with an unusual strength, when he deprives us of one. Eddie is a strong boy. This is a warm night. It would be a perfect shame if, with an able-bodied young man right on the scene, and a splendid ice house nearby, your decision to confiscate this road kill, *and throw it in the back of your truck, to spoil,* resulted in depriving a family of meat, that hasn't seen meat in a month."

"You're saying he'll carry it home," Briggs said.

"I believe he might try," Morrissette said. He turned his body so that he faced Garner and patted him on the right forearm. He began to gesture in the moonlight. Garner pointed at Briggs. He was shaking and his mouth was working. Morrissette shook his head. He looked back at Briggs. "Shake your head, Henry," he said, "and look very serious, please. I'll bet you've been scared, and you've needed a break. And I'll bet that you've gotten one, too. So give this kid one. God'll love you for doing it."

"I don't work for God," Briggs said. "I work for the State of Vermont."

"Henry," Morrissette said, "shake your fucking head. And shake it now."

Briggs shook his head. He holstered his gun. He held up his hands. Morrissette patted Garner again. Garner nodded hesitantly. He stood up. He bent down. He picked up the carcass. He hoisted it over his right shoulder and started east through the clearing. After about thirty yards, he shifted the load, and began to run.

"Thank you, Henry," Morrissette said in the moonlight. "God will reward you for this."

"Bunny," Briggs said, straightening up, "this is your last one for free. The next time you do this, I'm going to arrest you, and haul you right into court."

"No you won't, Henry," Morrissette said. "You won't arrest me, because you have an intuitive grasp of the world. You know exactly how much you can get away with. And I recognize that. It's how I've survived as a priest. I have the same miraculous gift, relied on it all of my life. If you catch me some night with a deer in my car, and some chef from the Mallett's Bay restaurant, and you find big money on him, then you will put the handcuffs on me and him too, and take the both of us in. I know this. I do. But I also know this: that I will never do that. Put myself in that position, or put you in it either. And you know that I know I will not do that, because you know that's not what I do. The Lord God made the birds of the air, and the fish in the stream, and the beasts of the wood, not only because they are beautiful, Henry, and because they bring the rich tourists to hunt and to kill them in their abundance, and give us their money to do it, but also in order to feed his poor children. Who sometimes get hungry when food's out of season. A mere technicality, I say, so long as the children don't starve."

2

In the mornings of what passed for midsummer in the Green Mountains, Briggs could tell again—he had learned the signals as a boy—that autumn was coming early. It always did, and that depressed him. There was frost on the lawn behind the house, and the leaves on the lower, longer branches of the maples were faintly tinged with orange at their edges. On the road at night he listened to the radio reports of Jim Lonborg, Gary Bell, and José Santiago starting, and Lee Stange and John Wyatt coming in from the bull pen, and was assured that it was still hot and humid at Fenway. But in the woods east of Canterbury he saw new clearings where farmers who'd been cold before were taking best advantage of the part of summer that lingered by cutting wood before the harvests that would start late in August, stacking the split logs on covered porches against the winter. In the fields east of Charlotte, he saw the grass and clover turned into bales of hay.

It was the damned length of it that got you, the damnable duration of the cold that seeped into your bones, when there was no longer any prospect of heading south in February. Toward the end of that drear month some warmth might be expected, and the sugar maples on the hills behind his house on the Richmond Road would surrender a small harvest of sap. But that was very little, fully eight months off, and for many years he had escaped before it came.

He sat in the kitchen on Saturday morning in his gingham shirt and khaki pants, gratefully drinking coffee and enlarging his paunch with Lillian's raisin bran muffins, tolerating her principal enjoyment of his semiretirement years: his accessibility to nagging.

"I must say," he said, spreading butter and then her homemade raspberry preserves on half of a muffin, "I didn't think it'd work at the time. I was very skeptical, when Leonard's boys said we should lay out all that money on that gravity-feed line. Didn't freeze? Okay, then it was sure to get clogged. But it worked. No more of that stuff, patrolling the buckets. Comes right in, nice, even flow, neat's you please. And a hell of a lot less spillage, although I presume we do lose something, just what gets stuck in the lines. But it's sure one hell of a lot less work."

"I don't see why you care," she said. "It's not like you did the work. It's Leonard's boys, do all the work."

"Well," he said, "but one way, the other, we end up paying them for it."

" 'Paying them'?" she said. "Did I hear you right?" The orange-yellow cat stood up suddenly on the fireproof mat in front of the iron stove in the kitchen, arched its back, stared at him, turned its back on him, flagged its tail to expose its anus, clawed at the rug, and lay down to sleep once again. The black and gold coon cat on the window seat regarded the performance with regal disapproval.

"You know," he said, "now I know that you explained it to me, and the doctor said you're right, but I still don't understand why somebody that can't stand to have a couple dogs around can keep two damned cats in the house all the time, that never go out 'cept they have to."

"Because I happen to be allergic to dogs," she said, "and I don't happen to be allergic to cats. It's not like it was something I *wanted* to do, Henry, you know."

"I still don't understand it," he said. "You used to come up here when we were in school, and we had Lady, and then Champ, and Punch and Judy. And it never bothered you then. Being around dogs, I mean."

"I wasn't allergic, then," she said. "You get over thirty or so, your body changes, I guess. It wasn't something I could help."

"I still miss the dogs," he said. "I like to have a dog around. At least one dog around."

17

"Sure," she said, "nothing but a bunch of mutts. Who'd feed them when you're gone, let them out and so forth? I'd have to do it, that's who, and it would make me sick. It's just like you like to have the Siller boys around. I'm surprised you don't want a horse. Those animals, those Siller boys, all they do make you feel like you're a country gentleman. Should be in a magazine. When all that we're doing's making Leonard and his boys rich. That's what we are doing. What you charge them, what they get, what they have to do? It's ridiculous, Henry. Just ridiculous. 'Henry Briggs, gentleman farmer.' Honest to God."

"Lillian," he said, "the place has to be kept up. The place is a farm. It has to be kept up by farmers. I haven't been a farmer since nineteen forty-nine. I wasn't much good at it when I was doing it. I was glad when I could stop. Even Dad was glad. Meant he could stop trying, teach me to do it right. Now I got two choices. I can start up doing it myself again, which I don't want to do. Or I can get somebody else to do it. Those are my two choices."

"That's all right," she said. "I guess if a man can afford to pick and choose what he wants, if he can look at an offer that'd put him to work and say: 'No, I don't want to do it,' well, I guess he can get someone else to do the other kind of work that he doesn't like either. But I don't see any reason why he has to go and say to them: 'Look, you take most of the money.' I don't see that at all. What you're letting Leonard do to you, well, he must be laughing at you. Laughing at you, 'hind your back, the way he's screwing you."

"Lillian," he said, "I was on the road over sixteen years. My old job means: on the road. I know what it was like, and I was lots younger then, and it's even harder now and I'm older. I want to be in one place, two places at the most. I told you: You want Florida? We'll go down to Florida and get ourselves a place."

"Oh, sure," she said. "Go down there with all your other no-good, washed-up buddies, and spend the whole winter drinking rum and fishing, playing golf and lying. No, thanks. I'm staying here."

"Okay then," he said, "then here we are, and here we'll stay. But that means I either pay Leonard's boys, or someone else's, cash, in which case there's tax problems. Or else I sit down with Leonard, and he says this is what he wants, and I say this is what I want, and we figure out the difference between he wants and what I get, and that he pays to me and gets his share from the land. Which means my life is simpler, and that's how I want it."

Around eleven in the morning he put on his windbreaker and his boots and went out of the warm kitchen onto the long wooden porch. He stood there for a moment, resting his left hand possessively on the stove wood corded between the white posts that supported the roof, pausing to survey the valley to the south where the brook ran shallow but clear between its gravel banks. He could see all the way down to the village—the gradually sprawling general store, the gas station, the creamery, the small white Congregational church with its assertively tall steeple that everyone in town admired, because it took all the lightning seeking to strike somewhere in the flat—and even make out vaguely the shapes of houses and barns scattered along the road leading south and west among the hills to Charlotte. A flock of crows veered east out of the woods behind the house and banked north over the barn, making a big racket. Satisfied that everything remained in order, he stepped off the porch and followed the path—in the winter, two widths of the shovel, twice as wide as the Thomas boy who used it thought necessary, or fair, for three dollars a storm (Henry had a way of quelling the kid's occasional feelers for more money: "You know, won't be long now, Jackie," he said, " 'fore long the trucks be heading north again from Florida, and the Sox'll be playing again." And the boy remembered that good tickets free to Fenway Park were precious things to have in still, hot Vermont summers that started too late and ended too soon; he stifled his greed)—out past the barn to the sugaring shack.

In the winter it would be quiet and cold inside. It had the light from one grimy western window and one dirty, naked, hundred-watt bulb. Starting in late February it would be hot and sticky—boiling the sap drove off more than water; there would be a heavy trace of sweetness in the air as well, and the cause of it would cling to glass and clothes, even to his skin. He bent and opened the iron door, where the hardwood then would burn low over a thick bed of red coals, those closest to the door whitening in the extra oxygen. He saw no sign of rust. He closed the door and straightened up, uncovering the empty vat; when he did that in the false spring, he would release a cloud of heavy steam that

19

would hide his face and upper body for a few tropical seconds during which he would not be able to see. There was no rust there, either.

He detoured through the red barn on his way back to the house, entering through the door at the southwesterly rear corner, latching it carefully behind him. He heard the swallows rustling anxiously above him; two flew through the slatted light that filtered through the crack between the loft doors at the front. The loft and three of the ten stalls were filling with hay baled from his fields by Leonard Siller, stored in Knox's barn under the agreement providing for the haying rights themselves. Siller survived in the dairy business in the same way as Carter Boyd and Mike LaFreniere and Joe Maleska: he leased enough pasturage to support a herd of Jerseys large enough to produce milk in volume sufficient to interest the big distributors, thus making a living without enslaving himself to mortgage payments on too much land.

Leonard was realistic: "I can do it," he said, "because I've got neighbors with land, who don't want to farm it, and I'm under fifty years old. But I'll be the last one, the last one to do it. My sons'll have to sell. You and Bessie Roche, and Sam Jackman and Ed Cobb: someday we'll all be too old to live around here, and then someday we'll all be dead. And when that day comes, well, our children or our widows won't have no choice but sell. And it won't be to folks just like you or us, either, that one reason or another don't get their livings from the land. It'll either be to people who could farm it, but can't buy it, not from what they'd get from farming, or from people who can buy it but don't give a shit for farming. You know which one'll get it. The one who's got the money.

"I tell you, Henry, day'll come. Day'll come when maybe some new lawyer'll buy the Cobb place, and it won't matter, not one damn, if he's a politician too, because he will want the money. He'll take one look at Ed's big barn, and that nice steep slope behind it, and he'll look at that Interstate coming up from Brattleboro, and he'll see that barn remodeled into a big dorm for skiers, bunch of New York Jews with lots of money sitting around a fireplace with drinks in their hands at night, 'stead of a bunch of guys like me, with shit on our boots, turning in early, feeding cows in it. And the house'll be an inn, with dancing every Friday night and the weekends, too. You think he'll leave up fences, when he puts in his ski lift? You think, if some New York outfit

20

shows up to buy him out, he'll give up a fancy profit so my cows can graze the same place where they want the swimming pool?

"We're dinosaurs, Henry—dinosaurs is what we are."

Briggs heard the swallows rustling back into contentment.

When he reentered the house, Lillian asked him as she always did whether everything was all right outdoors. She had a sarcastic tone that infiltrated everything she said to him. He believed that he probably deserved it, after all the years on the road, and had not begun to resent it until one night at the Whipples' when he noticed it was missing from her other conversations. He kept his judgments to himself, as he had learned to do when his work year ran from February through September, now and then into October, and prudence about contracts kept a man careful about what he said to others.

"You know the boys check it out every day," she said, never taking her eyes off the television screen. "The sugar house, the barn—they go through it every day. I think if you don't trust them, well then, we're giving away too much money. And if we do trust them, makes no sense for you, be doing their jobs for them."

"I still like to check, myself," he said. He kept his voice mild. "The boys don't own this place, you know."

"They might as well," she said. "The Sillers get all the good of it. All we get's the tax bills."

"You see things sharper when you own something," he said. "And besides, I'm in no hurry. I've got time to notice things. You're working for another man, you're liable, put things off. Not go through the barn today, make sure everything's all right. And that's the day you miss, of course, that day the first smell of a hayfire starting should've set your hair on end. When you still could've done something about it."

"Henry Briggs," she said complacently, "there's been hay stored in that barn since the first year your father died, and that was nineteen fifty-nine. Leonard's never had a wet bale that he put into that barn. You've just got a thing about it, that's all—you and your damned fires."

He supposed that she was right, but she had never been awakened into terror in the middle of the night in a sixteenth-floor bedroom of a hotel in Detroit, where the smell of thick smoke and the sound of alarm bells roiled around together in the brain, threatening at first impression ambitious plans for a career, almost at once blocked out by the vision of imminent death. " 'The first thing' I thought about?" he had replied to Russ Wixton's question: "The first thing I thought was: 'Holy shit, if I get burned, I might not pitch again.' But that thought didn't last too fuckin' long, I can tell you that. Pretty damned fast I started thinking about more important things, such as: 'How the hell do I get out here, with my fucking life?' "

"How'd the broad take it?" Wixton had said.

" 'The broad,' " Briggs had said.

"Yeah, the broad," Wixton said. "I was in the bar last night. I saw her pick you up. Not a bad-lookin' gash. Little old for me, maybe. Must've been at least nineteen. But a nice paira tits, and her ass wouldn't stop. She in the sack with you, the fire alarm went off?"

"Right," Briggs had said. "She said she thought she smelled smoke, I told her her ass was on fire. I didn't have anyone with me."

"Come on, Hank," Wixton had said. "I saw you leave the bar with her. I know she went with you. And I got to talking with Fritz in the lobby, stayed up 'til the alarm rang. And I saw her come down the fire exit, looked like you threw her clothes at her. And then, fifteen seconds, twenty the outside, out you come after her, looking stupid. What'd you do, stop on the landing so she could leave first?"

"You know, Russ," Briggs said, "you print that, you're gonna go a long time between drinks, you're with this team. I'll tell all the other guys, you know, how far they can trust you. It will not help you, pal of mine, the *Champlain Prospect* always knows the score, the old *Valley Press* does not."

"Oh, for Christ sake, Henry," Wixton had said, "if I printed half the stuff I knew, the opposition wouldn't worry me—someone'd have me shot."

The next morning, Wixton's story in the *Valley Press* was headlined: "Accident from Occident, Other Sox in Night of Fear." He quoted Henry Briggs: "This picture flashed in front of me. I was never going to see my wife and family again. I was going to die in a hotel fire, just when the kids are beginning to grow up. And all this great stuff that's happened to me in baseball, you know? I have been so lucky. It was all going to end, just like that. Thank God it was just an electrical short. Thank God they got it put out."

"Yes," he said to Lillian as a woman in a blue dress on the television show jumped in the air and clapped her hands when she was shown a dinette set. "Well, I believe I'll go down to Whipple's. See who's hanging around."

"Uh-huh," she said. "Well, just don't drink too much of that old beer, all right? I don't mind you going down there every day to eat lunch with your pals, if you can't bear to stay home. But if you keep drinking that beer, you're going to have a bigger belly on you than a cow's. You may think your morning walks are the same as doing work, and you're only thirty-nine, so you can get away with it. But they're not. Those walks aren't work, and you don't get the other exercise you're used to anymore. And that's why you're getting fat and sloppy. Because you don't do any work. You know what'll happen to you someday, you don't cut this out. You'll have a nice big heart attack. And that'll be the end of you—you're too big for me to lift, to drag you in the car, so you'll be dead before they get here. 'Fore the doctor gets here." She sniffed. "Not that I think much of him either, far as that goes. I don't see why it's so hard, get a decent doctor here."

"I'll be back," he said. He took off the windbreaker and hung it on the peg near the door. He went out and took the path leading east toward the garage, down close to the Richmond Road, gazing at his orchard on the opposite side, the apple trees green against the sky. The crows were wheeling furiously against the sky high above them and the cemetery on top of the hill beyond, maneuvering for swooping dives in screaming teams of two or three toward one of the trees at the far end of his land.

3

The side of Whipple's IGA Store faced the Richmond Road down the hill from Briggs's house. The building fronted on Union Street and faced the road going west to Charlotte (everyone who lived in or near the town pronounced the name *Sha-lott*). The first objects seen by a new arrival coming from Charlotte to Occident were the three Gulf gasoline pumps on the island in front of Whipple's store. The store itself had begun in the 1890s as a two-story frame building with clapboard siding, gradually expanding to the east with an ell that housed the lunchroom. The one-story addition to the south accommodated the refrigerator chests of dairy products, beer, and wine. Its shape owed less to architecture than to the faulty economic theories that had prompted the more acquisitive farmers of the area in the nineteenth century to buy up land cheaply from neighbors beggared by the post–Civil War collapse of the wool industry, and then add on to their houses in helter-skelter fashion to make room for indoor sidelines of carding wool and spinning, and processing of poultry and dairy products, in order to profit by increased volume while diversifying lines. The theory had not worked for the farmers—their spacious houses survived them and their fine ideas, for purchase by weekending city folk who liked to ski and pose as squires—but it had worked very well for Whipples selling manufactured goods.

Across the street, on the northerly side of the road to Charlotte, was the flat-roofed, brick-front, cement-block creamery, its unloading docks crowded with shiny tanker trucks. On the southerly side of the Charlotte road was the Congregational church. There were three stone houses set back from the Richmond Road south of the church.

Across the street from the houses there was an Amoco service station, operated by Wilson Carmichael; he justified his existence, and competition with Paul Whipple, when he opened it in March of 1951 by offering repairs, lubrication, and tires, which Whipple did not sell. He also sold fishing and hunting licenses, guns, fishing tackle, and fresh bait.

Paul Whipple sold licenses, ammunition, and tackle but believed that Occident residents in the market for firearms were most likely to purchase them either from Sears or from one of the sporting-goods stores in Burlington. He therefore preferred to allocate his shelf space to canned goods, dog food, toilet paper, magazines, ice cream, beauty aids, power and hand tools, sturdy clothing, pharmaceuticals, meats and poultry, canned and frozen vegetables, bread and pastries, cereals and tonic. He refused to sell bait.

Carmichael opened on Sundays, when both Whipple's store and his gas pumps were closed; Carmichael's willingness to do this saved Whipple the bother of leaving his chair and the Cleveland Browns games in the fall on the radio to go down to the store to answer emergency calls from idiots who should have realized on Saturday afternoon that they were nearly out of gas. After a first year of competition uneasily spent by both Whipple and Carmichael, Whipple perceived that Carmichael had no intention of adding a dairy case or putting in a line of overalls and shampoo, while Carmichael in his diffident daily visits to Whipple's lunchroom demonstrated by his greasy appearance that he spent most of his workday in the lube pit and appreciated both the convenience and the choice of merchandise in Whipple's store.

Whipple deduced—it would never have occurred to him to ask whether Carmichael had a wife, or whether her health was good, just as it would never have crossed Carmichael's mind to have put similar questions to Whipple—that Carmichael must have a woman somewhere up where he went each evening into the highlands; he occasionally purchased Tampax. For some reason this made Whipple feel better.

Carmichael took extreme pains when the timing chain broke on Whipple's 1950 Cadillac Coupe de Ville, thus sparing Whipple the trouble and no small expense of having it towed to Burlington for repairs. Carmichael himself drove his own Ford pickup to Burlington and secured genuine Cadillac parts, installing them with impeccable skill. He charged Whipple only for the parts, not for the labor or time. He did not point out to Whipple that the repair slip carried only parts charges, considering that he did not need to.

He didn't. Whipple took note and thereafter lost no opportunity to recommend Carmichael to grocery customers whose cars were acting up despite repeated visits to other mechanics, and Carmichael's repair business doubled in a year. Whipple during that year several times considered giving Carmichael a 5 percent discount on his goods, not on his meals, but in the end rejected the idea on two grounds: it would confuse his own checkout girls, and besides, by then Carmichael seemed to be doing pretty damned well for himself. Whipple and Carmichael did not become friends, but they got along.

Henry Briggs parked his own Jeep Wagoneer in the gravel parking lot and climbed the three wooden steps to the side door of the lunchroom. Directly ahead of him there was a row of seven high-backed booths along the wall. To his left there was a low counter. Seven men sat at it, four of them tanker drivers that he knew from conversations, but only by first names, and one he had known a long time. They ran regular routes north and east of Occident, collecting raw milk from farmers under contract to the creamery, and considered their three-day-a-week visits adequate for membership in the community of Whipple's store. The one Briggs knew as Floyd tipped his gimme cap (it said *Shakespeare* in red script on the front, with a spinning rod bent nearly double against the reel seated on its grip, behind the lettering) back over his thinning black hair and said: "Henry, you old bastard. Didn't see you for a while."

Briggs nodded to him. "Floyd," he said, "Jean, Maurice. Ah, Lester. Didn't see you there. Been on the job, usual. You'd've been fishin', you'd've seen me."

Maurice winked at him. "You are the devil, Henri," he said. "This I know for sure."

Henry smiled. "Just business, I'm afraid," he said. "Nothing interesting." He turned right at the pinball machine and went into the main store, ducking his head at the doorway, easing his frame through the narrow aisle to the counter on the southerly side where the sporting goods were sold. He waited for a few minutes while Paul Whipple finished trimming strip steaks for a rather stylish woman in tight jeans and Tretorn sneakers. She kept up a steady stream of low chatter that Whipple seemed to be ignoring, tossing her long black hair and flashing her large diamond ring. Whipple wrapped the steaks in white paper and scribbled a price on it. The woman accepted the package and turned toward Briggs on her way to the cash register. Her gray eyes opened wide and she gave him a flash of a smile. "Excuse me," she said, "I'm afraid I can't get by."

Briggs compressed himself against the counter and she brushed past him, looking up at him from under her lashes. "Thank you," she said.

"My pleasure, ma'am," he said as Whipple, wiping his hands on his apron, approached from around the meat counter. They both watched the woman walk toward the front of the store. "My, my," Briggs said, "who is that?"

"I know, Henry," Whipple said. "But I won't tell you. Lillian's a friend of ours. Can't stop you doing what you want to, but I don't think I should help."

Briggs turned to face him. Whipple, his eyes small and scant behind his gold-rimmed glasses, allowed a smile to play around the corners of his mouth. "Paul," Briggs said, "I'm surprised. I really am surprised. All these years you've known me, and you'd think bad things of me."

" 'S why I do it," Whipple said. "Known you a long time. You come in here to buy something, or you just come to jaw?"

"Couple boxes Remington Express," Briggs said, straightening up. "Number six, I think."

Whipple pulled a rolling step-stool from under the counter and locked its wheels at the shelf directly in front of Briggs. He clambered onto the stool with difficulty, keeping his balance by holding to the upright that supported the shelf. "Oughta make you get these yourself, goddamnit," he said. He took the two boxes of shotgun shells off the top shelf, stepped off the stool, released the wheel lock, and sent it rolling toward the front of the store. He put the shells on the counter in front of Briggs. "Goin' gunnin', are you?"

Briggs shook his head. "Paul," he said, "if I was, I wouldn't tell you. You'd just, the minute I walk out of here, you be on the phone to Montpelier, telling them the warden's goin' huntin' out of season." He took his wallet from his pocket. "How much I owe you for these?"

"You hurt my feelings, Henry," Whipple said. "Saying a thing like that. Twelve-eighty."

"Right," Briggs said, counting out the money. "I knew alligators, spent my winters down south there, got more feelin's'n you got." He handed the money to Whipple, who rang up the old register on the counter and deposited the cash in the drawer.

"I did hear, though," Whipple said, resting his buttocks on the shelf behind him and folding his arms over his apron, "Father Morrissette got himself a nice doe, night 'fore last, over the Notch Road, there. Had it right in the trunk of his car, there, someone come up and pulled him right over."

"Bunny Morrissette?" Briggs said. "Heard about that one myself. A road kill, I assume."

"Ay yeah, of course," Whipple said. "Asked Bunny myself. 'Oh absolutely, Paul,' he said. 'No doubt it was collision, driver drunk and ran. Must've been just the slightest brush, you know? Deer must've been jumping the road, landed on his antenna with her chest. Speared herself. Just a small puncture wound. Doubt there'd even be blood on the car.' "

"Uh-huh," Briggs said. "I don't suppose Bunny said if he had his gun."

"Matter of fact, he did," Whipple said. "I asked him exactly that. And you know what? So'd the warden. And it was *that* gun."

"The one he uses for night target practice," Briggs said. "That old thirty-thirty Savage with the flashlight taped the barrel."

"That's the one," Whipple said. He shook his head. "I said to Bunny: 'Did he smell it?' Bunny said: 'Of course not. Man the cloth tells someone he's been out target shooting, course he believes the guy.' And then Bunny says to me: 'You know, a man in my position doesn't have much time, all the work he does, clean his gun and so forth. All that work with the poor families, haven't got enough to eat. Only time I get to practice is at night, up in the hills. But this warden, know what he said to me? Said: "Father, ordinarily we have to confiscate these road kills and the state gives them, the poor. But it's late and all, and I was wondering, you'd do me a favor. You wouldn't know a family now, could make good use this meat? Save me the trouble, hauling it, blood in my truck, too?" ' Well, Bunny said he was very cooperative. ' "The very thing I had in mind," I told him,' he said. ' "That Garner family, up the Notch. Don't believe those kids, that woman, that they've had a decent meal, had some meat with their potatoes since Tom had his heart attack." So I told him,' Bunny said, 'that I'd take it over to them. And he said: "Much obliged." ' "

"Yeah," Briggs said. "And if a couple nice thick steaks should end up on the table at Saint Mary's Rectory, well, Father Morrissette's entitled, all his dedication."

"Exactly," Whipple said. "I was impressed, myself. I might even go to Mass, you know, next Sunday at the school. After Reverend Glennon makes us sing the hymns and all. Just to let the father know I like his style."

"Right, Paul," Briggs said. "You got a sack, these shells here? I can just see you kneeling there, and following the pope."

Whipple laughed. He bagged the shells. "Gonna have a bite to eat?" he said.

"Thought I might," Briggs said.

"Join you, a few minutes," Whipple said. "Got a few things to attend to, but as soon's the kid comes back. Take the usual booth, down in the back. The one with the leg room."

The tanker drivers were paying their checks when Briggs returned to the lunchroom. Lester, squinting against Lucky Strike smoke curling from the cigarette stuck to his lower lip, stuck his change into the pocket of his dark green wool uniform pants without taking his eyes off Briggs. Floyd clapped Briggs on the shoulder and winked at him. "Business is good?" he said.

"Tiring," Briggs said, "tiring. I didn't used to travel up here, the bad times of year. Always on the road, of course, but the road was always clear, and someone else was driving. Coming up on two years now, since I've been doing that. 'Less you count last, of course. But I still miss it, just the same. Life's just not the same."

"Don't pay as good, for one thing," Lester said.

29

Maurice nudged him in the ribs. "And the young lay-*dies*, Henri? They are not in the woods?"

Briggs gave him a light shot on the shoulder with the heel of his left hand. "Maurice, you old rogue," he said, shifting his gaze to Lester and changing his tone to cold, "*no* one's in *my* woods."

He went to the booth in the back. Huddled in the bench nearest the door was a small woman in a dark gray dress and orange kerchief, her head bent over her chest, one thick strand of black hair streaked with gray drooping out from under the kerchief. She looked up suddenly when he reached the booth. There was panic in her eyes. She was nursing a baby at her left breast. She pulled the lapel of the coat to cover herself. "*Please*," she said, hissing.

Briggs backed away. "I'm sorry," he said. "I didn't know you were here."

"I can be here if I want," she said. "Mister Whipple said so. You can ask him, if you want. If you don't believe me."

"I believe you, ma'am," Briggs said. He retraced his steps to the third table from the back and folded himself into it. He put the bag of shotgun shells on the table. When the young woman behind the lunch counter finished loading the dishwasher and looked up at him, he smiled. "A Miller beer, okay, Marie?" he said. "I'd come over there and get it, but I may be here for life." She smiled at him and held up the plastic-covered single sheet menu. "No, thanks," he said. "I'm waiting for your dad. I know what I want anyway, but I'll wait for him, to start."

He heard creaks and packing sounds behind him, with an under-tone of muttering. The woman in the kerchief was leaving, the baby wrapped in a dirty blue blanket and lolling in the crook of her right arm, a small quilted lavender valise clenched in her left. She stopped at his booth and stared at him. She was short; their eyes were nearly at a level. "You lousy rotten bastard," she said. "I know who you are, famous rich man. I hope you're happy now." She walked rapidly away. When he turned his gaze back to the counter, Marie was shaking her head. He was still pondering the encounter when Whipple came in from the store, registered surprise at his location, and nodded his head toward the back booth.

"I was going to," Briggs said, when they were seated in the back

30

booth, "but there was a woman sitting in here with her tit out—baby having lunch. And she didn't feature my company." Marie brought two Millers and waited expectantly. "I'll have a plate of hash and eggs, please," Briggs said, smiling at her.

"Pork chop," Whipple said, pouring his beer and not looking at her. "Plate of them hash-browns, go with it. That's the Lyman woman," he said, raising the glass of beer and drinking half of it. "Ahh," he said, wiping his mouth, "first of the goddamned day. Always tastes the best. I let her. I dunno. I feel sorry for her, though she is one mean little bitch. I suppose she isn't thirty, but she's had about enough bad luck, last a hundred years.

"She got herself, she's one them Garners there, live up there in the Notch? That don't pay their honest bills? Don't know what her first name is. Judy. Joanie. Somethin'. Well, doesn't matter anyway. Matters is her state. I don't know how the hell she met him, but she got herself tied up with this Lyman fellow, drove a logging truck. From up around in Montpelier. And she run off with him, and they got married. Guess they got married, at least. Know they went to bed. And then when she was knocked up, this was only just last year, he come down the mountain one night and the rig jackknifed on him. So there she was, alone.

"So she figured, I'm guessing, she more or less assumed she'd stay with his family there. Well, they didn't have a pot they could piss in for themselves, much less a spare one for her, and furthermore they didn't like her any more'n her family'd liked him, so they put her out. And she come back down to the Notch, and her own father locked her out.

"Well," Whipple said, "Martha Glennon got wind of it. Now there is one fine woman, I must say. Like to drive her husband nuts, practicing what he preaches, always got four, five strays hanging around the parsonage, they figure out their next square meal comes from, how to get it for themselves, 'stead of moochin' off of Everett at Martha's invitation, and I don't blame Everett none for getting some upset about it, havin' all them underfoot 'round his house all the time. Oh, he's come over here, once, twice, when they've got on his nerves, and you could see by lookin' at him, he was mighty cross. As he had a right to be. But Everett don't complain none, no sir. Everett keeps his peace. Galls him, but he does it. Credit where it's due. But still, Martha's a fine woman. She's what we all should be.

"So she was in here one day, in the store, I mean, and she says to me that Everett and this Lyman woman do not get along. Apparently the baby crying, interrupting him. And she wouldn't go to church—said she don't believe in God. I could see why Everett's mad. Take God's food, sleep in his bed, but don't pay him no heed. So I said to Martha, well, if it'd help some, I wouldn't object if she come over here, the mornings, stayed a couple hours so he could work in quiet, have his lunch and so forth. And Martha said that'd be fine. So that was how that happened."

He paused and drank more beer. "'Course, it wasn't fine," he said. "It was an improvement for Everett, and some help to Martha, there, but the little bitch looked at it like she's being sent to jail. The first day she come in here, she comes up to me and says: 'Well, Mrs. Glennon says I have to come here every day. So that is what I'm doing, and my baby's doing, too. Because me and Pooky have to do what Mrs. Glennon says, 'cause we got no place to go. But you just let us know if we're being any trouble, and we'll go out, sit in the cold, and we won't bother you.' I half set out to tell her then: 'Okay, go on outside.' Wasn't me that knocked her up. I didn't wreck the truck. I didn't lock her out of her house when she come back to it. I'm just trying, do a favor, and for this I get abuse. But what the hell, am I right? She never caught a break."

"Can't she go on the welfare?" Briggs said. Marie brought their plates. Whipple without speaking indicated that they wanted two more beers. He picked up the ketchup bottle and poured a large pool of it next to his pork chop. Marie returned with the two beers and a bottle of Worcestershire sauce. Whipple poured Worcestershire sauce into the pool of ketchup and mixed the combination with his fork. Then he put the pork chop in the mixture, turning it so that it was coated on both sides. Then he spooned the hash-brown potatoes into the puddle of sauce and stirred them vigorously. Briggs drank his first beer at one pull and poured the second. He mashed the poached eggs into his hash so that the yolks mingled with the grease shining on the diced potatoes. He poured ketchup over the food and mixed it in with his fork, salting it heavily as he went along.

"She could," Whipple said, cutting a chunk off the pork chop. "One these days she's gonna have to. No question about that. Everett's a fairly patient man, but his good will's gonna run out, and then she'll have to go. She don't want to, 'course. Mean she'll have to go to Burlington, some place like that, where they got a place to stay. Ain't no place like that here, any town this size. And she doesn't want to do that because of course they've all got rules. Cramp her style a bit. I guess she's got this idea if she keeps on screwing drivers that come in the creamery there, she'll get herself another man. The girl's not overbright."

"She's not spreading her legs, Lester Belcher, I hope," Briggs said. "That little piece of shit. You know that asshole, all these years, still thinks he could take me if he got me from behind?"

"Oh, probably," Whipple said. "What I hear, she's not choosy. Sneaking in the cab bunks after dark and all."

"Well," Briggs said, "Lord loves us all. That's what I heard, at least." They both ate steadily for a while in diligent silence. When Whipple finished the meat he had cut from the chop, he picked up the bone, ran the strip of meat and fat remaining on it through the sauce, and gnawed it clean. He put the bone back on his plate and wiped his hands and mouth with a paper napkin. Marie brought a plate of white bread. "Two more beers," Whipple said. He took a slice of bread, buttered it, folded it in half, mopped up the remaining sauce, salted the bread, and ate it in three bites. Briggs buttered a slice and used it to wipe his plate clean of yolk and ketchup. He washed the bread down with beer. Marie delivered two mugs of coffee with cream. Whipple and Briggs each added three spoonfuls of sugar. Marie brought two tulip dishes of bread pudding. Briggs and Whipple ate silently, digging the last raisins out of the bottoms of the glasses by tilting them to the spoons. "You want some pie?" Whipple said. "Got good peach pie today."

"Maybe later," Briggs said. They picked up their coffee mugs.

"Ed Cobb was in, first of the week," Whipple said.

"Haven't seen him in a while," Briggs said.

"That's what he said about you," Whipple said. "I said the same thing myself. 'Seen Lillian, time to time. She's been in the store. But Henry's been kind of scarce. Hasn't been over the hall, even, I bet over a month.' You should come over the hall now and then, Henry. Boys'd enjoy seeing you. 'Must be his new job.'"

"Boys from the hall don't like it a lot," Briggs said, "they run into me out in the woods, when they're not s'posed to be in the woods. What we should do is get together and go gunning. Must be, what, good twenty years, you and me and Ed did that."

Whipple shook his head. "Me," he said, "I couldn't afford the outfits you wear. And Ed, it's been so long since Ed's been out, he'd show up in coat and tie, with his shoeshine and his briefcase. And I never went gunnin' with no warden. Have to check with Everett— probably against my religion."

"Huh," Briggs said, "only thing against your religion's losing money."

"Well, that's more'n you can claim, just the same," Whipple said. "Haven't seen you around a lot, lately."

"Things to do down Boston," Briggs said. "Couple banquets I agreed. I didn't get back, Saturday, last week, Sunday the week before. 'S why I haven't been over."

"You like doing it?" Whipple said.

Briggs blew on his coffee. "I dunno," he said. "I got to do something. Lillian's used to just being here. Lillian's got her routine. But I'm used to a different life. Sixteen years, piece of another one—sort of gets in your blood. Got to keep moving. Blood all settles in your feet, brain starts to go to sleep. Besides, even if I didn't want to do what I'm doing, what the hell can I do here? Don't want to farm, for God's sake. I wanted to do farming, I wouldn't've pissed my father off all those goddamned years, throwing his apples at the shed, 'stead of letting them get ripe to pick."

"You miss the ball," Whipple said.

"Yeah," Briggs said. "I miss it a lot. And all the other old-timers that I talk to, the banquets and that stuff? They all feel same way I do. It gets in your blood. From Washington's Birthday right on to Halloween, you're on the road a bunch of guys you get to know damned well. Don't always like 'em—always don't like some. But you know them. Have a few beers after a game, maybe play a hand of cards. Gets comfortable out there. And then it stops. All of a sudden it's over, and all you got to show for it's your pages in the books."

34

"Plus a fair amount of money, of course," Whipple said.

"Not as much as people think," Briggs said. "Enough to get by on, sure, you hung on to some of it. But not enough so you can go to Vegas every week. Besides, it's all tied up in management, if you had any brains. If I knew anything about handling money, I wouldn't've played ball. If the guy that handles my money knew anything about baseball, he'd be doing that. I'm comfortable. Lillian and the kids shouldn't ever have to worry, something happens to old Dad. Course I don't think Ted's ever worried in his life, about anything—geez I wish he'd settle down. If he doesn't keep his grades up, the good padres at Saint Michael's're gonna kick his ass right out into the fuckin' lake. And Sally? Well, she's doing all right, but she's been serious about the same guy since she was thirteen, and that's seven years ago—I pay her bills down at Marlboro there, but I doubt she's ever going to do much, all that art she's studying. You and Evelyn, with Paul Junior, you've at least got that, look forward."

"Oh," Whipple said, "no question there. Young fellow works his tail off. Don't see him much. Don't understand what he's doing when we do. Don't agree with him, of course. Had one fierce row at Christmas, I can tell you that. Brought his girlfriend home here. Jewish dame. Against the war, like all of them. She's done her work on him, though. Boy's just putty in her hands. But he's working hard, all right."

"Well, that's what I mean," Briggs said. "I'm more like you and your son'n I'm like mine, and Sally, and their mother. I've got to be doing something. They're not the problem in my house—I'm the one that's the problem. I get, last year I got so goddamned bored I thought I was gonna explode. But is it, is what I'm doing the answer? Dunno. Haven't been at it long enough. Do for now, I guess."

"That's what was on Ed's mind," Whipple said. "That's what he was talking about."

"Ed?" Briggs said. "Hell, Ed's spent years getting where he's gotten to. He's not gonna give that up, I should think. Got his practice, legislature sure doesn't take up much his time. He's got no cause to kick."

"He's not," Whipple said. "It was you he was asking about."

"Can't imagine why," Briggs said. "I appreciate what he did, but that was all I wanted. Something to keep busy."

35

"Had something he thought he might want to talk to you about," Whipple said. "Asked me, he was sounding me out about doing it. If I thought it'd be a good idea."

"Well, what is it?" Briggs said.

"I think I'm gonna let Ed tell you that," Whipple said, "he decides he wants to. He wasn't sure in his mind, I think, which is why he come to me. I told him I wasn't sure, you'd be home, but I reckoned Lillian'd know and he should call her up." He paused. "Lillian'd know that much, wouldn't she?" he said slyly. "Maybe not exactly where you were, or who you were with, but at least when you'll be back from there."

"You know, Whip," Briggs said, "I don't mind a little kidding now and then, and I got to admit I had my moments, I was younger. But I'm not the only one that ever did a couple things, wouldn't want his wife find out. Like for example: I know a guy that got himself a good dose of the Japanese clap on R and R from Korea. I know a guy did that. And that same guy, well, he was not so young when he went to a convention back there four, five years, Chicago. And when he woke up with a big headache he needed a new watch, and he didn't have the money to buy it with, because the woman that he spent the night with helped herself to that, too. And he hadda make up this cock-and-bull story that nobody believed, about getting held up on the street."

"Yeah," Whipple said. "Well, anyway, that's what I told him. I said to Ed it seemed to me, he had a proposition for you, you're the guy to make it to. He said he'd think about it."

"And you're not going to tell me what it is," Briggs said.

"Nope," Whipple said. "Far's I'll go is say I told him I thought you'd be nuts to do it, and he said he thought so, too, but he still thought he'd ask. 'One man's nuts,' he said, ' 's another man's balls.' So you can wait and see."

Briggs pulled out his wallet and put four dollars on the table. He added three quarters from his pocket. Whipple grimaced. "You don't have to tip her like that, you know, Henry. Not when you're eating with me. I pay her what she's worth. The other customers, you know, they haven't got your means. But Marie don't realize that. She thinks if you can do it, then that must mean that those who don't, well, they must be cheap. They're not. They just don't have the money."

36

"That's all bullshit, and you know it," Briggs said. "But it doesn't matter—we've been through it all before. At least a hundred times. I've known her since she was a baby. I know there isn't much that she can do, but what she can do, she does well. Always cheerful, I come in. Always has a smile. Even though it must be awful lonely, locked up inside herself in there, no company except herself."

"She's perfectly contented, Henry," Whipple said. "I can tell you that. Me and Evelyn, we know how she's feeling. We can tell. She's fine."

"Yeah," Briggs said. "Well, just the same. Don't change my mind none. I know lots of people that could do a lot of things, if they approached life like Marie does, 'stead of griping all the time. And if I wanna tip her, then I'm gonna tip her, right?"

"Yeah," Whipple said. "Well, we gonna have another beer now? Or are you gonna let me get back my customers?"

Briggs began the procedure of unfolding himself from the booth. He picked up his sack of shotgun shells. "Don't think I'd better, Whip," he said. "I got some work to do with these and I think I need my head."

"Got another owl?" Whipple said.

"Looks to me like," Briggs said. "Down behind the orchard, probably one of those big oaks. I thought I heard him two, three weeks ago. And then the past few mornings, crows've been raising hell over there. So I thought I'd go and check."

"Think he needs your help, do you?" Whipple said.

"Hell, no," Briggs said. "I'm just a good landowner. Like to keep things orderly, at least when I'm around."

4

the day had become warmer with the noon. His boots were heavy and hot on his feet. He decided that summer remained in the first part of August in Vermont, although he had not seen it most Augusts of his adult life, but only between lunch and sunset.

The Siller boys had parked their beat-up red Chevrolet pickup alongside the porch, blocking the steps. Briggs had to cramp his way around it to reach the porch. He assumed they had come to cut the first crop of hay. He went into the house. Lillian was sitting at the kitchen table, a cup of coffee in front of her and the telephone in her hand. The television softly murmured conversation between two handsome young men in a soap opera; they were sitting in a bar and appeared to be angry with each other. Lillian fluttered her right hand at him. He returned the salute.

He put the sack of shells on the table and moved the coon cat aside from the middle of the window seat. The cat glared at him. He sat down and untied his boots. He placed them on the hooked rug and stood up in his stocking feet. He walked around the table to the door leading into the attached shed and fetched a pair of moccasins. He returned to the window seat, where the cat had resumed its position, and moved the cat again. The cat got down and marched over to the stove rug where the orange-yellow cat slept, curled up in a ball. The coon cat cuffed the tabby cat with its left front paw. The tabby cat opened its eyes and offered feeble resistance with its right front paw. The coon cat pounced on the tabby, and they began to roll around silently until the tabby acknowledged reality, stood up, and retreated under the table, rubbing against Lillian's legs. The coon cat lay down on the stove rug and curled up in a ball.

Lillian spoke into the handset. "Well, it isn't true," she said. "She's simply got it wrong. As usual, I might add. I was there for Mass on Sunday, and he never said a single thing about the President. Not one single thing. All he said was that what's happening in the cities is something we all should think about, where the country's going. He said we're all losing sight of the fact that what we do in our own life, when you put it all together, is what makes this country. And we have to start thinking about that, and paying more attention."

He put on the moccasins. He had not worn them for a while, and they had stiffened up. He reproached himself. He must have wetted them and allowed them to dry improperly. He flexed each one when he had it on his foot, standing up and lodging his heel securely on the sole. He sat down again and pulled the laces taut.

"Well, I can think of a reason," Lillian said. "She's anti-Catholic—that's all. Always has been. When I got engaged to Henry, she was talking all over town about me behind my back. And Henry, too. That he was marrying a Catholic. 'Henry liked high school so much,' she was saying, 'he's marrying a Catholic so he can go there all his life.' And: 'I bet Henry forgets someday, and just goes in the locker room and puts his gym shorts on, when he's going there for Mass.' She's always been that way, and so has her whole family." She paused.

"Yes, I know she's a good woman, and I like her very much. But she does have that blind spot, Evelyn, even when you're in her house. Martha Glennon is a bigot, and that's all there is to it."

Briggs went around the table again, past the door to the shed, and through the hall into his study. He went to the desk and took a small brass key from the center drawer. He used the key to open the glass doors of the mahogany gun cabinet to the right of the desk. He removed a Winchester 12-gauge pump-action shotgun from the rack and snicked the action closed. Then he opened it again. The chamber glowed dully with oil. He leaned the shotgun against the desk. He used the key again to open the top drawer of the cabinet. He removed the Magnum revolver, a box of shells, and the cowhide belt and holster from the drawer. He released the cylinder and spun it smoothly against the oil. He loaded the revolver with six bullets and pulled six more from the Styrofoam block inside the cartridge box. He put those in his pants pocket. He buckled the holster belt around his waist and put the revolver in the holster. He closed the drawer and locked it. He closed the doors of the cabinet and locked it. He put the key back in the desk drawer. He carried the shotgun back out into the kitchen.

Lillian was still talking on the phone. "I'm sure she did," she said. "That's exactly what I said. Back when it was Joe McCarthy, the Catholics were trying to ruin the country and get us into war with Russia. 'So the pope can run the country.' Now it's Eugene McCarthy, and the Catholics're trying to run the country. Get us to lose a war with Russia. So the pope can run the country. It doesn't matter to her, what's going on. If there's a Catholic that's involved in it, she knows what it is. It's the Catholics again, trying, wreck the country. I do the best I can, you know, to like the saintly Martha, who does all of her good works. But it's pretty hard sometimes, when everything that's bad that happens, it's my Church's fault. If you talked about niggers like she talks about Catholics, or Jews as far as that goes, everyone would say that—that you were a bigot. But she gets away with it. Because she sticks to us."

He went over to the window seat and laid the shotgun on it. He returned to the doorway and took a canvas vest with deep pockets from the peg next to the windbreaker. He put the vest on.

Lillian said into the phone: "Wait a minute, Evelyn." She put her left palm over the mouthpiece. "Where you going now?" she said.

"The orchard," he said. "I think there's something going on there that I need to take a hand in." He walked to the table and opened the sack of shells. He took a dozen from the top box and went to the window seat.

"Evelyn, I'll call you back," Lillian said. She put the handset in the cradle.

He stood in the late afternoon light filtering through the bay window and loaded the Winchester with six Number Six shells. He put six more in the left bottom pocket of his vest.

"Where're you going?" she said.

"I'm going 'cross the street," he said. "I'm going to go across the street and up the hill, through the cemetery. And then I'm going to come down the hill and to the orchard from the back. And see if what I think is going on, is going on. And if it is, or if it did, then I am going to finish off the business. And then I'm coming home."

"And what do you think's going on?" she said.

"I think I got a big old owl, or maybe two or three, nesting in the big oaks out behind the orchard. And I think, in fact I know, that I got a flock of crows that don't know damn-all about owls. Which generally means that when they spend the day dive-bombing them, there's some wounded crows around. Either someone shoots them, and disposes carcasses, or else somebody doesn't and they die and rot. After which the raccoons come, and they have a good old time. Then they run out of crow meat and they look for something else, some other easy pickin's, and that means we got raccoons looking in our windows, going through our trash. Which I'd just as soon not have. They know how to use their hands."

"And what's the pistol for?" she said.

"The *revolver's* for in case I meet a big old bear," he said. "Bears're active in the summer. Winter's when they sleep."

"I don't want you shooting anything big," she said.

"Oh, for God's sake, Lil," he said, "I'm just being cautious. Case one of them got restless, a rogue out of his den, in a rambunctious mood. But I don't expect to see one. Let alone shoot him. And then have to drag him back here, gut the son-a-bitch and salt him. I'm just being on the safe side. I'd rather have this thing, and not need it, 'n need it and not have it."

"Because it's maybe all right for you to hike it out of here, every day," she said, "come back, you're good and ready. But you're not leaving me with some animal to skin. And then try to cook strong meat so it won't taste like what it is."

"Do I look like Father Morrissette to you?" he said.

"What?" she said.

"Bunny's been jacklighting deer again," he said. "Caught him, other night."

"That's what Martha Glennon told Evelyn," she said. "I don't believe a word of it."

"I do," Briggs said. "Bunny's been jacking deer ever since I can

41

recall. He's famous for it. Good at it, too. Now Bunny, you were married to him, Whip'd never clip you on another piece of steak. You'd be up to your armpits in buffalo, probably, you had Bunny around. Wouldn't be a bear for miles."

"Well," she said, "if you're worried about bears, isn't the long gun better?"

"Good point," he said. He put the shotgun back on the window seat and went back into the study. He unlocked the second drawer and removed a box of deer slugs. He put three in his top right pocket, replaced the box in the drawer, and locked it. He went back into the kitchen. He racked open the action of the Winchester, dumped out the shells in the magazine, loaded two deer slugs in first, added three shot shells, and closed it. "Think I'm all set now," he said.

"You saw a pheasant or something," she said.

"A rabbit or something," he said. "Pheasant's out of season."

"I could make a stew," she said. "Carrots, turnips, potatoes. Onions. It would be delicious. Little red wine, let it simmer, day or so—remember how it tasted?" She stood up and moved toward him quickly. She kissed him on the mouth and clung to him. "Remember, Hank, how it tasted? How you loved my rabbit stew?"

He disengaged himself slowly. "Won't be here tomorrow night," he said. "You forget: I got to work. Light's dying. I'll be back before it's dark."

He had learned it early in his youth—exactly when, he could not remember. It was easier and smarter to walk a half-mile down the Richmond Road to the cemetery entrance on the left, and climb the plowed road up the hill to the granite pylon commemorating the Civil War dead. It was shorter to cross the road and labor through the shaded field into the orchard, but the noise he made frightened off whatever game had been there. Often he had heard the sound of drumming wings, as the birds took off.

He went down the road, the shotgun cradled in his right arm. He saw the sun setting to his right over the Adirondacks. He stopped for a moment at the culvert to look into the dark brook. Then he went on another four hundred yards to where the iron gates hinged at stone pillars closed the cemetery road. He went up around the pillar to the north and regained the road. He walked in the center of the road, his weight crunching the gravel, the sky turning darker, the gun comfortable on his arm, the air clear but smelling already of wood smoke, and he thought about the players running in the outfield, the pitchers making long tosses, the batting cages ringing with foul balls, and the summer still enduring farther south where it was warm.

The hill had gotten steeper since the days when he climbed it with Whipple and Cobb and Ford Thomas. He thought of that when he came to the Thomas headstone on his left, sheltered under a tall black maple that kept some of its leaves in the winter. He stopped in front of it and did the closest thing he ever did to praying for the dead: He thought about Ford—MAY 11, 1930 / AUGUST 15, 1951 / IN THE SERVICE OF HIS COUNTRY—and what it must have felt like to awaken from a sound sleep out on bivouac on the Kansas plain to see a roaring half-track coming out of the darkness to crush you.

Luck was strangely distributed. The bones of a fine athlete and crack shot had been in the ground for sixteen years. But Ford's brother, Winston, two years younger, was still going strong.

There was something wrong with Winston that had prevented him from playing sports and excluded him as well from other normal, high school things. He seemed to go through life at an angle, dodging obstacles different from those other people faced, dealing with strange problems that they could not imagine. He was just able enough to graduate, and close enough to normal so that he was taken in the draft, but marginal enough so that there was never any doubt that he would be a combat infantryman until the day that someone shot him. But he served a full two years in Korea, uncomplainingly enduring the worst of the Chinese counteroffensive, collecting battle stars enough to cover the left side of his tunic, surviving in grade long enough to be discharged as a master sergeant, returning home with a petite Japanese bride he had met in Kyoto—he introduced her as "Elida," soon shortened to "Lida"—to the initial respectful amazement of those who'd known him.

The amazement subsided and the respect ebbed quickly, too; he had pulled off things that no one had thought he could do, but he had not changed. He took up carpentry and roofing and crabbed out a living doing poor work with his hands. His shingling leaked and the floors he repaired were not plumb, and when he installed cabinets the doors sagged and the hardware fell off. When his customers complained he did not reply or object, or blame the results on poor materials or green lumber. He stood humbly with his eyes lowered and listened until they were finished, and then he nodded and indicated he would try to make things right. He did try, and they never were.

"It's very simple," Whipple said when Briggs reported what a lousy job Winston had done on his garage doors, "Winston's not a good workman. It's not that he don't want to work. It's not that he don't know how. He's as willing as a horny bull. And he understands what you want done. But he ain't competent. It's not something he can help, and he knows it. That's why he won't answer you, when you chew him out."

But Winston was still alive, as silent as his older brother, maybe, but alive all the same. "Can't figure it, Ford," Briggs said to the headstone, and resumed his walk up the road. Punch would have been less respectful; he had had a large bladder for a medium-size mongrel, half brindle German shepherd, half some kind of hound, and he had loved to piss on headstones.

At the top of the hill he looked down the gradual slope to the northwest. Someone with a plot there had had a death in the family in the past day or so. Near the tumbledown stone wall at the edge of the brook, there was a fresh grave. He went down the hill in the diminishing light, pausing at the bottom to peer into the dimness under the trees to read the name on the gravestone: LIGGETT. He made a mental note to ask Lillian which of the Liggetts had died; it would give him the pleasure for once of plainly implying she had shirked her duty to keep up on such events when he was away from home and brief him when he returned.

He put the shotgun on top of the wall, muzzle pointing away from him, and climbed over the smooth stones. He picked up the shotgun and waded into the dark water, the current over the gravel and slippery rocks strong against his ankles. He avoided the deep pool eroded in front of the large boulder half-on, half-off the northwesterly bank, chiefly because he knew it deep and strong enough to reach his knees, and perhaps cause him to slip, but partly out of consideration for the big brown trout that lived in it.

A long time ago, Lillian, four months pregnant with Sally, had

44

followed him out to the brook one summer day during the All-Star break. Ted was about four then, and Briggs had decided that showing him the big brown would be better entertainment than subjecting him to the frustration of being unable to catch a baseball. The boy had sat on the tall grass of the bank and ignored his father, playing with the Tonka bulldozer that went everywhere with him, and saying: "Vroom, *vroom*," over and over.

The big brown's struggle with the hook did not interest him. He had glanced up politely when his father brought the fish ashore and displayed it, but then he went back to his toy. Briggs was removing the barbless hook when Lillian came down to the bank. "Are you putting him back again?" she had said.

"Uh-huh," he had said. He had dipped his hands in the brook and picked up the fish carefully, so as not to rub off its protective slime, and had lowered it back into the pool, holding it in the July-sluggish current until it moved its tail, showing that it had recovered from its most recent trauma.

"I don't see why you keep throwing him back," she had said. "I could make a nice dinner with that. How many times've you caught that fish, anyway?"

"I don't know," he had said. "Judging from the way he keeps getting caught, same lure, he doesn't recall either. Ten or a dozen, probably. Why kill him? He's old. Not too smart, but old just the same. He's never done anything to me except cooperate in a few thrills. Maybe some day Ted'll catch him, I'm away. Then you'll get your wish."

"I don't like fishing," the boy had said abruptly. "I'm never going to fish. I want to go back now."

So far as Briggs knew, the boy had kept his word. There was that about the kid, at least: You could count on what he said he planned to do, even if you didn't like it. Especially if you didn't like it.

One evening before a game in Comiskey Park, Briggs had sat musing on his stool in front of his locker in his T-shirt, pants, and socks, his uniform shirt hanging from his right hand onto the floor, his gaze in the middle distance. Bill Parmalee, the bull pen coach, had interrupted him. "Hank my friend," he had said, "you in a trance or something? Morales been taking you, his gypsy friends again, so they put a spell on you?"

"No, no," Briggs had said. "I'll drink the rum with Gus all night. But when it comes to his damned voodoo, he does that alone. No, I was just, I called home from the hotel, and I talked to my wife, and she and the baby're fine. Then I talked to my boy. And he said he's fine, but it's like he's doing chores, I'm home or I call up. I can't figure him out.

"You saw him, Father's Day game. He seems like a normal kid. But it's like he's the one on the road, and I'm the one who never knows where he is, even in the same house." He had sighed. "I don't know what to do about it."

"Simple," Parmalee said. "Retire."

Briggs had started putting on his shirt. He snorted. "Retire?" he said. "You kidding? In the first place, why'd I want to? I'm just getting into the swing of things now. And in the second place, where could I make this kind of money? Raising cider apples?"

"Well, that's something else," Parmalee had said. "But the answer to your problem is that you're exactly right. He *is* a normal kid. He don't like his father. He resents it when you're gone, because you're not there, take care his mother, and he thinks he has to do it, and he shouldn't have to. And when you're there, he resents that, too, because he's the one that's been taking care of her all the time you're gone, and who the hell you think you are, coming back and getting into bed with her."

"She lets him sleep in our bed when I'm out of town," Briggs had said.

"Well, make her cut it out," Parmalee had said. "That only makes it worse. My second wife, the twat, did that, with her son from her first marriage. And I tried to tell her: 'Josie, that is not a good idea.' Kid was eight years old, the time. I said: 'He's gonna start getting hard-ons, you know, three, four years from now, and he should not be sleeping with his mother when that thing stands up.' And she wouldn't listen. Not that it made that much difference to me—we only lasted two more years. But the kid turned out lousy, and that didn't help. It didn't help matters at all."

Briggs had followed Parmalee's advice when he got home. "I *have* to," Lillian had said. "It's hard enough for him's it is, you gone all the time. Then he sees me letting Sally stay in our room, so I don't have to go far for her feedings, and he wants to sleep there too. I can't just throw him out. It'd break his heart."

"In the first place," he had said, "Sally is a baby. In the second place, Sally sleeps in her crib, not in our bed. In the third place, you're giving him habits he shouldn't be getting into, that aren't good for him. There'll be problems when he's older. So I want you to cut it out." She had agreed at last. Then she said: "But how will you know, if I keep my word?"

He didn't know. He had never known. The hostile distance between him and Ted remained unmeasured in the boy's thirteenth September, when they left him for his first year at Phillips Exeter, a decision Briggs had made over his wife's sullen objections, not only because he knew the education available in Occident was poor but because he wanted to get his son out of his wife's bed, at least for most of the year, and that seemed the only way to be sure that he was doing it.

He climbed up the bank of the brook and went into the sparse line of oaks that bordered the orchard. He walked slowly, the gun ready, making an effort to breathe silently, listening and inspecting quadrants of ground in front of him. There were tracks in the grass that rabbits had left in matched pairs, and a fox had browsed there too, quartering back and forth among the trees, sitting motionless at one point and then bounding forward in several great leaps to a spot where blood and gray fur showed he had caught a squirrel on the ground. There were chickadees active in the oaks. He remembered the day when his father had caught him plinking the small gray and white birds with his .22, loaded with shot shells.

"You don't go halfway, do you, son?" he had said, hitting him hard on the shoulder. "First you take my gun without asking me. Then you start putting those damned shot shells through it, and fuck up the rifling. And what do you use the shot on? Animals you can't eat, that never hurt a thing. You're a little shit, you know that?" Then he had grabbed the rifle away and carefully hit Henry in the face with the butt-end of the stock, knocking him down onto the carpet of fallen leaves.

The blow had driven his inner cheek against his teeth, making it bleed. He sat on the ground then and put the first two fingers of his right hand into his mouth, bringing them out red. He had looked at the blood and then back up at his father.

"Hurt you, huh? Good," his father had said. "Consider yourself lucky. Dick Boyd told me he caught Carter, doing the same thing. And

47

you know what Dick did? He give the kid a taste of his own medicine. Made him walk back the house ahead of him, and shot him in the backside with one of those bird loads. Stung his ass pretty good. 'He won't do that again,' Dick said, and I believe he's right. And you better not again, either, 'cause that's what I'll do next, if I catch you at it."

Off to his left there was motion in the open place between the oaks and the apple orchard. He made out three black forms on the ground and turned to approach them. He found three crows. One, its head nearly torn off, was obviously dead, but two, a yard farther away, were slowly bleeding to death. The one nearest to him lay still on its back, its chest ripped open in two deep gashes. The other flopped helplessly, its left wing torn from the bloody socket. He kicked the mortally wounded crow over close to the one with the damaged wing, released the safety of the gun, and fired twice at the birds, the circular pattern of shot peppering the grass around them as they bounced from the impacts. He chambered a fresh shell and relocked the safety. He picked up the two birds he had shot, and the one that had died, carrying them by their feet in his left hand.

It was getting dark faster than he had expected. He followed the dirt track where the trucks would come in among the orderly rows of apple trees at picking time, pausing at each of the three little intersections to look down between the files. The arrangement of the trees had always reminded him of church. If it had not been for the bees in blossom time, the orchard on a sunny day would have made a place of worship far better in his estimation than the hushed, hot church in the village where the Reverend Glennon condemned sin every Sunday while the Briggses and the other thirty or so families sweated out their shirts.

About a hundred yards from the road, near the westerly edge of the orchard, the bulkhead structure built over the opening of the fruit cellar looked like a ski jump for elves. The bulkhead was new, erected in 1963, steel he had purchased reluctantly to replace the wood his father had used when he built it forty years before. The wooden structure had not been as geometrically precise or functionally efficient. It was a small windowless shed, about five feet high, made of boards left over from major barn repairs. On its easterly wall Briggs's father, in the summer the boy turned ten, for his son's birthday had displayed a resignation to reality that Briggs recognized only later.

Abandoning his annual threats of punishments to follow any repetition of the boy's practice of using unripe apples as baseballs, Roy Briggs had painted a white rectangle one foot wide by three feet tall, the bottom of it about eighteen inches from the ground. Then he had taken his tape measure and carefully located a place exactly sixty feet, six inches from the wall of the shed. There he had made a mound of dirt about eighteen inches high, and in the center of it lodged a one-foot length of sidewall cut from an old car tire. "Now, happy birthday, son," he had said, "but I want a present, too. You can have this, I want you to. And in exchange I want something. Only the dwarf apples, all right? Or a tennis ball or something. But leave the good ones on the trees. Only windfalls and the dwarfs. Will you do that for me?"

Henry remained embarrassed by his acceptance of the gift. He stood at the edge of the orchard with the three crows in one hand and the shotgun in the other, and he remembered his complaints—the distance from the mound was a good ten feet longer than the sandlot field at school, and the zone itself was smaller than even major leaguers used.

"I know," Roy had said. "Did that on purpose. You hit that target from this distance, and hit it every time, fifty feet'll seem like twenty, and the real strike zone'll look big. Besides, maybe you keep at it, some day you'll be good enough to face that kind of distance." Not until several years later—and hundreds of healthy apples—had Henry entirely appreciated his tenth-birthday present.

He paused again when he got to the bulkhead. Something four-footed and large had climbed onto it, disturbing the accumulated pollen and dust. It had sat down, swished a long tail once, and then jumped back down toward the brook. He bent to examine the spoor in the fading light. The paw marks seemed to have been made by an animal with a large center pad and three forward flanking pads. He went around to the back of the bulkhead to seek more tracks, but in the light could find none within a twelve-foot radius. Dogs could have smelled what had been there; at least someone would have known.

He continued out to the road, the dark coming fast now. He made his way across and went up the driveway toward the barn. The Siller boys had left. The smell of the burning hardwood from the house lay welcoming in the still air. He went to the garage, opened the trash bucket nearest the door, and dropped the dead crows in. He replaced the bucket cover tightly and went up to the house, unloading the shotgun as he walked. Between the barn and the house he saw a cock pheasant standing watch while two hens browsed the low shrubs beside the sugar house. He stamped his feet on the porch and went inside.

"Any luck?" Lillian said. She was making beef stew on the stove, and the smell of it made him suddenly and desperately hungry. "How long 'fore that's ready?" he said. "Oh, say, an hour," she said. "I asked if you had any luck."

"Manner of speaking," he said. "The old owl nailed three of those crows. Hadda shoot two of them—he'd finished one by himself." He removed his vest and took the shells from the pocket. He put them in his shirt pockets. "Looked to me like there's been something big out in that orchard, past couple nights or so."

"Evelyn said they saw a lynx up in the Notch," she said. "Someone did, I mean. Did you see a pheasant for me?"

"This was no friggin' lynx," he said, unbuckling the holster and picking up the shotgun and the bag of shells from the kitchen table.

"Well," she said, stirring the stew while adding a cup of red wine, "whatever it was. Did you happen to see my pheasant? My mouth just waters for pheasant."

"No," he said, "I'm a warden. Pheasants're out of season. Guys in my line of work don't shoot things out of season. I'm gonna put the guns away. And dry my moccasins right, for once."

5

the deep still darkness outside made the lights in the house and the fire glowing through the stove door into aspects of shelter as reassuring as the roof and the walls. Lillian served the stew from the crock in the center of the table into the broad white soup plates. She put a plate of fresh cornbread between them, and he poured each of them a glass of red wine from a Gallo jug. The orange-yellow cat was back on the stove rug, and the coon cat slept on the window seat. He finished his first plate of stew and helped himself to a second, along with a fourth piece of cornbread. She looked at him wistfully. "I never know," she said.

"You never know what?" he said.

"I never know whether to be flattered, and glad that you've got such a good appetite, or worried about your weight."

"My weight's all right," he said. "I'm six two. I can carry two ten, easy. I'm not saying it's all solid as a rock, but it's not too much to weigh."

"And it's also *what* you eat," she said. "I can always tell if something's bad for you. If you like it, and eat lots of it, it is."

"You're a good cook," he said. "And you're no featherweight yourself, since we're on the subject. What do you do, I'm away? Make all the doughnuts you won't make while I'm here, scarf them all up 'fore I get back?"

She giggled. "Evelyn called me last Thursday morning. Said Marie's tutor's car'd broken down, so she'd had to pick her up and she was going to take her back. And after she dropped her off, she'd stop in here. Evelyn, I mean."

"Whip treats that kid like shit," he said, buttering the cornbread. "I like Whip, and I've known him all my life, and I realize he can't help how he feels that she can't talk. But, god*damn*, she can *hear*. And she's not stupid. She can hear when you talk about her as though she wasn't there, and she knows what it *means*. When you don't say 'please,' and thank her when she does something for you."

"He thinks it's his fault," she said. "Or else it's Evelyn's. Or maybe both of theirs. Something they should've done. Something they shouldn't've done. 'It eats at him,' Evelyn says. 'It just eats at him every day. That he's got a child that isn't perfect. *Right*'s the word he uses.' Even Paul Junior, as well as he's done. Paul has his moments with him, too. 'He won't let him be a man. He just won't let it happen. When Paul Junior comes home, it's like his father can't wait to get at him. Start a fight. Bring up a subject he knows they'll disagree on, and then just start digging him about it.' And I guess there's a real problem with Paul Junior's girlfriend, Dana. Evelyn's kind of closemouthed about that, though. I don't know what it is."

"She's Jewish," he said. "Whip'd like to think it's because she's 'one of them damned liberals,' and that's the main reason he gives for not liking her. But when he talks a little longer, he gives it all away. Martha Glennon doesn't like Catholics? Paul Whipple doesn't like Jews. Not that he really ever knew any Jews, or anything like that, or one of them did something to him. He just doesn't like them, is all, and when he sees Paul Junior's girl, he sees one. Doesn't like her in his house." He paused. "He also doesn't like her in Paul Junior's bed, which is where he thinks she is. And, of course, he's right, but they hide it from him and he can't say anything."

"In this day and age?" she said.

"This is not Whip's day," he said, "and it isn't his age, either. It all just came along and rolled over him, 'thout his permission. Far's he's concerned, he was perfectly satisfied with nineteen fifty, 'fifty-one, and if he can't stop things from changing, well, that's all right—he doesn't have to like the changes. And he doesn't."

"Well," she said, "Evelyn won't admit it, if she knows that's what it is. She says it's politics. She says Dana just gets his goat every time she comes. She doesn't know whether Dana starts it or Paul does, it always happens so fast, but every time they come to visit, inside a half an hour, that girl and Paul're at swords' points. 'I dread it,' she said. 'Isn't that an awful thing? My own son comes home, and we're all going to be together, and I just dread to see it coming? Because I know there'll be a fight.'"

"That what she had on her mind, this week?" he said.

"No," Lillian said. "I don't think so, at least. She was just feeling social. I made a batch of cinnamon rolls, twelve of them. And you know, we ate the whole batch? I didn't have any lunch. Just a tuna fish sandwich for dinner." She sighed. "I hate it when you're away."

"Oughta be used to it by now," he said. "After all these years. I'm home a helluva lot more'n I was when I was playing." He got up. "You want coffee?"

"Please," she said. "It wasn't so hard then. It wasn't in the winter, so much. When the kids were little, and we all went to spring training, well, that helped. And then, when the season started, it was April. And I had them with me. Now, with them gone away, and you gone away, I'm here by myself. You're away half of the time."

"Not half," he said, delivering the coffee to the table. "Not even close to half. Besides, if Teddy keeps fucking around, you'll have him back with you pretty soon. I wish I knew what makes that kid tick. Or why he doesn't tick—that'd be more like it. I've tried and tried, to figure it out, and I can't do it."

"You were away *five* nights last week," she said. "Four the week before that."

"I have to patrol," he said. "You know that. Poachers get wind that I'm staying home, they'll shoot everything but their own dicks, and what they can't eat, after they've skinned it for pelt, they'll feed to their dogs and go out and shoot more. All these woods'll be one mausoleum. And then I had those dinners to do." He sat down again.

"I don't see why you keep having to do those things," she said. "You're retired now. I could see it when you were still playing. Part of your responsibility to the team. Especially when you were with Boston. But that was years ago. It ever end?"

"It's only been two," he said absently, "I've been out of ball. What, six? Since I left Boston."

"Well, six, then," she said. "Whatever. It was a long time ago. Doesn't this sort of thing ever end?"

"I hope not," he said. "It's one thing to live in Vermont."

"I like Vermont," she said.

"And it's another thing to have your degree from the University of Pittsburgh," he said. "And to've put in some your best years in the National League, that nobody's ever even heard of in Vermont. Under forty, that is. Let alone who was a star in it, when I was going good. I got to keep my name before the public. I got to keep reminding them they know me. That I'm a famous person. Whatever the hell that is. At least so I'm told. That if I do, it'll do me some good. No one's ever told me just exactly what good."

"I just wish you didn't have to do it so often," she said. "If it was places nearer to home. It worries me, having you drive all around all the time."

"It'd be nicer," he said. "But on the other hand, nobody else asked me, do anything. I got to have something to do. Everybody does."

"It also worries me," she said, "you *being* out there on the road by yourself all the time. It worries Sally, too. She said to me, on the phone the other night: 'Dad's not getting into trouble, is he?' They remember, Hank. They know it's lonely on the road, and things can happen, and it's not like they don't forgive you. Haven't forgiven you. But they still remember. You have to remember, they look up to you. Or want to, at least. If you'll let them."

"You know, it's the damnedest thing," he said. "When I was growing up, it was the grown-ups' job to keep the kids in line. And now things've gotten all turned around. Now that I'm a grown-up, the kids're keeping us in line. Who the fuck appointed them, see over our private life? Sally been's humping Cal since she was fifteen, the latest. Where the hell does she come off, getting pious about us?"

"She has not," Lillian said.

"Oh, bullshit, 'she has not,'" he said. "I used to sit out there on the porch after you'd gone to bed, I was home in the fall, and I'd see that black Camaro come up the hill and turn right, into the orchard. And the lights'd go off, and pretty soon the crickets were getting drowned out by the springs creaking. They were fucking their brains out under those trees. It's a wonder she didn't get knocked up. He must've used a rubber. Kid's smarter than I thought. I wonder where he bought them. I was his age, I was too embarrassed. Course I didn't have my own car. Would've had to buy them from Whip's father. If I'd've had my own car, there wouldn't *be* a Ted around to drive me halfway nuts. I would've gone to Burlington and bought myself some Trojans. That's probably what Cal does. I'd've left the little bastard in a condom, 'stead of you. Thrown him out the window in the bushes, after we got finished, and good goddamned riddance, too."

"You're awful," she said.

"I'm realistic," he said. "And since I am realistic, I don't take kindly to a lot of happy horseshit from Sally about how I live my life. Fresh, or secondhand. Especially from a green kid crowding twenty-one with absolutely no idea of how she's going to make a living—if she ever has to make one, God forbid. Diddling around down there, taking god-damned art courses, for Christ sake. Can she type? Can she keep a set of books? Take shorthand? Teach? What the hell can she do that anybody'd hire her to do, and pay her money for?"

"She's ahead of where you were at the same age," Lillian said. "Closer her degree, I mean."

"When I was her age," he said, "I was making a goddamned living. It wasn't a good living, and there wasn't any guarantee it ever would be, but I was making one. And when I got a vacation from the way I made my living, I went out and got temporary work, to improve my living. That's why it took me eight years to finish school. So she finishes in four. Big deal. What's she finished? She's finished finishing, is what. She went out of here with stars in her eyes, and when she comes back here now, that's still all she's got in them. I kind of doubt the day'll ever come when I'll drive down to Boston to see Sally warming up in the bullpen for the Sox. She hasn't got the velocity, even if they do start playing women."

"They'll straighten out," Lillian said. "Wait and see—they will. I think Ted's going to . . . well, I think he'll do just fine. College, it's just that college isn't his real cup of tea. He likes being out in the world, with real people. He'd be a good salesman."

"Oh, for crying out loud, Lil," he said. "What's the kid ever sold?

Except to us: a bill of goods. When they tossed his butt out of Bates, for God's sake, at first I was scared shitless he'd get drafted. Then I thought: 'Hey, wait a minute. He gets drafted, he'll have to do what people tell him. For the first time in his life. He's smart enough to figure it out, not maybe right off but fairly damned soon, that they've got something that we never did have: a way to punish him if he doesn't do as he's told. So he'll shape up, for the first time, and he'll do it. And they'll find something he *can* do, without killing himself or them, and this whole thing could turn out to be the best thing, ever happened. More'n we ever managed, at least.' After that, I was *praying* he'd get drafted, but of course he never did. The kid is nimble, Lil. He's quick. Doesn't work much, but he's shrewd. Too shrewd for our good, certainly, and probably for his own good, too."

"Henry," she said, "he might've gotten killed."

"Nuts," he said. "He's too smart. He would've been a clerk. But of course he lucked out. A whole goddamned two years on the loose, and they never even bothered him."

"They were only taking the twenty-year-olds," she said. "It wasn't anything he planned."

"Oh no?" he said. "Well, I notice soon's he turned twenty, he was back in school again, got his Two-S deferment back. You see maybe any planning in that? Teddy's lazy, not stupid. He doesn't want to work at anything, except whatever it takes to get him out of work."

"Driving a truck's hard work," she said.

"Driving a truck is not hard work," he said. "Not for the brains involved, it isn't. I admit it's a little hard on the social life, getting up at three in the morning to go down to the terminal and load up the papers, and then drive around in the dark dumping them off all over the place. Not that it seemed to affect him much—gave him permission to sleep all day. But you're all by yourself when you're out on the job, nobody giving you orders, and if you got the brains of a milk-wagon horse, you can do it without any sweat. But what the hell's it lead to? After twenty years on the job, what do they give you? A bigger truck? With a radio in it, so you don't have to carry your own? No, the only thing it gets you is a big, soft belly, good for lots of beer and coffee, and doughnuts, too, of course, and a bunch of friends to go hunting with, or maybe take in a game."

"Do you want to go to bed?" she said. "Since you're going away again?"

"Sure," he said. "Always ready for that. Least there's something we agree on." He stood up and began to clear the dinner dishes.

"Oh," she said, finishing her coffee, "Ed Cobb called, you were out, over in the orchard. I forgot to tell you."

"I'm not surprised," he said. "Whip said he might. Just surprised he didn't come here. He say what he wanted?"

"No," she said. "I assumed you knew. Just that he wanted to come down and see you. He has to go to Boston tomorrow. I told him you'd be gone Monday."

"Which means I'd better make myself scarce next weekend, then," he said.

"Why?" she said.

"You know Ed," he said. "When Ed wants to see you, it never occurs to him, maybe you don't want to see him. He thinks it's an honor or something."

"Well," she said, "he is the Speaker."

"I don't care if he's the king of fucking England," he said. "Who I see, and when I see them, those're things I like to decide. He'll show up here next weekend—just wait and see."

"Do you know what it's about?" she said.

"No," he said, "I don't. Whip knows, but he wouldn't tell me. But I can't think a single thing that Ed could want from me, that I'd want to give to him. I've known too many guys like Ed. Always on the lookout for some way that they can use you. You think they're asking you to visit a sick kid because they feel sorry for the kid. So you take your afternoon, and you sign a dozen balls—because the sick kid's always in a playroom with ten other little sick kids when you get there to see him, and you can't leave them feeling bad—and you blow the whole day there with the parents taking pictures. And then about a year later, maybe a little sooner, you find out the prick that asked you did it so the sick kid's father'd give him all his legal business. Or buy stocks from him or something. And that's the way Ed is. My job? He expects me to be grateful for it. And I am. But he also expects me to think he didn't get any mileage out of giving it to me. Which I know damned well he did, and that means he thinks I'm stupid. That's the way they all are.

Sitting around all day and scheming, how they can use somebody. Ed's just not as bad, and sometimes he gives something back."

"He said he'd call you back, on Friday," she said, coming over to the sink and linking her arm through his.

"I will bet you," he said, "I will bet he doesn't. On Saturday he'll just show up. If I'm not here, he'll wait. He knows sooner or later, I'll have to come home, and he'll be waiting to ambush me."

"Well," she said, snuggling her head into his back, "then we have something in common."

6

Shortly after eleven on Saturday morning, Ed Cobb arrived at Briggs's house. Briggs was sitting at the kitchen table drinking coffee and reading the *Champlain Prospect*. When he saw the Chrysler come up the driveway and stop next to the porch, he put the mug down on the paper and said to the cats: "Well, you're my witnesses. Said he'd be here, and he is."

Cobb got out of the car. Briggs went to the door and opened it as he reached the porch. "Come in, come in," he said. Cobb nodded. "You want, what, an hour or so?"

"An hour," Cobb said. "That should do it." He took the chair Briggs had vacated. He tapped his right forefinger on the newspaper. "*Prospect*, huh? Surprised you're not reading the *Valley Press*. Our friend Russ'll get all depressed, I tell him old Henry's deserted."

Briggs moved his coffee mug to the place mat opposite the one at the chair that Cobb had taken. "I read the *Press* when I'm working," he said. "Days when I take a short lunch. Since it changed hands the damned thing takes less'n five minutes, read it from cover to cover. After I've finished, know less'n I did, 'fore I opened the thing. Russ Wixton's the only thing in it worth reading, and he doesn't write, Saturdays. So I take them off, 'long with him."

"Good," Cobb said, nodding. "Plausible, plausible, may even be good enough, save Russ from a big burst of tears."

"You want some coffee, Ed?" Briggs said. "I'd offer you a beer, but it's still a little early. Don't want to give you bad habits."

Cobb snorted. " 'Bad habits,' " he said, "I wish it was that. You know something, Henry? I'm almost forty now, and I'm not in shape, and I'm in the wrong line of work. And it's too late to change."

"Should've gone into mine," Briggs said. "In that, you don't get to decide. Some guy who never could do it—he's the one who decides."

Cobb snorted. "Yeah," he said, "but at least you know who he is. In my business, in my business it's like getting goosed in an elevator. You know somebody did it, but as long's they all keep straight faces, no way to tell who it was."

Briggs laughed. "So whaddaya want, Ed?" he said.

"I apologize, dropping in on you like this," Cobb said. "I would've called you, yesterday, but I hadda put down this rebellion, and that took half the day. And then of course I had about two hundred calls, return. So, I just took a chance."

"I didn't get back 'til yesterday afternoon anyway," Briggs said. "Besides, I figured from what Whip said that you'd probably be in touch. Lil had some things to do in Burlington this morning. Wanted me to come, but I said, no, I been on the road enough the past few days. And I figured you'd drop by."

"Got a new broad for yourself, have you, Hank?" Cobb said. "Gotta hand it to you, pal. Some of us start to slow down with age, but you just keep on, going right at it. Or is it 'coming' I mean?"

"I protect the animals, Ed," Briggs said. "I stop people from fishing with dynamite, and I don't let 'em kill off the beavers. Just what you told me to do."

"Yeah," Cobb said. "You always protected those beavers. I bet you protected more beavers, your time, most guys've ever dreamed of."

"Okay," Briggs said, "think that, it makes you happy. Anything else on your mind, you come on a Saturday, bother a man when he's annoying the people, minding his business at home?"

"Yeah," Cobb said. "I was thinking about maybe getting season tickets next year. Think the Sox still'll look good?"

"You're asking me?" Briggs said. "The guy so smart that he gets hurt five years before they decide, try to win the damned pennant? What the hell did I know? Getting hit in a game that meant nothing at all, I should've stayed on the bench. Whaddaya really want, Ed?"

"You could've helped them," Cobb said.

"I couldn't've helped anybody, this year rolled around," Briggs said. "Tigers knew it last year, 'fore I did, but anyone with any brains could see I was through. Be kind of funny, though, wouldn't it? If it didn't hurt so much. All those years I hadda work my ass off, trying to save games I didn't have a chance, and then they finally get some people that I really could've helped, and what am I? Washed up. Could've been a friggin' hero, people coming up to give me baskets full of money. And instead I'm back in the woods, and nobody knows my name."

"Oh, they know your name, all right," Cobb said. "I'm not saying you wouldn't've been, you know, a lot better off, otherwise, if things'd worked out different. But you're not exactly a stranger now, either. People've heard of you. They remember you."

"What do you want, Ed?" Briggs said. "I know you want something—what is it?"

Cobb grinned. "Haven't changed that much, have you now, Henry? You're playing ball, you used to do that. Even in high school. Guy shows a little initiative, starts pushing you a little, first thing you do's drill him right in the head. I like that about you, old buddy. I'm sick of guys that pussyfoot, beat around the bush. Just come right out and say it. Say what's on your mind."

"So go ahead and do it too," Briggs said. "What've you got on your mind?"

Cobb shifted his position. He grinned. "Well," he said, "you being a former athlete and all, not to mention a good friend, I figured I could count on you for some free medical advice. I got this sort of a dull ache that never seems to stop. Throbbing. Like to drive you nuts. Me, nuts."

"Where's it located?" Briggs said.

"In the Second Congressional District," Cobb said. "I think I got Wainwright Disease."

"I'm sure," Briggs said. "Most Democrats have. It's been going around here for years."

Cobb settled back. "You know, I think I will take you up on that coffee. Straight black is how I take it."

Briggs got up and fetched another mug from the cabinet over the sink. He poured from the blue enameled pot on the stove. He placed the mug in front of Cobb and sat down again. Cobb nodded. He sipped.

"You've got kids," he said. "You get any that antiwar shit's so popular everywhere now?"

"Some of it," Briggs said. "I don't pay much attention. I'm not around here that much, after all. Neither're they, far as that goes. Pretending they're going to school. And then when they're home, they're out most of the time. When they're here, they don't tell me that much. Sally and I get along all right, when we get along at all, but art is what she likes. I'm a regular scholar of art. I saw a calendar once, had a picture van Gogh did on it. Flowers. I think he was drunk when he did it. But that's how I recognize art. If it's a picture of flowers, and isn't a photograph, well, you can't fool me, kid—I know art when I see it. And that's all I know about art. Ted? I don't know what Ted thinks. I don't know *if* he thinks. Well, I know what he thinks of me, but what he thinks of other things? Mystery to me. Never did like mysteries that much. Read comic books on the road. Now on the road, *Valley Press*."

"We got a *lot* of it, Burlington," Cobb said. "President's in big fuckin' trouble. You know what's gonna happen, Johnson takes the pipe? The party's gonna be so split, the Republican *walks* in. These fucking idealists, you know what they're gonna accomplish? They're gonna make Richard Nixon President, United States."

"I don't follow politics much," Briggs said. "Do they have that in some comic book?"

"There're times, lots of times, when I think they should," Cobb said. "There're times when I think that must be what explains it. We're all in a movie cartoon, taking turns being Roadrunner. Seeing who can get squashed the flattest. But I still stay with it. It's what I know. Man has to master a trade, and then stay with that trade 'til he dies.

"Same with you," he said. "You may sit there and claim you don't know politics, but you know a hell of a lot. A lot more, at least, than the people I talk to, that think they know all about it," Cobb said. "I can't talk any *sense* to some of these assholes. They won't listen to me when I tell them they're cuckoo, just keep trying to bull their way through things. And of course they got stomped, and then they blame it on me. If I'd've been a friend of theirs, I'd've stopped them before they screwed up. Their priorities're all screwed up.

" 'All right,' I say, 'all right. I agree with you, all right? Just say we

62

agree. We should not be, we should get out, we should pull out of Vietnam. But that's not the point of this election. That is not the fuckin' point of *any* damned election, what we should do on an issue, or what we should say we will do. The point of this election is exactly the same point that it was, the last election, and the election before that. The point is always whether we win, got it? *The point is whether we win.* What we want, never mind what all the jokers with the signs and banners think, what we want to do is to win this thing, local, state, and national. And for that what we need's not some pious bastard that makes women come in their shorts, 'cause he's so handsome, kind, and nice. What we need's a guy, the guy, who can win. Just fuckin' *win's* what we want.'

"And they don't listen," Cobb said. "It drives me fuckin' nuts. We finally get the point in this state where we got an actual chance that we control Montpelier, state house, assembly, both, and now when some one of our guys decides he wants to be a judge, he can run as one of us, come right out and *admit* it, and sometimes even can win. Which, and I can't seem to get this through these people's heads, is what politics is about. How it works. That's how you build a party. By making it respectable enough and winning often enough so that someone in his right mind, with some ability, and money, doesn't, when he registers, automatically go the other side. Because we look ridiculous. The way it used to be, and not that long ago.

"I'm telling you, Hank," he said, "I can see it happening, right in front my face. There aren't that many of us, that realize what's going on. We got these goddamned kids, and the teachers egging them on, and every day it seems like there's ten more of them'n yesterday, and they've all got ten friends, they smoke pot with and bang. Slogans. Fucking slogans. They think if they've got a slogan, well, they died and went to heaven. If we let these fuckin' migrants come in here and bed down at the colleges, and then let them get the point where they outnumber us, that've been here all our lives, the day is gonna come when they're just gonna throw us out, and run things to suit themselves. And they'll lose, of course, but these jerks won't *mind*. They think it's honorable, 'if you stand up for something.' Just so long as when they lose, they lose with the right guy, and his goddamned bumpersticker's tough enough to last longer'n the bumper does, surviving winter after winter of salt and slush and shit. But still hurling defiance. That no one cares about. *Then* they will be happy.

"Well, I know what's gonna happen," Cobb said. "For a few years they'll get their thrills. And then they will lose interest, or they'll go someplace else. And the rest of us, that built this party, that we got thrown out of, we'll be sitting on our thumbs, out on the manure pile, too old to start all over, and worse off'n before."

"I see," Briggs said.

"I'll be *damned* if I'll just sit on my ass and just watch it happen," Cobb said. "I got too much of myself invested in this. Too many years of my hardworking life, that I know I won't see again. If I was wrong, well, I won't admit it. *Damned* if I will admit it. Maybe they can beat me. Maybe there's too many of these long-haired crackpots, and it's already too late, and I should've thought of this, seen it coming, I mean, a long time ago. Well, I didn't, but now that I have, well, by Jesus, I am going to fight. If they're gonna beat me, all right, let 'em beat me then. Let's see how good they are."

"I don't see . . ." Briggs said.

"Bob Wainwright," Cobb said.

"Yeah?" Briggs said.

"Bob Wainwright's the answer," Cobb said. "He's not all of the answer, maybe not even a very big piece of it. But he's part of it. And that's what you have to deal with, in my line of work: you have to deal with the parts."

"Well," Briggs said, "like I say, I don't follow politics much. Hell, before you gave me my job, half the time I didn't even vote. That's how much I know."

"Doesn't matter," Cobb said. "I did give you that job."

"But I don't, still," Briggs said, "I don't see how Bob Wainwright's the answer to your problem. Cripes, he's been in Congress ever since I can't remember. My father used to vote for him. Never even met the guy, but always voted for him."

"That's exactly what I mean," Cobb said. "Bob Wainwright's been going to Congress from the Second District for twenty-eight whole fucking years. Fourteen whole goddamned terms. And you know how many times he's had opposition? Twice. *Twice*, goddamnit. Once from his own party, when the guy there before him for twenty-two years got out of bed at age sixty-four and dropped dead, and old Dick Carlisle, may his soul rest in the bosom of Eugene V. Debs, decided he had as much right to the seat as change-purse-mouth Bob did, and once after Bob's seventh term in nineteen fifty-four, when some rich bitch from Bennington decided she was the new, or maybe the original, Margaret Chase Smith, and nobody else wanted the thing, so she got our nomination. Otherwise, if Wainwright votes for himself, he wins, and if his wife votes for him too, which I understand she maybe doesn't, always—I heard they don't always get along—then that gives him two votes, and he wins, two to nothing.

"Just by being there," Cobb said. "That is how he wins. People look at him, and shy away. 'Run against Bob Wainwright? You'll get licked, for sure.' And so they won't do it. But nobody's ever run against him, really. How do they know they'll get licked? If you keep giving the guy free rides, how the hell can you say he's unbeatable? Nobody's ever tried. Really tried, I mean."

"I don't see where this is all leading," Briggs said.

"I, we, want you to run against Wainwright," Cobb said.

Briggs stared at him. "You're out of your mind, Ed," he said.

Cobb grinned at him. "Now I will have that beer," he said. "Let's you and me talk about this."

7

ow, the first thing I am telling
you," Cobb said, "the first thing is that you're full of shit, when you say
you know nothing about politics, all right? You know Don Beale, right?"

Briggs shrugged. "I know who he is," he said. "I know what he is,
too. Collared me one night, the Legion Hall in Charlotte, and starts
buying me beers. Before that I never heard of him, but he seemed like a
pretty nice guy, giving me all this crap how I should've had a ring, just
bad luck I didn't. Well, that happens to be my opinion, too. But
naturally, all the time we're talking, I'm trying to figure out: What
does this guy want? Because usually—hell, always—you meet some
jocksniffer like that, he's got something he wants. But he fooled me.
Gets up from his stool, hands me his card, says to come up and see
him, he'll give me a rate on a car. Well, we didn't really need a new car
just then. The Buick was running all right, and with me on my way to
Pittsburgh, you know, well, I wasn't going to be home much. At least
not 'til fall. Didn't need another one. But I thanked him, said I'd keep
him in mind when I did, and he went out the door.

"Well, it couldn't've been more'n two weeks after that, guy calls me
up on the phone. And I said to him what I said to him before: still
didn't need a car. And he said: No, no, wasn't that. I guess he's pretty
big with the Little League up there? Wanted me to do a banquet.
Uh-*huh*. Free, of course."

"Sponsors a team," Cobb said. "Uniforms, all of that stuff. Also a CYO basketball team, and a couple of troops of Scouts, and he ran this big benefit dance, send one the high school basketball teams to a tournament at Syracuse. He's into all that stuff. Very civic-minded guy. He's been doing it for years, and so'd his father and his grandfather before that."

"Probably doesn't do his business any harm, either," Briggs said. "Sounds like advertising to me."

"So what if it is," Cobb said. "The basketball team still went to Syracuse—wouldn't've without him. Got their asses kicked, of course, all those black kids from New York, but still, they did get to go. The old folks still get to sit in the park Sunday nights, hear John Philip Sousa and smile. The little kids get to play baseball, and the bigger ones, well, you follow me. I've known Don Beale a long time, Hank. Ever since we were in law school."

"I hate lawyers," Briggs said.

"Lots of people do," Cobb said. "Just keep in mind what you just said. I'm coming back to it later.

"The thing of it is, Hank," Cobb said, "here's Don, third generation of his family that's been doing good things for people around here for over sixty years—"

"—and selling cars as a result," Briggs said.

"—and selling cars as a result," Cobb said, "without which most of those good things they do, they could not have done. Because they wouldn't've had the dough. But, did you know who he was?"

"Not until he told me," Briggs said.

"Okay," Cobb said. "Now, Don has got a brother. Near as anyone can tell, he never did a decent thing for anyone, in his whole life. He's a rat, is what he is. But everybody, *everybody* knows who he is."

"I don't," Briggs said.

"Uh-huh," Cobb said. "Now Hank, we've been friends a long time. So you can tell if I'm bullshitting you, and I can tell if you try it on me. Tell me you never heard of Earl Beale."

"Ahh," Briggs said, slumping down in his chair, "this's why I hate dealing with lawyers. He was the kid that fixed the games, few years back, for Saint Stephen's."

"*Right,*" Cobb said. "You're an honest man, Hank. I got to give you that. But you see the point I'm making? Earl was a ball player. Not in your sport, not close to your level, and the only thing he ever did was something very wrong, and he got caught and went to prison. Years and years ago. But everybody knew his name before he disgraced it, and everybody, after that, is never going to forget it. Not for the rest of their lives. Now, if they remember Earl for that rotten thing he did, ruined his own life and humiliated his whole family at the same damned time, for which a lot of people that he never met will never forgive him, how long do you think those people will recognize your name? As being of a guy that so far as they know never did a thing except make himself famous, and his family proud of him, and give everyone who lived in this state something he could brag about. 'I'm from Underhill,' or wherever the guy's from, and when the guy he's talking to says: 'Never heard of it—where the hell is that?' the guy from Underhill swells out his chest and says: 'Don't you know anything? It's right next door to where Henry Briggs grew up. You must've heard of Hank. Why, I recall when he was young, *God*, he could throw that ball. Strong as an ox, and good control, and blah-blah, blah-blah, blah.' How long will they remember *that*?"

Briggs shrugged. "Probably quite a while," he said.

"You bet, 'quite a while,' " Cobb said. "You gave people something, Henry. You gave them a lot. And as long's you walk this earth, they'll remember you for that. People don't forget those things, and if you go out now and say: 'Well, there's something else I want to do,' they will listen to you, and if they see you're a nice guy, along with former major leaguer who gave them lots of fun, they will say: 'Time for a change. I'm voting for Briggs.'

"Henry," Cobb said, "you see what I'm telling you. What you did was good. What Earl did was bad. I did Earl a favor once, though he's no friend of mine, because his brother is, and you do things for your friends. I've done a thing or two for you, too, and you don't even have a brother that I owe. Earl I don't want for a friend—still got him just the same as my responsibility awhile, because I didn't have a choice. Happens that I *do* want you, and I want something from you. But you're resisting me. Well, I guess that evens out the thing—have to help the guy I don't like, can't get help from one I do. But *my* kind of politics, the kind I have to play as a Vermont Democrat with some small hope of survival and maybe even prospering, I don't have the margin to write off reluctant friends. There aren't enough of them. So when a guy gets finicky, like you seem to be doing, well, I have to hunker down and keep at him. I need all the friends I can get, and excuses won't do. I really need you on this."

"Ed, Ed," Briggs said, "you're asking a hell of a lot."

"Well, I guess I'll just hope you'll pardon me then, Hank," Cobb said. "I'm talking in confidence with you here now. I have to, draw what I guess must be a little clearer picture. To give you the right perspective.

"When Earl got out of jail, he had two things in the world, and he needed another one real bad. On paper he had a college education, just like you and me. Well, most of one. He hadn't finished his class work when they packed him off to jail, but he was pretty close. Could've done it if he'd wanted, but he was too good for that, I guess—didn't bother trying.

"The second thing he had was a prison record. Which took care of him getting the thing that he needed: a job. Don was desperate to get Little Brother out punching a time clock, and I could understand why. 'Jesus Christ, Ed,' he said," Cobb said, "and Don seldom gets upset enough to forget his Holy Name pledge not to take the Name in vain, 'if he gets loose out on the street tomorrow, he'll be back behind bars before Sunday. I can get him a job with a guy that owes me a favor in Boston—I don't want that bozo 'round here. But my guy can't hire him with that damned record—Earl'd be handling money, and the bonding guys'd go nuts. So can you do something for me? I know it's a lot, but I need it.'

"Don was wrong about it being asking 'a lot.' It was much bigger than just 'a lot.' Getting a federal record expunged is radical surgery: 'Undertake only if desperate.' But like I said, Don's a good friend of mine and I'm cursed with a very good memory. I remember when Don and I gave it up on the office. He had that dealership for a living; all I had was the politics. Not the same thing at all. I really needed some money. Don and his father and some friends of theirs, they got me some, and I took it."

"For what?" Briggs said.

"Oh," Cobb said, "say, outdoor advertising? That bill that finally

69

passed last session? No more billboards on the highways? It started a long time ago, the goo-goos all upset, and I told Don and his dad, too, it wasn't going to die. And they said No, they knew it wasn't, but their friends were still determined. And if I could hold it off awhile . . . Well, running every two years like we have to do, it doesn't take a lot of money like it does in the big states, but it still takes some money, and also, you have to eat. So they had friends who needed me? Well, I needed friends I had, and they were two of my best. There were two hundred and thirty-nine other guys milling around in the Hall of Flags then, this was a few years ago, and if you stuck close to your personal project, tended it starting every damned January, not letting it out of your sight until after Memorial Day, you might be able to get something shelved. Year, after year, after year.

"It wasn't a big, major thing," Cobb said, "but it paid the rent, and when I did guys favors, well, they owed me favors back. The billboard bill was my pet dog. I kept it inside for years, even though it had support from a lot more guys than I did. There were six of them to one of us, but it's a funny thing: They tended to fight among themselves, just like the rest of us, and so sometimes they needed reinforcements to keep their dogs on the leash, and had to cut a few small deals with the enemy. And so we cut some deals. We're doing it today, though it's little harder this year since they chopped off ninety seats—a hundred forty-nine other fellas doesn't leave you as much slack, you need rope to tie things up. But we still do all right, when we're determined about something. Especially now, since we've been there long enough to get some clout. You got Danisi from Barre, and Shaw from Saint Albans, and Cobb from Burlington, and a few other guys like us, that just don't fit the molds, and a tourist comes on up there now, he won't know what is going on.

"Well," Cobb said, "all good things must come to an end, and the day came when brother Earl got out, and Don rang my bell for me. I could see his point. The only thing Earl really could do well was play basketball. He was good at that. But there's not a lot of call in the NBA for a guy that got convicted of rigging games in college. Even the Knicks didn't want him, and he was a holy terror at Saint Stephen's, right in the Knick's own bailiwick before the cops bagged him. Asshole doesn't understand this. He thinks it's because, you know, he lost a step in jail. But what matters is, he's out of work, he's almost thirty, and he's never had a job. Well, making furniture and stuff, but 'Federal Pen' on your résumé, it doesn't look so hot.

"Like I said, Don went nuts. This kid when he's in college had his name, Earl Wilson's column. Cadillacs like fleas on dogs, and blonds with mammoth tits. 'That's Earl, brother.' This is just what Don needs working in his agency. Convicted felon, big show-off? The customers'll love that, dealing with a crook, and the bonding folks? They just love that breed, and Detroit likes them even less. So when Don came to me and said: 'You owe me,' knowing it was certainly true, what do I say: 'Take a hike'? I do not. I say: 'What do you want, Don? I can do it, well, I will.' And that was what he wanted: no more record on Earl, at least that you can find. So I did it. Oh, it's still there, and if you knew exactly where to look, you'd probably find it. But if you knew exactly where to look, you wouldn't need to, 'cause you'd know it already, so that was good enough. Good enough's the most you hope for, in my line of work."

"Politics," Briggs said. "That is politics."

"That is *part* of it," Cobb said. "That is one part of it. There is another part, which concerns you more today. I want you to do something you don't really want to do. You can't think of a single reason why you'd want to do it."

"I can think of a lot of reasons," Briggs said, "why I don't want to do it. Lillian'd go batshit, for one."

"Well, that's fine," Cobb said. "I certainly understand. But I've got one, just one good reason, that outweighs them all."

"Let me hear it," Briggs said. "This'd better be good."

"Oh, it is," Cobb said. "A fairly long time ago, a friend of mine asked me to do something for him. And I did. You'd probably remember the Beachmont Motel, if you should happen to see it again. Down in Lafayette there, in Rhode Island?"

Briggs stared at him. He nodded.

"That night in 'sixty-one," Cobb said, "when you and Gus Morales had a night off in New York, and the two of you drove up to Providence for a banquet?"

Briggs nodded.

"And you picked up a couple of broads and checked into a motel nobody ever heard of, down the coast? And one of them, the only name the cops had was Patty Rios, and she died? Chugalugged a quart of vodka and got cardiac arrest? That ring any bells?"

"Yeah," Briggs said.

"Who'd you call that night?" Cobb said.

"Well," Briggs said, "I didn't call my wife, and I didn't call the team."

"No," Cobb said, "and a good thing too. What was it you had to say about lawyers, little while ago here? Didn't say anything like that that night, how you can't stand lawyers. No sir, not you, Hank. I was the first guy you thought of. Degree bothered you not at all. Matter of fact, I would bet the fact I was a lawyer that night, a lawyer that you knew, had quite a lot to do with your choice of me to call. Am I right on that? And a politician, too, a dirty politician that makes deals and cuts corners? Did that bother you that night? I tend to doubt it, Hank. All of a sudden you were in a big fat fuckin' *mess*. The famous bull pen ace was gonna get a good shelling himself, if he didn't get some help, and for that help you came to me. That was a smart move, Henry. You were in a situation where you were gonna need a whole damned squadron of lawyers, if this one couldn't help you out, and at least you still had brains enough to see you'd better get me quick. Am I right?"

Briggs nodded.

"So you took this lawyer's advice, anyway, and got your ass out of there, and I stayed on the damned phone half the night, end up talking to this Jimmy Battles guy—who was perfectly willing to do it, but wanted me to understand he was getting credit established—and then he did it. Didn't find the body until checkout time next day."

"That fucking Gus," Briggs said, "I hadda pay that other whore a thousand fucking dollars, because he fed too much juice to his, and she went and died on him."

"You should've picked your companions more carefully," Cobb said. "Good thing they didn't know your names."

"But this Battles did?" Briggs said.

"Henry, Henry," Cobb said, "when dealing with delicate matters, avoid asking too many questions. I suspect he did, but I sure didn't tell him. Only name he knew was mine—well, only new one, anyway—and he remembered it, the bastard. So last month he called me up, and

72

he cashed his chit with me. Wanted me to say I'd keep his soldier kid out of Vietnam. I didn't say I'd do that, but I did say I would try, and I did what I said I'd do, and I tell you, it was tough. But I got my Battles mortgage stamped 'paid in full,' in ink. Now I'm endorsing it to you. Pay me."

"This is not very pretty," Briggs said.

"Art was never my strong point," Cobb said. "Politics is a choice of enemas. You're gonna get it up the ass, matter what you do."

"Ed," Briggs said, "be reasonable. I'm not welshing on you. But you're asking me . . . Look," he said, "I was a goddamned *kid* that night. My name was in the paper six days out of seven every week, for eight months a year, and I thought I was a big man because people treated me that way. I was good at what I did, and I knew I was. But that didn't mean I *knew* anything, except what to do when some gorilla stepped up with his war-club in his hands and the bases loaded, and dug in on me. Hum that sucker right in there, just about ear high, and when he gets up off his ass where you put him in the dirt, well, if he doesn't back off then, stick it in his ear again.

"But that was all I knew, what to do and how to do it. Off the mound, outside the park, I was a stupid, asshole kid. If I hadn't've been, I wouldn't've gotten myself in the situation in the first place, where I panicked and called you. I didn't call you because I sat there and thought to myself: 'Jeez, I'd better call Ed because he's a lawyer and a politician, and he can put himself into a deep hole to get me out.' I called you because I thought: 'Ed's a friend of mine. I don't know what to do here, and he's smarter than I am, and maybe if I call him up he'll tell me what to do.' That was all I expected. Not that you'd make it go away, just make it disappear like it'd been a real bad dream. Just that you'd tell me what to do so I wouldn't go to jail."

"You didn't have any trouble, though," Cobb said, "going along with me when I said that if you'd sit tight, and do just what I said, maybe I could do that for you—just make it go away."

"Good God, no," Briggs said. "I wouldn't say I was overjoyed or anything like that. For one thing, I was too scared to be anything like that. And for another thing, well, Ed, let me tell you something: Even after you said that, I had no real idea of what was going on. I expected if I stayed put pretty soon I'd get a call from a lawyer in Rhode Island who would come down and go with me to report it to the cops, but stop me at the same time from making a bad thing worse. Which, as ignorant as I was, and I was pretty ignorant, was one hell of a lot smarter than old Gus Morales was—his idea was: Cut and run. Just deny it ever happened. When all kinds of people at the banquet we'd been to'd seen us with the hookers and probably'd used them themselves, too. But that was the extent of my brains. 'Tackle Gus if you have to, but keep him in the room. And when Ed gets a lawyer for you, do what that lawyer says.' And that was all, I thought.

"I was stunned when Battles called us and just said to us: 'Get out. Get your clothes on and get out. I'll take care of this.' I played dumb. 'Take care of what?' How did Battles know what'd happened in that room? The only one I'd told was you. I'd kept Gus off the phone, and my whore, the other one, was so drunk and scared herself that she'd been in the closet, ever since we figured out that the first one was dead. 'Just shut the fuck up and get dressed and just get out,' he says to me. 'I just had a call from a fellow that I know, up in Providence, and he says he had a call from a guy you know. Ed Cobb. And I called Cobb and talked to him. Cobb I can talk to. Now, I told you I'll handle this. Just get out of here.' And that was what we did.

"Now I know I owe you, Ed," he said. "I owe you big for that bad night, and owe you too another one for the job with Fish and Game. But you've got to let me try to pay you back by doing something I can do. Something I know how to do. Those're the only two things I've learned so far, really. How to pitch, and that the rules about the trapping and the hunting and the fishing, camping, so forth, have to be enforced because they make damned good sense, and unless we make people do what those rules say, it won't be long before the only thing we've got left will be rules no one obeys and nothing to protect with them.

"If you came to me and said I owe you, as I certainly do, and you said what I had to do was get myself back into shape and try to pitch three innings for you in a make-or-break ball game, that I doubt that I could do, but I would try, Ed, I would try. If you came to me and said you wanted me to forget something that I saw in some guy's truck, and what I'd seen was a big buck, around the end of June, well I wouldn't even ask you why you wanted that forgotten. The minute that you said it, my mind would be wiped clear. I might not like your reason, I might disagree with it, but I sure wouldn't say: 'Oh no, Ed, can't do that.'

"If you came in and ask me, though, to build you a rocket ship, or anything like that, I'd have to tell you that I can't, same's I'm telling you right now. Not because I'm saying that I don't owe you a thing—*because I don't know how to do it*, and I know I'll never learn.

"Christ, Ed," Briggs said, "you call me 'friend.' Thanks. I hope I am. But I don't know shit from politics. And I never will."

Cobb laughed. "There's a good many of us," he said, "who've suspected more'n once that there *isn't* any difference between shit and politics, except that no sane human being'd ever step in either one, if he had a choice. Lemme ask you something, all right? I came in here, we had a little back-and-forth about our pal Russ Wixton."

"I like Russ," Briggs said. "I've known Russ a lot of years. Always liked the guy."

"So do I," Cobb said. "Russ is unusual for a man, his line of work. Russ actually knows when it's in his own best interest, along with someone else's too, to keep his mouth shut when he knows some hot stuff that could hurt people. How'd you first get to know him?"

"He covered us," Briggs said. "You know that. He was with the *Valley Press* back when I broke in. He was with us quite a lot. And I was the local boy, so he spent a lot of time with me. The one long road trip that they sent him on each season, he was mine. I didn't want him to be that, like having a detective on your trail all day and night, but I did like the guy, and who else did he know? Then he went down to Boston there, with the *Commoner*, and he traveled all the time with us, Ed. Traveled with us all the time. Every trip, all season long. By which time, we were old pals. It's pretty hard not to know someone, couple years of that."

"And what was Russ writing about in those days?" Cobb said.

"Baseball," Briggs said. "You know that. Same thing I was doing, was what he wrote about. He was a sports reporter. In the fall, after the Series, he wrote about football. In the winter, hockey and basketball. In the spring, back to baseball. That was why I talked to him, and that was what he did."

"When you read Russ Wixton now," Cobb said, "what does he write about?"

"He writes about politics, mostly," Briggs said. "Sometimes he writes about the groundhogs and the weather, and the skiers and the leaf-peepers, or some trial or something. Whatever he seems to think's getting under people's skins. But mostly what he writes about these days is what you do."

"Is he any good at it?" Cobb said.

"Well, yeah," Briggs said. "I mean, at least I like him. I know more about varmints, 'n' shooting varmints'n he does, so when he gets on those kicks I more or less decide he ran out of ideas that day, but when he writes about stuff that I don't know, or don't know as much about as he does, yeah, I think he's still pretty good. He can still stick it to a guy when he gets pissed off at him. I must say I like that, when he gets pissed off."

"So he made a transition," Cobb said.

"Yeah," Briggs said. "I didn't think about it before, but now you mention it, he did. Hell, I didn't even notice it." He paused. "I couldn't even tell you when it was," he said. "All I could tell you is that I know Russ got fed up with Boston, or maybe homesick for here, must've been the weather wasn't bad enough in Boston, not enough cold and snow, bad driving, all that crap, and he came back to the *Press*. When that was I couldn't say. I was gone, don't know where I was, and I came back a few times, and he was still gone. And then I came back, and he was back. And then I was gone again some more, and I came back, he was still here, but just not writing sports. I don't know when that was."

"You didn't even notice," Cobb said. "You read him when it was sports that he wrote about, and then he wrote about some other things, and you kept on reading him."

"Yeah, I did," Briggs said. "Like I said, I know Russ. He's a friend of mine. I'm interested in what he does. I wouldn't go so far's to say that if it wasn't for him I would skip the *Press* now, though I wouldn't miss it much, but I would consider it. I guess I read it for Russ."

"What I want you to do," Cobb said, "is make the same transition. The following that Russ Wixton got, from writing about you, is an iceberg tip compared to the following that you got, from doing what he described. You can beat Bob Wainwright, Hank. I know you're a rookie, and I know the notion scares you, but you've been good and scared before, and you overcame it because it mattered to you. Now I'm

76

telling you, and I *do* know, too, you can stick it in Bob's ear, and knock him on his ass. And you owe me, pal, and it matters to *me*, now." He sat back in his chair and drummed his fingers on the table.

Briggs did not say anything for more than two minutes. Then he cleared his throat and said: "You, ah, want another beer?"

"I wouldn't mind," Cobb said.

Briggs got up and went to the refrigerator. He removed two beers, opened them at the sink, brought them to the table, where he gave one to Cobb, and sat down again. He drank half of his own. He sighed. He shook his head. "I got to think, Ed, got to think."

Cobb drank half of his beer. "Think as much as you want," he said. "You called me up when you came home and said you needed something. Anything, to keep you busy. Could I help you out.

"Well," Cobb said, "I wanted to. But what did I have? What does the Speaker have for a retired ball player, with time on his hands? Nothing came to mind. You remember what I said. I said I'd do my best. But the only thing I thought of was the poachers and the people who light camp fires next to deadfalls primed to light the whole state off. I told you it wasn't much, just the best I had, and I apologized for that. Said it wasn't fit for you. But you took it just the same, and were grateful for it. And you've done a damned good job. I've heard about the job you've done. People like you, Hank. You've got sense and you play fair, and they like that in a man. If you'd fucked up, I would've known. Instantly, by God, because it would've been my fault.

"Now I have got something. It's what the swordsmen used to call 'a foeman worthy of your steel.' " Briggs laughed.

"Okay, okay," Cobb said, "sometimes I get ornate. But I'm serious, Henry. This one's worth your time. Take a leave of absence. If you lose you can go back, protecting trouts and trees, and taking care of deer. Try it out. I think you'll love it. Furthermore, you'll win. And then I'll know a congressman, I can call anytime. Except of course I won't dare call, because I will owe him."

"I've got to think," Briggs said. "You've got to give me some time to think. I've got to talk to some people."

"Happy to," Cobb said, draining his beer and setting the glass down, rising out of his chair. "Give you a full month. Hell, six weeks if you want. Go to the bullpen. Warm up the arm. But when Labor Day comes, I'm soon after."

8

there was just enough bite in the wind off the lake to remind the experienced of what was on the way. It took a steak sandwich, preceded by a bourbon Manhattan on the rocks and accompanied by two bottles of Heineken at the Hunter's Tap in Shelburne, but Wixton arrived at the point just as the waitress brought coffee.

"The first thing to think about," he said, "is how your family's going to take this." He paused. "That is, of course, if you happen to give a shit."

"You got the question backward," Briggs said. "The main question's more, I think, whether *they* will give a shit."

"Because if they decide to," Wixton said, "they can murder you. When I first shifted over, sports to politics, I made a mistake. I confused confidence with naïveté. Hell, how long'd I cover sports? Over sixteen years. And I saw a lot of things I never put in the paper."

"I heard that," Briggs said.

Wixton grinned. "Point of it is," he said, "I know, *I know*, there had to've been a lot of pissed-off wives, and messed-up kids, who'd just loved to've given dear old dad a dagger in the back when he was least expecting it. Have him open up the paper some fine morning in Baltimore, see where AP's picked up that his wife's divorcing him for flagrant adultery. And there were lots of wives who could've done

78

exactly that. But none of them did. And you know something? If they had've, we wouldn't've printed it, and there wouldn't've been anything for the AP to pick up. So the Baltimores that morning wouldn't've *seen* something in the paper they could use to ride the guy, maybe get a little edge.

"Politics is different," he said. "In baseball you got a whole book of rules, and the game's between the lines. In politics the game is in the stands, out in the parking lot, on the street, and in the bedroom, you get home. The rule is: Anything goes. In sports it's how you play the game. In politics, it's how you live your life. Not the same thing, pal-o'-mine, not the same at all."

"So," Wixton said, "that's my first question, I guess: Lillian gonna stick your dick in the pump-handle hinge, if somebody asks her what kind of husband you are? Or is she gonna be loyal, and lie, and say what a saint you are? Because if she tells the truth—well, what I assume's still the truth—that you've had a rocky marriage, well, all those ladies knitting the afghans for the goddamned church socials're gonna see it in the paper the next day, and they're gonna set their lips and scowl at their needles, and then stick them into you. How's Lil feel about this?"

"She hates it, of course," Briggs said. He hesitated. "It's like everything else I've ever done. Anything she can't do with me, which is everything but stay at home and feed the goddamned cats, make the muffins, and talk on the phone, she is gonna disapprove of. Or anything I've ever even thought about doing, in this case."

The sky had turned overcast in the afternoon after Cobb had left the house. Briggs had made himself a sandwich and taken it with a beer into the study. He had turned on the television and was using John Wayne in *Red River* to help him think. "What'd he want?" she had said.

"What'd who want?" he had said.

"Cobb," she said. "I assume it was Cobb who was here. Nobody else I know of could get you drinking beer at home before it's even time for lunch. And you're not in the bedroom, sleeping it off, so I know it wasn't just you."

"What'd you do," he said, "go through the trash?"

"Would've been pretty hard not to notice," she said. "The wastebasket was overflowing. What'd he want?" He had told her. For a moment she had stared at him. "He wants *you* to run for Congress?"

she said. "He must've lost his mind. Or else he needs a fool, and thought of you right off. Are you going to do it?" He had said he didn't know. "Well, if you do," she said, "if you do this, you needn't think I'm going to join you, make a public spectacle of myself, too." He had not said anything. "You'd do just about anything, wouldn't you," she said. "Anything, to get away from me."

"The last thing she approved of, that I did," Briggs said to Wixton, "was when I signed with the Seals and went out to the Coast. That was before she figured out that the only way I had of making her into not-a-farmer's wife was by playing ball. And that meant I had to travel, and she couldn't travel with me, or sit in the bullpen, either. But by then it was too late."

"Will she pound the hell out of you," Wixton said, "if some reporter asks her, I mean?"

"I don't know," Briggs said.

"Well, you'd better find out," Wixton said.

"Would *you* print it, if she did?" Briggs said.

"Look, Hank," Wixton said, "we go back a long way. You know I don't print personal stuff, that I happen to know. Unless it's germane to the story. Which it wasn't, to how you played ball. But if one of my reporters talks to her, and she says it, well, there's a certain school of thought that says a man's family life *is* germane to politics. And you're gonna see lots more of that, too. I can't get beat in my own backyard by some out-of-town hotshot, you know. Which if you run, you'll attract, you know, New Yorkers and other exotics. Congressional races don't draw much attention, when they take place in the hinterlands. And old ball players, when they retire there, they don't draw maggot flies either. But when an old ball player announces for Congress, that makes 'em prick up their ears. A lot of political junkies are practicing baseball fans, too. And they love a story that lets them show off that: 'See, I'm a regular joe, just like you. I love my Cracker Jack too.' You run and they'll come, mark my words. And we natives will go red-alert, battle stations, because they've decreed we are national news, and they're not gonna whomp us at home.

"So that's one thing to think about," Wixton said. "You should also think about how your kids'll react. Because the press'll get to them, too. You get along all right? You and your kids, I mean?"

"Ahh," Briggs said, "a little of this, a little of that. But what could they possibly say?"

"They could say what she doesn't," Wixton said. "She could put them up to it. And maybe throw in on their own that you've been away so much, they really don't know you that well. Ladies' vestry won't like that any better'n if Lil said it."

"I don't know," Briggs said.

"Well, you'd better find out," Wixton said. "Lemme ask you something: Why do you want this job? Why're you even thinking about it? Beating Bob Wainwright's like beating the Yankees. They've got to have an off-year, which they don't ordinarily do, or else you've got to be awful lucky. Which nobody else's been yet—not when it comes to Bob Wainwright. He's old, which is plus him. Most of the old people get out and vote. Most of the younger ones don't. Or up until now at least, haven't. He's been there since Noah—plus him another one still. Incumbency plays like plunging necklines—they'll both always be popular. So why do this? Isn't this a stillborn loser? The job stinks. Everyone says so. Those that know what it is. So if you win, which you might well not do, what've you won that you want? A damned job you could do without? Isn't this idea a common-law dud? From the git-go, right from the gate?"

"Because I'm bored," Briggs said. "I like this thing Ed got me, out in the woods with the bears. It gets me away from Lil and her speeches, what a rotten bastard I am. But it's also lonesome, you know? It's not what I've gotten used to. I'm used to being out there."

"Well," Wixton said, "you can give a speech, I know that."

"Oh, sure," Briggs said. "You put me in some little town like Jericho, place like that, night before the Fourth, I can eat the ham-bean supper—they give you a choice of drinks: red Kool-Aid or iced tea—and the fireworks afterward—usually two sparklers and a couple cherry bombs—wave to all the people, and I am TNT. Then Tom or whatever mine gracious host's name is, takes me back to his house, which is where I'm staying, because if that town had a hotel it would be three rooms, at most, two registered to dogs. And we sit up pretty late for Jamesville, Proctor, Jericho, wherever the hell it is—and 'leven, eleven-fifteen, we finally call it quits. Having a couple of pops. It's not exactly Opening Day, or the Seventh Game, World Series—

although I never did find out what that's like, the World Series, I mean—but it isn't bad."

"Well then," Wixton said, "then you should do it, then."

"But I don't want to embarrass myself," Briggs said. "I, I knew the Tigers, what they were getting set to do to me last spring. I could've waited around and let them do it. Send me down. Let me come to my senses in Triple A in June. And that was when I quit. And it was hard. I don't want to get myself into something where people're making fun of me. I had enough booing to last me a lifetime. I don't want any more. People calling you names. It went with the old job. I understood that. I don't want a new job, that it also goes with, too.

"Sure, I can make a speech. I got one. Well, two, if you don't count the fact the short one's part of the long one. But neither one of them's about politics. They're both about baseball. The short one's about how lucky I was to play major league ball, and how much I owe my father, and how I learned the one thing that counts when you're a pitcher is basically the same thing that I learned outside of baseball."

" 'When you're out there on the mound,' " Wixton said, " 'the best thing you can have in this life is three fast outfielders behind you. And then when you get off the mound, and go out in the world, you learn that it's the same teamwork, in every phase of life.' "

"That's the one," Briggs said. "I guess you must've heard it somewhere."

"Maybe once or twice," Wixton said. "What the hell is the long one? The one I heard was short. No more'n four or five minutes."

"That *was* the long one," Briggs said. "You must've heard it around here. Did I put in the stuff about the best years in my career were the ones I had with the Red Sox, and I love you fans in New England?"

"Yup," Wixton said.

"That was definitely the long one," Briggs said. "The short one, the one that I give when they ask me to talk in Pittsburgh or something, that one I leave out about the Red Sox and New England."

"But you put in something about those loyal Pirates fans, I bet," Wixton said.

"Oh, absolutely," Briggs said. "They haven't asked me back to Cleveland—which I'm not surprised, since I was there about an hour—but if they ever do, I'll have something in there about those great Ohio fans. And that wonderful old big ball park, that very few customers go to. But it'll still come out shorter." He frowned. "And that's another thing that bothers me about the idea of doing this: I don't have anything, really, to talk about. I spent years playing baseball, for money, at the top level, the game. And when I stand up to talk about it, I'm finished in less'n ten minutes. How on earth do I talk about government? What do I have to say?"

"Tell me something," Wixton said, "when you make the short speech, and you make the long speech—does it make any difference?"

"Like how?" Briggs said.

"Oh," Wixton said, "the reception that you get. How they treat you afterward. Are they nicer to you after the long one, or the short one?"

"I never noticed any difference," Briggs said. "If there was one, it got by me."

Wixton nodded. "Well," he said, "that's what I mean. It's you being there that counts. Politics is just the same. So they can look at you and see if you got webbed feet or something. Gill slits. You spill your food on your tie when you eat? Dip your sleeves in the salad dressing? Butter your thumb or something? If you do, well, that's a bonus. 'Should've seen that asshole Briggs. Drunker'n a goat.' They would all like that. But if you don't, it's still okay. 'Seen Henry Briggs the other night. I was at this feed? Jesus, remember how that big bastard could pitch? And you know something? I was talking to him afterward. Just went up and introduced myself. Said I used to go to his games. He actually thanked me. He's a very nice guy. We talked for quite a while. Very damned nice guy.'"

"I'm a show horse," Briggs said.

"Well," Wixton said, "no more'n, say, the Budweiser Clydesdales. Maybe I missed it, them out on their rounds, but it sort of seems to me that the only time I see them hitched up to their wagon is when I'm at home, watching TV, and it's around Christmastime. Or down at the Rutland State Fair. Up here, Bud uses trucks."

"So you think that I should do it," Briggs said.

"Lemme put it this way, Henry," Wixton said. "If you had something else that you were doing, you know? You had some calls from maybe Tidewater, looking a manager, or say the Phillies, need a pitching coach. But from what you're telling me, those things aren't happening. So, try it out. Maybe you find out you like it. Maybe you meet some dynamite lady, get lucky again, like you used to."

"Tell me something, Russ," Briggs said, "I wanted to talk to you because you're an old friend and all. If I do this, after it's over, that still gonna be the case?"

Wixton sat back in the booth. "Hank," he said, "you look out the window, you will see the lake. The shore of the lake's where the land ends. That's the water's edge. Don't matter whether you like it—that's just the way that it is.

"Politics is the water, and friendship's the land. I'm the political editor. Plus the Sunday columnist. I tell my people: 'Down the middle. Throw it down the middle.' That's what Bob Wainwright can expect, and that's what you can, too. If you announce, maybe before, if the trial balloons go up, I will see they're fair to you. That's all I can do."

"Fair enough," Briggs said. "That's really all I was asking."

9

ted Briggs at twenty-four suffered from a prematurely receding hairline that left him with a sharp prow of dark brown hair leading back into long curls that flowed out over his ears and concealed the collar of his plaid flannel shirt. He had recently given up shaving but was having better luck with the mustache than the full beard; it was patchy. His eyes were dull and bloodshot at noon on Sunday, and he seemed to have a cold. He entered the Varsity Grille at Winooski furtively, as though apprehensive that he would be unable to recognize his father among the small crowd of young men and women who looked and dressed as Ted did. He picked Briggs out at the last booth in the back and sidled up to it, sitting down as though declaring he did not wish to be observed or, if noticed, acknowledged, and forced to perform introductions.

Briggs offered his right hand. His son hesitated for a moment, apparently searching his memory for the meaning of the gesture, then took it in his own and perfunctorily shook it. "Dad," he said. He yawned. He released his grip and sat back. He folded his hands across his stomach. He offered a lazy grin. "What's the bulletin?" he said. "You and Mom decided, have another kid? Thought we ought to know? Or you decided, leave the country, now the party's over?"

"Hasn't been over very long," Briggs said. "From looking at you, at least. My guess is not more'n an hour."

Ted glanced down over his clothes. "I, uh," he said, "no, that one's not over. Shirley and Janice just got back. Last night. From Oakland? Che got killed. Che Guevara? And there was gonna be this big sit-in anyway, but when they heard Che was dead, well, they just *hadda* go." He snickered. "They were both at Port Huron. SDS? I don't think they're ever gonna get over it. But the rest of us play along. I do, at least. So, a bunch of us got together. Stayed up all night talking. I didn't bother, go to bed. Just stayed up, and then came here. But it's still going on." He laughed and shook his head. "Fucking people," he said. "They're so innocent. So goddamned serious. But funny, oh yeah, funny. They don't mean it, but they are."

"Marathon, huh?" Briggs said. "Higher education's changed since my student days."

Ted showed him a portion of a crooked grin. "Come on, Dad," he said. "You were old when you went. You'd already raised your hell. Hell, you're still doing it. Just not with so many people around. One's about your limit. One at a time, that is."

"Nice to see you, too, Ted," Briggs said. "Always a pleasure, drive a few miles, take the kid out to lunch. Keep in touch with the next generation. See if they learned any manners. Or anything else, far as that goes."

Ted yawned again and slumped back in the booth. "Okay if we order?" he said, looking drowsy. "I'm fucking famished, you know?"

"Grass'll do that, I understand," Briggs said. "Sure, go ahead and let's order."

"Grass, my ass," Ted said. "What do you know about that stuff?"

"From experience," Briggs said, taking his reading glasses out of his pocket and picking up a menu, "not a hell of a lot. But we had some Latins when I played. I saw how they looked, heard what they said. Isn't it supposed to goose the appetite like a lightning bolt? Can't say I saw it helped their minds much, but they said it was dynamite before sex. Spoke very highly of it." He put the menu down.

"Surprised you haven't tried it," Ted said. "You sure don't need it for the appetite, but for the other thing, well, I'm surprised you've stayed away." He beckoned to a waitress.

"Been keeping in touch with your mother, I see," Briggs said.

Ted glanced at him as the waitress came to the table. Then he looked at her. "I'll have two cheeseburgers," he said. "Double order of fries. Two eggs over easy. A large Coke. And some coffee. You got any brownies or pie?"

"Pie," she said. "People come in early ate up all the brownies."

"Pie, then," Ted said.

"You gonna tell her what kind?" Briggs said.

The waitress looked at him with pity. "It's always apple, mister," she said. "We get it from Table-Talk, you know? Apple's all we get. All we ever get."

"See, Dad?" Ted said. "Good news at last. Make sure those Siller boys're picking those apples right. Now you know where to sell 'em. Oh, I forgot: You don't sell the apples. The Sillers do." He laughed.

"Right," Briggs said. "I'll save ten boxes out and send them to you. You can set up a stand right outside. Give you something to do when there's no party on." To the waitress he said: "I'll have a medium hamburger plain, and some coffee."

When the waitress had gone away, Ted leaned forward and rested his elbows on the table, dangling his hands below the edge and hunching his shoulders. "What's the angle, Dad?" he said. "What're you doing here?"

"Well," Briggs said, "that's a good question. I don't have a lot to do, you know? And the thought occurred to me, haven't seen you in a while, maybe I'd drive up and see if you'd found any time, crack the books or something."

"Uh-huh," Ted said. "You also had the thought that after you ragged my ass, you'd drive down to Marlboro and ream out Sally's. Right?"

"Gracious," Briggs said. "I was home all day yesterday and last night, after I called you. How'd your mother reach you this morning, you're rolled up in a rug with some broad that needs a shower, one toke over the line and all?"

"Simple," Ted said. "Party's at my place. Just called me on the phone. She does that now and then. Like when you're away, you know? She does it then a lot. Probably lonesome or something. 'I just like to hear your voice.' "

"Gee," Briggs said, "I think I'm gonna cry."

"She does that too, now and then," Ted said. "She gets to talking about when we were little. And when you two were young. And how she hopes we're not disappointed the way she's been. Gets herself all worked up, and then she cries." He paused. "I don't look forward, those calls," he said. "It's a royal pain in the ass sometimes, you're trying to get something done and she calls up. Whoosh, there goes an hour, and you know it's all gone the second you hear her voice. Forget about your class. You're not going to the seminar. You said you'd meet someone? You can forget that, too. You're not going anywhere. And furthermore, you're not gonna be able, call anybody that was expecting you and tell them you won't be there, because Mom has got your phone.

"And then you know what she does? After she's tied you up all that time? She apologizes." He altered his voice to a falsetto whine. " 'I'm really sorry, Teddy, for taking up all your time like this.' It's really sickening. Because she's not sorry at all. She just thinks you're pissed off, which you are, but she isn't finished with just that: She wants you to feel guilty about it. Doesn't work with me, though. I just say: 'No, Mom, no. Don't give it another thought.' "

"And also, I bet," Briggs said, " 'Could you spare an extra twenty, Mom? I'm a little short.' "

"Now and then," Ted said. "Stuff costs a lot. And some the guys here, you know, don't have much cash, their own. I can spring for a few beers every so often, I like to do it."

"You always were a generous kid," Briggs said. "Even before you were old enough to figure out somebody—not you, of course, but someone—had to earn the money, you were always generous. Very free with it."

"Hey, Dad," Ted said, "relax, all right? Face some facts, okay? We're better off'n most people. If I like a guy, and he's flat, can't I buy him a beer? If my girlfriend goes to U. Conn., and her family's kind of poor, can't I give her some dough to come up and visit me here? What'm I supposed to do, someone wants to flop at my place? Charge 'em rent? So we're paying for it? Big fuckin' deal. These people, you know, they know who you are. They may not know your record, what your *Earned, Run, Average* was, or other big, important things, like how you star-*ruck* out Mantle, but they recognize the name. You want them to think I'm cheap? Gimme a fuckin' break."

"I'm trying to," Briggs said. "I'm doing my level best."

"Oh, you always do," Ted said. "And you usually do all right, too. Who's your new lady?"

"What?" Briggs said.

"Your new lady," Ted said, looking sly, as the waitress brought the food. "Mom says she knows you've got one. Says you're out, almost every night."

"Oh for God's sake," Briggs said. "The deer season's coming up, all right? What's she expect a warden to do when the deer season's coming up? Assume all the hunters'll obey the law? Give everybody else the same chance they're entitled to themselves? Of course I go out at night. Or stay out there, on the road."

Ted began eating, taking large bites from the first cheeseburger and talking with his mouth full. "Yeah," he said, "well, I guess that means Mom's right."

"Where does all this come from?" Briggs said. "What's all mean, anyway? You trying to tell me, you don't want me up here? Makes you nervous to see me? It should. You're a lazy little creep, and I'm the one footing the bills. I've got a right to see how it's being spent. Wasted."

Ted nodded toward his father's plate. "You should eat some of your burger, Dad," he said. "Wouldn't want you wasting away."

"I already tried it," Briggs said. "I'd've wanted a lube job to eat, that's what I would've ordered."

"Hey," Ted said, "grease is good for you, man. Keeps you warm in the winter—'s why bears're so fat. So what'd you come up to tell me? You decided, get a divorce?"

"A divorce," Briggs said.

"Sure," Ted said, "it'd figure. You're out grabbing strange all the time. Mom doesn't like it, and she complains. But Mom's getting old—must be true; she told me herself—and maybe you're sick of her bitching. I've been kind of expecting it, you know? Like, for years. The two of you get along together like Florida and Maine—long's you're nowhere near each other, both of you're happy. 'S why she calls when she does. Always, when you go away. Make one of your 'speeches.' Right after you've just gone away. It's such a relief to her, you know? *She* doesn't know, that's what it is, but that doesn't mean that it isn't. She knows what you're doing, but she can't stop you doing it, and since you're not there, she relaxes. By calling me." He paused. "Or Sal," he said. "She also calls Sal quite a lot."

"So I can assume," Briggs said, "that when I get down to Marlboro this afternoon, Sally will also have a barrow load of shit to dump all over me."

"Nah," Ted said, shoveling eggs and fried potatoes into his mouth, "you know Sal better'n that. Well, she'll have it, but she won't dump it. Sal won't know she's got it. If Mom was trying, gear up Sal, to go and pound you on the head, well, Mom don't know Sal like she should, 'cause it'll never work.

"Sal is *nice*. She's not like me. She *likes* you, in her goofy way. She likes Mom, in her goofy way. If you told Sal her clothes were on fire, her stuff was all stolen, and you just ran over her dog, and then you said you were gonna, you know, put her eyes out or something, Sal'd give you a nice smile and tell you that was neat. Sal even likes *me*, sometimes—when someone hits her on the head, reminds her she's got a brother."

"Meaning: Sal won't give you money," Briggs said.

Ted shrugged. "She's pretty cheap," he said, "but that isn't what I mean. I mean—you know Cal's car? His old black Camaro?"

"I seem to remember seeing it once or twice," Briggs said.

"Right," Ted said, pushing his empty plates to the center of the table. "Well, when I'm driving the truck, all right? I happen to mention a couple the guys, I saw this nice Geeto, Carmichael's. And I mean, this was a real cherry car. Sure it was used, but damn, it was nice, and I asked old Wil, would he sell it. And he said he was, that was what it was there for, and then he gave me the price. And it was about nine hundred bucks more'n what a good GTO ought to cost. And I said: 'Mr. Carmichael, that's way out of line,' and he said: 'Not with that mileage.' Which I forget what it was, but it had a low clock. So I'm talking about this one night I was home, which I was about's much as you ever were, and Sal hears what I'm saying and says: 'Then buy Cal's car.' And I say: 'Oh, Cal's car's too old.' And she says: 'Oh no, it isn't, it's not old at all. It's only got about twelve thousand miles on it.'

"Well," he said, "I don't believe her, and that's what I tell her of course. Car's been around for three or four years, and Cal's never let it cool off. Got to have more on the clock'n that. And she says that no, it does not. So he comes by that night to pick her up, and I'm still up and I ask him. And he says he's been meaning to pick up a cable, maybe two or three years. The odometer's busted. The miles never change. No matter how much the jerk drives it.

"Well, Sal is the same way. That's what I'm saying. She thinks if you don't see the numbers changing while you're rolling, the numbers, well, don't count. That's the whole secret of Sal. Her odometer's busted. She thinks . . . I don't know what the hell she thinks. She thinks about art, is my guess. So, no, you won't get a load of shit from Sal. You could tell Sal you've decided, have a sex-change operation, and she'd say: 'Well, that's nice, Dad. I'll loan you a dress.' Sal's just plain dizzy." He hesitated. He nodded. "Yeah, I'd go a little further. Sal is an asshole."

"Tell me something, Ted," Briggs said. "Do you like anybody?"

Ted stared at him. "*Like* anybody?" he said. "You being serious here?"

"Trying to be," Briggs said. "The question too much for you?"

Ted snorted. He shook his head. "Honest to God," he said. "I cannot fuckin' believe this. I see you about twice a year, which is enough for me, and every time it happens, man, you seem to want to fight. What's the gig, you know? Let me in on it. I'm no different'n you were. I can't throw a baseball, maybe, but I'm the same kind of guy. Like my women, like my booze, whatever else you got, and like hangin' out with my friends. What's the beef, all right? Just what the hell is your beef? Is it: I'm spending your money? Well, shit, what if I am. You got it. I asked you, you remember, lemme go out the Coast last summer. You said: 'No.' No explanation, no apology. Nothin'. Just: 'No.' Why? I don't know. Is that right? I ask you for something, and you won't give it to me, and won't even tell me why?"

"That *ganja's* getting to your memory, I think," Briggs said. "You got an explanation. You got a short, simple explanation, which I think's the only kind you're fit to understand. It was that if I'd've wanted to raise parasites, I would've gone into mushroom farming. I wouldn't give you money for a summer off on the toot because it's time you got a real job. Made your own damned money, you hold mine in such contempt."

Ted raised his eyebrows. " '*Ganja*,' " he said. "Hey, where did you get that? You getting hip your old age, Dad? That what you're telling me?"

"Gus Morales called it *ganja*," Briggs said. "You kids all think you created the world. The stars and the moon and the planets. So therefore every day's the Seventh Day, and every day, you rest."

"Very cute, Dad," Ted said. "Very fuckin' cute. Still didn't answer my question, did you? 'Spose that comes from all the years, bullshitting the press."

"Ted," Briggs said, "skip the tactics on me, all right? Skip the goddamned tactics. You've been using this bit since Exeter, second year at Exeter. Whenever it looks to you like somebody's getting close to looking for an answer that you don't want to give, you start in with the breast beating. How that person doesn't love you. And then if that doesn't work, a few little digs, get the other guy mad about something else. Well, it doesn't work. It's all horseshit, and it fools nobody. I asked you a fuckin' question, as you'd probably put it, and I want a fucking answer. What is it with you? Not: What is it with me. What is it with you? There're only four of us. Two of us aren't here. So far you've pissed on the two who aren't, and the one who is. So, I'm asking you again: Do you like anybody?"

Ted sat back and laughed. The waitress brought his pie. "Sure," he said, "I like *every*body." He used his fork to detach a fair-size wedge from the slice of pie, and put it in his mouth. "But liking them don't mean, you know, I'm gonna let'em *shit* me. Which is what everybody, you come right down to it, really wants to do. And, by the way, let's keep in mind whose idea it was, send me, Exeter. Wasn't mine, Dad, wasn't mine. That was your brainstorm, from start to fucking finish. So, the way I look at it, I learned something, Exeter, that you don't happen to like, well, that's poetic justice, Daddy, and I think you deserve it."

"Really," Briggs said.

"Oh yeah," Ted said. "I used to, I was driving the truck, you know? After I got old enough so you couldn't fuck me over all the time like you used to. And I had lots of time to think, about that and other things. You get that, and pretty soon you figure it out that the guys with the shortest routes always take the longest to finish. And they're getting the same pay. And you start to think: Why is that? And then you figure it out. You got it backward. They don't take the longest to finish because they got the shortest routes—they got the shortest routes because they take the longest to finish. So the smart thing to do's get back late every day, and then they'll shorten your route. So I did that, once I figured it out, and after that I had plenty of time, read the paper every day. Which's also all bullshit, what all of them're doing. Just like what you did for me.

"Johnson, Fulbright, McCarthy—the whole bunch of them," he said. "That's what they're all trying to do. Shirl and Jan come back from Port Huron, right? 'We're gonna take over the world. Now the people will listen. Now the people will care.' The Students for a Democratic Society are gonna run the world. Horseshit. Nobody cares. They're all in it for something themselves. You look at me, right? Am I gonna get called? I'm supposed to, when I get out. So, well, it's possible. I might and I also might not. I might get married instead, have a kid, miss out on the whole big parade. Will any of them care, I do? About me? Are you shitting me? They might say it matters, matters to them, but all that really matters to them is whether somebody who hears them'll vote for their candidate, because they were there when they said it. If I get my ass shot off, will any of those guys actually care? Uh-uh. So I went back to school. I may not know enough to suit you, but there is one thing that I do know: how to cover my ass."

"That's what I thought," Briggs said. "You given any thought to what you're going to do, you happen to finish some day?"

Ted grinned again. "Me?" he said. "Plan out the rest of my life? Hey, I'm a chip off the old block, Dad. I take after you, you know? No, of course I haven't. What would you say, for Christ sake, if I asked you that?"

"I'm going to run for Congress," Briggs said.

10

"Well, he seemed a little surprised," Briggs said, initially distracted as he always was when he and Sally were alone. "You know how Ted can be," he said. He hesitated. "Am I permitted, is it permitted, to admit you despise your own son?"

Sally shook her head. "Don't worry about it, Dad," she said. "Ted can be pretty loathsome at times. I'm sure he does it on purpose. Don't let him get on your nerves. What did he say when you said it?"

"He laughed in my face," Briggs said. "Nothing like a vote of confidence from your son."

"He can't give anyone a vote of confidence, Dad," she said. "He doesn't have any himself." She sat up straight in the ladder-back chair across from him at the table in the Waterfall Inn, the light from the tall white candle in the hurricane chimney modeling her face under her straight dark hair. "That's why he tears everyone else down. Because he's so down on himself. He's trying to get company."

"And that, I suppose, I did too," Briggs said.

She laughed. "*Look*," she said, "if *you're* going to start now, I may get upset myself. What's going on with self-pity these days? Is it some new kind of flu, that one person gets and then everyone's got, you get it wherever you go?"

He allowed his shoulders to slump. "Sorry," he said. "You must be right. I guess he did get to me. I do hate to admit it, though."

"It shouldn't surprise you," she said, "and it shouldn't bother you, either. Ted was shocked. What you said to him shocked him. Everything always shocks Ted. He doesn't know very much, except that he doesn't know much. Just that he's always one step behind. And he's scared to death someone will see it, so he always tries not to be shocked. Even though he always is. That's his defense. He tries to make the other person feel ridiculous for saying what they did that shocked him. What did he say?"

"At first he didn't say anything," Briggs said. "He looked like I knocked the wind out of him. Then, when he finally believed I really meant it, after he laughed in my face, he said: '*You*, run for *Congress*? You don't even read the papers, 'cept for the sports section. You don't, have you got any idea, what's going on in the world? They'll make a fool out of you. They won't have to make a fool out of you. You'll make a fool of yourself.'"

She nodded. "He's a real treat to have for a brother, too," she said. "He's always so righteous about everything, and so cynical at the same time. I told him, I don't know why I tell him things, but I told him Cal was ditching this semester to work New Hampshire for McCarthy, and you know what he said? 'Sure he is. Somebody told him the reason there's no ginch around New Haven this winter's because all the girls've gone north.' And like a jerk I tried to tell him that no, Cal's serious. He spent a lot of time last summer, and over Christmas break, talking to Paul Whipple, Junior, and his girl, and he really believes Paul is right, and the other people that he knows, the ones at Yale, are right. About the war. And that if everybody really gets together on this, they can do something here.

"But I got just what I deserved, for trying to be serious about something with Ted. And the second I did it, I knew it, knew that I'd made a mistake. I should know better by now. He said Paul Whipple's an asshole, and anyone who listens to him must be an asshole, too. 'Cal just doesn't want to get drafted. Well, neither do I, but that doesn't make me a saint.'"

"Well," Briggs said, "you make me feel a little better, at least. Every time I have one of these dustups with Ted, I start thinking I'm the only one and it must be all my fault."

"It isn't," she said. "He makes Mom feel bad, too, and she always falls for it. He eggs her on, when she calls him, just to get her going—he tells me all of this, like he's proud of it or something, and he thinks that I should laugh. And of course I always know when I get one of those calls from him, what he's going to say. Because she always calls him before she calls me, and he makes her cry, and then the minute she's over what he did to her, she calls me, and *I* have to get her calmed down. Which isn't easy, as you know. And then as soon as *she* hangs up, about an hour later, and always at the worst possible time—when I've got an exam coming up, you know? I always, now I always make one of my roommates answer the phone, and say I'm in the library. Anyway, then after she gets through with me, *he* calls up. To brag."

"I can see I should've said no when she started paying the bills," Briggs said. "At least after I quit playing, and I was home to do it. Could've learned a lot from those phone tabs."

"Yeah," she said, "but what could you've done about it, once you learned it? Could you've stopped it from happening again? Only if you stayed home all the time. I don't know. I'm not there, and Ted's not there, when you two're alone. So I don't know how she is, when she's supposedly got what she wants. But if she's anything with you in the house like she is with us on the phone, I would go away too. Just as often as I could."

"This is not what I expected," Briggs said.

She shrugged. "You've got a bad marriage, Dad," she said. "You and Mom've got a bad marriage."

"Ted told me the same thing. Basically the same thing," he said. "Not exactly in those terms, but that was what he meant. Did Ted call you after I saw him?"

"If he did, I didn't get it," she said. "I've got a paper due on Modigliani Thursday, so I went to the library right from church, and that's where I was all day. I didn't even stop for lunch. All I could think of was the duck I had here the last time you came down, and I want to lose some weight so I thought: 'Well, I'll skip lunch.'"

"Ted assumed I wanted to see him to tell him we were getting a divorce," Briggs said.

"So did I, when you called," she said. "That's exactly what I assumed. I guess I can understand why Mom wouldn't want to. Even if she didn't love you, well, she's still a Catholic and I think she still believes. But you're not. What's holding you back? You don't call us up and bitch about her, but you can't possibly be happy."

"Well, for one thing," he said, "if the thought ever crossed my mind, I couldn't now. Not when I'm running for office."

"That's not it," she said. "It's something more than that."

"My father owned that place," he said. "He inherited it from his father. His grandfather bought it with the pay he saved from fighting in the Civil War. I don't farm it, and I don't want to farm it, and I'm never going to farm it, but that is where I live. Even when I'm not living there. So long as I'm on this side of the grave, I refuse to turn it over to anybody else, no matter how long or well I've known them. That's not what I tell your mother, and I'd like it if you didn't, either, but that's the way it is. She's not the woman that my mother was, and I'm not half the man my father was, but that place is still my home. Nobody drives me off it. Not her, and not anybody else. She got my dogs out of there, but she's not getting me out. Not until I'm dead."

"Was she really going to have them, have them put to sleep?" Sally said.

"I don't know," he said. "I honestly don't know. She said that she was going to, if I didn't take them away. What the hell could I do? If I'd've been home all the time, it might've been different. But I wasn't. And if they made her sick—certainly looked like she was sick; certainly acted like it—well, what else could I do? Carter gave them a good home. But I still miss those dogs, and I'm not gonna leave the place. Until I'm good and dead."

"Are you going to leave it to Ted?" she said.

"Now there's a thought, isn't it?" he said. "Well, in the first place, I don't figure I have to worry about that for another forty years, if I'm lucky. Maybe in that time, Cal will've decided that his Sheffield degree doesn't necessarily mean he's got to spend his life building a new Panama Canal, and if you're still together, and I've outlived your mother, maybe I'll leave it to you. Maybe, likelier, she'll outlive *me*, and then it'll be her decision. But it's going to take six guys and a long black car to get me out of there, no matter how much commotion there is while I'm still in the place."

He laughed. "Besides," he said, "if I left it to Ted, he wouldn't have it for long. The minute that he got it, the first thing that he'd do is throw the Sillers off the land, and the second thing he'd do would be put in a crop of marijuana, and the cops'd have him in the can before he got his harvest in."

"He does do a lot of grass," she said. "He's always after money. I've told Mom and told Mom: 'Look just don't give it to him.' But, since I can't tell her why . . ."

". . . and she still does," Briggs said.

"She still does," Sally said. "It's very hard to know what the heck to do with her. She's *so* demanding, and she doesn't understand how hard she makes these things. But to make her understand, you'd have to tell her that she doesn't, and she couldn't handle that. I think, well of course there isn't much of a chance that when I finish here, there'd be something for me there. In Occident, I mean. And there sure won't be anything for Cal. He'll probably have to go in the service anyway. So we'll be somewhere else. We'll have to be, that's all. But if, you know, even if something did happen, and there would be something there, I would not go back there. Not for anything. Someplace else may not be better, but it will be someplace else." She paused. "You remember the plaid shirt?"

He laughed. "Remember it?" he said. "How could I forget? I've been taken by surprise a few times in my life, some guy that couldn't hit the fastball got around on one, probably started swinging when Morales threw it back to me, threw back the pitch before, and I got set and threw the next one, and away she went. Okay, that happens. But to get in a fight with my *kid*? About a *shirt*?"

"That was Mom," she said. "When you were living in Pittsburgh. 'Now you notice, next time you see your father, if you ever do, you notice what he's got on. And think whether you've ever seen it before.' And of course we hadn't."

"Well," he said, "you knew I was staying down there, during the winter. Doing my best, finish school. Gets cold in Pittsburgh, too, you know, not just up here in Vermont. And the cops? Well, you can't run around Pittsburgh naked any more'n you can run around Occident bare-ass. Of course I had clothes down there. Cripes, I thought I was doing pretty good, just driving up all that way to spend Thanksgiving with my loving family. Sure, I expected the usual battles with Lil, but with *you*?"

"It wasn't the shirt, of course," she said. "It was that you had another life. Which she wasn't in, and she was mad about it. Well, we weren't in it either. So she got us on her side."

"She's always done that," Briggs said. "One of the things that Lil's always done is treat life like she's fighting a war. And the one with the most troops wins. So she's always lining up people. Those who're with her, and those who're against her, and keeping score all of the time. She never really comes out and fights the damned battle. The battle's always tomorrow. Today is always for more recruiting, more workouts, and more training. And as soon as you kids got old enough, way she looked at it, to fight, she started putting you through your paces, lining you up against me. And since I wasn't there, a lot, she didn't have much trouble getting you lined up. Well, I know whose fault that must be. Must be mine, I wasn't there. All of a sudden, you two were grown up. You grew up when I wasn't looking."

"You were someone who came on visits," she said. "I didn't hate you for it. At least I don't think I did. I didn't think about it much, one way or the other. I lived there, and you came there, and then you went away. I guess when I was little I must've wondered why you kept coming in and going out, why you just didn't either come and stay, or stay away, and I knew we were different from the other families. But it wasn't, you know, *bad,* and I guess I always knew that when I got big enough, I would do the same thing you did. Only come to visit. It's easier, now. It'll get even easier, soon. And then, when you're in Washington, and she's up in Occident, it will be fairly nice. No one will expect as much. We'll get along much better."

"Oh," he said, "so you think I'm going to win? You're the only one."

She frowned and shook her head. "I don't think it, Dad," she said. "I know it: You will win."

"Even though all I read's the sports pages?" he said.

"It wouldn't matter if you didn't even read them," she said. "Some people, well, you and I were born lucky. Ted and Mom? They weren't. And they know it too, and they resent it, and when they're not blaming you for it, they're blaming me."

"My catcher was like that," Briggs said. "Gus, I hung around with Gus because I felt sorry for him. Nobody else on the team would. He was always needling people, daring them to give it back to him, and when they did, even if they didn't use the word, he would say they were calling him a nigger. Or that they were going to, soon's he left the room. So the only time Gus was ever comfortable was when he was going out and acting like he wanted to give people an excuse for calling him a nigger. Which some of the black and Latin guys did more than once when I could hear them. 'Pay no attention to Gussie today—he's niggering it up again.' He used to do it himself. He used to call it, when we'd go out and get a skinful, he called it 'niggering around.' But it was all right, I guess, when he said it.

"Ted reminds me of Gus. He wants me to cuss him out so bad, almost seems like it's my Christian duty to take all the reasons that he gives me, and cuss him out some more."

"Sure," she said. "I don't know why that is, that stuff with luck, and I know it isn't fair. But just the same, if I want something, chances are, I'll get it. Or something pretty close. And you're the same way. If Ted wants something, or Mom wants something, you can almost bet that they won't get it, 'cause they're always out of luck."

"It's an interesting theory," he said. "A lot of guys I played ball with, said something like that about Gus."

"They're right," she said. "And so am I. If you go out there and just be yourself—and you can be so charming—well, Mister Wainwright was down here, when the new building opened with the Farmer collection. And he made a speech, and came to a party, and he seemed like a very nice man."

"That's what everybody says," Briggs said. "Even Ed says that, that Bob Wainwright's a very nice man." He paused. "And, after all this time, he certainly knows what he's doing down there in Washington, better'n I ever could. Knows his way around Congress like I used to know mine around the ball parks. Ted's right—about that part of it, at least. He may be a disagreeable kid, but now and then, he's right."

"But Mister Wainwright isn't charming," she said. "And he's not on the right side. You've never been on any side, so you get to choose. If I were in his shoes, and I heard that you were running, well, I would be worried.

"I think you'd be a good congressman, Dad. I really, honestly do. Because you don't have a program, and you don't have an agenda, and you don't have a whole list of things you want to do. So you can go out and tell people that you want to know what they think. And really mean it. Everybody says that. All the people that come here, they look at us and they think: 'College students. They must be against the draft. They must be against the war. They must be for civil rights. They must be against this, and they're for the other thing.' So they get up behind the microphone, and you can just see the gears working, and they stand up there and spout just what they think we want to hear. And as a result, we're supposed to follow them. Like they were Jesus Christ or something, and we were stupid sheep. It's humiliating. And what really makes it that way is that lots of us do it, do exactly what they think we will, when they lie to us like that.

"Well, you don't have to do that. You can go out and say to people: 'Look, I was a ball player, and I'm a warden, and I never had to lie to anybody to do either one of those things, and I'm not going to start now. So, what's on your mind?' And they'll tell you. And if you don't think that they're right, you can say to them: 'Well, I don't happen to think that's right, and I'm not on your side on this.' And you should say that, if you don't. They will respect that. They will respect it, Dad, because everybody else is telling them what they think they want to hear, and they're sick of it. I think they'll vote for you, if you're not like them. I will, anyway. And I'll help you any way I can."

"Son of a bitch," he said.

She giggled. "No," she said, "you had lunch with him, Dad—this is dinner."

101

11

the Siller Boys had raked the yard but not yet burned the brown leaves. At 5:30 in the morning, there was frost on the piles, and on the long green grass that had bent under their weight. The sky was high and clear, the kind of limitless heaven that outfielders purely hated because fly balls disappeared into it on their ascent and did not reappear until they were out of reach near the turf. He could smell the maple smoke from the wood stoves clearing their throats for the winter. He got into the green pickup and drove down the hill to the village. The store was not open but the lunchroom was. He parked the truck and went around to the front of the store. There was a bundle of morning papers wired together on the cement porch. He climbed the stairs to the porch, the Magnum weighing on his hip, and muscled a paper out of the bundle. He returned to the entrance to the lunchroom and went in.

There were four men from the creamery at the counter eating breakfast. The booths were vacant. He stood at the counter until Marie had finished refilling their coffee mugs. When she smiled at him, he said: "Morning, Marie. Coffee usual, please?" She took a fresh mug and filled it with coffee, topping it off with cream. She set it down on the counter and put a spoon next to it. The pupils of her eyes were almost black. "And," he said, "three over-easy with hash-browns and sausage, whole-wheat toast. Okay?" She looked up inquiringly.

"No, no juice, thanks," he said. "I'm going over to the booth. You just set it on the counter when it's ready. I'll come over, pick it up."

He took the coffee over to the booth in the back and sat down, unfolding the paper. He stirred three sugars into the coffee, spreading the paper open on the table when he had finished the first page. He had read large portions of the stories at the top of the front page (there had been a shotgun murder in Dorset that appeared to be the result of a domestic disturbance; the widow was in custody. The Burlington City Council had approved a highway bond issue. Amtrak disputed reports it was neglecting roadbed maintenance on the Conn River line north of Burlington. State Assemblyman Joseph Danisi, D., Barre, said he intended to introduce a bill at the next legislative session to establish a commission to review local zoning regulations, saying it might be time to think about state codification governing land use "before it's too late, and we wake up some morning and discover we've been strip-mall-developed right off of our own land"), but he had not turned to the pages where the stories were concluded when Marie placed his breakfast platter on the counter. He got out of the booth and fetched it. He was about to sit down again when Paul Whipple entered the lunchroom.

Whipple registered surprise by lifting one eyebrow. He stopped at a vacant space at the counter and rested his hand on it. He did not look at his daughter. She poured him a mug of coffee and positioned it so that the first two fingers of his left hand had only to close on the handle. He picked it up and went back to Briggs's booth. "What the hell're you doing?" he said.

Briggs used his fork to spear one of the three fat sausages and to break the yolk of the first egg. He cut the sausage in half and raised it on his fork. He raised his eyes to meet Whipple's. "Cleaning fish," he said. "Something the matter, your eyes?"

"I don't mean the breakfast, for pity's sake," Whipple said. He sat down opposite Briggs. He nodded at the paper. "Where'd you get that?" he said.

Briggs put the sausage in his mouth and nodded toward the front of the store. Through the meat he said: "Bundle out front." He swallowed. "Don't worry, Paul, I'm gonna pay for it. You're just a little late this morning, so I thought I'd get something to read."

"I'm not late, goddamnit," Whipple said. "I'm here exactly the same time I always am. It's you that's early. And that's not it—about paying for the paper. Never saw you read the paper in here, mornings." He squinted. "Cobb's been talking to you." Marie brought a platter to her father.

"Wait a second, Marie," Briggs said. He lifted his breakfast and removed the paper. He set the platter down again and folded the paper, dropping it on the bench beside him. She put a breakfast of eight thick pieces of bacon and four pieces, halved, of buttered white toast in front of her father. She went back to the counter and brought him a ten-ounce Coca-Cola glass filled with tomato juice. Whipple did not look at her, or speak to her.

"Ed come by to see me," Briggs said. "Week or so ago."

"Yup," Whipple said, seizing the first piece of bacon with his fingers and biting off half of it. "Said he might do that."

"Well, he did," Briggs said, finishing the first sausage and dividing the white of the first egg with his fork. He folded the half-egg over itself until he had it all on his fork, and ate it.

"You gonna do it?" Whipple said. He swallowed the second half of the bacon piece and picked up another one with his right hand. With his left hand he picked up half a slice of toast and ate that first.

"Dunno," Briggs said. He picked up a piece of his toast and looked without expression at Whipple. "Think I should?" He bit off some of the toast.

Whipple shook his head. He ate the toast in two bites. He frowned. "You know Ed Cobb's well's I do," he said. "Know him better, in fact." He ate the bacon.

"Didn't ask you that, Paul," Briggs said. "Didn't ask you that at all. Asked you, think I should do it." He ate the toast and started work on his second sausage and egg.

"Yeah," Whipple said. "So you did." He frowned. "Don't know why a man'd want to do a thing like that," he said. "Didn't understand it when Bob Wainwright ran. Had a perfectly good operation goin' over there. Thrivin' business. What he wanted that Washington grief for, beat me all to hell. Dad didn't understand it, either. Said to me: 'Makin' good money, that bank. No reason at all, go and leave it.' Figured the guy, you know—this's what Dad thought, at least—

104

thought maybe old Bob'd gone simple early. Happens to people some-times. Fool idea. Didn't know what to make of it when he up and did it. Didn't know what to make of it when Ed said he was thinkin' askin' you about doing the same damned thing. Didn't know what to make of it at all. Thought about it some since. Still don't.

"'Must be some weakness in the family, there,' Dad said. This would've been when Bob ran. 'Something secret. Something we don't know about. Something in the blood. Thin blood. Makes them act like that. Just as well young Bob and Jane didn't have the kids. First thing you know, one of them'd decide, wanted to be governor.' I think Dad was right."

"Did you vote for him, Bob I mean?" Briggs said.

"Well, sure, we voted for him. Voted for him every time," Whipple said. "Every time he run."

"Why?" Briggs said. "If you thought there was something wrong with him."

"Well," Whipple said, scowling, "Wainwrights asked us to. His father and Bob both. That's why. Man asks you to do something, doesn't cost you anything, of course you're going to do it for him. Wasn't like we had something against them, either one of them. They always traded with us, every chance they could. Paid cash, too. Cash on the barrel-head."

"But if you thought they were crazy," Briggs said. He finished his second combination of egg and sausage and his second piece of toast. He drank some coffee.

"Huh," Whipple said. "What's that got to do with the price of bananas? Far as that goes, I think they're all crazy. Every last one of those people. No one but a crazy man'd want to leave his home like that, his family, his business. Just the fact he wants it, or even says he does, that's enough to prove he's crazy. In my book, at least. Might's well vote for the crazy man you know. One you don't know, well, he's probably crazy, too, but maybe in different ways. Might do something down there, take years to straighten out. Least the Wainwrights, man and boy, they never acted that way, once he got in office."

"So the fact that I'm thinking about running against Bob makes you think I'm crazy," Briggs said. "That what you're trying to say, Whip?"

"Makes me wonder," Whipple said. Three pieces of slab bacon

remained on his platter, along with two slices of toast. He picked up the Coca-Cola glass and drained the juice without removing the glass from his lips. He set the glass down. He picked up his coffee mug and drained that. He shifted the mug to his left hand and slammed it down on the front edge of the table. Briggs finished his coffee and got out of the booth. He took Whipple's mug and his own over to the counter, where by now eight milk drivers and two different creamery workers perched over their food. He set the mugs on the counter.

Marie brushed a wisp of hair back from her eyes and brought the coffeepot. She filled both mugs and topped them off with cream. She looked up, gratefully. Briggs said: "Thank you, Marie." He returned with the mugs to the table.

"Goddamnit, Henry," Whipple said, "I told you and I told you, there ain't no goddamned need to be acting like that. She's perfectly able, wait on the customers. Not much she can do, but she can do that."

"Whip, you old bastard," Briggs said, sitting down, "that kid's got ten customers 'sides us. She's working the grill. She's making fresh coffee. She's making the toast, and she's cleaning up. You're too cheap to hire a short-order man and you give her no help on the counter. All right, 's your business, I guess, you want to sit on your ass and just watch, 'til she falls down on hers. But I'll be damned if I'm gonna help you, help you speed it up."

"Man oughta mind his own business, 's what I think," Whipple said. He stirred sugar into his coffee.

"So do I," Briggs said. "And I think it's my business, decide whether I want to get off of my ass now and then, give somebody else a hand."

Whipple drank, his brow furrowed. He put the cup down, nodding. "Well," he said, "you're runnin', all right. That's pretty clear. Already starting to meddle, other people's business. You asked me why we always voted for Wainwright? Well for one thing, because he kept his nose out of things, didn't concern him."

"Well then," Briggs said, "if I do, then will you vote for me?"

Whipple cleared his throat. "Well," he said. He took a paper napkin from the black metal dispenser at the back end of the table and wiped his mouth. "Don't see how I can."

"Why not?" Briggs said. "Understand, Paul, I'm not pushing you here."

"Hell you're not," Whipple said.

"No," Briggs said. "I just need to know, that's all. If people like you, 've known me a long time, if I talk to you, and you say you can't vote for me, well, that could change my mind."

"Doubt it," Whipple said. "I go up to Siller's place, talk the bull, that mean he won't chase the cows anymore? 'Now, you just stop that there, you hear?' Doubt it. Nope, you've made up your mind."

"And you won't vote for me," Briggs said.

"Can't," Whipple said. "I assume you're goin' Democrat. I'm Republican. Can't vote for Democrats, at least the first election."

"I'm not talking about the primary," Briggs said. "If I run I won't have opposition, that. I'm talking the general election. Me against Bob Wainwright."

"Mmm," Whipple said. "I'd have to think about that some. Like I say, Wainwrights've always treated us fair. Got nothing against him at all."

"Whip," Briggs said, "if it's trade you're talking about, the Briggses've given you one hell of a lot more trade in our time'n Wainwright has in his. He only buys something when he comes through for votes. Just to keep you happy. Otherwise his business, well, they do it, Canterbury. The Briggses live right here, and this is where we trade."

"Well now," Whipple said, "that may be true. But it don't change the facts. Now Bob, I expect that he'll be in, order up his turkey for the holiday. Probably the next week or two. And he don't have to do that. He could buy it somewheres else. But he says our birds're fresher, which I think they probably are—got Joe Maleska and his wife up 'til all hours, week before Thanksgiving, Christmas, slaughtering fresh birds. We sell 'em soon's they're plucked. And Bob, he buys from us. Does it every year."

"How many's he buy from you?" Briggs said.

"Well, just the one," Whipple said.

"Sure," Briggs said, "gets his Christmas somewhere else. Probably tells the guy there that his birds're the freshest around."

"I ain't so sure of that," Whipple said. "There's just the two of them. Never did have kids." He mused. "Bob's smarter than I thought, maybe. Didn't think of that." He shook his head. He cleared his throat. "Anyway," he said, "I doubt it. Bob's mighty careful with a dollar. Might just buy the one. Freeze what's left for Christmas."

"Yeah," Briggs said, "must taste real fresh, then. But the Briggses buy the two. Don't they, Paul."

"Oh, yeah," Whipple said. "Oh yeah, you do that."

"Well then," Briggs said, "if buying turkeys is buying votes, then the Wainwright household's entitled to one from the Whipples, and the Briggses're entitled to two. I guess you and Evelyn'll have to vote for me, and Paul Junior can vote for Bob."

"Huh," Whipple said, "doubt Paul Junior'd vote for either one of you. 'Less you come out for downright surrender, over Vietnam there."

"Well, I'm not about to do that," Briggs said. "You can work out that business yourselves. But if I do go after this, Whip, I'll expect your help, you know."

"Yeah," Whipple said. "You, ah, you know something, Henry? Assuming that you do, you know, this thing you got in mind, you ain't got much of a tinker's damn chance."

"Sure, I realize that," Briggs said.

"And you're not goin', improve it," Whipple said, "you go around badgerin' the few friends you have got. Like you've just been doin' to me."

Briggs did not say anything.

"See, Henry," Whipple said, "I can take it, take it from you. And I will. Because you and me, we've known each other a long time. And I watched you, you made a big name for yourself, see if your head'd get big. You were just a young kid then, same as I was, but I was right where I'd always been, mostly, 'cept for the time in the service, nobody knew me from Adam. And you were just off there, out in the limelight, people fallin' all over you.

"I remember," he said, "the first year or two, the boys at the Legion Hall laughing. 'Well, it just didn't happen yet, that's all. Just wait around, and it will.' And I said no, it wouldn't, because I'd seen you, and you hadn't changed, I could see. Always back here at the end of the season. Always remembered your friends. You know I never asked you, not once, get me tickets a big game or two?"

"I never thought about it," Briggs said. "If you had've, if there was some particular game . . ."

"Well, you had no reason to," Whipple said. "The games that *you* called *me* up for—three, four a year, sometimes more?—all those games suited me fine. Always day games, didn't have to stay over. And usually Sundays—I didn't miss work. And the boys at the hall they'd say to me: 'I 'spose if you called him for tickets some time, he'd get them for you right off.' And I said: 'I'd never call Henry for tickets.' All started laughing at me. Said I didn't call you because you'd high-hat me. I didn't 'cause I knew you would. And that's when I said: 'Got no need to call Henry. Henry calls up and invites *me*.'" He paused and smiled. "That shut 'em up, oh you bet. Changed their tune some with that one."

"Well," Briggs said, "I always thought, hoped anyway, that I did the right thing by my friends. Too bad some of the guys that I knew over there, too bad that they didn't call me. Wrote me a letter, that was the way they felt. None of them ever did."

"I knew that," Whipple said. "I knew you'd oblige if you could. But I didn't tell them, see, Henry? I didn't say what I knew: 'You guys weren't so damned ready, assume one your friends went bad, you might get more enjoyment from life. 'Course you might have to swallow some bad words you said about him, but you might have a little more fun.' No, it was better the way that I did it.

"Got a confession for you, Henry," he said. "I didn't always go to all the games you got for me."

"Well, I knew that," Briggs said. "You asked me once if it was all right, you gave them somebody else."

"And you said it was okay, so I did it," Whipple said. "I'd take those tickets to the hall, and I would say to this one, and the other one next time: 'Got two good seats, Chicago, Sunday. Henry sent 'em up. Evelyn's got me roped in for that damned bean supper here. Think you could use 'em? Certainly hate to see 'em wasted, and I know Henry'd be obliged.' And they'd *grab* 'em. And I'd say: 'Just remember while you're down there, sittin' in the catbird seat: Henry Briggs don't forget friends. Just remember that.'

"So," Whipple said, "this is what I'm tellin' you, and I want you to listen. You got a lot of friends 'round here. Some you don't even like. They'll never come right out and say it, thank you for the ball games. They'll never tell you to your face what they all think of you. That it was not the ball games, but the way you didn't change. There's lots of people you don't know, that you did favors for. They maybe were small change for you, but they were big for them. You think one of those bastards in his seat at Fenway Park—so close the field the ump is asking where's his name, the lineup card—you think one of those bastards ever said when someone asked him: 'Got these tickets from Paul Whipple, runs the IGA'? My arse they did. Every single one of them did the same thing that I did. 'Say, mister, where'd you get those tickets? These're damned good seats,' and every single one of them just made like it was nothing: 'Why, I'm a friend of Henry Briggs. Grew up with Henry Briggs. Up home there in Vermont.' 'Oh, what kind of guy is Briggs? Looks like one mean bastard.' 'Bullshit he is—that's pure bullshit. Old Henry's best there is.' That is what they said.

"Well," Whipple said, "now they're stuck with it, all those things they said and all the bragging that they did. They'll never come right out and say it, not again they won't. But once they said it, they believed it." He pointed his finger at Briggs. "*And they'll act as though they did*, if you, dumb bastard, let them."

"I see," Briggs said.

"Now," Whipple said, "makin' a big show, readin' the paper, tellin' people how to run their family business, givin' them a lot of shit how they got to vote for you because you always traded with them: That's not gonna do it. Because that's a different Henry. That's the Henry we expected when he made the major leagues—and we weren't lookin' forward to the day when he come home. Well, that Henry never showed up. It was the old Henry come back, and even though we don't say much, we were all damned glad to see him.

"This morning here I think I catch a glimpse the other Henry, one we didn't want to meet. Get him outta town, Henry, 'fore he does you harm. We're all comfortable, the old one. Like him a good deal. If he tells us he is runnin', well, we'll know what to do. We may think he's got a screw loose, now he's gettin' old, but Henry is a friend of ours, and if he says he wants this thing, well then by God, he oughta have it."

"Jesus, Whip," Briggs said, "I think I'm gonna make you my campaign manager."

"The hell you are," Whipple said. "You do anything like that, I sell one less turkey a year, and I turn a good profit on them. Besides, I don't know shit about politics, and that's more'n enough, suit me. No, what you do now's concentrate on people, *don't* like you. The ones you *know* don't like you. There aren't that many of them, but there're a few. And everyone knows who they are. You win one them bastards over, you might even start to roll." He paused. He glanced at his Timex. "Christ on a crutch," he said, "listen to me. I'm gettin' excited 'bout this. Just look at the damned time. I got to open out front. Probably lost ten or twelve dollars already, sittin' here jawin' at you." He slid out of the bench. He looked down at Briggs. "I'd start with Wilse," he said. "He doesn't like you at all."

Briggs started to slide out of the booth. "Got to go to work myself," he said. "I'll see him sometime this week."

"Good," Whipple said. He started toward the store.

"Whip," Briggs said. Whipple turned around. "Thanks," Briggs said. Whipple dismissed him with a wave. Briggs waited until Whipple had vanished into the store. Then he asked Marie for his check. He put two dimes on the counter while she added it up. "For the paper," he said, indicating the coins. She picked them up and put them on top of the register. When she turned around he was going out the door, leaving her with her eyes open wide, staring at a two-dollar tip.

That night he got home after eleven. The house was quiet, as the woods had been. The only light was the one that glowed above the kitchen table. He opened the door of the wood stove and stirred the bright white ashes. He inserted three more pieces of wood from the box beside the stove and closed the door. He went to the refrigerator, unbuckling his gunbelt as he went. He got a beer and put the gunbelt on the table. He sat down, twisting the cap off the beer, and felt the stove heat welcome on his back and stiff shoulders. He drank some of the beer. He bent down and untied his bootlaces, loosening the ones below the first eyelets, and removed the boots. He tilted back in the chair and put his stocking feet on the table, crossing his legs at the ankles. He drank some more beer and thought.

When he had finished the beer, he stood up and slid the bottle into the trash, making no noise. He picked up the gunbelt and returned to the refrigerator, getting a second beer. He padded into the study, the gunbelt in his left hand, the beer in his right. There was some moonlight through the westerly window. The sugar house was a black, indeterminate bulk under it. He used his left elbow to hit the light switch inside the door. The lamp beside the desk came on. He sat down at the desk and put the gunbelt far forward into the center compartment under the pigeonholes. He opened the beer and drank some of it. He leaned forward in the desk chair and took his wallet out. From it he removed a scrap of paper with a number written on it. He pulled the phone over to him with his left hand. He sighed. He took another drink of beer. He began to dial Ed Cobb's home number.

12

four years before, winning his thirteenth term as congressman, Robert D. Wainwright, R., Vermont, had surprised none of the minority leadership by again waiving his seniority privilege to move to larger quarters with a better view in the Longworth Building. He responded as he had in 1959, 1961, and 1963, saying that he appreciated the courtesy, but he and his staff had "grown accustomed to the cozy if limited space" at the easterly end of the south corridor on the first floor, and were apprehensive as well that "our rather medieval notions of filing and storage, while comfortable for us, would certainly baffle any Capitol employee's most conscientious effort to reconstruct elsewhere."

Leadership staff every two years perceived his self-effacement as a shrewd if minor tactic to accumulate negotiable debts from newer legislators from larger states who would be grateful for Wainwright's deference. Wainwright's chief assistant, Andrew J. Prior, corrected that error each time. He did so when he talked to Russ Wixton.

"Look at him sometime," he said. "Hell, look at *me* sometime." Wainwright, in his seventies, sufficiently resembled Prior, in his late thirties, so that those who seldom saw Wainwright publicly prominent frequently mistook Prior for him. Both were lean, sandy-haired, under six feet tall, and habitually attired in neat dark suits and scuffed black shoes.

"He looks like just what he is," Prior said, in September 1967, "or what he used to be. He's a Vermont banker. You know that breed, Russ. You must know them—you live there. When you become treasurer of a little bank that your grandfather started in Canterbury, Vermont, eighty years ago, you know your father didn't redecorate the office when he got it, and so you didn't, either. Even if you wanted to. The directors wouldn't like that. Neither would the customers. They would wonder whether a man who spent money on his own comfort like that was the kind of guy they ought to see to practice thrift. And when you take your place in Congress, you don't go in, take it apart, and put in a swimming pool. That'd be against your nature. Voters wouldn't like it. They would wonder if a man who'd waste taxpayers' money on luxury for himself is the kind of man they want in Congress, voting on tax bills.

"That suite's like his car. A black 'fifty Olds Eighty-eight was good enough for him when his father's DeSoto died out after he came down here, and if that hadn't rusted out under him nine years ago, he'd still be clunking around in it instead of the black 'fifty-eight Pontiac Chieftan he's clunking around in today. He's not complicated—he's cheap. Just, plain, cheap. If he wants something, he will tell you. If he doesn't ask, he doesn't."

Prior did not cite, as he could have, the most persuasive proof of Wainwright's parsimony: At the conclusion of each session, to the despair of his staff, he regularly returned to the Treasury between 30 and 40 percent of his office budget, saved by his refusal to add additional assistants or to pay those he had for the heavy workload and long hours that the personnel shortage created. He used his postal frank to send out only one constituency newsletter each session; the only boast he ever made consisted of the laconic report of the actual sum he had saved.

Congressman Wainwright kept Vermont hours in Washington. He was never in his office after 6:00 P.M., when he went home for dinner alone. He was proud of his ability in the kitchen, and had confided more than once to Prior and his constituents that the meatloaf he made on Saturdays was even better heated up in the middle of the week. Now and then he varied his diet from that or corned beef hash that he also prepared himself. "Well," he would say on such occasions, "think I'll go home now, treat myself to a pork chop." He arrived in the building each day by 6:00 A.M., having breakfasted at home. Prior pretended to believe his explanation that he preferred his own oatmeal, raisin toast, and tea to the morning menu offered in the House cafeteria: "Besides, I can't stand the smell of those damned grits."

Prior infrequently became bitter in the privacy of his small brick house in Bethesda, usually when his wife, Helene, mentioned her continuing wish that he made enough money to allow them a larger house. "Well, I don't, and I won't," he would say. "When you work for a man who's too cheap to eat for dimes in the House dining room the food the Treasury's mostly paying for, your chances of a big raise from him are mighty small, my dear. Hell, I don't know how he justifies the extra cost of raisin bread. Whole wheat's much cheaper, better for your bowels, and you get a bigger loaf."

Then she would ask him, again, why he did not seek another job. And he would say: "Well, it's not that I'm in love with him. I can tell you that. It's because everybody that pays more thinks that I agree with him, and nobody else in his right mind wants a skinflint running that kind of office for him."

Prior did like the lulls that interrupted the congressional year. Wainwright did not belong to the Tuesday-Thursday club of congressmen who spent each weekend either on fact-finding tours to desirable destinations, or pressing the flesh in their districts. "The people who elected me didn't send me down here so that I'd go gallivanting back and forth all the time. Put me down here to work. No need for all that other."

Prior and Helene agreed that Wainwright kept to his efficiency apartment on the Hill because his wife, Jane, lived at home in Canterbury and did not like Washington. Prior and his wife agreed that either of them, married to either of the Wainwrights, would have welcomed such separation. But Wainwright did observe extended recesses. He went home on the Thursday that preceded each legislative holiday, and did not return until the following Tuesday. He expected Prior to brief him by telephone each morning, not later than 7:15, and to call him again in the afternoon, not later than 5:45.

"I don't see why," Helene said. "Why you have to call him twice a day, when he knows nothing's going on. I don't see the point to it."

"The point is," Prior explained, "the point is that it means I have to be in the office all day, so it's really never closed. And that means he can tell the people that he's always on the lookout in case someone tries something sneaky. And it also means they know from that that he's getting full value for their dough he spends on staff."

"Well," she said, "I suppose so. And from your point of view, I suppose it must be better, better than spending the whole day cooped up in this little bandbox with three screaming kids."

During the Christmas recess in 1966, Helene had taken the children to visit her parents in Elgin, Illinois, the plane tickets a present from her father. Prior had joined them only for the holiday itself. He took five days of vacation to stay over for New Year's, and then returned to Washington. "Boss wasn't pleased," Prior told her. "Said he 'sposed I needed some time off, but he begrudged it. I know he wasn't pleased."

"Really," she said. "I should think he would be. We're beginning to live just like he does. He should be very flattered." In the spring of '67, she acquired a Tupperware franchise, making enough profit from three house parties a week to defray babysitting costs and build a tidy new bank account for herself. She declined to apportion any of the money to household expenses. "No, this is for us," she said. "I haven't decided yet whether it's to rent a summer place this year, or to just keep saving until it's enough for a down payment on a new house. But it's certainly not for you to have more lunches at the Carroll Arms, while that miser's out of town."

"I don't pay for those," he said. "Norman pays for those."

"I don't believe you," she said calmly, and put in a load of wash.

The day after Labor Day Andrew Prior left the office for lunch at the Carroll Arms at 11:45. "I'm meeting a couple guys, the National Committee," he said as he left the office. The receptionist was Emily Poitrast. She had gotten her first job at Canterbury Savings in 1938, acting as a teller and part-time as secretary to Robert Wainwright, Jr. When he was elected to Congress, he invited her to Washington, and she took the job eagerly. As soon as Prior was out the door she muttered to her typewriter: " 'I'm sorry, Mr. Prior's not in. He's over at the Carroll Arms, getting himself blotto. Can I have him return your call, assuming he can talk?' "

★ ★ ★

The Carroll Arms behind the Capitol since World War Two had declined in the eyes of men from a relatively comfortable residence-lodging hotel into an establishment where government officers renting the small rooms on the second through fourth floors would not describe the business that they conducted in them, beyond making strong averments that the transactions were "official." The building had been taken by eminent domain and marked for demolition at some unspecified time in the indefinite future when some unidentified individual or committee of some unknown agency decided what would be better suited to whatever needs it had. The General Services Administration in the meantime managed it aloofly. The bar and lounge in the half-cellar, down three steps from the sidewalk, operated under private management in discreetly boisterous seediness while those decisions were pending, dispensing large martinis and frosted seidels of draught beer to overflow luncheon and cocktail-hour patrons who visited for drinks and camaraderie, and sometimes ordered food. The waitresses appeared to have acquired from their immediate predecessors sufficient data about John Quincy Adams, Henry Clay, and Joe Cannon to convince them that the current crop of pols and hangers-on was inferior to the group long gone before, and often greeted those who asked: "What's good?" with the "personal opinion that the beer must be all right, 'cause we don't get too many complaints, and the booze must be all right, too, because we sell lots of that. But if you mean: 'What's good to eat?' Well, I understand, the sandwiches, down the Monocle."

Prior descended into the lunchtime uproar shortly before noon. Ferdie Norman was standing in a cluster of men at the bar, all of them in gray or blue suits and well-barbered middle age. Norman held a martini in his right hand and looked over the rim of the glass, his eyes beetled under his flushed forehead, at the tall man opposite.

Norman had retired as a colonel in the Air Force at the age of fifty-three, taking the promotion (from lieutenant colonel) and his pension because he could "do arithmetic." He had honed that skill during twelve years of assignment to the Pentagon, where he had done the calculations that enabled generals to defend ever increasing appropriations to Undersecretaries of Defense, who had in turn passed them on by rote to Secretaries testifying before Armed Services Committees.

117

He had learned that proffered numbers were accurate if they simultaneously reflected the interests of the Air Force (its commanders wished to have more men and equipment under their command; the more equipment, the more men, and therefore, the more commanders); the manufacturers of weapons (their executives desired to report profits pleasing to stockholders, who would acquiesce accordingly as manpower was increased); and the members of the Congress who sat on the Armed Services Committees (whose staff assistants made it clear that appropriations requests would be most favorably received by congressmen and senators whose constituencies could expect more jobs when contracts were awarded, and most hostilely received by congressmen and senators whose constituents could shortly plan for layoffs).

Norman had learned that the most accurate estimate of the number of dollars adequate to preserve and improve America's preparedness was therefore almost always the largest one available. He had learned always to propose that number to his superiors, and felicitous results had followed. Applying that experience to his individual case, he had elected to retire, with commendations, soon afterward, accepting not only an advisory staff position with the Republican National Committee but also consulting assignments with companies involved in the aerospace industry. Ferdie, looking past the tall man's left shoulder, spotted Prior and nodded. He looked back to the tall man, said something, picked up a check from the bar, looked at it, dropped it back on the counter, signed it, and motioned with his head toward a booth along the easterly wall.

Prior made his way through the shoulders and the din. He reached the booth and sat down opposite Norman. Norman drank the last of his martini. He set the glass down solidly on the wood. "Andy," he said, "glad you made it. Got a lot to talk about. Talked to Jerry. Be along in a minute. Cleaning up a few things, the office. Lemme get Barbara here, order us some drinks." He fluttered his left hand in the air.

"Andy," he said, leaning forward, "we got problems. Before Jerry gets here, lemme brief you—that all right?" The waitress brought two martinis, straight up, and set them on the table. "We got two kinds of problems, I recognize. Maybe there's more, I dunno.

"The first one we got," he said. "Well, maybe this doesn't concern you that much, but I think it's connected, you know. So lemme backtrack a little bit here, and you just kick in when you're ready." Prior drank some of his gin.

"Neil Cooke was in town, day before yesterday. He took Jerry to lunch. Now you know how Neil is, and you know how he acts. Always like it's post-time, and the bugler is playing. But damnit all, the guy's not dumb, no matter what you say. Nobody who made that much money can possibly be dumb."

"He married that fucking woman," Prior said, drinking some more gin.

"Nobody's perfect," Norman said. "Besides, and you know this like I do, you would've done the same thing."

Prior shook his head. "Not unless," he said, "not unless I had a paper, she'd stay home and mind the kids."

"They haven't got any kids," Norman said.

"Then: She would stay home in New York," Prior said. "I keep trying, tell the man: 'This broad's on our turf, and she's trouble. She's looking for something to do. And sooner or later, she's going to do us, and we had just better start planning.' And the man always says: 'She's not trouble yet.' Which just goes to prove what I'm saying."

"Well," Norman said, "maybe that's what I am saying. Neil's telling Jerry he thinks Nixon. You can guess what old Neil thinks of that."

"Neil thinks he died and he's in heaven," Prior said. He finished off his first martini. "I don't envy Nelson, if he thinks that Neil's for him. Once for Nixon, always Nixon. Those guys never change. They're like dogs with rabies. They may nuzzle up against your leg, and ask you, scratch their necks. But when the chips're down, boy, they've still got the disease, and the only way to cure them is to shoot them."

"Exactly," Norman said. "Now, Jerry, you might imagine, he's got no quarrel with this." A burst of laughter erupted around the bar behind him. "Fuckin' Drayne," he said.

"Dick?" Prior said. "He in here again?"

"Of course he's in here, goddamnit," Norman said. "You can bet your ass he's in here, you hear that shit go up. Bastard's holding court. Anytime that someone gets it, right upside the head, and it's one of ours, Drayne's the guy that wrote the line. Bastard's everywhere. Teddy takes the bows and credit, but old Dickie wrote the line."

119

"He's a funny bastard, though," Prior said.

"You're as bad as the rest of them," Norman said. "You guys from New England, you got no sense of outrage. You think he comes from the same place, he must be all right. You like the son a bitch so much, whyn't you go and listen?"

"Don't need to," Prior said. The waitress brought two more martinis. "All I have to do's go back my office and sit down. What Dick says, it travels fast. I'll have everything he said, before the sun goes down. And besides, you got it wrong—he's from Pittsburgh, I think. Some place like that, anyway, nobody ever heard of. He just worked in Boston."

"Second thing," Norman said. He scowled. "You know how Neil Cooke is. Him and his damned wife've got joint custody of pols. He doesn't mess with her stuff, and she doesn't mess with his. So getting out of him, what she is going to do, well, I had teeth pulled easier, without novocaine. But he did say some stuff."

"Which is?" Prior said.

"Which is basically that your guy is her target now," Norman said. "Neil said she's hooked up with some car dealer named Beale, operates out of Burlington, and he's thicker'n thieves with the Speaker up there, some gunslinger name of Ed Cobb. This is trouble looking for a place to happen, baby doll. She's got time on her hands, and money. Cobb's got targets to pick and needs her, or as many like her's he can get."

Prior laughed. He drank the second martini. Norman drank his down. "I'm serious," he said.

"I hope you are," Prior said. "I hope this dame from New York's got this in mind. Bob Wainwright will eat her up, her and anyone she picks, to be a stalking horse."

"You know what worries me about you?" Norman said. "You don't have a sense of danger. You should be in Vietnam. You don't know what quiet means. It doesn't mean the other guys're beat, and that they've gone home. It means they're lying low, and piling up supplies. It means they're scouting out the bushes, looking over the terrain. Setting up an ambush, so they take you by surprise."

"Ferdie, Ferdie," Prior said, "you don't know Bob's district. Second's a well-settled place, just like the whole state. There isn't anybody in it, that could take Bob on. It's suicide to think about. The guy would just get crushed. You know how long he's been here. And he's just like his district. They think they're voting for themselves. He is just like them. There isn't anybody, just like him, that can compete with him. They all got other things to do. That's why they don't run."

"You know," Norman said, "I bet that's just what Lyndon's saying, right this very minute. 'I know my people. They know me. They will vote for me.' Well, I hope Lyndon's wrong, and I'm pretty sure he is. But if he's wrong, then you are. And that should worry you."

The waitress returned to the table. Another burst of laughter came from the bar. Norman scowled again. "You guys wanna order?" she said. "Or don't you want to die?"

13

the two-story houses along High Street in Canterbury had been built during the late nineteenth century. The yellow ones had white or black gingerbread trimmings. The white ones had gray or black blinds. Tall maple trees and oaks flanked the houses, and there were glider swings attached to some of them, iron seats suspended by rusty chains from the thick lower branches, the dull red springs exposed year after year to winter. The leaves were turning colors slowly; some had already fallen, littering the worn floorboards of the porch, and the cushions of Bob Wainwright's father's glider.

Robert Wainwright sat in his late father's home office on the first floor of his white house on High Street, the black phone back in its cradle. The handset and the base were yellowed with oil and grime from his hands and his father's. It was the shag end of 1967, but yellowed tax demands levied on Canterbury Trust—mortgaged properties during the Depression—he remembered his father's mournful countenance, when he had to present such a default: "I know it, Cyrus. Times're damned tough. But you got to come up with the money some way, or I'm gonna have to foreclose you"—long since paid, hung out of the pigeonholes of the rolltop desk. The dark came early to Canterbury as the year declined.

He got up, switching the light off, and made his way through the gloom into the kitchen. There was a shaded lamp suspended over the table, and the iron stove showed orange fire behind the carboned glass. He went to the table and sat down. He could hear his wife moving jars around on the rough wooden shelves his father had built in the cellar. Then he heard her ascend the creaky stairs and open the door into the hallway. "Don't forget to shut off the light," he said. The click of the old switch against the white china fixture constituted her reply.

Jane Wainwright came into the kitchen using her flowered apron to wipe dust from a one-quart Mason jar of stewed tomatoes. She took it to the sink and rinsed it briefly under cold tap water. She dried it and held it to the light. She nodded and set it down on the counter. "What did Andy have to say?" she said. "Has war been declared since you talked to him this morning?"

"In a way, yes," he said. "Or looks like it's going to be."

"Really," she said. She unsnapped the wire clamping the lid airtight on the jar and opened it. She peeled off the red rubber ring she had used to seal it the previous August, and discarded it, limp, into the wastebasket. "I'm surprised the President would do a thing like that. Without consulting you, I mean. Is this another war, or just the same old one?"

"This is a new one," he said. "The President isn't involved. That is, if Andy is right. This's going to be a private war. Two people invited. I'm one."

She took a blue enameled saucepan and cover from the cabinet next to the gas stove and poured half of the tomatoes into it. She covered the pan and put it on a burner. She used a wooden safety match to ignite a low flame, stooping slightly to regulate it to her satisfaction, and blew the match out. "Who's the other one?" she said.

"Don't know yet," he said. "Don't think anybody does. They're trying to decide. Find someone to oppose me."

She glanced at him. "This year?" she said. "After all these years, someone's going to run?"

"What Andy says, they're trying," he said. "Trying to find some-one."

"Who is this?" she said. "You haven't made any enemies in the party. Least that I know of. I thought everyone was happy."

"Not them," he said. "The damned Democrats. What Andy says, it looks as though some damned woman name of Cooke that lives in Manchester has got it into her fool head to put up a man against me."

"Do you know her?" she said.

"I don't think so," he said. "I never heard of her, I think. I thought I knew most of the people, live down there, and I do. Must be one of those damned newcomers. She's from New York." He paused. "Probably a Jew. Some damned New York Jew bitch."

" 'Cooke' doesn't sound like it's Jewish to me," she said.

"Oh," he said, "you can't go by that. Those sheenies change their names all the time. Look at Rockefeller there. Now, he's a Jew. You know he has to be one. But back when the old man was robbing everybody, he didn't want people to know that that was what he was. So he changed his name. They're all the same. Sneaky. That's why they're always getting their names in the paper all the time, for giving their money away. That's the tip-off right there. Only Jews do that."

"Of course that might not've been her maiden name," she said. "Is she married, do you know?"

"Oh, she's married, all right," he said. "Her husband's some rich bastard with the National Committee. Republican, I mean. New York. Apparently he still lives there. But now she lives up here. Nothing to do with her time. Andy says she's tied up with that bastard Cobb."

"I thought you got along with him," she said. She went to the refrigerator and took out a covered Pyrex casserole dish. She closed the refrigerator and opened the dish. She used a spoon to taste the contents, nodded, re-covered the dish, and took it to the stove. She put it on a second burner and lighted a low flame under it.

"I get along with him when I see him," he said. "There's no point in not. But I wouldn't do the son of a bitch a favor unless he could make me. And he knows it. He's one of that crowd with Danisi. And that damned renegade Beale. They put out all this guff about how what we all need's a *real* two-party system. Well, that's nothing but a smokescreen. Beale's game, and Cobb's game, and that crowd that runs with them, all they're really after is the power that we've got. And they think they see their chance now, all these newcomers moving in.

"I was against all that damned development eight, nine years ago, when everyone got so excited about building all these new highways. All the trade that they'd bring in. All of a sudden every dumb son of a bitch owned a piece of land too steep to plow was going to be a rich man, never did a tap of work. But no one'd listen to me. All they could see was dollars. People coming up with dollars, spending them all here. Well, they came, all right. But they weren't like the ones we got before, their damned sailboats at Mallett's Bay. Those bastards went *home* in the winter. *These* bastards come *up* in the winter, and then pretty soon they decide they'll stick around for spring. And pretty soon it's summer, and they've heard about October and the goddamned leaves, so then they stay for that. And all of a sudden decide that they live here. So now we've got them to contend with."

He slapped the table with his open palm. "Gets me," he said, "their attitude does. Thinking they can just come in and start running things. Well, who the hell do they think they are? Who the hell invited them? Who asked them what they think? Why should we give a goddamn? Why should we pay any attention? Well, now we do. We've got no choice."

She sat down across the table from him. "I think you're getting all upset about nothing," she said. "What exactly did Andy say?"

"Huh," he said. "Well, to start with, Andy was drunk."

"He wasn't," she said.

"Yes, he was," he said. "He'd been drinking, anyway. The son of a bitch always does that. The *minute* I leave town. He doesn't dare to when I'm there. Come back from lunch with liquor on his breath. But the minute I leave . . . I swear, I bet after he drops me off at the station, sees me get on the train, he goes right back to the Hill and sits down in a bar." He pondered. "I should fire that son of a bitch."

"Oh, don't be silly," she said. "Andy's a good boy."

"Andy's a damned nuisance," he said. "You know he's asked me three times, three times the past three years, for a raise? And I've given him two. And I bet he asks me again this year. For another one. The son of a bitch's making over thirty thousand goddamned dollars a year. He's got the health insurance. It seems like he's always going on vacation, and then every time I check, he's still got more leave coming. Well, I say if a man his age can't raise a family on thirty-one thousand dollars a year, put something aside, well, he doesn't know how to manage his money."

"It's very expensive to live down there," she said. "You told me that yourself."

"It's expensive," he said. "It's just like everything else that's expensive. It is if you make it that way. Just where the hell do these young people get the fool idea that they should have steak all the damned time? Paying over a hundred thousand dollars for a house."

"But that's what houses cost down there," she said. "I read that in the paper. It's one of the most expensive places in the country. To live. Man's got to have a place to raise his family. Hasn't he got three, three children, I mean? He has to have a house."

"Well," he said, "whose fault is that? Didn't he know that, he got married in the first place? Whose decision was it, have three god-damned kids? Not mine, I can tell you that much. And I say: If you have three kids, and you don't know you're going to need a house to raise them, and you haven't figured out that houses cost too much and you can't afford them, well, then that was your decision and you've got to live with that. These bankers, the bankers down there must be crazy, giving these kids wet behind the ears eighty-, ninety-thousand-dollar mortgages. And *thirty years* to pay. It's a lot of foolishness. Of course they're going to be strapped all the time. Wanting more money'n they're worth. I tell you, it's just another sign of the way this country's headed. Nobody saves anything anymore. It's all get, get, get, and gimme, gimme, gimme. No wonder the budget's in the damned mess it's in. I tell you, we've let the thieves in to count the cash drawer, and they're taking it, right under our noses. Serves us right. We're going to go to hell some day. Mark my words, we will."

The tomatoes began to bubble in the saucepan. She got up and turned the heat down lower. "Oh," she said, lifting the cover off the pan and taking a spoon from the drawer next to the stove, "you've been saying that for years. Ever since I can remember." She stirred the tomatoes.

"And it's been true for years, goddamnit," he said. "Everybody thinks, all the Democrats at least, that what this country's all about, the government at least, is one big free ride for every lazy son of a bitch that never did a goddamned honest day's work in his life. Look who we've got running it. Lyndon Baines Johnson. Him and that bumpkin drawl. A fake if I ever saw one. Probably learned it from his father while he taught him to steal cattle. All this horse manure about how he grew up so poor. Well, I don't believe a word of it. And even if it is true, he sure ain't too poor now. He is a rich man.

"Him and his goddamned wife there—God, I can't stand that woman's voice. Radio stations, television stations, big ranch on a river down there. Well, where'd they get all that stuff? Man never held a real job in his life. First he was a teacher, but he gave that up. Didn't pay enough, most likely. Couldn't see a way he could get rich doing that. Although try telling that to those bastards in the NEA today, think any damned fool with a college diploma oughta get twenty thousand dollars a year for teaching a bunch of snot-nosed kids that two and two makes four. Sure. And don't forget some extra for some-one 'to counsel' them. So they don't go out in the woods without knowing how to make babies, goddamnit. Why the hell do we need teachers to tell kids how to screw? Why the hell're we paying people good money to teach them that? My day, kids didn't have any trouble, figuring that out themselves. No trouble at all. But now we're teaching them, and paying people to do it. Bunch of damned nonsense.

"That's the whole goddamned trouble with the way we go about things now. That's why the country's in the sorry shape it's in. Because you've got a bunch of people running it that never did a damned thing in their lives but suck off the government tit. Never met a payroll in their lives. That's how Andy thinks. Just like everybody else. The money doesn't have to come from anywhere, you see? It's just there. Like water. Someone says they want some money, they control a lot of votes?

" 'Well, hell, yes, here's some money. Take as much you like, and if it turns out that's not enough, come back and we'll get you some more. It's not like it was ours.' It's one big candy store. I said, when that goddamned Tonkin Gulf thing went through, I said: 'Has anybody here bothered, study this damned thing? Has anybody figured out what this whole thing's going to cost? How're we gonna pay for it? Anybody thought of that? Anybody asked the President if he intends to ask us, if we're going to have to go back to our people next year and tell them we're raising taxes?' And did anybody listen? No, of course they didn't, and we're spending ourselves broke. If this country, if I'd've run the bank the way we run this country now, the examiners would've marched up here in short order, and put it in receivership. And me, probably, in jail. And goddamnit, I would've deserved it. It would've served me right. It's irresponsible."

She lifted the top off the casserole and stirred the contents. The aroma of pineapple rose into the room. She tasted from the spoon and nodded. She replaced the cover and returned to her chair. "Well, anyway," she said, "what was it Andy said?"

"Well," he said, "as I say, Andy'd had too much to drink. I asked him how long he'd been out of the office, how long he'd spent at lunch, and he hemmed and he hawed, but he never really answered me. Good long time, I bet. He was slurring his words, but I wasn't 'sposed to notice because he'd had lunch with Norman. And a guy named Jerry."

" 'Norman,' " she said. "I don't recognize that name."

"Ferdie Norman," he said. "Name's actually Ferdinand, but nobody calls him that. He's an old boodler from way back. Got his practice flying a desk for the Air Force over at the Pentagon. He's a boozer and he buys whores for anyone wants one. They put him on the National Committee when he left the service. Must've been afraid he'd have to pay for his own desk. He's a lobbyist. All the goddamned defense contractors fall all over each other, hiring those lying bastards as soon as they retire. Supposedly to get them votes in Congress, they're such experts on defense. Well, that's a load. They're getting thirty, forty thousand dollars a year in retirement, and they're getting another fifty, maybe more, in what they all call 'fees.' Just bribes. Deferred bribes, for all the lies they told us, they're in uniform. And that's how they do it, this so-called work they do on us. They take out people like Andy and fill them up with hooch, and then the silly little bastards're supposed, come back to us, and fill us up with bunk. Well, it doesn't work with me, and Andy's bright enough to know it. So he only does it when he knows I'm not around. I'll bet he'll have himself a good headache tomorrow. I hope he does. He earned it, when he should've been at his desk. Thirty-one thousand dollars a year, and he still can't get his work done. How the hell does he think fifteen hundred more'll do it? And why should he have it, anyway, he can't do his work?"

"Robert," she said, "what did Andy say? What did he actually say?"

"What I just got through telling you," he said. "This woman named Cooke's a Democrat, and her husband's a Republican, and they both've got too much time on their hands. So he's in New York, still, with Nixon, I guess, or maybe with deep-pockets Rockefeller, and she's in

Vermont, and she's tied up with Cobb, and they're looking, make trouble for me. Because apparently this guy Jerry, Vito I think's his name, on the staff of the Committee, he told Ferdie that the husband'd stopped in on his way to 'the island.' Probably Long Island. All those Jews go there. Talking strategy, or some sort of bull, showing how much clout he's got. And apparently somebody asked him how his wife was, and was she with him. And he said she was and let it slip that she's got a new hobby. Instead of gumming up everything he tries in New York, she's moved her domicile to this place they've got over in Manchester, and now she's getting ready to start making trouble here. 'Like what?' someone asked him, and I guess he tried to play cute, but he didn't make it work. Said he really wasn't sure, they don't discuss that stuff that much, but apparently from what Ferdie and this Jerry guy gathered, she wants herself a pet congressman, for her very own."

"Well," she said, "even if that's true, it could be Ransom's seat."

"It could be," he said, "but isn't. That much they got out of him. Did he know which district? And he said he thought the Second. So it's mine this bitch is after, soon's she finds someone to do it."

"Well," she said, "but can she? I mean, you've held it a long time. Twenty-eight years is a long time. And I think you must've done a good job. So far no one's complained."

"Well," he said, "if you don't count the first time, when Dick Carlisle ran against me, and that time twelve years ago when that crazy dame from Bennington decided it was hers. But I had an advantage then, in both of those elections. Even Dick knew it was pretty likely people wouldn't want to take that seat away from the party always had it. Even though Dick had been in the state senate for years. And everyone could see that that crazy dame was crazy.

"But now," he said, "a lot of people that knew me because of Dad, well, they're dead. And this is not, not like in Chicago, where most dead people vote. So I don't have them to count on. And the people I'd met through the bank, doing business with the bank, well, they may still have their mortgages there, but they haven't seen me in there for years, and may've forgotten who helped them.

"And this woman isn't the only stranger that's moved in, past few years. There's lots of 'em, up from the cities. Good many of them lefties. Might be hard, convince them, they should vote for me. What if they say: 'You help the niggers?' What do I say then? Do I say: 'Look around you, and then tell me: How many you see? Why should our tax money go to help other people's niggers? Is that really what you want?' Or do I say to them: 'Oh, nuts. They're not here. The fact that they're not here is why you moved up here. Don't give me no more of that crap.'

"I don't think so, Jane," he said, "I do not think so. People don't always think straight, they get pencils in their hands, ballots in front of them. They vote the way they always voted, which is fine if they're my people. But if they come from somewhere else, goddamned automatic liberals, well, if this Cooke dame fields someone who talks like them, like the way that they are used to, I could be in trouble."

"Oh," she said, "I just don't think so. There's not enough of them yet. And besides, you like to worry."

"What you call 'worry,' I call 'thinking,' " he said. "It's how you get where you want to go, and how you stay there afterward. This goddamned thing in Vietnam—if somebody'd done some 'worrying' about that mess, before we got into it, well, it might still be a big mess, but we wouldn't be involved. And I try to tell people that. People that I know down there. And they just look at me and say: 'Why're you so worried? Republican, Republican state, it's all Democrats that got us in.' They think because they're Democrats they might get voted out. And Republicans are safe. But I'm not so sure of that. I think everyone that was in office when this whole thing got started, well, if it's a problem in their district doesn't matter which party they are. If they're in, then they go out. Maybe, anyway."

"That's not a problem in the Second," she said. "Least not from what I see."

"Well," he said, "it hasn't been. But sooner or later, enough of those coffins come home, sooner or later somebody's going to get up on their hind legs and say: 'This has got to stop.' When I was over to Occident, dropped in to see Paul Whipple, other day in his store. And I sort of felt him out about that, not because I had anything in mind or anything, but his boy's the right age so I know he's thought about it. And he didn't want to answer. He just dodged the question—asked me how the ham was. Well, is that because Paul's afraid his boy'll die? Or is it because he's getting ready, blame me if it happens?

130

"Suppose that's what it is, that he's going to blame me. And then what? Suppose that someone happens, happens to be running against me. Might say he's against the war, and if he gets elected he'll work to keep kids out. What do I say to them then? Did I vote for the damned war? Well, you could say I did. Once we sent our troops in, naturally I did. I may've been about the worst choice the navy ever made, far's supply officers're concerned, but when people got mad at me because something got stuck in the pipe the boys needed out at sea, I knew why they were mad. And I was concerned all along that once we started sending troops, we'd send more and more. But what do I do when we start doing that? Holler that we should abandon ones already there? Let them take a beating without trying to help them? Can't do that, can we? So if Paul Whipple loses his boy, or gets real afraid he might, then maybe someone up against me, if he says the right thing he can get Paul Whipple's vote. And I won't even know.

"So," he said, "no, it's not a problem right now. Not one for me, at least. But it could become one, time a year November comes, if that bitch, that bastard Cobb, if they find somebody popular, give him lots of cash, and turn him loose on me."

"Is there anybody like that?" she said. "Popular, I mean."

"Not that I can think of," he said. "Not right off, I mean. There might be, one the dairy co-ops, or some state assemblyman that didn't show much when I met him 'cause he's having an off day. But that's the whole trouble with being down in Washington—you don't know who's coming up, and by the time you find out, well by then it's too damned late."

"It isn't Cobb?" she said.

"I thought of that," he said. "I doubt it. I don't think he'd do it. I don't like Ed Cobb at all. I think Ed Cobb is shifty. But because I think he's shifty, I don't think he'd take me on. Ed Cobb likes sure things. Victories. Only gets into a fight that he thinks he will win. Besides, I think what he's planning is: top job in Montpelier, and then a nice judgeship. Ed Cobb likes his comfort. Doesn't want much Washington. So what he wants to bother me is someone that's well known. Not a politician, might decide: 'Now, governor.' Or: 'Think I'll be a federal judge.' No real politician. Not to get my job. Cobb's a real one. He's picky. Doesn't create competition. He wants the kind of man that people don't mean when they say: 'Well, he's a politician.' The kind people have in mind when they call us names. What he wants, him and his pals—that Fenian, Shaw from Saint Albans, and Danisi from over in Barre—is power. Power and control over big money. That's what those pirates want. And that smiling crook, Don Beale, up there in Burlington—buying up the real estate as fast it's on the market. Those boys're in it for the money, and the money's not in Congress. The money's in the state Houses, and that is what they want. No, I don't think Cobb's likely."

"Maybe you should call Russ Wixton," she said. "See what he's been hearing."

He shook his head. "No," he said, "if I ask Russ, he'll think I'm worried, and he'll put it in the paper. And the next day, all over town: 'Bob Wainwright's jittery.' And that'd be all they need. If they need anything. Once they find out you're worried, then you're like a deer in deep snow. The dogs come at you in packs. And run you 'til you drop." He grinned. "Besides," he said, "if Russ hears anything, he'll call me right away. Russ's memory is good. Russ remembers who he called when he needed some money, fast, and no one'd give it to him."

She shook her head. "Oh dear," she said, "I'll be glad when this next winter's over."

"And that's what you say, every year," he said. "I don't mind the winter much—just glad I'm around to see it. What I mind is being hungry. Is that ham ready?"

"Should be," she said. She got up. "It's lasted pretty well this year. Should be three meals left in it."

"Good," he said. "Best thing that came from this Fourth of July. I told Whip that when he asked me: 'Stood up pretty good.' "

14

On the morning of the second Monday in September, Briggs left his truck at Whipple's when he finished breakfast and walked down the street through a thin drizzle to Wilson Carmichael's garage and store. There was a heavy-duty rusted-out red pickup truck at the pumps; Carmichael in soiled blue coveralls and a dirty Red Sox cap was tending the nozzle of the regular-grade pump and watching the gauge. When it hit $9.90, he reduced the flow, and when it reached $10.00 he shut off the pump and replaced the nozzle in its receptacle. He went around to the driver's-side window and collected the money, eight singles and two dollars in coins. He put the money in his right breast pocket and stood in the rain and watched the truck depart, ringing the bell activated by the black air hose stretched across the lot, and then he watched Briggs approach.

"Wilson," Briggs said.

"Henry," Carmichael said.

Briggs came up to the island where the pumps stood and leaned against the premium-grade pump. "Like to talk to you," he said.

Carmichael sucked food from his teeth. He nodded in the direction that the pickup had taken. "Ever' time Jake comes in here in that thing," he said, "figure it's the last. Said to him, good many times: 'Don't make a lot of sense, you know, paying extra for the no-lead to put in this thing. Paul Whipple sell you regular, three or four cents less. She's beyond pamperin'.' Don't seem to matter to him."

"What is it?" Briggs said, "Forty-three cents? It gives him peace of mind, it's maybe worth it to him."

Carmichael snorted. "Jake Garner can't afford no peace of mind," he said, "not at any price. You seen how he paid me. Ever' time he comes in Mondays, always gives me change. Ten bucks' worth gets him through the week. Friday night, Friday he might have cash, 'cause that's when he gets paid. Then he'll fill the damned thing up, twelve, thirteen dollars' worth. Won't see him 'til week from Monday. Comes again to see his daughter. 'Just ten dollars, Wilse.' Don't make any sense."

"Well, why doesn't he go to Whipple?" Briggs said.

Carmichael spat on the cement apron that surrounded the pump island. "Dunno," he said. "Don't like him, I guess. That's the usual reason, people don't give you their trade. Whip's givin' charity, his daughter. That'd be his reason." He paused and spat. "Don't know what yours might be, never see you here."

"Yeah, Wilse, yeah," Briggs said, "but we been all through this. I told you when I took this job, I'd split the gassing with you, give me same terms as Whip does. And you didn't want to do that. So I buy it all from Whip."

"Well," Carmichael said, "but them weren't no terms. No terms I could live with anyways. Bad enough, state wants a discount, but then you got to wait, and then you wait some more, they finally get your money to you. Can't do that, do business that way—sell it cheap, then not get paid. Tanker truck pulls in here, he don't pump 'til he sees money. Have to give him money, not some bills the state owes to me."

"Well, sorry about that," Briggs said. "That's the way it has to be."

Carmichael gave him a sharp glance. "Didn't have to be," he said. "I'd've taken care of you all right."

"Oh yes it did," Briggs said. "That kind of taking-care-of is the kind that I don't need."

"Nobody ever would've known," Carmichael said. "You'd've paid in cash and got receipts, I'd give you the discounts. You could get it back, I bet, lots faster'n I could. And plus the other thing."

"Wilse," Briggs said, "when I steal something, if I ever do, it's not gonna be discount gas for my personal car."

"Wouldn't've done you no harm," Carmichael said. He spat again.

"Oughta tell you, though, case you're wonderin'. That truck of yours there ever breaks down, I don't think Whip can fix it, and I ain't gonna touch it here."

"Right," Briggs said. "Look, is there any chance we could go in? Seems to be raining out here."

"Yup," Carmichael said. "Come along."

The two-bay garage and attached store and office were set down in a slight declivity from the fuel service area. The roof sagged in the center. There was a large picture window in front, lettered CAR-MICHAEL'S SPORTS & SERVICE. The building siding was clapboard, most recently painted white, but the weather and time had two years before exhausted the life of the paint; bare wood showed through in places. The wind had collected brown leaves and heaped them along the foundation. Carmichael opened the faded red door and set the bell above it to jangling. He went in like a bear to its cave, shoulders hunched and rounded, head lowered, and shuffling. Briggs followed, ducking his head at the door.

There were three windows in the southerly wall. The gray light, augmented by the light from three white globes hanging on chains from the ceiling down the center line of the store, fell onto three long dusty glass cases displaying fishing lures, creels, landing nets, insect repellent, fly-casting reels, spinning reels, bait-casting reels, spools of monofilament spinning line, braided bait-casting line, coils of fly-fishing line, clip-on flashlights, hook-removing pliers, folding knives and pocket tackle boxes. Hip boots and chest-high waders were paired in front of the display cases, flanked by stacks of tackle boxes. Wall racks of fishing rods filled the spaces between the windows.

In the center of the store there was a long, locked display case filled with revolvers, semiautomatic pistols, boxes of cartridges and shotgun shells, Outers gun-cleaning kits in red metal cases, telescopic sights, boxes of bull's-eye paper targets and larger targets showing life-size drawings of woodchuck, rabbit, squirrel, and fox. Six brands of hunting knives were fanned out on their sheaths at the front. On top of the counter was an eight-by-twelve-inch sign declaring the availability of fishing and hunting licenses. Flanking it were a stuffed pheasant on the right and a mallard drake decoy on the left. In front of the center cases hunting pacs and leather-top duck boots were paired.

On the interior wall separating the store from the garage there were large poster calendars depicting jumping fish, and whitetail deer leaping fallen logs partially concealed by shaded snow; the calendars advertised Heddon lures and Winchester rifles. There were four chromium chairs with red plastic cushions against the wall under the posters. There was a door leading into the service area next to the chair farthest from the front. There was a sign on the door that read: INSURANCE REGULATIONS PROHIBIT CUSTOMERS FROM ENTERING THE SERVICE AREA.

Behind the center counter there were two more chairs against the wall. Above them three dozen leghold traps in various sizes hung on their chains from wooden pegs. Red-and-black plaid wool and canvas hunting jackets were displayed on hangers next to canvas fishing vests, hung over the same pegs—caps and blaze-orange bibs hung on the pegs as well. There were two more chairs between the back of the center display case and the large, scarred oak desk, where Carmichael sat on a tattered straw cushion in an oak swivel chair. The desk was littered with yellow copies of repair orders, a black ledger, three oily spark plugs, a water pump, a starter motor, a Bendix drive, and a black anodized circular ashtray with a coiled spring lining its rim; it was filled with butts. At the corner to his left there was a black telephone on the sliding shelf above the top drawer. Behind him, in the corner to his right as he faced the outside door, there was a tall brown iron stove shaped like a refrigerator. On the wall behind his chair were locked racks of rifles and shotguns, with wooden cabinets below them. There was a Philco table radio on top of the cabinet behind Carmichael's chair. In the southeasterly corner there was a small rack containing six hunting bows; below it there was a small glass case of bow-hunting accessories.

Briggs took one of the chairs along the wall behind the center counter after Carmichael had sat down behind the desk. Carmichael opened up the top right-hand drawer and took out a gray metal cashbox. He opened the lock and then lifted the cover. There was a small compartmented tray on the top. He reached into his breast pocket and removed the money he'd received for the gas. He put the quarters in the tray. He smoothed out the bills and put them in the bottom of the box. He shut it and replaced it in the drawer.

"This's quite a place you've got here, Wilse," Briggs said. "Never dreamed you had so much stuff."

"Could've," Carmichael said. "I been here near fifteen years. Since I got home, Korea. You'd ever seen fit to come in." He reached into his left breast pocket and took out a pack of Viceroys and a matchbook. He paused. " 'S the trouble with this place, in fact. Put your finger on it. I got too much inventory. Damned stuff keeps me broke." He lit the cigarette and exhaled a large cloud of smoke. He used the embered tip to move the butts around in the ashtray until he had a clean spot. He rested the cigarette between the spring coils so that the coal was over the ashtray.

"But that's the way it is," he said. "Remington, Winchester, Ruger, all them boys, they don't care if all you sell, place like this, is Moss-bergs for the shotguns, Hi-Standard twenty-twos. Some bastard gets it in his head, get himself a nice new rifle, well, he goes up the road a ways, get a better price. Doesn't think of coming here. Then when he needs bullets, well, 'no need of all that travelin', just to get a box of shells. I'll just stop by and see old Wilse. Wilse'll fix me up.' You want the better kinds of ammunition, sell the people buy those guns, well, you got to take a certain number of the high-priced guns, too. It's like everything else—there's a catch to it." He paused. "Suppose you never need shells, your own gun."

Briggs patted the Magnum on his hip. "Wilse," he said, "the state provides the brass. I'm not gonna come here and buy it from you, when they issue it to me for nothing. Not allowed to, in fact—they get a better price on case lots'n you could hope to match."

"Uh-huh," Carmichael said, "and some goddamned politician gets a rake-off on the contract. No, I can't beat that."

"So," Briggs said.

"But you still do some gunnin', your own stuff, I bet," Carmichael said. "State give you shells for that, too?"

"No, as matter of fact, they don't," Briggs said. "And, now that you mention it, I've kept meaning to get me some buckshot. You got any Western Express?"

Carmichael stared at him thoughtfully. "Winchester," he said. "Same damned thing of course. Same damned company."

"That'll do, then," Briggs said. "Whatever you got'll be fine. Gimme a couple of boxes."

Carmichael stared at him. Then he swiveled the chair around and reached for the latch on the cabinet nearest his chair. He opened it and bent to inspect the contents. He brought out two boxes of shells. He shut the cabinet and put the boxes on the side of the desk nearest Briggs. "That'll be fifteen," he said. He clasped his hands across his stomach. The air bell rang as a green Ford passed the picture window at the front of the store.

"Shit," Carmichael said. He lifted himself out of the chair and shambled toward the front door. "That's the trouble with this business. Any bastard gets himself two bucks together, gives him a perfect right, come around and pester you." He went out into the drizzle, jangling the doorbell.

Briggs leaned forward and took out his wallet. He took three fives out and fanned them on the desk. The smoke from the Viceroy spiraled up from the ashtray. Carmichael returned with a five-dollar bill in his right hand. He sat down at the desk and repeated his ritual with the cashbox. "Ev Glennon must've gotten a good plate, Sunday past. Martha actually bought five dollars." He put the money in the box. He noted the three fives on the desk. He looked at Briggs. "Yours?" he said.

"No, yours," Briggs said. "For the shells."

Carmichael nodded. He picked up the money and put it in the box. Then he put the box away.

"You keep it all together," Briggs said. "The gas and the gun money both."

"Yup," Carmichael said. "I first started out, I kept 'er separate. But it didn't make no sense. I was always takin' from the gas to pay for guns or fishin' gear, and when I had a good week selling huntin', fishin' stuff, season opening or some damned thing like that, well, seemed like that was the same week I didn't sell much gas. So after a while I just looked at her and said: 'Well, shit. The hell with it. What I spend buying stuff, I haven't got no choice. Got to have stuff to sell. And what I make, from selling stuff, well, first I got to live, got a family to support. So when I'm buying, I take it out, and when I'm selling, I put it in, and when the end the year comes, hope to God I got enough left, get some Christmas presents." The Viceroy had burned down to the filter. Carmichael stubbed it out in the ashtray.

"Well," Briggs said, "but marking up the shot shells, extra couple bucks, that should tide you over when things get a little slack."

Carmichael stared at him. "I don't sell no groceries, Henry," he said. "I don't sell no meat that I doubled when I marked up. I don't sell no bath salts for twice they get in town. You go in there and buy lunch, have your breakfast there, your wife comes in and buys her order at the prices that he sets, well, I figure then he can afford it, set his prices low on shells. We're both sellin' convenience, but he's got more kinds to sell. Unless you get your car fixed here, or buy a lot of gas, I got to ask you the full price. I got to stay in business." He took the Viceroys out again and lighted another one. He rested it on the ashtray. The smoke curled up.

"And of course it's a convenience," Briggs said, "for your customers to come in here and get their licenses while they're stocking up on hooks, or maybe buying shells."

"Sure is," Carmichael said.

"Of course that convenience you offer them," Briggs said, "that's a convenience that you have to ask the state to let you offer."

"What's that supposed to mean?" Carmichael said.

"Well," Briggs said, "I'd hate to think a man had to buy a box of shells, or a fishing tackle box, he came here to get his license. That wouldn't be right."

"Well," Carmichael said, "I don't know's I like the sound of this, Henry. Most the people I sell licenses, sure, they generally see something they been needing, while they're in the store. And if they see, you know, new knife, a better tackle box, a hat or extra shells, well, what am I supposed to say? 'Hey no, you can't buy that—you just bought a license'? That wouldn't make no sense. They'd think I'm a crazy man. And, I'm doin' the state a favor here, let's just keep that in mind. I sell the licenses, my place, that's one less office to rent, one less lazy bastard to pay. Not that Montpelier minds doin' that, but the taxpayers oughta, I think. And if it brings in a little trade, well, there's nothin' wrong with that."

"Got a very good point there, Wilse," Briggs said. "I give you the benefit there. Just have to remember, I got a job, and licensing's part of my job. Making sure it's all, you know, all done according to Hoyle."

"Yeah," Carmichael said. "This what you had on your mind, you said you wanted to talk? Spend your whole morning in this place, 'stead of out doin' your job?"

"Nope," Briggs said. "Come in to get your opinion on something. See what you might have to say."

"For instance," Carmichael said.

"I'm thinking of running 'gainst Wainwright," Briggs said. "How's that idea strike you?"

Carmichael lapsed into his stare again. The Viceroy smoke plumed up from the ashtray. "The hell do you want to do that for?" he said. "The hell makes you want to do that? Ain't the tit you're on now, ain't it good enough for you? Chasin' around all over the place, makin' sure that some poor bastard didn't shoot too many ducks? Why the hell should you run against Wainwright?"

"Would you vote for me if I did?" Briggs said.

"Nope," Carmichael said. "I'd vote for you for ball player. Do that in a minute. They had you now, comin' end of October, might stand a chance at that thing. But you were pretty damned good at that job, and everybody knew it. You had experience. You don't know nothin', Wainwright's job. You'd probably screw up."

"Well, fair enough," Briggs said, "but suppose I could convince you that I did, that I could do it better."

"Be damned hard," Carmichael said. "Be a damned hard thing to do."

"Okay," Briggs said, "but let's suppose I did it. Would you vote for me then?"

"Nope," Carmichael said.

"Is it the French kid?" Briggs said. "Is it because of your boy?"

The Viceroy burned down to the filter. Carmichael stubbed it out, and lit another one. "Nope," he said. "I'm over that, Henry. I admit at the time, when you testified there, I thought what you said turned the tide. And I guess I blamed you, too. I know for sure my wife did, when we lost our boy. And for what? Still thought that French boy, he should've been punished, punished more'n he was. Let him out to join the service? Shit, what sense that make? I never did a damned thing wrong, and I hadda join the damned service. No, he should've gotten more.

"But I'm over that now," Carmichael said. "Got over it some months ago. And one of the things I finally saw, after that, was that you had to do that. Had to get up there and say what you found, say whether what French said'd happened really was what'd happened. Not saying I agreed with you then, not saying I agree now. But, wasn't my job, it was your job, and you did what you had to do. It was just a damned bad thing that happened. No, I don't hold that against you."

"Then why is it?" Briggs said. "If you've been voting for Wainwright all these years . . . ?"

"Haven't been," Carmichael said. "I turned twenty-one in time to vote for Truman, 'forty-eight. Had a lot of respect for that man. I was healing up too fast, after Italy. If he hadn't had the balls, drop that thing on Hiroshima, I knew where I'm headed next. And next time, I get killed. Knew it sure as my own name. So he runs for office on his own, and I voted for him. And goddamn the man if he don't turn around, right in his tracks, and ship me out to Korea. The Reserve money looked just fine, after World War Two. Never even crossed my mind, they'd call me up again, and see if maybe this time they could get me killed.

"Well," Carmichael said, "that's the last damned time I voted. I dunno, maybe I did vote for Wainwright that year. Might've. Probably voted for someone. But never since then, not one single soul. Damned if I'll encourage the bastards."

"But you still speak your mind, from what I hear," Briggs said. "The boys of a late afternoon."

"I got my opinions," Carmichael said, "sure. And I'll say what I got on my mind. But when it comes to votin', well, I don't do it. Got better things to do with my time."

"If I do decide to run," Briggs said, "and the question comes up in here, would you put in a good word for me?"

"Yup," Carmichael said. "Here and at the Legion Hall, far as that's concerned. I've got no problem with you, Henry. I at least know where you stand, and I respect that in a man. Unless you start slingin' bullshit, you won't get no guff from me." The smoke from the Viceroy curled toward the ceiling.

"Fair enough, Wilse," Briggs said, getting up. "Guess I'll be going to work."

15

On the morning of the second Sunday in September, Ed Cobb arrived for the meeting at Beale Chrysler-Plymouth before Caroline Cooke did. He parked the 300F in his usual place and found Donald Beale waiting at the door to admit him. Cobb wore a double-vented brown Harris tweed jacket, a white wool turtleneck, tan twill jodhpurs, and shiny brown riding boots. A pair of brown riding gloves stuck out of his lower left-hand pocket.

"Oh, my dear sweet Lord," Beale said. "What on earth're *you* trying out for? Halloween's not 'til the end of next month."

"Just shut the fuck up, all right, Donald?" Cobb said, shouldering his way past Beale into the showroom. "Just shut the fuck fucking up."

"Well," Beale said, closing the door and locking it, "you can't tell me you expect to go around in that getup and not have your old pals *notice* it. Good Lord, man, I knew you wanted to be governor, but you've got more'n that in mind. You want to be a damned *duke*."

"Hey," Cobb said, looking at the red Barracuda convertible parked where the Mercedes roadster had been, "what'd you do with the hot car?"

Beale ostentatiously peered through the showroom window, shading his eyes against nonexistent glare. "Yup," he said, "here they come now. Your faithful pack of hounds, as I live and breathe. Oop, I think they're on his trail. They're on the scent. Yup, that's it, all right.

142

'Tally-ho' and 'View halloo': All that great British stuff. That fox doesn't have a prayer. What was it Oscar Wilde said, something about the inedible pursued by the unspeakable?" He turned around and studied Cobb. He shook his head. "Oh my goodness, wait 'til Wixton gets ahold of this. First he'll wet his pants. Then he'll go home and change, and then he'll go to the office and write a column that'll have all the farmers lying down in their fields, pounding the cornstalks with their fists, tears running down their faces, they'll be laughing so hard. Anybody got a picture of this, Ed? Nice eight-by-ten for the front page: 'Speaker all in style, as he takes a stile'?"

"You son of a *bitch,* Beale," Cobb said. "Goddamn you anyway. Gwendolyn made me dress up like this. She's making me let her teach me to ride. Says I'm all out of shape, don't get enough exercise, and this's perfect for me, 'til the skiing season starts. Now, what happened the hot car, the Mercedes Earl stole and brought here?"

"Well," Beale said, "she's certainly got a point about the shape. Merciful heaven have pity on the horse, though. I hope *he's* in shape. He'll have to go to the bonecracker tonight, that is what I think. Have his poor spine realigned, get those vertebrae set right. I mean, it's one thing if *you're* henpecked—that was your decision. But the poor horse, he had nothing to do with you getting a young second wife. All he's ever done's mosey around the pasture, little grass here, little more grass there, 'maybe if I act real good, I get some oats tonight.' They probably cut the poor old nag's testicles off too, when he got to be one or two and had an eye out for the ladies. Should've done that to you, maybe. Then you wouldn't be going out now, torturing poor, dumb animals. I can just see that horse now. Nice and peaceful in his stall, nice and shady in the barn, and he looks through the door, and the guy comes in, takes him out in the yard, '*Oh*-kay, another job. Got to go to work. Well, oats tonight for sure. Couple carrots, apple? Maybe sugar, too.' Takes it all in stride. And then he gets one look at you, and he says: 'Holy Mother of God.' And tries to run away." Beale's face was red. His body shook. He had to wipe his eyes.

Cobb waited until Beale had put his handkerchief away. He shook his head. "I got to hand it to you, Don," he said, "I never met another man, enjoyed his own jokes as much as you do. Are you finished now, you cocksucker? I asked you where the car is."

Beale shook his head, his body still shaking with laughter. "I," he said, "I never made a joke as good's the one I'm looking at. It's Gwendolyn made that joke, and I must say, it's good. Best one I've seen in years. Be sure and thank her for me." He rubbed his eyes with his fingers. He took a deep breath. "I sold it."

"You sold it," Cobb said. "You're making fun of me, but at least I'm gonna *ride* the horse. *You're* the horse's ass. Who'd you sell it to? You sell it to Caroline?"

Beale shrugged. "She said she wanted to buy it," he said. "You heard her yourself. Said it's her husband's favorite car, the whole wide world, and she wanted it for his birthday. You were here, Ed. You heard her. Asked for first refusal. So, I let her have it. And she snapped it up."

Cobb shook his head. "I hope Mr. Cooke's a real good driver," he said. "I hope he doesn't get stopped, and he doesn't get in an accident, and I also hope he's lucky, and no one resteals that car. Because the minute a cop puts his hand on that thing, he's gonna snatch it back and say: 'Whoa, Earl Beale had something to do with this thing. It's gotta be hot, I just know it.' And that cop will be right."

"Then that will be Mr. Cooke's problem," Beale said. "I bought that car for real money. I put a lot more into making it run like a watch. I got a bill of sale with that car. I sold it for a fair price. Somebody clipped it, before I got it, that's got nothing to do with me. If somebody clips it, after I sell it, that will have nothing to do with me."

"You must've fallen down in the shower, hit your head," Cobb said. "You sold that car to Caroline Cooke. If something bad happens, she blames you. And that means she blames me, 'cause I introduced you. And that is the end of a beautiful friendship, one that I need very much. I could kick you right in the ass for this, Donald. That was a dumb, stupid thing to do. You made three or four thousand dollars—"

"About twenty-eight, actually, twenty-eight hundred," Beale said. "Those parts were more expensive'n we bargained for."

"—which you could've made the same, from anybody else on this green earth of ours, that's a sucker for old cars, and then when something happens, 'Hey, can'tcha take a joke?' But no, you don't do that. What do you do instead? You sell it to the one person that I cannot offend. I may be henpecked, like you say, but it hasn't affected my judgment the way money seems've to yours."

"Caroline," Beale said, "Caroline would've been angry with me if I hadn't sold her that car."

"So let her be pissed about that, for a while," Cobb said. "You could've told her something. Told her you ran a dynamometer on it, found out the block was cracked, so you sold it a collector who isn't gonna drive it and don't care if it leaks oil. Anything. Better having her pissed a little while, 'cause she didn't get it, than permanently pissed because she did, and it was hot."

"Yeah," Beale said as Caroline Cooke's blue Healey pulled into the lot. "Well, what's done's done. Now don't say anything to her, all right?"

"Say anything?" Cobb said. "You outta your mind? The hell would I say to her? 'Gee, Caroline, I'm awful sorry you bought that car from Don, because it's hot and you're gonna get in trouble, and when that happens, I hope you won't blame me'? Is that what I'm gonna say?"

"Just keep your big mouth shut," Beale said, "that's all I got to say."

Caroline Cooke got out of her Austin Healey 3000. She wore a gray tweed jacket, a white blouse, jeans, and riding boots. Beale opened the door with a flourish. "Madame," he said, executing a low bow, "how veddy pleasant to see you this day. Remark the influence you've had upon my worthy friend, Brother Cobb. Twinnies, as I live and breathe. Oh, absolutely top drawer, first chop, and pip, pip, I must say."

Caroline looked at Cobb. "Nice outfit, Ed," she said. "I didn't know you rode."

"Neither did I," Cobb said. "Gwendolyn seems to be under the impression that I used to, in a former life or something. So I love her, and I'm playing along."

"Very nice," she said, fingering the tweed. "Suits you very well."

"Well," Beale said as Cobb stared at him, grinning, "so much for my fun and games. Let's all go on upstairs, shall we now?"

In Beale's office they took their usual seats, Cobb and Caroline opening the containers of lukewarm coffee Beale offered to them. "You have some news for us, Ed," Caroline said. "Is it going to be good, I hope?"

"I think so," Cobb said. "I definitely think so. The major thing is that he's running. Briggs is in. He called the other night at some

godawful hour and said: 'Okay, count me in.' He's got some reservations still, but that's natural enough. The only thing, really worries
me, and at the same time makes me happy, is that I'm afraid even
though he acts like he knows he can't possibly win, that's not the way
he really feels, way down in his gut. It's hard work, running for office.
It's pretty hard to do it if you believe you're gonna lose. So, from that
point of view, way he's acting is good. But still, I hate to think the guy,
you know, 's just going to come crashing down a year from now when
Wainwright whips his ass. From that point of view, it is bad."

"What were the reservations?" Caroline said.

"He wanted me to tell him he could have his old job back, 'when I
take the gas pipe.' I told him no, of course. Man that's run for
Congress can't be out in the woods, issuing citations for unauthorized
camp fires. 'But if that does happen,' I said, 'if you do lose, you will be
protected. I dunno what it'll be, something up in Montpelier, most
likely, but it'll be a better situation for you. We're not going to forget
you, just wash our hands of you, if that's what's on your mind.' Didn't
seem to console him. Said he's gotten so he really likes the job he's
doing now. I said that was something we could think about a year from
now, if it becomes necessary.

"But, he's in. He's thought about it, and he's talked to his family and
a couple people he trusts, and seems like they came down about fifty-
fifty, the idea. His son thinks he's an asshole to do it, but then his son's
a little prick, I guess, and anything old Dad does's just further evidence that old Dad's a jerk. So that didn't bother Hank much. His
daughter thought it was a great idea. And I guess Paul Whipple, the
guy that runs the store down there, I guess he really acted like he
thought Hank could win. Which kind of surprised me. Not so much
that Whip'd be behind him—those two're old friends—but that
Whip'd actually come right out and tell him that. He must think a lot
of Hank."

"What about the wife?" Caroline said.

"Ahh," Cobb said, "well, nothing different'n expected. I asked him
that, how Lil took the idea, and he said she as much as told him she'd
divorce him if he won. 'You think she means it?' I said. He said: 'Look,
I got home here less'n an hour ago, and everybody's gone to bed. Cats
included. The same bed. My bed. Before I can go to bed, first I have to
take off all my clothes, and brush my teeth and that shit, and then I

have to go into my own bedroom and boot two cats off my bed before I can get into it myself. The coon cat isn't gonna like this. The tabby takes it all right, but the coon tries to claw me. So he'll try it, and I'll swat him, and that'll wake Lil up. And she'll start complaining about all the noise I make, and I'll tell her again, for the nine-thousandth time, that I refuse to sleep with cats, and if she doesn't like it when I throw the cats out, then she shouldn't bring them up in the first place. And we'll have a nice fight for ourselves. We do this instead of saying our prayers.

" 'Then, tomorrow morning,' he said, 'I'll get up in the dark, as usual, because Lil'll still be asleep, and I'll shower and shave and go back to the bedroom and try to get dressed in the dark. Which is hard enough by itself, but even harder when you have to do it without making any noise. I mean: total silence. Here you've got a woman that can fall asleep in the middle of the day with two televisions going and the damned tea kettle sounding like a locomotive right behind her left ear, but when I buckle my pants in the morning, the noise wakes her up. You know why I eat breakfast down at Whip's? You think I don't know how to scramble an egg? No, it's because I might clank the skillet on the stove, and that's enough to wake Lil up, way the hell the other end the house, on the second floor. Hell, I think breaking the eggs might do it. So, she says she'll divorce me if the day comes and I win? This is a threat? If I wasn't planning to work hard before, you can bet I'll do it now.' "

"Will he stick to that?" Caroline said. "If the going gets tough and the heat goes on, will he change his mind?"

"Nope," Cobb said. "You got to push Henry pretty hard to get him to make a decision. But you'd better be sure, when you start doing it, that's the decision you want. No changing your mind down the line on that boy. He makes up his mind and that's it."

"Okay," Caroline said, "sounds good so far. Except for one thing."

"Which is?" Beale said.

"Which is this business of him consulting friends," she said. "That could bring some trouble."

"Oh, for heaven's sake, Caroline," Beale said, "naturally the man's going to talk to some people he respects, before he makes a decision like this. Let's be reasonable, here."

"No," Cobb said. "No, I agree with her, Don. I'm a little concerned

147

about it, too. That's what I meant when I said that the major thing was that he agreed. The minor thing is what he did on the way to agreeing. That I don't like quite so much."

"I don't see what the problem is," Beale said. "I should think both of you'd be glad, the guy's gone out and he's asked around and so forth. Shows you he's taking the thing seriously. I just don't see a problem with that."

"Well," Caroline said, "I can see at least two problems. Potential problems, at least. The first one is that the other side gets wind of our plans before we're all set to go. That's dangerous. Gives them time to corral all the money, start a nice little whispering campaign, prepare to go on the offensive. Ordinarily, a new guy takes on an incumbent like this, one that's been in as long as Wainwright, ordinarily the challenger's the aggressor and the incumbent plays defense. Oh, you get a certain amount of counterattacking, naturally that happens, but the matchup is that the guy that's got the office runs on his record in it, and the guy that's trying to take it away from him, he runs against that record. So if he gets wounded before he has a chance to attack, he may never recover.

"The other thing," she said, "the other thing is that since we're trying to do something that nobody's tried before, Tom Calley is essential. That's why we're spending so much dough on him. There is no one better, and that's why he costs so much. But Calley insists on total control. Before he comes in, you agree unconditionally to do what he says."

"Briggs'll do that," Beale said. "I think he will, at least."

"Well," Cobb said, "but you don't see what Caroline's saying, Don, see? If Hank's already committed himself to positions, before Calley gets a chance to study the district and figure out what he thinks'll work and what'll send us down in flames, what Calley comes up with isn't much good to us, see? Hank'll be locked in."

"Actually," Caroline said, "it'll never come to that. The minute Calley finds out his expensive advice from down in Boston's getting exactly the same respect, but no more, as the homespun wisdom that he's getting from the cracker-barrel sages at the general store, Calley'll be out of the game. Tom is paranoid. He thinks every race he gets into has to be a winner, because, well, he says it: 'Losing's like impetigo.

148

Scabies. Maybe leprosy. You can't have a little bit of it, and have people think, "Well, that's not much." You get any of it, you got all of it. You can't afford to lose.' And he's convinced that when his candidate starts 'free-lancing,' as he calls it, the fight's as good as lost."

"Has *he* ever lost?" Beale said.

"Sure," Caroline said. "When he was young he started off backing a bozo who shared his liberal ideas. And the guy got creamed. Calley learned a lot from that. It took him two years to get another contract. 'You learn a lot, going hungry. Fry your principles some time and lay them on some toast with some tomato, lettuce, mayo, and then tell me whether what you've got really is a BLT. You're in politics, but you still like bacon in your sandwich? Fine, then learn to bring it home. If the people that're voting tell you that they don't want any niggers in their schools, well, calling them a bunch of rednecks, bigots, bums, and racists isn't going to do you any good. Even though you think that's what they are. You've got to choose between the courage of your convictions and whether you want to win. You can preach at them, and they'll picket you and you won't have to buy any vegetables, or wait for the free ones to ripen: Every time you stand up, you'll get a supply, maybe along with some eggs. And then when election day comes, they'll wash their hands and go and vote. For the other guy.' "

"So he wants his people to lie," Beale said. "Well, that may work down in Boston, but it sure isn't gonna up here."

"Not lie," she said. "Not lie at all. That's even worse than telling them what you really think's the truth, if it's a truth that they don't want to hear. 'People can tell when you're blowing smoke at them. You don't believe it? Don't say it.' No, Tom doesn't advise his candidates to lie. What he does is pick issues where he finds that the electorate actually disagrees with the incumbent, but doesn't maybe realize it, and then put together position papers, talking papers, for his candidate to attack where and when it's least expected. You know who's a master at that technique? I hate him, but he's a master. Lyndon Baines Johnson. During his campaign with Jack, civil rights was like a phrase that stuck in his earwax. Never seemed to hear it. Only clue you had that LBJ did hear it was that little wink he had, for his seggie pals down South. And that message was damned clear. 'Now, Jack has to say all that stuff, him being from the North and all, but you and I, we're good old boys, and you know with me in those secret meetings, young Jack won't do anything rash.'

"Then Jack gets shot, and before you can say 'Booker T. Washington,' Lyndon's up in front of Congress, pushing civil rights. Why? Did the angel of the Lord tap him on the shoulder and say: 'Lyndon, you've been bad?' Not at all. Lyndon'd graduated to first violin, and Lyndon liked that just fine, but now all of a sudden, he had to win the North, and he didn't have Jack to help do it." She sighed. "Poor Hubert. The nicest man in the world, and he sold his birthright for a mess of barbecue. Now he looks like he's been rode hard, and put away wet, as a friend of mine likes to say. I've seen whipped dogs with more dignity.

"Anyway," she said, "those're the things that bother me. Now that Briggs's in, we can start planning, but we have to start doing that right now, and make up for what we couldn't do before he came in. You've got to keep him clammed up, now, much as you can, at least. No confidential chats with reporters. No hypothetical questions floating around in the air. No local experts with cowshit on their feet telling him what he should say. Just life as before, 'til we're ready."

"And when'll that be, may I ask?" Beale said.

"After the first of the year," she said.

"That's a pretty long time," Beale said. "Get the guy up on tiptoe like this, and then tell him he's got to wait two months or so before he gets his first kiss."

"Well," Cobb said, "but we couldn't very well get going until we had our guy, could we?"

"I know," Beale said, "I know. It just, it's just that all this stuff, this guy that does the polling and all that stuff, I'm not sure it's the way that it'll work up here. Most of the people Henry'll be asking for their vote, well, they at least know who he is. Either they like him or they don't. They're not about to change the habits of a lifetime, vote against Bob Wainwright because Henry's got a better idea how to stop Russia from attacking. If they vote for Henry, it'll be because, and only because, they think he's the better man."

"And that's what Tom Calley's going to tell us how to achieve," she said. "How to make them think that." She stood up. "I'll have twenty thousand dollars in two weeks," she said. "Calley gets fifteen in front. That'll mean either right before, or right after, Thanksgiving, he'll have some preliminary data. Population profiles, income distributions, all that arithmetic. And then it'll be time to take Mr. Briggs down there and see if those two get along. I'll be in touch."

"Hey," Beale said, standing up, "aren't you even, don't you want to go over to Occident, else have Henry come over here? So you can at least meet the guy, I mean? Don't you want to do that?"

"Don," she said, "I'd love to. But I've got to go to New York. Next week we've got an opera party. Then it's a Library dinner. Then two dinners in one week, one for the Natural History, one for the Metropolitan Museum. Then we take the boat down to Florida and fly back up for more parties. It goes on like that until Halloween. And that's when Neil's brother every year puts on a party for all the kids in the family. My dear nephews and nieces. They go out trick-or-treating, just in the building, naturally—even on Park Avenue, the kids don't leave the building—and then when they get back the place is a graveyard. Headstones in the living room, fog rolling through the halls, skeletons and ghosts just where you'd least expect them—in the bathroom, for example. And the damned things *move*. Neil's brother's company does set designs, Broadway productions, TV ads. So he really has good stuff. It's very realistic. If he had a Nixon monster, it would even frighten me."

"Why do you have to go?" Cobb said.

"Well," she said, "for one thing it's a good chance to arm-wrestle people who've got it into giving money. They're off their guard at a kids' Halloween party, much less'n they'd ever be at a Carnegie benefit. Much likelier to give a grand to some guy they don't know, different state, if a witch asks them."

"You're the witch at this thing?" Beale said.

"Indeed I am," she said. She grinned and hissed. " 'Auntie Caroline, the witch.' One of Neil's people knows a makeup artist. I went home one Halloween like that, Neil'd been in Washington, some mischief of his own so he had to miss the party, and when he came into the bedroom all the lights were off, and I'd stuffed pillows in the bed, and he took off his jacket and tie and went into the bathroom and turned on the light, and when he came out I was just sitting there on the loveseat, with a flashlight under my long, pointed chin, and my snaggle-teeth and white eyes, my black, conical hat, and it scared the hell out of him. 'See?' I said, 'See?' I've really got the cackle down pat. 'See what happens to people that go sneaking around for Dick Nixon?' I thought I was gonna have to get him rushed to the hospital." She laughed. "So, first to the hereafter, and then, I hope, to the banks, and then to the *here,* after that." She fluttered her fingers. "Toodle-ooh," she said, "double double," and left the office.

"You're sure she's right in the head," Beale said to Cobb.

Cobb laughed. "Better than that," he said, "she's right on the money. Those're the hard ones to find."

"What she said about Briggs," Beale said. "Doesn't that look like a problem? He's awful friendly with Wixton."

Cobb shrugged. "He's probably already seen Russ," he said. "They're old pals, and go way back. I can dragoon the guy into this, and he'll listen to me, to a point. But dumping his old friends is beyond that point. He knows it, and I know it, too. It's contrary to the man's nature.

"Let's keep our focus on what our goal is, and why we need people like her. We need ladies like that because they've got money, or because they know where to get it. We do not need them to tell us about us, because we know more about that. They do not. And we do not need them because they are smarter than we are, or know more about this state than we do. On those topics we'll let the nice lady talk. We will not act on what she says. You had a solid idea, when you suggested Henry, and I was able to use it. But Henry has some ideas of his own. That's why he was a good idea. All I've done is get him. I haven't changed him. I know when a job is too big. If I were you, I wouldn't take it on. And if she does, she will fail. This is the word of the Lord."

16

briggs met Cobb in Donald Beale's office on the morning of the second Sunday in October. The gray sky was spitting early snow. The black-haired woman he had seen in Whipple's store was seated on the couch. Her mink coat was open over a gray wool suit. Her face was deeply tanned. Beale was hearty. "Henry," he said, "nice to see you again. Wish the Sox'd had you coming back this year. Maybe not, though, you're coming through like this for us. This is more important."

The woman stood up. "Caroline Cooke," she said, extending her hand. "We're a little differently dressed, from the last time I saw you, but it's nice to meet you after all these years. My father would be jealous. He was one of your big fans."

Briggs shook hands with her. "He may be sick to his stomach instead," he said, "he finds out what I'm doing now. Back in those days, most of the time at least, I knew what I was doing. I couldn't always *do* it, but I did know the drill. Now I'm a rookie all over again, and I never practiced for this."

"That's what she's for," Cobb said. "Caroline and Tommy Calley—they'll get you up to speed. Caroline, explain him."

She took a deep breath. "You need a reason to listen to me," she said. "I know who you are; you don't know who I am. You're entitled at least to that much. I'll start at the beginning.

"In most respects I'm a perfectly intelligent person. I eat right, I sleep right, I balance my checkbook every month, and I live within my budget. In two respects I am a complete fool. I admit it. But neither one of them was all my fault. My father made me a Red Sox fan. Why a perfectly decent man who lived all his life forty miles from New York would do a damned thing like that, I will never understand. I think he had a mean streak that he otherwise hid, and what he did to me and my brother was his one indulgence of it. Better he'd've worked nights, and come home in the morning to sleep days in the attic, tucked into a nice casket, or hanging upside down like all the other vampires.

"The other strange thing that I did was marry a Republican. Neil Cooke is a carbon of my father. A gem from all points of view. Well, he can take baseball or leave it alone—goes to games with me to be nice, but football is his sport; he never recovered from college. Here's a grown, adult man who still thinks Y. A. Tittle was the Second Coming. Still, he treats me well, makes lots of money, doesn't fool around. I consider myself lucky.

"Except where politics are concerned. There, forget it. Election years I think I should wear a garlic necklace, and never go anywhere near him without a crucifix. I keep expecting I'll wake up some morning and find two little fang marks on my neck, and have this irresistible urge to go out and vote for Nixon."

"Nixon," Briggs said. "I thought he quit."

"He did," Cobb said. "Once and for all, after Pat Brown whipped his ass. But he's resurrecting himself. I think the guy's part cat."

"Nixon is Lazarus," she said, "only with bad motives. He can hide them for a while, long enough to convince people who don't pay attention that he's really a nice guy. For a while. Sooner or later, he'll disillusion them again, but that'll be after they vote for him, and then it'll be too late. One of these days, and pretty soon, too, it's going to dawn on all the kind and decent Joes who vote Republican—and there are some of them, quite a few, in fact, hard as that is to believe—that George Romney is a jerk. A nice jerk, but a jerk. And what they're looking for is someone who'll take on Lyndon on his own terms, elbows in the clinches, kidney-punches and eye-gouging, shots below the belt. Well, when that day comes, they know where to find a guy who can kick ass. My God, when Neil got back from his last trip to Washington, you'd've thought Jesus'd been sighted that day, strolling on the towpath. The only other time I've ever seen such a look on a person's face was when my father gave my little brother *two* sets of electric trains. It was *sickening*."

"You don't think," Cobb said, "you don't think if Romney pulls out, Rockefeller comes back in?"

"Look," she said, "Neil loves Rocky. But Neil is from New York, and he is also smart. What he wants is to win. And there is no way Rocky runs and wins. Not after 'sixty-four. You put him up down south, in California, and everyone who still loves Barry either sits down on his hands or spite-votes Democrat. No, if George takes the pipe, as he's bound to do, doesn't matter what the Rock does. Nixon's the one.

"Now," she said, "what this does for us, well at this point, who can tell? If it's McCarthy, or it's Bobby, and it isn't LBJ, well, either one of them'd rather run against the Trick'n against Doctor Frankenstein's monster. If it's Lyndon, then we lose. Our troops won't backlash-vote for Nixon because we will have no troops. We will have *no troops*. So if, like you hear, old Lyndon's sulking, and he doesn't go again, and it's our old pal, the Hump, well, he's the nicest guy on earth. But, him against the Trick? Well, that's all a house of cards. Humphrey just won't shut his mouth, but he will not piss on Lyndon—and if he did, he'd lose the South. So Tricky just makes fun of Hubert and says he can end the war. Nice, huh? Nice if you are them. Not so nice if you are us."

"But there is one good thing about this," Beale said. "From our point of view, at least? Just the people in this room?"

"Yeah," she said. "It's about the same kind of good thing that the nice plump missionary sees when the cannibals catch him. He knows he's gonna get boiled alive and eaten, but at least God will be pleased because he's helping feed the hungry. The good thing is that we're as free as the Indians were in the woods, when they still owned them. In one state, we run alone. We get a guy like you, Henry Briggs, we've got a blank slate. We can write what we want on it—no howls from Washington. This one's gonna be like a fire in a Mexican whorehouse. Everybody grabs their pants, their own if they're lucky, and bolts for the nearest exit, never mind your dignity. If you think you can win a district kicking FDR to hell, well, just hope old Eleanor's not listening from up there in the sky, and go out and speak your piece."

"I don't have a piece," Briggs said.

"*Good,*" she said. "This is not the kind of situation where we want some goddamned ideologue with an agenda of his own. Ed—the first thing that you told me, Ed, was that this champion will *listen.* Isn't that right, Ed?"

"I was never a champion," Briggs said. "Poor planning on my part."

"Kiddo," she said, "stick with us. By the time we get through with you, you will *be* a champion. You will've won the Series, the Seventh Game. Would you like six no-hitters on your plaque at Cooperstown? Six no-hitters it will be, if you behave yourself."

" 'Behave' myself?" Briggs said.

"Tell him, Ed," she said.

Cobb shifted in his chair. "You're so eloquent, my dear," he said. "Why don't you do it?"

She nodded. " 'Let the broad do the dirty work,' " she said. "Nothing ever changes. Okay then, I will do it. I came back up here specially to meet you. I might as well get my money's worth. Ed asked me to call Tommy Calley, once you said you'd go. So I did. You'll see him end of next month.

"Now let me tell you about Tommy. Tommy's very strange. He's got these big dark circles under his eyes, and bags, so it looks like he's never slept. Maybe he never has. No one's ever seen him do it. I think, myself, that he sleeps like a horse. Standing up. While you or I, when it takes a phone call a long time to go through we just sit and drum our fingers on the desk? I think that's when Tommy sleeps. And he's overweight, so he looks like all he eats is coffee, sacks of burgers, and popcorn. Which is all I've ever seen him—eat, I mean. He smokes like a fiend. His fingers're all yellow, and his teeth, well, if they were ever white I never saw them that way. Tommy's idea of a big night's three other operators, just as smart as he is—if there is anyone like that, which I tend to doubt—four six-packs, and an argument no one can win.

"The first thing that Tommy said was: 'What are his bad habits?' Which I happen to've heard something about. Along with everybody else, I gather, in the western hemisphere. And Tommy said: 'All right, that we can live with. Long as it's women, and his wife don't change her mind. If it's boys, or if she does, then get somebody else. Either someone else to run, or somebody else to help.' "

156

Briggs shook his head. "It's the strangest thing," he said. "When I was doing it, nobody ever said a word. And now, since I stopped doing it, that's all I ever hear."

"You're saying you're on the reservation now, Hank?" Cobb said, looking skeptical.

"What choice've I got?" Briggs said. "You got me out where the only available females're bears and stuff like that. I admit some of my ladies weren't Miss America, but you've got to draw the line someplace, and bears're over mine."

"Well, anyway," she said, "Tommy had more to say: 'And another thing: No other bad companions. This guy's a former ball player? Sometimes they make friends along the way with shady characters. Like bookies and high rollers: He's used to hanging around with any of those guys, anyone someone can say is "Cosa Nostra, baby," he cuts it out, as of today—I don't want the Mob around.' "

"This guy missed his calling," Briggs said. "Should've been a preacher."

"Tommy's not a moralist," she said. "He's a realist. He knows what will maybe win, but what makes him so valuable is that he knows for sure what loses. By the time Tommy gets through analyzing your district, he'll know more about what the voters will put up with, and what they'll shoot on sight, than Ike knew about the Germans. And Ike had boats and planes.

"Next thing that Tommy said was: 'Will he take directions? I don't want some wise know-it-all that's gonna spring it on me some day, he's for recognizing China. Unless I say that he's for something, such as recognizing China, then he hates what I hate, too, when I tell him: "Hate this now." '

"See, Tommy is a player," she said. "You are his jukebox. Tommy scouts the crowd, and he decides what they will like. Tommy puts the money in, and you sing the songs he plays. That's how he wins elections, when his candidates allow it. And that's how they lose elections—they ignore what Tommy says. So, if you're for going back to the gold standard, tell Tommy, and he will plug it into your district and see if being for that gets you more votes than you lose. And if it does then he will write the best damned speech there is. Or have someone do it. But if it doesn't, you will shut up, and do whatever else he says. Same thing with every issue, every other issue. If Tommy reads it that your people are against the war, then you will stand up on a flatbed and raise hell about the war. If Tommy reads it that your people think that we can win, then you will grab that microphone and say: 'Geronimo.'

"Now," she said, "that is not easy, and I know it isn't. What you're doing, in effect, is putting your own mind in trust. You're a celebrity, your own right, and the routine's a lot the same. But if you think you played hardball, and you know how it's done, let me tell you, this is different. This game *really* hurts. You sure you're up to it?"

"Frankly, no," Briggs said. "For one thing, I go nowhere the last two weeks of this month or the whole of next. It's deer season. Bow season starts next Saturday, lasts for sixteen days, during which time I'm in the woods making sure nobody takes a deer with a thing that makes a big noise, or tries to put one down with anything less than a thirty-pound pull, or goes back out after he gets one, looking for another, or forgets to look for antlers. And then we give the Bambis two weeks off before gun season. So I'm not leaving after this week."

"Oh, he's up to it," Cobb said. "Don't let this modesty fool you. I convinced him that it was his civic duty, you know? That he owes it to this country, that's given him so much, to step forward at this time and give the voters, the Second District, the choice they haven't had. A new face. A fresh vision. A man who's seen this country whole, and knows where it should be heading. A hero of the national pastime, an example to our children and a legend to all."

"One of a new generation of Americans," she said. "Born in this century. Tempered by war. Disciplined by a hard and bitter peace. Proud of our ancient heritage. I like it. I like it. We should get a torch for this guy, let him carry it around to every meeting we can find."

"Hey," Briggs said, "I liked Kennedy. I may not know much about politics, but I liked what I saw. I got a letter from the White House, the year that I got hurt. One from his brother, too, and some guy named O'Neill. I liked JFK."

She nodded. "Figures," she said. "But that's the whole point, you see? So'd everybody else. Okay, so he didn't carry this state. Cows're all Republicans—they outvoted us. Those of us here, then. But even the cows're sorry now. Everyone was, after Dallas. So, give them a chance now, to make partial amends, and I think they'll jump at it. Gladly."

She stood up. "I gotta go," she said. "Got to catch a plane, and I hate missing planes."

"Going back to Florida?" Cobb said. "Wish I didn't have to work. Must be very nice."

" 'Work'?" she said. "What is this crap? You're a politician. Politicians don't *work*—everyone knows that. But: no, not Florida. Boat's in a marina anyway. In the Dismal Swamp Canal. We tried to take it down last week, but that's as far's we got. Cable broke on the pedestal steering, which it wouldn't've if Neil'd ridden herd hard enough on the yard in Stonington, and the boatyard down there had had brains enough to send for the part. But they didn't, and it did, so we left the thing there and flew home. No, I'm going to New York. Got a party there tonight. Which I've been dreading until now. But not now— tonight at that goddamned party, I'm gonna have something to *say*. 'All you other guys may have egg on your faces and soup on your ties in the states that you come from, but we've got a comer up in Vermont, my friends, and we're going to show you some *real* stuff.' " She grinned. "*This* one I'm going to enjoy. *Then* I'll fly down to Norfolk, and Neil'll pick me up there." She left in a swirl of mink.

"She's something, isn't she?" Beale said. "She ought to be on the stage."

Cobb gazed at Briggs. He sucked his teeth. "Yeah," he said absently to Beale. "But I got to ask you, Hank, all right? You gonna have trouble with her?"

"Trouble?" Briggs said. "How could I have trouble with her? I think she's dynamite."

"That's the kind of trouble I mean," Cobb said. "That's exactly the trouble I mean. You put one move on that lady, you're finished. Dead in the water and sinking. This is not the kind of broad you're used to, you butter her up like a Parker House roll and the next thing you know, you're in bed. The reason she's so valuable is because she keeps things separate. And that means she doesn't go to bed with her clothes on, I'd bet, and she doesn't play politics naked. She's a lightning rod, and she knows it. Opposition looks at her and they think just what you're thinking."

"Hell, what I'm thinking, too," Beale said.

"Well, you're breathing, aren't you?" Cobb said. "Any man didn't react like that to her, I'd call the coroner. But the minute, the first time she hops in the sack with a guy whose name is not Neil Cooke, that minute she becomes useless. And she knows it. The enemy'd smear her from here to Washington, and the guy she did it with would get ruined, the same time.

"So," he said, "she sees you drooling, or fiddling with your zipper when she's talking business with you, she'll be *gone*. She likes you, and she wants to help, and we really need her help. But she will not deliver if it starts to look as though her position's jeopardized. Keep in mind with her at all times that she's like a battleship. As long as she's with you, the other guy'll be getting hit with her artillery. And she's got a lot of it. She's got a lot of money. She can raise a lot of money. And she's got the contacts, too. But if she decides you're dangerous she can turn those guns around, and she will murder you. Understood?"

"Understood," Briggs said.

Cobb nodded. He looked at Beale. "I should feel good," he said. "So, why? Why do I have the feeling I just gave a new revolver to some guy named John Wilkes Booth?"

Beale shrugged. "Maybe you just did," he said. "How about if we start right now, teaching him to shoot it? And who to shoot it at? Then he won't foul up."

"Oh-kay," Cobb said, "good point. Now I already worked out some things on the phone with Tom Calley. He thinks, and I think, and Caroline thinks, that the best thing's to wait to announce. Maybe a month or so. Right now the New Hampshire primary's the thing everybody's pointing for. Well, waiting to see what's gonna happen, after Christmas, I mean. Assuming anybody around here starts paying some attention, politics, after the tree's taken down. But if anything grabs them, that's what it'll be—who else wants to be President now. So what we do is use January, and as much of February as the big-leaguers'll let us, to get you a higher profile. Which, since you're starting from ground zero, far as politics're concerned, shouldn't be too hard. Week after next, we'll go down and see Calley. He'll have his research by then."

"No," Briggs said. "We either go this week, or after Thanksgiving. First, second week in December. You need to get your ears flushed out, Ed. I already said it's deer season."

"Cut it out, Hank," Cobb said. "You're among friends in this room. I got you that job. I can get you leave. You've got something else you have to do."

"No," Briggs said, "I won't do it. I've been on this job one full year now. This is my second deer season. Deer're the most important part of this. The biggest chunk of our tourist trade. Last year they took seven-oh-four with the bows, and then came the full gunnin' season. Seventeen thousand, three hundred and eighty-four bucks, plus thirty-two, thirty-two does. That's twenty-one thousand deer harvested, and that makes 'legal' important. Last year I brought in eight guys for selling deer to people who can't shoot, but who don't want to admit it. Last year I arrested fourteen assholes, for shooting from roads, or near houses. Last year I had two kids, got shot by mistake. Those kids did not bleed to death, either. Is this important? I think it is, regardless of what you may think. And furthermore, I do a job when I take it, and I took this damned job on. And anyway, I may not know shit, when it comes down to politics. Fine. But I know, I think, how most people think, when somebody wants a new job. The first thing they ask is how he did the last one. Well, this's the one that I've got, and if you want me to run against Wainwright, I think that question could be important. If someone asks it, I know my answer, and that answer's gonna be truthful. 'I did what I said I would do.' "

"There will be rumors, you understand," Beale said.

"How could there be, so soon?" Briggs said. "I wasn't sure myself until I called Ed that night, and that was, what, three weeks ago? Month at the outside?"

"See?" Cobb said to Beale. "This kid's got a lot to learn."

"So teach him, teach him," Beale said. "Stop wasting his time here. Man's got things to do, besides listen your complaints. This is the man's day off."

"Yeah," Cobb said. "From the night he made that call, Don, there were no more days off. But, okay, rumors're already out there. Not: that *you're* running, Hank. Just that someone is. Russ Wixton at the paper, I saw him Thursday night, having a drink at the Sportsman. Just before you came in. And he was all over me, see if he could make me say: We're running against Bob. So I gave him a few dance steps. I said: 'What makes you think that?' And he tells me he picked up something—which I know he got from you, and I know what it is, too.

161

But I gave him not one thing." He paused. "If you start improvising, Hank, you're gonna tailspin here. This is a delicate device that we're fooling with here now. If I call Calley and tell him, it's got to be this week, he'll probably see us, but he'll resent it. We could get off the wrong foot."

"This week," Briggs said, "or December. Otherwise count me out."

Cobb did not say anything.

Beale cleared his throat. "Ahh, Ed," he said, "what'd be the harm, huh? It seems to me as though the sooner we get started, the better off we are. You know it's just a matter of time until Bob Wainwright starts to catch on. You know that Prior fellow, one that looks like him. He's a vulture for gossip. Aren't we better off if we spring it on them first, before they can get set and dug in to fight us off?"

"Oh, Prior," Cobb said, "that little beauty. Sneaky little bastard. Always prowling around, sniffing around, looking for the angles. I don't know how the hell they stand each other. Bob sits there in his office, or he's in the Capitol, and what I get is that there's no one less in touch what's going on. Only thing he thinks about is cutting the budget. Which is about as popular an operation down there these days as free castration is. But because he's got Prior, he can get away with it. That kid is like a beagle when there's something going on."

"Too bad we don't have him," Beale said. "We could use a man like that, one with no ethics at all."

"What would you use him for, Don?" Briggs said. "Politics or selling cars?"

"I'll ignore that," Beale said.

"So okay, then we go early," Cobb said. "I say to Wixton, Turner's spa, I see him tomorrow morning drinking coffee, eavesdropping, I tell him confidentially that we've got something brewing, but he can't print it yet. And promise him an exclusive, as soon as we're all set. Which in due course, a couple weeks, I will give to him. After we've seen Calley, and after you're in the woods. Because you don't lie to Russ if you want to keep your ears. Shit, look at what he does to our honorable mayor, every time poor Joseph pokes his head up above the trench. And you know why that is, Hank? Because Joe lied to Russ once, and Russ can be very mean."

"I know him pretty good," Briggs said. "From when I was playing ball. We've had a lot of drinks. I don't think he'd harpoon me. Known him a long time."

Beale snorted. Cobb shook his head. "Henry, Henry," he said, "a friendly reporter's no more dangerous'n a friendly water moccasin, all right? Engrave that on your brain today, right up near the front. Where you see it every morning, minute you wake up. What you're telling me's what I know: that he knows the dirt on you. And the instant that he finds out, you're the guy we picked, from that moment on, my friend, all that he'll be waiting for's a good excuse to print it. Take my word for it. You come out for being faithful, he will chop your balls off. And grin while he's doing it. Because you will be lying, and that will be his excuse."

Briggs grimaced. "Well," he said, "I don't know's anyone'd believe me if I did say that anyway, but okay, I won't do that."

"So, okay," Cobb said, "we already got the rumors, but they're not specific yet. Fine. Those're good, in their own way. Get people curious. Stimulate their interest, so when it does come time, announce, well, it won't be unexpected, but it will add to the importance. Get us better coverage. Which we want to be in a position to exploit, all right? I'll shoot for Wednesday, Boston, the exploratory meeting. That all right with all concerned?"

"Well, just try to keep me out," Beale said. "I'm the original Vermont bankroll man. I think I need to know all I can about this little frolic. I'm paying for the hot dogs and the beer, so far at least. Sure, I want to hear the band."

"I'm not sure I can," Briggs said. "I'm 'sposed to work on Wednesday. And why Boston anyway? Why don't the three of us just meet here, way we're doing now?"

"Henry," Cobb said, "we're not meeting here because it's not the three of us. The fourth one is Tom Calley, and Tom Calley is in Boston. Okay?"

"So let him come up here then," Briggs said. "Doesn't this guy work for us? Four guys for a meeting, three of them go there?"

Beale coughed. "Well," he said, "as I understand it, there's always been some doubt when Calley gets in a campaign, just who's working for whom. If you follow me, I mean."

"Besides," Cobb said, "Calley doesn't fly. He's afraid of airplanes.

You want the guy to go somewhere, it's got to be important. Say: the presidential level. And even then he gripes. Says his time's too valuable, get taken up on being scared, or wasted riding on a train. So if we want to see him now, and believe me, friend, we do, then we go where Tom Calley is, and hear what he has to say."

"Why's it have to be so fast?" Briggs said. "We've got lots of time."

"Henry," Cobb said, "face the music. Donald's band is tuning up. We have not got lots of time. After the general rumors die down, the specific ones will start. And that will be very soon. And then, when it turns out that you *are* the candidate, everything you do in public will be scrutinized. So, until the time you announce, but while you're getting ready, we can't have you doing things that will make you look like an asshole, all right? When the season opens on you, after the one on deer closes, you want to look like a statesman, not some fucking jerk. What you do and say, the meantime, that becomes important. You've made a decision. So, Wednesday get your ass in gear and drive it down with us to Boston. Look at it the way you did, spending the winters in Pittsburgh with coal soot all over your meat. It's necessary, all right, pal? It's for your education."

17

early on the following Wednesday morning Briggs was in his banquet-speaking uniform: solid-gold-button blue blazer, gray flannels, black alligator belt with solid-gold buckle, blue-and-white-striped broadcloth shirt, collar pinned with a gold clasp, solid blue silk tie tacked to his shirtfront with a small solid-gold baseball, heavy hexagonal initialed gold cufflinks, solid-gold ID bracelet on his right wrist, solid-gold Rolex Presidential watch and band on his left, and black tasseled Bally loafers with gold accents on the instep straps on his feet. In his breast pocket he carried a dark red silk ancient-madder pocket square. In his inside pocket he carried a solid-gold Mont Blanc pen. He had packed his pigskin overnight valise with a fresh shirt, shaving kit, socks, and underwear. He was at the bay window, drinking his third cup of coffee, his gray cashmere double-breasted overcoat over the back of his usual chair in the kitchen, the bag concealed beneath it, when Lillian in her robe emerged bleary from the bedroom.

The cats rose up to greet her and rubbed against her legs. She yawned. "Well, I see you're really going," she said. "All dressed up for the prom."

He did not turn to face her. "I told you again I was going, last night," he said. "I did expect them 'fore now, though. Thought they'd be here by eight. Ed must've gotten tied up."

She went over to the kitchen television and turned on the "Today" show. "Really," she said. "I didn't know lynch mobs went out this time of year. Must've been after I went to bed. Before you came home's what I mean." She went to the stove and poured a cup of coffee, returning to the table to sit down.

"They probably got distracted," he said. "Run into Ted on his way back, Winooski, decided to string him up first. Wish they'd've called me, needed extra rope or something. That'd give him a reason at least, to start another fresh fight."

She yawned again and drank some coffee. "Oh, I don't know," she said. "I think you get some blame, too. You bore him so he baits you. And you always fall for his game. I don't know which one of you's worse. You, I guess—he's younger. You're old enough to know better, let him do it to you."

"Least he can't make me cry," Briggs said. "Hasn't brought that one off yet."

"I know," she said. "I know, but I can't help it. I always go into things with him hoping, 'maybe this one'll be different.' And it never is. None of them are. They always end up the same way. Ted goading you, you yelling at him, Sally and Cal leaving early. Not that I blame those two at all. I wouldn't stay 'less I had to. I just dread to think of Thanksgiving coming. Four whole days of you fighting."

He did not say anything. A metallic green Chrysler Imperial sedan with a dealer plate on the front pulled into the drive and up to the porch steps, Ed Cobb driving. Donald Beale was in the passenger seat. "They're here," Briggs said. "Gotta go." He went over to her chair and bent to kiss her cheek. She pulled away irritably, brushing at her jaw as though he had been a mosquito. "Right," he said, straightening up. "Well, I'd guess I'll be home pretty late." He took his coat and grabbed the bag. "Packed a change, just in case."

"Well, least there's a good reason this time," she said, "you do come back late tonight. Coming all the way back here from Boston. Last night you were late, later'n get-out, and that was just the next town."

"Yeah," he said. He put his coat on, settling it over his shoulders. "That's the funny thing about asking people's help. Sometimes takes longer, you think."

"Huh," she said, picking up the coffee cup again, " 'asking people's help.' Buying them beer's what you mean. And having a lot for yourself." She laughed. "Getting drunk with a bunch of damned farmers," she said, "and you like to pretend you've got class. No wonder Ted laughs at you, honest to God. Out 'til all hours on a weekday night, getting yourself good and plastered, and then here you are, bright and early next morning, all spangled up like a show horse, off to wow the slick city boys. I'll give you one thing, Henry, didn't know you had it in you: Whatever the audience wants, you can give them. Any disguise that they want. Hay sticking out of your ears? You can do that. More gold than a whore? Do that, too. I think I'll start saying what Martha says about Everett: 'Everett found his true calling. Preaching the Lord Jesus Christ.' Only I'll change it, of course. I'll say: 'It took him a while, but Hank knows what he is now: He's a real politician.' You'll wind up President, Henry, you will. You'll do whatever they ask. What if they ask you, what if they say: 'Hey, Henry, put this dress on—get you elected for sure.' Will you do that, Henry, if they say that? Just how far is it you will go?"

"Have a nice day, Lil," he said. He went out and closed the door. He got into the back seat of the Imperial and shut the door. "Whoosh," he said as Beale said "Good morning."

Cobb looked at him in the rearview mirror as he put the car in reverse. He was grinning. "Another tender parting, Hank?" he said. "Bride a mite upset?" He turned in the seat and backed the car down the hill to the garage, turned around, and headed onto the road.

"I'm thinking of putting a bounty out on her," Briggs said. "Also: No closed season. Wonder if Bunny'd take care of it, huh? Doubt you could get much lean meat off her, but Bunny can always use cash, help his needy friends out."

Beale turned in the passenger seat. "Not a real good weekend?" he said.

"Ahh," Briggs said. "They're all the same. My fuckin' son calls home and starts to jerk my chain. Lookin' for money of course. When that doesn't work, and it usually doesn't, he insults his mother. Lil cries on demand, so that's two things I'm mad at: one at Ted for being vicious; her, being weak. Well, I got to sound off at someone—there's a short end to my long rope, too. So I get to the end of it and I explode, never at her, just at him. But that means he gets to hang up all offended, his own father yelling at him. And that leaves me to deal with her flooding, which somehow's completely my fault. Well, I don't want to yell at her. Hell, I don't want to holler at anyone. So what I do? Go out, have a few drinks, leave her cry to sleep by herself. And then the next morning, what do I get? It sounds like a record of Ted, but it's coming out of her mouth."

"Well," Beale said, "if it's any consolation, Henry, you are not alone. And here's some good news: You can't win. Used to be my family, my wife, the kids, and me, we'd all pile in the car the morning and drive to Dad and Mum's. And this was back when Earl was playing—at first he would fly home to join us, and Dad and Earl and I would go and see Albertus Magnus play Saint Stephen's, years before Dad got too old. It was a real nice outing there."

Cobb hit the signal to turn right at the intersection in front of Whipple's store and headed east at sixty through the faded-green and brown fields between Occident and Charlotte, the softly sprung big car heeling slightly to the right on the forty-mile crowned blacktop. About a mile from the village a herd of some thirty Holsteins had crowded into one corner of an eight-acre pasturage near the barbed-wire fence at the road. Some of them raised their heads and stared at the car as it passed. Most of them proceeded placidly about the business of searching out and eating what fresh grass remained.

"Then Earl started to become better known. His schedule was crowded. He had more important things on his mind than his parents, and holidays. So he stopped flying up. And Dad was really hurt, you know? It really hurt his feelings. It wasn't that he said anything. He kept things to himself. But he *was* hurt, and I could see it. Everywhere he went, you know, he'd bragged about Earl. And now Earl had no time for him. Dad really took it hard. We stopped going to the games. We just sat and talked instead. Kids were some help, underfoot, begging for his attention—they got his mind off Earl a little, cheered him up, you know?

"Then, well you know what happened next. Earl got in big trouble. And I know the doctors told me that the two things weren't connected. 'After all, he's seventy-six. These things have to be expected.' Well, the docs were wrong, that's what I say—they had to be connected. Earl got arrested; six weeks later, Dad had his first stroke. And they said it was a mild one, that he'd make a full recovery. Then they said he did. But that was a lie—he didn't. Anyone who knew him could see that. He shuffled when he walked, and he got tired easily. Dad always walked and stood up very straight, shoulders back and all. Now all a sudden he stooped. He had to use a cane. His mind started to fail. Not much at first, but it did. Just little things you had to know him pretty well to notice. He always was, for example, a stickler for inventory. And every manager we had had the same question to ask: 'What's he need inventory for? What's he do with it? Knows every part, in every bin, that we've got on the shelves.' And whenever I would want, you know, to heckle him some, I'd ask him, in all innocence, why he needed it. And that would set him roaring. 'For the goddamned government. Every time I take a leak, I'm supposed to keep a record. Goddamned IRS, goddamn them, what went in and what went out, and how much I kept myself.' Well, no more of that, after the stroke. After that we needed those books, for our own information.

"Then," Beale said, "there were the years when Earl really couldn't come. Dad was fairly frisky, after the first one. He'd had some time get used to it, Earl being in prison and all that. He couldn't change it, so he pretended to laugh it off. I overheard him talking on the telephone one day. 'Nope, just Don and his family. Earl can't get away.' Must've been someone he knew, and knew pretty well, too. I heard him laughing. Bitter, but still laughing. 'Well, it's his mother's fault, you know. I've had to tell her that. "If you'd've baked a cake for him, and put a hacksaw in it, might've done some good."' But when the actual day rolled around, he wasn't laughing anymore. He was really in the dumps. He'd been so proud of Earl, prouder than of me. And then right before that Christmas, well, he had his second stroke."

The Imperial reached the intersection with Route 7 in Charlotte, and Cobb turned it smoothly south toward Vergennes, accelerating to eighty. "He was never really right after that," Beale said. "In the spring he made a couple tries at coming to the office, but he tired so easily, and so fast, that I had to take him home. That summer, the second summer Earl was in the jail, we actually had to go out and buy Dad two air conditioners. One for the big bedroom and one for the closed-in porch. That alone like to've killed him. Spending all that money for some damned-fool blamed machine, and then running up the electric every time you turned it on? And this for a man who always claimed, and seemed to mean it, too, that heat didn't bother him? No one I could name at least could ever claim they saw him without his shirt and tie and coat, and his hat when he went out, on the hottest day of the year. I think that's when he realized, fully understood, that he was really sick, and he was not going to get better: when he had to sit there in his chair and hear the cool air being made.

"I thought," Beale said, "I actually thought, you know, that that was the worst time. As bad as it could get, Dad sick and Earl in prison. But I was wrong. Earl got out at the end October, after Dad had two more strokes, and we didn't even know it because Earl didn't bother to call. And besides, we all had enough on our hands with Dad, without thinking about our jailbird, Earl. Dad was in-and-out, you know? Drove my mother nuts. One minute you'd be sitting there in the same room with his actual body, seventy-eight years old, surrounding the mind he had as a boy, then as a young man, then a young father, time spinning around like a top and the damnedest things coming out of him, and he'd get you to laughing. He'd be a little kid showing off, pleased as punch at himself. And then bingo, like lightning, he's back in his real mind, glaring at you, thoroughly insulted. 'Now what the hell're you laughing at? Have all of you lost your damned minds?'

"Well, because of that," Beale said, "because you never did know when he'd flip, you'd had to plan, and then make sure you did, everything just like you done it before. Close as you could, anyway. Because if you didn't, and he snapped to, he'd know that you skipped doing something and he'd get all upset. Sometimes he'd be sad: 'You all think I'm dead. Just waiting for me to be dead.' And sometimes he'd be mad: 'I know I'm sick, you know, you fools. I'm not too far gone to know that. But don't think that means you can stop doing things, you figure I won't probably notice. You can bet that I'll notice, bottom dollar on that. Got a kick or two left in me yet.'

"So," Beale said, "just in case he might be lucid, just in case he might come to, we had the regular Thanksgiving, the year that Earl got out. And Earl without calling or sending a letter, showed up big as life, like he'd never been gone, just borrowed somebody's car and came up. He gave Mum a big kiss and a hug and some flowers. Thought to God she'd faint dead away. Then he says, 'Hi, Donsie,' 'Julie, how's it going? Think I'll go in and see Dad.' Jaunty as you could please. Not a care in the world. I'd written to him about Dad several times; I thought I should even though he never wrote back. So he knew the score, what the situation was, but I guess maybe he didn't believe it. Or it hadn't registered on him. Couple of minutes, and out came Earl again. He had a big grin on his face. The rest of us, Julie, Mum, and me, were in the living room, trying to come to grips with things, and Earl came out the front room and said: 'Christ, the old man's gone loony.' I happened to be sitting right where I could see past Earl, see Dad sitting behind him.

"Earl's timing was just about perfect. Dad snapped in about a second before Earl said he was nuts, and his mouth just fell open. So did Mum's, and so did Julie's. I was speechless, too. And Earl says—Dad was still listening, mind you, he still knew what's going on, not that he would for long—'What's the matter with you people? Don't you know what's going on? The guy that scared the whole world shitless, everywhere he went, well, he's on another planet, guys. Old Dad's porch light's gone out.' "

"Jesus," Briggs said, "what'd you do?"

"I didn't know what to do, actually," Beale said. "Well, I did, I knew exactly what to do. But my mother was there, and I didn't know how she'd take it. Earl was her youngest. He was her favorite. As many the bad things he did that hurt people, never once did my mother say: 'Boo.' So I looked at her. She looked like she'd been stabbed. And I said: 'Okay, Earl, you're leaving. You're leaving right now, and if you don't leave, I'll go and get Dad's gun and shoot you.' Which I really think I would've, if he hadn't done it. He looked at Mum, found no help there, picked up his traps, and left.

"We didn't see him again until Dad's funeral. The following April that was. All full of contrition he was then. Course Earl being Earl, some things never change, he made a big show of that, too. Dick Carlisle had the body, he and Dad were good friends but it was strictly personal—he stopped buying our cars when Dad died—and Earl showed up second night of the wake, very humble, with some quiet tears. He went up to Monsignor, Monsignor Roach, all the way down from up Burlington, and Monsignor was no kid himself then, but he'd led the rosary for Dad. And Earl pulled him aside, where Mum could see him, of course—never miss a chance to grandstand—and asked him to hear his confession. So he could receive the next day, for his Dad, that he never meant to hurt so bad.

"I thought I was going to throw up. I looked at Mum, and she just shook her head once. 'Let him put on his show,' I took that to mean. So I did. I figured he'd throw himself in the grave the next day, or pull some other big stunt. But I guess he went out and got drunk or something, after Monsignor absolved him. The effort must've been too great—he never showed up at Carlisle's the next morning, or the church for the Mass, or the cemetery. Nor come back to the house afterward.

"I didn't hear from him about two months—sometime in the early part of the summer. Then I get a call at work. My brother was on the phone. Knowing Earl I figured this had to be some bail bondsman he primed to say that, so that I'd take the call. But no, it really was Earl, and he wasn't in jail. Not then at least. He was in Nashua, on his way up to see me, and he'd had two flats in a row, and would I spring for a couple of tires since he didn't have the cash on him. No surprise there: If he was coming up to see me, it stood to reason he'd run out of cash— that was always what brought him around. Well, lucky for Earl I'd gotten to know Steve Grace pretty well. Steve runs White River Plymouth north of where he was, and I told Earl to sit tight and I'd ask Steve to send a guy down with a tow truck, bring him in and fix him up.

"Ended up costing me close to a hundred-fifty bucks, because naturally the car Earl'd borrowed was a beat-up old Cadillac that took the biggest doughnuts Firestone ever made. And I hung up and sat there, waiting for Earl to come in the way a man waits for the hangman to come, or the priest for the walk down the Last Mile.

"I finally went home around ten that night," Beale said. "Earl didn't show up for three days. Some cock-and-bull thing about seeing people, whether they'd give him a job. I figured that, as usual, he'd had a dame with him, planned on dropping her off while he came up alone to see me. But she'd done something extraspecial for him that night, so he'd had trouble breaking away." Beale laughed. "That's the beauty of Earl," he said. "You never have to wonder if he's telling you the truth. If the news is good, he's lying. Just assume that. If the news is bad, it's true. Well, partly; if he tells you things're bad, then you know they're worse.

"This particular time, I knew it was very bad, because what he told me was that no one'd give him a job. I not only believed that; I also believed this meant he hadn't been able to find anything worthwhile stealing, or any shady, easy, way to make big money fast. Because if he had, he wouldn't even've looked for a real job.

"I'm sure Earl's going to die someday, just like the rest of us—he doesn't believe that, of course, just the opposite. And I'm also sure he's not going to die rich, another thing we disagree on. But both of us know that when he wants to get money, the first thing he tries is dishonest. Or illegal. Or worse. So if he was losing his touch in that line, he was in serious trouble.

"So I said to him: 'Well, there's lots of work around, Earl. Jobs going begging all over the place. What kind of thing interests you? Short of a bank presidency or something, I mean.' And he said, Well, no, he realizes he couldn't go around expecting to land something big; he'd reconciled himself to that. But that's what made him realize what a big problem he had: once people found out that he had a record, they wouldn't hire him to do toilets. And that's when I called up Ed here, and asked him see what could be done. About the record, I mean." Cobb increased the Imperial's speed to just over ninety, but otherwise did not react. "And Ed, I'm glad to say, was able to help me out."

"Help you out?" Briggs said. "I thought it was Earl, had the problem."

"You got it wrong, Hank," Cobb said. "Don had the problem. He gave me the problem. Earl doesn't *have* problems. Earl *is* the problems. Anyone's got him has problems."

"Which is the point that I'm trying to make," Beale said. "The stuff you're going through at home, well, look at it this way: It's very disagreeable, but extremely good basic training for this new thing you're taking up. Just ask Ed here. He's been at it a long time.

"What you've got with your family," Beale said, "well, the details're different from what I've got with mine, and if you talk to enough people, as you're going all around, sooner or later you'll start to wonder how in hell all these normal-looking people could have managed to find so many ways of getting into trouble. It's as though everybody needs a hobby or something. If we're not born into a family with an Earl to keep us entertained, we do what Ed did with Gwendolyn there, the lady sparring-partner—"

"—the queen of the Roller Derby," Cobb said.

"—we marry ourselves one," Beale said. "And if that doesn't do it, well, we can always screw up on the job, or cheat on our wives with Jim Beam, or cheat just a little bit more on our taxes'n the people who look at 'em stand for.

"It's like we've got this sixth sense; it tells us comfort's bad for us. We need a lasting itch or something, in a place we can't reach. It's the only way that we can think of to maintain our alertness. In your case, you married this woman. Now, I've never even met her, but Ed tells me she used to be a real looker. Now he says she's pretty fat, and she gives you lots of grief."

"This is true," Briggs said. "The fact she gives me lots of grief: Well, that something I used to do had something to do with that. Stopped doing it when I retired, I didn't have much choice, but I gave her plenty of reasons, 'fore I reached that point. The fact she let herself go so she looks like my first catcher? That was all her idea. The woman isn't forty yet, but she looks sixty, easy. Well, maybe fifty-five or so. She's got our wedding picture, framed and sitting on the bureau. I look at it sometimes and wonder: 'Hey, the guy I recognize. He's a younger me. But who's that good-lookin' girl with me? Did I know her once?' It's confusing."

"Then you've got the son," Beale said. "Apparently just annoying the wife, so that she'll nag you all the time didn't quite meet your expectations for problems you can't possibly solve. So you have the boy to help her, and the two of them can keep you amused. Good for you. This means you're a lucky man. You didn't have to start looking around for something more to help you to full misery. Like drinking too much whiskey, too much whiskey every day. Or screwing up a nice career, like some lawyers I could name who took their clients' money, or some doctors that I heard of that helped healthy patients die.

"Now," Beale said, "you get upset when your wife and kid get on you. They anger you. You think they're wrong, and that you don't deserve it. And you want to stop this. Well, you're wrong. It doesn't matter whether you deserve it—what matters is, you need it. And stopping it, or trying to, that's the wrong approach. I know that because of Earl, now that my mind's clear on him. You can't stop it; you're not going to; this is permanent. Or as close as we ever get to permanent, in our mortal toil. So what you should be doing with them is what I try to do with Earl: Earl's the confounded wild animal. I'm just the wild animal's trainer. He didn't ask to come in the cage with me; I sure didn't want the job. He'd chew me up if I'd let him, if I dropped the gun and the whip. But as long as I don't, he can't do what he'd like, so mostly he stays on his stool. He can snarl at me, as much as he likes, but as long as he can't see his way clear to a clean bite out me, I'm in control of the cage.

"Ed," Beale said as the Chrysler passed a second sign announcing the date and the place of a weekly service club luncheon, "I realize you don't go to Rotary much, and we never see you at Kiwanis. But where they've got those organizations and they put the signs up, they've also got kids, dogs, and cops. So why don't you back off the throttle a little, huh? It's Boston we want, not the lockup."

"Yeah, yeah," Cobb said, but he began to ease off the gas. "It's just that we got that late start there, you know? Just trying to make up some time."

"Anyway," Beale said, talking to Briggs, "that's what I'm trying to tell you. I don't know what this Calley guy thinks. I've never met the boy genius either. But I'm telling you, regardless of that, or whatever he tells you today, the first thing you need if you want to get votes is some common bond with the voters. Now, that sounds simple, doesn't it. Well, you can ask Ed, if you want first-hand knowledge, or you can ask me, who's just watched, but I believe, and firmly believe, that's the secret of every election. At least every one that's a fight. And that is a secret Wainwright doesn't know, because he's never been in a real fight. I think that gives you an advantage. You go into this with your baseball thing, and it looks like it's your hole card. But that's 'used to be' and the campaign is 'now,' and therefore you need something more. People will come up and talk, because you played the ball and they've known your name for so long they're confused: They think they know you—along with your name. But now you're asking them to do something for you, and the ball's irrelevant to that. What they're really asking you, when they come up and talk, or you go up to them, is not whether they know you—they know that they do—but whether you really know them."

"Well," Briggs said as Cobb slowed to fifty a mile from the center of

Vergennes, letting the big car coast down, "to tell you the truth, most of the people I've talked to so far, I do know them, more or less. Knew them when I was a kid. And they seem to remember me, too."

"I don't mean the guys at the Legion," Beale said. "I don't mean the people at Whip's IGA, or the rest of Occident, either. Those aren't the people I mean. I mean the people up in the Notch. I mean the ones in Canterbury, all the Canterburies. You've got a whole bunch of small towns in this: Winslow and Proctor and Brandon; Addison, Dorset, and Coryville. Most of those people've never met you. Only a few've ever seen you. And I'll bet not more'n a dozen or two of those who recognize your name right off, soon as they hear it, will also remember right off how come. So, what you've got to do, while they're wracking their brains, those that have brains to wrack, is capitalize on the time you're getting. Make them see who you are. And it's not, you're not just a ball player, back from the big time—that is what you used to be.

"No, what you are now is a man who understands problems, problems that they've had or are having, too. You don't want'a stand there, say: 'My wife drives me nuts, and my kid hates my guts, so I know you've thought "murder" too.' That is not what I mean. You're going to say: 'This life can be tough, and not much we can do's going to change it. Or the government can do, as far as that goes, to change all that's bothering us. But there are *some* things the government can do, to change *some* things, and it should be doing that. When it gets tough, when the last thing you need is losing your place to the bank, or hocking yourself broke, to pay for a sickness, then I think that government should give you some help, more'n your friends can afford. And that's what Bob Wainwright doesn't think, doesn't support, and won't vote for, and that's why I should replace him. Because I will do those things, for all of us.' "

"I dunno, Don," Cobb said, the speedometer needle pegged at thirty-five as the big car rolled through Vergennes. "That works all right 'til a wise guy stands up and says: 'Hey, but won't that mean more taxes?' Or 'filling out forms and getting inspected, and putting up with carloads of shit?' I tried that approach, when I ran the first time, and where I was shaky, it cost me. A win is a win, even if it's a squeaker, but I'd've won bigger, I'd've said less."

"Sounds like my old trade," Briggs said. " 'Aw right, Briggsie, heresa ball. Don't make it more exciting'n you needa.' "

"True, true," Beale said as the car moved out of the center and Cobb began moving the speedometer needle steadily back toward the high end, "but Hank's not in a situation here, anymore'n you were, where he has the option to get by without saying anything. Wainwright, unopposed, has always had it. Henry, against him, does not. The people that've been voting for Wainwright for centuries, who couldn't give you a good reason if you put a gun to their heads, they're going to need a good reason before they stop doing that. *You* know he's a vacuum; *I* know he's a vacuum; but that vacuum sucks up their votes. So Henry needs a magnet to hold them back before they do it, or a rope if a magnet won't do it. And I'm telling you, as I see this thing, it's the same as when Oaksie, or any of my men, tries to whammy a guy that's driven Fords all his life into trying a Plymouth for a change. Well, we can do it on price, at least the first time, if that's what it takes to persuade him, but money's not part of Hank's dealing. And that's why I'm saying: Find your common ground. Then stand there and talk to them on it."

The state police car moved up beside the Imperial shortly after Route 7 became hilly and curving north of Middlebury, and the trooper turned on the flashing lights. Cobb looked over at him in momentary surprise. The cop motioned with his right forefinger toward the shoulder of the road. Cobb nodded and sighed and started braking down from eighty, flicking on his right turn signal as the cruiser pulled in behind him. Cobb put the transmission in park and shut off the ignition. "Shit," he said. He began reaching for his wallet, lowering his window as he did so.

The trooper, in a brown tunic, a broad-brimmed hat, and Sam Browne harness holding his revolver holster so that the lower tip brushed the outside seam of his fawn trousers, put his hands on the windowsill and stared impenetrably into the car through his sunglasses. "Sorry to bother you, gentlemen," he said. "I'll need to see your papers."

Cobb handed the trooper his license. The trooper did not look at it. "The registration, too, please," he said. "Need to see both of them. This is a dealer car?"

"Oh," Beale said. He opened the glove box. "Forgot which car we had. It should be right in here." The document was on top of the owner's manual for the car. Beale handed it to Cobb, who handed it to the cop. The cop looked at it and frowned. He leaned down again and peered in at Beale. "This," he said, "all this does is say about six plate numbers. One of them matches the plate on this car. But the paper doesn't say what kind of car, anything about it."

"That's right," Beale said. "We've got six sets of plates that we slap on the various cars that we're taking out on the road. Customers trying them out. Hell, I'm just lucky this happened to be one of the cars had the sheet in it. We don't see them stopped very often. Sometimes get careless about that."

"Yes, sir," the cop said. He looked at the sheet again. "You work for," he said, "you know these Beale people? This 'Beale Chrysler-Plymouth' thing here?"

"I own it," Beale said. "It's a family business. Been in the family for years."

"Never heard of it," the cop said, continuing to study the paper.

"Just south of Burlington," Beale said. "Right on the main drag up there."

"Don't get up there that much," the cop said. "When I do, it's just passin' through. I'm from down Athens myself. You got some identification?"

"Driver's license," Beale said. He began to reach for his wallet. "That good enough?"

"Good enough for me," the cop said. "Business card'd help too, since you say you own this place."

"Say," Cobb said, "is there any way, you know, we could speed this up a little? We've got a meeting down in Boston that we're late for, and . . ."

The cop held up his hand. "All in good time and order," he said. "We go by the book with these things, sir. And you don't mind me saying so, more speed don't seem to me to be just what you need today." Beale handed him his license and his business card. The cop examined them. He compared the signature on the driver's license to the signature on the dealer-plate document, and the address on the document to the one on the business card. He handed all three back across Cobb to

Beale. "All this seems all right to me, sir," he said. "Now, you're saying this gentleman's driving this car because you want to sell it to him?"

"Well," Beale said, "I wanted him to try it out. Sometimes you get a customer who doesn't know he wants a new one. So you let him try it out like this, hoping that he'll fall in love."

"Yes, sir," the cop said. "Well, if I was in your place, Mr. Beale, not running your business or anything, but I'd suggest to my customers like this gentleman here that a lead foot like his is one in the grave. And I bet you don't sell many cars to dead folks. That won't help your business at all.

"Now," he said, reading Cobb's license and then glancing back into Cobb's face, "your name's Edward Cobb, is that right?"

Cobb fidgeted. "Yeah," he said, "like it says. Just like it says on the license."

"Uh-huh," the cop said. " 'Edward S. Cobb, R.F.D. Nine, Alexander, Vermont.' That's just up north a bit there, Essex Junction, am I right? North and east off of Fifteen?"

"That's right," Cobb said.

"Thought so," the cop said. "Pretty country up there. Great mountain views. In the early part of the fall, I'd guess, it's just beautiful, you happen to have the right location. Have you got the right location there, sir, so you see both the valleys from your place?"

"Oh, yes indeed," Cobb said. "All but takes a man's breath clear away, that foliage starts changing colors."

"Well," the cop said, "that's what I figured. Last time I was up there, that's all there was. Big houses with great mountain views. And I imagine you'd like to get back to that nice house of yours."

"Certainly plan to," Cobb said. "It's certainly on my agenda."

"And your family, most likely," the cop said, "I'd bet. Back to your family—you got one?"

"Oh, yes," Cobb said.

"Wife and kids, I suppose?" the cop said.

Cobb sighed. "Just the wife, Officer," he said. "The kids're in Jonesville, their mother."

"Oh, sorry to hear that," the cop said. "But you still go and see them, I'd guess. Probably still think a lot of those kids, no matter what bad luck you and the mother may've had."

"Oh, faithfully, faithfully, Officer," Cobb said. "Why, I'm practically a lodger there. I don't think the neighbors know yet we're divorced, I'm there so much with the kids."

The sunglasses hid the cop's eyes, but the frown lines on his forehead and the bulges at the hinges of his jaw suggested they were squinting. "Well, that's very nice, Mr. ah, Cobb," he said, "and that's why I know you'll appreciate this, what I got to say to you now." He bent and rested his forearms on the windowsill, so that his hands were clasped, Cobb's license between his two thumbs and his forefingers about four inches in front of Cobb's nose and their faces less than a foot apart.

"This thing that I'm holding my hand here," he said, "it's a license to *drive*, Mr. Cobb. The State of Vermont says you can *drive*. It doesn't say: 'Go out and kill people.' Now this may surprise you, Edward S. Cobb, but there's people like you, and people like me, that live down the road in this town. And some of them use it, this road you're on, and some of their kids use it too. The kids ride their bikes, and some ride their horses, and some bring the cows home along it. Their dogs run alongside of them. The folks that're older, they, they drive on it, too. Mostly in cars, sometimes on their tractors, sometimes in wagons with horses. And it's very unusual, Mr. Cobb, my experience at least, that any of them does what you were just doing. Which was well over eighty. The speed limit on this stretch's forty per hour. Most of them seem to be satisfied with that. They maybe haven't got meetings in Boston, or big houses up north of here, and they, most of them anyway, couldn't afford a big fancy fast car like this is. But they've still got their reasons, good enough least for them, so they observe the speed limit. Because, like I said, they got families, too—don't want them hurt, see them killed. Not by them, Mr. Cobb, and not by you either, down from your mountaintop home, trying out this big luxury car."

Cobb did not say anything.

"Now, Mr. Cobb," the cop said, "got to ask you a question. Did you have the slightest idea, Mr. Cobb, how fast you were going back there? Or isn't that something that you thought about? You want to answer me that?"

"Now that you mention it, no, I don't," Cobb said. "It's my turn now to ask you some questions." He removed his right hand from the wheel and gently but firmly pushed the cop's hands away from his face. He took his left hand from the rim of the wheel and reached into his jacket pocket. He produced a black morocco pass case and flipped it open. "What I want you to do, Officer, is read this. I assume that you can do that. And then when you've finished, I'll ask *you* some questions. Not many—just one or two."

The cop shifted the license entirely to his left hand and opened the credentials case with his right. He stared at it. "Mr. Cobb," he said, "you'll have to forgive me." He closed the case and returned it to Cobb. "I see from those papers and those nice gold seals that you're Speaker of the Assembly."

"That's right," Cobb said.

"What I couldn't see on it," the cop said, "is where it says it's okay for you to hit ninety where the speed limit sign tells you 'forty.' Is that on there, sir? Did I overlook that? And if I did so, will you show me it?"

Cobb sighed again. "I don't recall that being on there," he said. "Not in so many words."

"Well, that's good news for me, at least, Mr. Cobb," the cop said. "Thought my eyes must be going bad there. And now that I had a minute to think, seems to me that you're also a lawyer. Didn't the papers say that, one time or another I saw them? I'm not a lawyer, myself. Didn't have that advantage in life. But I have read the statutes, we have to do that, and I think got them down pretty good. And I don't recall one, the parts about highways, and the public safety and that stuff, that says anywhere: 'Mr. Cobb, since he's Speaker, he can go ninety, regardless of what the sign says.' Do you think I missed something there?"

"Very likely," Cobb said. "Look, I told you we're late, and I showed you who I am. And you're still gonna write me up. Okay, we understand each other better now. Just gimme the ticket and lemme get going. Never mind any more of these games." He paused. "And while you're at it, write nice and plain, especially your name and badge."

"I'll do better than that, Mr. Cobb," the cop said. "I'll give it to you right now, so you can be writing too. The name's Ronald Fairchild. Barracks B, Addison. Badge number two sixty-five." Cobb took out his pen and memo pad from his right pocket and began to write that down.

The cop stepped back from the car, took his ticket book from his back pocket, and started toward the back of the car.

Briggs opened the right rear passenger door and got out of the Imperial. The cop had put his ticket book on the trunk lid and was taking a Parker Jotter from his pocket. "Uh, Officer Fairchild," he said, "before you get started. Wonder we might have a word?"

18

briggs returned to the Imperial and got into the back seat, shutting the door behind him. He reached over the bolster of the front seat with his right hand and presented Cobb's license. "Here," he said, "put this in your pocket for now. You can put it in your wallet later. Just start this damned thing and get out of here, five miles under the limit, before Fairchild changes his mind."

Cobb took the license and put it in his shirt pocket. He turned the key in the ignition, looking into the rearview mirror as the cop slowly got back into his cruiser.

"Get going, get going," Briggs said. "Just do what I tell you, all right? Five miles, at least, under the limit. Never mind looking back to see what he's doing—he already told me what that'll be. He's gonna let you get 'round the next curve, maybe the next two or three. And then he might follow us, or he might not, or he might make a call up ahead. So, steady, and easy, and nice, is what does it. I don't think I can pull this off twice."

"Is that what he said to you, Henry?" Beale said.

"That," Briggs said, "and that I oughta pick my friends better."

"Never mind what *he* said to *you*, Hank," Cobb said, "what in hell did *you* say to *him*? That guy had a hair across his ass like I never saw in my life."

"Well, he didn't," Beale said, "before you provoked him. Before that he was just tough. It was after you murmured all your sweet nothings that he suddenly became so mean."

"Will you shut up, let Henry talk?" Cobb said. "What the hell did you say?"

"Oh," Briggs said, "I guess I just wanted to see if I could pay you back a little, getting me my job."

"You use the baseball thing?" Beale said.

"Not that," Briggs said, "not that at all. Doubt it would've meant much to him. He looks like the *Field and Stream* kind of guy to me, never heard of the damned *Sporting News*. No, what I told him, and showed him my badge, I reminded him that I'm a cop, too. Sort of, anyway."

" 'Reminded him'?" Cobb said.

"Yeah," Briggs said. "We met once, sort of, late last spring. Worked close together, in fact. But it wasn't the kind of thing, lot of people around, nobody's name meant too much. And I was dressed different, had my gun and driving the truck. So today he didn't make the connection. I wasn't sure I did myself, matter of fact—not until you got his name. But then I figured: 'Hey, it's at least worth a shot. Ed don't seem to be doing so good on his own.' And it worked."

"What'd you do for the guy," Cobb said, the Imperial lolling along at thirty down the hill into town, "save him from a horny catamount or something?" The main road divided at the town green, the right fork sloping down toward the village center, the brook, and the college campus beyond, the left climbing past the Middlebury Inn on the knoll to the left, aiming for Brandon to the south.

"Nah," Briggs said. "It was that damned Carmichael kid thing there. The one that got shot up the gorge? And the kid, Tony French, kid that did it, took off and hid in the woods?"

"Oh yeah," Beale said. "Three-day manhunt or something. Papers had a regular Mardi Gras with it. Would've thought it was the Boston Strangler or something. I remember that."

"Yeah," Briggs said. "Well, I didn't do a hell of a lot. Was pretty new on the job. But green as I was, I'd still spent more time in the woods'n those stonecutters' kids in cop hats. Funny, huh? They go out looking for some guy, doesn't matter who it is, what he did, or what he's done before. The first thing they do's get the riot guns out, load 'em up with the buckshot, and practice looking grim. Then they go down to the kennels and leash up six, eight bloodhounds, plus a short platoon, German shepherds, and then all march off into the woods. Dogs're barking, guys're yelling, blowing whistles, everything. Breaking branches, cooking dinners, and news guys from here to there. It's like a Chinese New Year's parade—only thing missing's the fire-breathing dragon, the witch doctors bangin' on pots. And every hour on the half, the guy in charge of this production gets up with a bullhorn and tells all the TV guys and the ones from radio that they ain't caught nothin' yet except eight cases poison sumac and a snakebite that they're looking at but they don't think it's fatal. And he acts like he's surprised.

"So all I really did," Briggs said, "all I really did was take a couple cups their coffee, and one their cinnamon rolls, and sit down on a rock—this'd be the third afternoon and I was getting sick of it, wanted go home and go to bed—and try to think what I would do if I was who we're looking for. And when I thought I knew, I went up to the captain there and offered some advice. 'Look,' I said, 'your men're tired. They could use a rest, hot meal, maybe wash their hands. So if I could suggest something, not trying, mind your business, how 'bout leave three or four of them and send the rest home for the night. I'll stay up here with your guys, maybe roam around a little in some places that they might've missed. I'll take a walkie-talkie, so if your guys sleep in shifts, well, I'll have backup if I need it. Nothing turns up by the morning, we haven't lost a thing. But what we gain is rested troops, and that might help a lot if we're back on this tomorrow.'

"So he went for it," Briggs said. "Allowed as how 'that would be best, the men.' This captain, cripes, must've been fifty, had a belly like a horse, most wilderness he'd seen up close in years was mold on stale bread, and here he's being the kindly Commander, for my benefit— and the reporters, too. But what he's thinking is: 'Ahh. Martini. Hot shower, steak, two beers, and then bed.' And also, of course, naturally: 'Goddamn this fuckin' hillbilly kid, got us trapped up in the woods like this, takin' shits off logs.'

"I tell you," Briggs said, "I wasn't really, you know, worried about it happening, but the longer that circus went on, the more chance there was that one of those trigger-happy highway patrolmen, never fired a shot in anger and he's always wanted to, 'd get so frustrated and pissed

185

off at that French kid he'd shoot him on sight if he saw him. And he would've gotten away with it, too. Tony French had two guns with him when he went out with the Carmichael kid and the other lad there, forgot what his name was, to go fishing up at the gorge.

"Now you know, Ed, and I know, too, that that was not uncommon. Get a bright day, fish not biting, lots of people did that. Us among them. Put the fishing poles down, climb back up the gorge, sit there and wait for the snakes to come out, lie on the rocks in the sun. And then just plink at them with your good old twenty-two. It's senseless—they're just water snakes, even though they're big, but snakes is snakes and boys is boys and potting snakes is fun, and it's been going on since Cain and Abel pegged the first rocks at one those slimy-looking things that got Mom and Dad in trouble. So we're not gonna stop it now. Even though it's dangerous, up at the gorge, because of ricochets. You miss a snake and bounce a hollow-point off the rocks of those sheer walls, you're lucky if it doesn't billiard off them, right at your fool head. Or at one your buddies' heads. You're sure not gonna hear it, not in time to duck, not with the noise those turbines make up the line, and the water coming out, and anyway, the slug's deformed by every fresh impact—so you don't know where it's coming from, or any idea where it's headed.

"Well, Tony French wasn't lucky," Briggs said, "not that day at least. And Wilse Carmichael's oldest there, his luck was really bad. And that was really all of what that whole show was about: Three boys went fishing. One brought guns, and acted stupid with them. One got killed. The shooter ran, the third one came for help. There's a name for that kind of thing. It's called: 'an accident.' Not 'a prison break.' Not 'a train robbery' or 'a bank holdup.' Not 'a maddened mass killer at large.' A bad damned accident, for sure, but still an accident, with less dead bodies on the ground after it was over'n you find after two carloads of drunken skiers smash. We weren't looking for a murderer, armed to the teeth. We were looking for a backwoods teenager, scared shitless and hiding, hiding in the woods.

"Well, I wasn't sure all those cops still remembered that, and I was also more'n just a little bit afraid that if the French kid thought he was surrounded by a posse, he'd panic, and open up on those cops, and then he'd really be in trouble. If he lived, I mean.

"So the army retreats," Briggs said. "This is just about dusk. Bugs come up. Surprising how many mosquitoes you get up the gorge, a warm spring night. You'd think that white water moves so fast they couldn't breed in it. What you don't think is we'd had some rain, quite a lot of it, and every little hollow had a nice warm puddle in it where the bugs could drink and fuck. So I went back to my truck and got my trusty bottle of pure oil of citronella, smeared it all over me and my cuffs and hat as well. Looked like I was ready to be rolled in breadcrumbs and fried. Smelled like a big fat candle that choked out on melted wax, but I figured stuff that worked in the mud of New Jersey, doing basic at Fort Dix, it oughta work up here. Go back to join the troopers—guy you just met was one of them—and they're all spreading on the nice clear stuff that doesn't make you greasy, doesn't make you stink, and don't stain your clothes, either. Course it also don't keep bugs off, but I didn't tell them that. And after about twenty minutes, what I figured'd happen, happened. They got tired of swatting mosquitoes and went back to sit in their cars with the windows all rolled up. Rather sweat their nuts off'n soil those pretty uniforms."

He laughed. "Reminded me of some infielders I had. And also a *lot* of guys that settled for singles when they could've had doubles—and maybe scored me some runs—if they'd've been willing to slide in the dirt, or get grass stains on their ass, for that little extra. Had one kid playing short behind me at Pittsburgh, and about the third week the season—he was small and quick, like most good shorts, and I was 'bout as big as I am now—I went up to him at his locker after we'd blown the game on two hot ones he could've had if he'd've dove, and I grabbed him by the T-shirt, picked him right up off the floor. And I said to him: 'You little shit. You just cost us a game, me personally a win, because you think Picture Day's forever and you don't want to get all mussed up. Well, lemme tell you something, rook: The team pays to wash the suits. This is not the Sally League. And if you don't get your suit dirty, while we're out there on the field, you're gonna find it's all bloody by the time you take it off. 'Cause I'll be in the runway, waiting, when you come in off the field, and if you're still looking sharp, and we've lost another game, I am gonna punch your face until your nose disappears.'

"Funny," Briggs said. "After that when something shot back through my wickets too fast for me to get down and pick it up, I'd just turn around and smile, and there'd be my shortstop, two feet behind second, throwing from his knees. Writers began calling him 'Dirt-drawers,' and it stuck, and I never saw a kid who liked embarrassment so much.

"Anyway," Briggs said as Cobb kept the big car steady at fifty in the rural fifty-five zone north of Brandon, "I give those four cops about an hour, sit and smoke and scratch their bites, and then I went up to Fairchild's car. By now it's getting dark. He rolls the window down about, maybe an inch, all this tobacco smoke comes out, and—by now we're on a first-name basis—I say: 'Ron, I'm getting kind of stiff, just standing around here. Think I'll take a stroll around, stretch my legs a bit.'

"He looks at me. 'Yeah,' he said, 'well, if I was you, I wouldn't. Not with that crazy kid out there, in the bushes with his guns.'

"'Ahh, I'll be all right,' I say. 'He's long gone from here by now. Besides, I'll get my flashlight there, and my flares and whistle too. I got the walkie-talkie, if I fall and break my leg. Got my weapon right here, too—he shoots at me, I can assure you, I'll be shooting back. Just lemme bum a couple butts off you, case I have to smoke off the bugs. I'll be perfectly all right.'

"So that satisfied him," Briggs said, "He shook out a couple of Luckies, and off I went. Having told him the exact opposite of what I figured was the case. That French kid hadn't run for the next county, soon's the third kid went for help. He'd lived up in the Notch all his life. It was wilder country, hundred yards from his house, 'n it ever thought of being, up around Huntington Dam. Power company built there, they clearcut all around it just to get equipment in. That's why it had such good hunting—rabbits, pheasants, woodcock, deer—all that nice low browse that came up after the trees went down. Lots of hiding places, too, for small animals, and big. That French kid wouldn't leave a buddy who got hurt out in the woods. If there was someone else who could go and get some help, as there had been in this case, then French would stay beside the body until that help either came, or he knew it didn't matter. And even then, I kind of thought, he still would not've run. Unless the people he was waiting for showed up armed to the teeth, and looked to him more like a posse than a rescue team. Which of course had been exactly what he'd seen: the U.S. Army coming for him, not to help but hunt him down.

"See, those people up the Notch," Briggs said, "those people know a lot. The stuff they know is different from the stuff most of us know, and they're a little weak on some things that we think are real important. But what's important to them, that stuff they really know. And if you'd had a nickel, I'd've bet you buck against it he saw that brigade a good mile off. Long before they could've seen him, at least—bet your ass on that. Those cops're good at spotting things, but just familiar things. It's a lot easier picking out a big Chrysler doing ninety, on a paved road, by itself, than it is to spot a young kid hunkered down behind a deadfall tree, in an old rainwash that's overgrown with brambles. And it's a lot harder, if the only people you've ever chased through the woods've been city boys escaping from the workhouse, who don't know the woods because they've never been in them before, than it is to catch a Notch boy in woods he knows—if he's afraid of you. They thought he ran because he felt guilty and was scared. Well, he probably did feel guilty, and you can be sure he was damned scared. But not: scared of taking the blame, the punishment for what he did. Scared of being shot down like a mad dog in his tracks.

"They also," Briggs said, "they were also figuring he'd run like they would've, if they'd been him. But this kid was an experienced hunter. Hell, I bet he didn't know what the words 'hunting season' meant. Not to us, at least. To him the hunting season was any day his father or his mother said: 'Get meat.' So if these cops were going to hunt him now, he'd really make them do it. And the way that he would do it was the way the game ducked him.

"See, you flush a smart old rabbit, he doesn't hightail it for Montpelier. He's never been in Montpelier, isn't curious about it, and sure can't read a map. The way that he got old was by always staying smart, and never going very far from territory he knows better'n the guy or dog that's chasing him. Or the fox, if it's a fox. He zigs this way, he zags that, he ducks behind a stone wall, he jumps over a brook, and then he dives down a hole. Catches his breath and watches careful, and watches a long time, too—because he knows that you're smart, too. Maybe smart enough to stop, just wait silent in your tracks until he comes out again, and gives himself away. Smart young bunnies, smart young deer: That's the big mistake they make, that turns them into someone's dinner and stops them from getting old. Leave the hiding places that they know, or come out of them too soon.

"So the way to find Tony French wasn't by going out on maneuvers or bivouac. The way to do it was to convince him it was safe to come out. Then he would."

"How'd you do it?" Beale said.

"Well," Briggs said, "I don't know how much gunnin' you did, when you were growin' up, but me and Ed there did a lot, 'til Ed there finally give it up, he was such a lousy shot."

"Huh," Cobb said, "only reason I quit was the lousy company. Spend all day tramping through the woods with farmboys never read a book and very seldom took a bath, all so's I could go home with a bunch of dead animals and get guts on all my clothes."

Briggs laughed. "Actually, I was kidding, Don. First part of his life, Ed here was a pretty decent hunter. Had the makings, anyway, he'd've listened to someone. But then his father sent him off to prep school there, and that's when Ed discovered that meat didn't come with fur and feathers, feet, and tails and stuff, and fish had no heads or fins. And none of it was ever bloody, raw, or even really fresh. If it wasn't in the meat case, cold, when you bought it at the store, it was frozen in the freezer or it came out of a can."

"You're partly right," Cobb said. "Until I was about twelve, I lived with a bunch of savages. Couple of them, I suspect, moved on to cannibal."

Briggs reached forward and patted Cobb on the shoulder. "Now don't get all upset, Ed," he said. "Want you to know, we didn't think any the less of you for it, when you stopped goin' gunnin'. We approved of it, in fact. Meant the chances of one of us getting plugged by you mistaking us for deer were considerably reduced, and that made us feel much better. Remember that day when you got that new Winchester twenty-two? The semiauto there, with that nifty Weaver scope? And you lighted off the first round at some vicious big brown sparrow— naturally you missed it, and a damned good thing it was: Those things attack if they're just wounded and they think you've got them cornered.

"Anyway, you wanted that first spent cartridge for a keepsake. Isn't that right, Ed? So that sweet little semi spit it out onto the ground, and you had us all helping you look for the damned shell. But you forgot the semi reloads automatically. And you didn't set the safety, either. So there's old Whip down on his knees, and you're bending down yourself, and has my memory gone bad, or did that thing go off? You know, I swear it did, Ed. I'd take an oath on that. It went off about two inches next to Whip's old nose, and scared the living shit out of him." Beale had begun laughing quietly, his body shaking with the effort of suppressing the noise.

"Go ahead, you guys," Cobb said. "Go ahead and have your fun. Just keep in mind when you get through, I know some stories too."

"Hey, Ed," Briggs said, "don't get the wrong impression from me, now. It isn't you I'm laughing at—it's Whip's damn fool reaction, makes me grin like this. Hopping around and yelling, calling you bad names—wasn't 'asshole' one of them? 'Fucking goddamned asshole'? 'You tryin' get me killed?'"

"Shut up," Cobb said. "I'll stop and let you off right here. You can walk your ass to Brandon, call your bride and get picked up. If she decides it's worth the trouble, wants you back there all that much. Get down to Boston, I'll see Calley, say you got cold feet."

"You can't do that, Ed," Briggs said. "And I wouldn't have to walk even if you did. All I'd have to do is just wait on the shoulder there. And inside five minutes, maybe ten, my pal Fairchild will be along. All I'll have to do is wave, and he'll stop and pick me up. 'I made that crazy bastard stop and let me off,' I'll say. 'He's driving like a maniac. Going a hundred easy. Just barely missed two head of cattle, school bus full of orphans, retired couple towing an Airstream behind their Mercury sedan, and the entire membership of the First Methodist Ladies' Choir practicing carols on the lawn. I think you'd better chase him. I'll be glad to testify.' The next time you talk to Calley it'll be from some jail cell. Your whole career'll be in shambles, right straight down the toilet."

Cobb scowled and turned on the radio. "Think I'll get the eleven news," he said. "See if anybody in the world is talking sense today."

"Anyway Don," Briggs said, "before Ed become a conscientious object-or, and gave up shooting things, he learned, if he remembers, the same crap that we all learned. He didn't do it as well, not that it mattered, because most of those tips we got from the old geezers down the store were worth about as much outdoors as fancy French cologne. Goddamned wooden duck calls, and the turkey calls and stuff: Somebody takes two pieces of hardwood and bores one out after he turns it on his lathe. Then he fits the second piece inside it nice and tight, and when you pull it back and forth, it screeches or it squawks. And that's supposed to drive the pheasants absolutely crazy to get laid. So crazy that they lose their minds and walk up to your gun.

"We believed all that shit, Don," Briggs said. "That was the only thing they were actually good for, any of those gadgets that we paid four bucks apiece for: Since we couldn't make the noise they made, we believed the guy who said that that was why we came home skunked. So we paid out our money, and it never dawned on us, even when we still got skunked, that the purpose of the gadget was not to fool the birds and beasts into getting themselves shot—it was to fool the stupid boys into parting with their cash. And from that point of view, they worked great.

"Anyway," Briggs said, "there was one animal noise that we could make by ourselves. Without store-bought equipment." Cobb was decelerating into Brandon, taking the gentle slope toward the quiet center dominated by the Brandon Inn, overlooking the common and the white wooden buildings around it. "He could make a noise like a squirrel."

Beale guffawed. "He still can," he said, "and he still does, too, now you mention it. When he gets all mad and gets to spluttering, he sounds exactly like a squirrel. That is exactly what it is."

Cobb drove at twenty through the center of town. He scowled, but he said nothing. "Well," Briggs said, "so can I, only I do it on purpose. And that's how I got the French kid to give up. Just exactly that kind of thing. Talking to the squirrels, same's we did when we were boys to get them 'round our side the tree."

"Sure," Cobb said. He used his tongue, teeth, and cheek to make a clicking sound. "Not sure it ever worked, though we did get our share of squirrels. But I doubt they thought what we thought they did—that we were other squirrels. Likelier it seems to me they came around to see what kind of asshole'd do that. Had the same effect of course—sense of humor can be dangerous, even for a squirrel."

"That's the one," Briggs said. "Well, I remembered that. Hell, we used that squirrel sound for everything. Calling our dogs—worked fine for that. Signaling to each other when we didn't want to scare the other animals—they probably had a good laugh, listening. But we all did it, everybody did, and I wasn't sure, but I figured, you know, the kids from the Notch did it, too.

"So," he said, "most of the search party'd worked upriver from the dam. Theory was the kid would've run away from the cops coming up from downriver. Which I thought he probably did—until he found a hidey-hole where he squinched down and let them by. And he doubled back behind them, back to where he started out, and got down low to the ground. And that was where he still was, watching. Waiting just as long's he could, and then waiting some more.

"Now that territory up there," Briggs said, "up around the dam, it's funny how you learn to listen around all that constant roar. It's something like when I was pitching. You first get up there, seems like the only thing you can possibly hear is the noise. It isn't. You can't hear the noise unless you strain. Thirty, forty thousand people can be screaming bloody murder in the stands, but when the other guys' best hitter comes up and says under his breath: 'I'm taking your ass downtown, pal, just throw the ball and duck,' all you can hear is *him*. And you think: 'Okay, my friend'—you don't say this; it's just what you're thinking—'we'll see who does the ducking here.' And throw it right at his ear.

"Well," Briggs said, "I got probably about half a mile, maybe a bit more, southwest of the dam. Downstream and downhill. Could still hear it, of course, but not really distracting. Crickets, night birds, maybe coyote—something howling long way off—and once or twice a good sharp scream: Something big'd caught something smaller, broke its neck with one good shake. Those sounds *were* distracting, not what I was looking for. But even though I didn't hear it—body shifting in the brush, someone taking a deep breath—and I didn't see it either— one branch moving in no breeze, one changed shadow from the moon—I still knew that I was there. I was where he was. It was like I felt the kid. Couldn't've told you where he was within twenty yards or so, but I knew he was there someplace.

"So I stopped," he said. "Kind of kicked my foot around the base of a big white pine—sitting on a possum-playing possum isn't my idea of fun; the first thing he does is piss—and when I'm sure it's vacant space, sat down and leaned my back. Not a sound. I know the French kid's out there, and I know he's watching me. I don't see him, but he sees me. He can't make out my features, wouldn't know me anyway, but he knows I'm looking for him, and that makes him afraid of me. This I do not want. So I make the squirrel sound."

Briggs made the clicking noise. "Now he's not gonna think I'm a giant-size squirrel, offering acorns or something. I'm not under that kind of impression. What I'm hoping he'll think is: 'No guy that sits down, don't try to sneak up, and then pretends he's a squirrel, no guy who does that can be too dangerous. What the hell does he want?' So I do it again. I don't expect him to answer. Just think a bit more. He's got to be tired, he's probably hungry, lived on berries and roots for three days—wouldn't dare to shoot anything. The only thing he's not's thirsty; got a whole cold river for that. I make the noise again.

"See," Briggs said, "I'm getting confident." The Imperial left Brandon behind, and Cobb took it back up to fifty on the Rutland road. "It's hard to judge time in the woods, especially after dark. But I figure, least ten minutes, I've been sitting there and making those silly noises. And he hasn't shot me yet, which he easily could do. So progress is being made.

"Now," Briggs said, "I am no kid, and I know that, but recently I was. Lil says it's not that recently, but that's another thing. When I was a kid, Ed, and you were one, too, I used to smoke the cigarettes. Remember cigarettes?"

"Gwendolyn made me give them up," Cobb said. "Said I could be too fat, or I could smoke the coffin nails, but no fair daring heart attack with two things every day. Guess I was a lucky one—didn't bother me that much, even though I thought it would."

"It was the surgeon general's thing, did me," Briggs said, "back in 'sixty-three. That damned report came out? We were in L.A. when I read it. Scared me half to death. Threw my cigarettes away, and then I went half batty. But damnit all, I made it stick. I sure had good friends, then—put up with me during that."

"I never took it up, the first place," Beale said. "Never had to quit."

"You see, Hank?" Cobb said. "That's why you never met this guy 'til

194

fairly recently. When we were all growing up, little creeps like he was, beating their meat down at Cranbrook, they weren't allowed to meet coarse guys like us, like we were then, at least. His idea of raising hell was taking two desserts. Cutting daily Mass, or maybe having impure thoughts."

"I knew lots of guys who did smoke," Beale said. "Just never appealed to me, was all. I didn't like the taste."

"I did," Briggs said.

"So did I," Cobb said. "I fuckin' loved the taste."

"But even more than that," Briggs said, "it was the smell I loved. Not the rotten stale one of the room the morning after—the one that comes when you light up. God that smoke smelled good. I miss it to this day. The first thing that I always did, finished gunnin' for the day, as soon's we came out of the woods, I lit myself a smoke."

"Fire?" Beale said. "Was that why you waited?"

"Nah," Cobb said. "I bet there never was a fire, a forest fire, I mean, that someone started with a butt he didn't fieldstrip. Never mind that Smokey Bear shit that you hear all the time. That's just to keep the folks alert. There ain't no truth in it."

"I agree with you," Briggs said, "about the cigarettes. Camp fires that you didn't douse? Sure, they start a few. But lightning's usually what does it, almost every time. No, the reason you don't smoke in the woods is because animals don't smoke. And the animals not only know this, they've got damned good smellers on them. So when they smell tobacco smoke, they know they've got visitors. And I don't care how much you use, the musks and all those oils supposed to mask your human scent, the minute you light up a smoke, they've got you pegged for miles. One guy on a deer stand that gives in and has a smoke, he can ruin a day's hunting, everyone for ten, twelve miles. That's the reason you don't smoke. Smoke gives you away.

"Unless," Briggs said, "unless what you're hunting's not something to shoot, but a kid who's scared to death and'd like a smoke himself. Especially a Lucky—nothing smells as good as those. A menthol, Salem, Newport, that possibly might do it, but if the kid's like most kids, and he ever took a drag, and he's been three days without one, well, a Lucky drives him nuts.

"It did, and he came out."

"You just sat there and smoked, and it flushed him out," Beale said.

"I just sat there and *lit* it," Briggs said. "I didn't smoke the thing. Blew the smoke right out. I was scared to death I might inhale it, go back to where I was before. Took about six puffs and just blew that smoke right out, and pretty soon I hear some rustling and I said, a normal voice: 'Tony, my name's Henry Briggs. I won't let anybody hurt you. I just want you to come out so we can fix it so they don't. You want the rest of this smoke here, I'll give it to you. And then I've got another one, which can be all yours.' And then there was some more soft noise, and he was standing there. Nice fat gibbous moon that night—warm summer on the way."

"Did you talk to him at all?" Beale said.

"Sure," Briggs said. "Soon's he had the first one burned down to his teeth, I started asking him some questions, and gave him the second one. It was what I'd figured. Just what I'd figured it to be. And I told him I'd get up at the inquest, or a trial, if there was one, and say what he told me. And also that what he told me jibed with what I'd seen myself. Which it did, and which I did. Prosecutor didn't like it whole lot. Neither'd some the cops. They looked at him and they saw this big, rangy, bearded, mountain man that kept them out three days, and said: 'That's a killer there.' But they were wrong. He wasn't that. He wasn't overbright, and books weren't too familiar to him, but he could read, and write, and think. Knew right from wrong, in other words, and that he'd done nothing wrong. Stupid, sure, and thoughtless, yup—just never thought he'd miss, probably never had before, when he fired down on that snake."

"What'd you do with him?" Beale said.

"Walked him back to where the cops were," Briggs said. "Took his guns, of course. It was about nine-thirty, getting on toward ten. Cops were all asleep in their cruiser cars. Put him in the backseat of Fairchild's machine. Then rapped on Fairchild's window, woke him up, and said: 'Hey Ron?' His partner woke up too. He rolled the window down. 'Yeah,' he says. 'What do you want? Time is it, anyway?'

" 'Just wanted tell you, I'm headed home. You guys take over now.' 'Hey,' he says, he's awake now, 'you can't just run off like this. You said you're gonna stay. What about the French kid, huh? You just giving up?'

" 'Not what I said,' I said to him. 'Not what I said at all. All I said was "heading home. You take over now." You turn around and look, your back seat, you'll see Tony French. You wanna take these firearms here, keep them in the trunk, you should all be fine. Just radio the captain there, tell him the kid walked in and you're bringing him back down. Oh, and have somebody call his family. Possible they're worried.' And then I went home."

"And Captain Hiller," Cobb said, the Imperial holding steady at fifty in descent through the foothills of the Green Mountains north of Rutland, "called a big fuckin' press conference. Took the credit for the cops."

"You should be glad he did," Briggs said. "Should be today, at least. Fairchild said to me back there: 'I still don't know why I should do this. Let that bigshot politician go, so he just does what he damned pleases. Doesn't matter he gets caught—he still always farts through silk.'

" 'Well,' I said, 'I got one reason, pretty good—at least I think it is. Captain Hiller and yourself, too, you guys looked pretty fine on TV one night, in the papers the next day. And there's at least a couple people think the captain and his stalwart troopers might've overdone it some, hogging praise they didn't earn.' "

"What'd he say?" Cobb said.

"He was all right about it," Briggs said. "He said: 'You may have a point.' "

19

Calley Consultants operated out of two thousand square feet of office space on the third floor of the Park Square Office Building in Boston. The marble-floored arcade on the street level had not been cleaned for a while, and the small shops lining it were evenly divided between vacant spaces and dimly lighted stores offering shoe repairs, greeting cards, and laundry and cleaning services.

Briggs squared his shoulders and entered the elevator, emerging into the greater dimness of the third-floor corridor and taking one useless trip to his left before locating the Calley office at the end of the corridor to his right. The reception area was windowless; the only light was from a brass lamp with a dark brown shade on the unoccupied desk. Briggs saw three wing chairs upholstered in fabric, and an elliptical coffee table with three heavy glass ashtrays and a number of discarded newspapers. He said: "Hello?" There was no answer. He sat down in the chair farthest from the door. Behind him he could hear a phone ring, the sound stopping midway through the fourth ring. Some time passed.

The entrance door opened and a lanky man, coatless, with dark hair, a bow tie, and suspenders came in. He had a key on a large metal ring in his right hand. He closed the door before he noticed Briggs. "Oh," he said. "You here for something?" He went behind the desk, opened the top drawer, and dropped the keyring in.

"I think so," Briggs said. "Henry Briggs. There're two more guys with me. They're parking the car."

They had arrived well behind schedule in Boston; Cobb had insisted upon detouring through Springfield, Massachusetts, because he liked the pot roast served at The Fort Restaurant. Beale had had a good deal to say about losing more than an hour of valuable time for pot roast. Briggs had kept his mouth shut, except to try the pot roast, which was good.

Another dispute had arisen when they left the Massachusetts Turnpike at the Prudential exit. Beale had demanded to know where Cobb planned to park the Imperial. Cobb had identified his choice as the Motor Mart Garage in Park Square, "right near the fucking building where we're going."

Beale had exploded, saying that the ramps and turns of the Motor Mart had been built to accommodate Model T Fords and similar cars of heights greater than their lengths or widths, and forbidding Cobb to risk the long, low, wide Imperial by driving into them: "I'm still planning on selling this thing to someone, you know. Just because I let you drive it like a maniac doesn't mean I actually want it wrecked."

Briggs had opened the right rear door when Cobb paused at a traffic light at the intersection of St. James and Clarendon, obtained the office number and floor of the Calley offices, and said he would meet them there.

"We're supposed to meet some people here."

The man gazed at him. "You're not," he said, "you're not selling something, are you?"

"I don't think so," Briggs said.

"Office supplies?" the man said. "Magazine subscriptions? Plants? Coffee service? Anything like that?"

"No," Briggs said.

"Because we already get all that stuff," the man said.

"Yeah," Briggs said.

"I ask, who you're meeting?"

"Mr. Calley?" Briggs said.

"What's he look like?" the man said.

"I don't know," Briggs said. "Never laid eyes on the guy."

"Okay," the man said. "Try it another way. What're you meeting him about?"

"I don't know," Briggs said. "Well, it's politics. But he's the one, supposed to do the talking. The other people that're coming, that's why we all came down. See what he's got to say. But he's never seen them, either—least I don't think he has. And then he's going to tell us. I just don't know what."

"What're their names?" the man said.

"Hey," Briggs said, "you Calley?"

"No," the man said.

"Well, fine," Briggs said. "If you happen to see Calley sometime today, and I still happen to be here, you can tell him Mr. Briggs's waiting to see him. And if my friends've shown up by then, well, I'll introduce you. And if you don't happen to see Mr. Calley, or I don't happen to be here, well, just go and fuck yourself. All right?"

The man stared at him. He picked up the phone on the desk. He dialed three numbers. "Security?" he said. "Yeah. Calley Consulting. Third floor. Got another camper in here, 's what it looks like to me." He replaced the handset in the cradle. He sat down behind the desk and folded his hands. "I just called Security," he said.

"You're a very bright boy," Briggs said. "I bet, I bet if you wanted you could call the Avon Lady. Order out for pizza. Get a cab."

"You could save yourself some trouble, you know," the man said.

"Ah, I wouldn't want to do that," Briggs said. "Been too long since I had trouble. I could use some trouble."

"All you got to do's just stand up, walk out of here. Security guys get here, well, I'll tell them that you left."

"Save you the trouble," Briggs said. "I will still be here. They can see it for themselves."

"They'll make life hard for you," the man said.

"I doubt it," Briggs said. "I gave you my right name. Told you why I'm here. They can check my story. Just ask for Mr. Calley. He don't know my name from Adam's, I'll leave on my own."

The man studied him. He picked up the phone again. He dialed one number. He cupped his right hand over the mouthpiece and muttered into it. The entrance door opened. Cobb and Beale came in. Beale shut the door behind them. Briggs stood up. "Where'd you end up parking?" Briggs said. "Out by Fenway Park?"

Cobb looked disgusted. "No," he said, "Nervous Nellie here made me put it under the Common, and we hadda wait about ten minutes for a car to come out, 'fore we could get in, and then ride around in the dark tryin' to find the place he left."

"That's all right," Beale said. "Takes a little extra time, find a safe place to put it? Least I know when I get back, it won't've been remodeled."

The man at the desk said "just a second" into the phone and held it off to the side. "Who're you?" he said.

Cobb took one step forward. "Ed Cobb," he said. He indicated Beale. "Don Beale. Here to see Tom Calley. He's expecting us."

The man studied Cobb. He nodded. He put the handset back to his ear. "Cobb's here," he said. He squinted. "Yeah," he said. He looked up. "No, *two* other guys. Yeah, one says his name's Briggs." He nodded. He put the phone back in the cradle. He stood up. "Have a seat," he said. He vanished into the gloom of the corridor behind the reception desk.

Cobb and Donald Beale took the wing chairs to Briggs's right. "They give you a warm welcome too, Hank?" he said.

"Few minutes," Briggs said. "Nothing serious."

"But nowhere near as rough as that cop out there this morning, right?" Beale said. Briggs grinned, but Cobb said nothing.

The entrance door opened. A heavyset man with a handlebar mustache came in. He was wearing a blue shirt with a red silk tie pulled down from the collar. His dark trousers were baggy, held up by a wide belt buckled with a winged-wheel Harley-Davidson emblem. He inspected them. "Well," he said, "this must be the Vermont contingent. Follow me."

He walked past the reception desk and into the corridor. Briggs stood up and waited for Cobb to take the lead followed by him and Beale. When they entered the internal corridor, the man had disappeared. At the end of the corridor they were blinded by light from three large windows. They stopped for an instant. The corridor, narrowed by file cabinets, branched to the left and the right. There was no one in sight.

Cobb cleared his throat. Donald Beale nudged Briggs in the ribs. Briggs glanced at him. Beale nodded toward Cobb, who cleared his throat again. There was no response. "*Hey,*" Cobb said, his voice coming out as a roar, "Caroline Cooke told us you're smart. Have I got to call her up now? Huh, friends? Give her the word you're stupid?"

The heavy man appeared at the door of the office at the end of the corridor to the left. "Down here," he said. He disappeared again.

"You'd better be there when I get there," Cobb said. "I can do this, and I'll do this, but I don't like doing this, and I don't like rudeness. You disappear on me again, you Cheshire cat, I'll have your head on a pike."

The lanky man appeared at the door of the second office down the corridor. Cobb waved his hand at him. "You get the hell back in there, sonny," he said. "Get the hell out of my way." The lanky man retreated and shut the door. Cobb whacked it with the heel of his hand. "And stay in there, you son of a bitch. You just get up on your tire swing in there, have yourself a damned banana, and don't come out 'til I say so."

Cobb slowed his pace as they reached the office at the end. He entered it cautiously. The others followed. "As I live and breathe," Cobb said, "the sanctum fucking sanctorum."

Calley sat at the head of a long oak table haphazardly surrounded by seven battered oak chairs. "Gentlemen," he said. He gestured languidly with his left hand. "Make yourselves comfortable."

Cobb pointed to a chair at the side of the table. "Don," he said, "put this down the other end." Beale placed it so Cobb faced Calley. Cobb sat down carefully. Briggs and Beale took seats flanking him.

"Now, Mr. Calley," Cobb said, "these two gentlemen are Don Beale and Henry Briggs, case your memory needs refreshment, and it slipped your mind, why we're here. We got something in common, the four of us today. We are here because Don Beale here's paid you money. And so've some other people. I asked Don to do that. Caroline asked the others. Mr. Briggs here's your new client. And that is why you got the money. Not because you are good-lookin', not because your teeth are pearly, but because you got some money from some friends of Henry Briggs. To advise him. Not to treat him, not to treat us, to some of your ego games. Have I made myself clear so far?"

Calley grinned. "You've made it clear," he said, "that you don't understand the situation. I told Caroline you didn't, and she said I was wrong. But Caroline's the one that's wrong. She gave you the wrong impression. We're not looking for work. We weren't looking for work. I

202

took this on as a favor to her. And I asked her to make sure you understood that. Which she clearly didn't.

"This is a hopeless shot," he said. "I don't deal in those. If I affiliate myself with an obvious sure loser, the guy invariably loses. And then publicly blames it on me. I deal in images, you see? So I know how to make them, and I start with my own. You got it right that some people want me to be Mr. Briggs's advisor. Within limits, I was willing. But those limits have been reached. He has to understand that. My first client's always myself. When it looks to me like my own image's getting jeopardized, I start to get nervous. The worst kind of jeopardy is staying with a loser.

"So, this wasn't my idea, Mr. Cobb, meeting with you guys today. I advised me not to do it, but Caroline sweet-talked me into doing at least this. And then you made me get ready for it on the hurry-up, which I hate to do because then I'm never sure that I have got it right. Except this time—this time I am.

"I said I didn't like it when you said I had to do it, and I won't pretend I like it now. But I did it, with my teeth clenched—I'm doing what you wanted. And that's all I'm going to do unless heaven sends a message pretty soon I can't ignore."

"So give the money back," Beale said. "We'll find someone else."

"In the first place," Calley said, "I've spent or earned the money. So I can't give it back. Another problem with this was: I didn't know the district. Now I do, but that cost money. You don't get that money back. Even though what I have learned is just what I said it is: You have got a hopeless cause."

"He doesn't seem to think so," Briggs said, nodding toward Cobb. "He told me: an uphill fight. But nothing like: It's hopeless."

"Well, Mr. Briggs," Calley said, "then one of us is wrong. He is, or I am. I can live with that. I've been wrong before. Maybe Mr. Cobb has, too. I have no way of knowing that. We've profiled your district, all right? We've done a phone survey. Eight hundred people— well, eight hundred numbers, anyway. You've still got party lines up there, so dialing one number often got us two or three responses. More bang for the buck, as Curtis LeMay used to say. Unfortunately, from your point of view, the majority of habitual voters are entirely satisfied with Mr. Wainwright. I'm not saying they like him. I'm not saying they admire him. All I'm saying is that they have no complaint against him. They don't—in an affirmative way—they don't expect much from their congressman, and as long as he doesn't deliver much, they're satisfied.

"This leaves you with two alternatives," Calley said. "You can set out to educate them. Make them see that they *should* expect something from their congressman, and, by extension, their government. My guess is: That won't work. They prize their independence. They'll resent even the suggestion that they need governmental help, and they'll vote against you for making it.

"The other track," Calley said, "is to out-Wainwright Wainwright. Tell them you'll do more of less. Which of course immediately raises the question of: Why should they change? If they're satisfied with the bump on the log that they've got, why move to a newer bump?"

"They haven't had the damned choice, since after World War Two," Cobb said.

"That's essentially true," Calley said. "But all that does is move the question back one step. Why is it that they haven't had a real choice, in all those many years? Most likely because they haven't wanted one. You offer them one now—will they want it? Well, if you find a thirsty man on his hands and knees in the desert, and you offer him some water, he will grab it from you. But if you meet a man on his way to the bathroom in a beer house, and you offer him the same water, he will turn it down.

"There simply isn't any core of discontent about Wainwright that seems promising to tap. He doesn't show the negatives. Well, he does, but in the Second, negatives are positives. They don't think much of him, and that's the way they want him, their congressman to be: someone they don't *have* to think much about. Anything you do try to do will contradict that attitude. You'll be asking them to think about something they don't want to think about. They won't like it. So they'll either tune you out, or else they'll vote against you. You don't have a prayer, chum. I'm sorry, but you don't."

Donald Beale started to get out of his chair. "Siddown," Cobb said. Beale sat down. "We wanted to pray," Cobb said to Calley, "we would've stayed in Vermont, and gone to the churches of our re-spective choices, and put our dollar in the free-will offering plates.

But we didn't want to do that. Prayer's got nothing to do with Congress. This is a political matter. Politics is what you do. So we came down here. It's not your political job now, to tell us how Henry's going to lose. It's your political job to tell us how Henry's going to win."

There was noise in the corridor. Two guards in brown uniforms entered Calley's office. Both of them were young and black. Calley waved them off. "It's all right," he said. "Everything's all right."

"We got a call," the first one said, "you had an intruder. Mr. Esterly called down."

"That's the fellow," Calley said, gesturing toward Briggs. "His name's Henry Briggs. He's not an intruder. He's supposed to be here. We get a lot of browsers in here. Most of them reporters, snooping on our clients, and we have to bounce them out. But Leon always overreacts. Everything is fine."

The second guard frowned. "Briggs," he said. "Didn't you play ball?"

Briggs nodded. "I thought so," the guard said. "Jesus. You could throw."

"Thank you," Briggs said.

"I seen you, man," the guard said. "Seen you, good God, must be, ten, twelve years ago. First year you were around."

"My rookie year," Briggs said. "Fifteen years ago."

"And you're just *mowin'* 'em down," the guard said.

"I used to throw pretty hard," Briggs said.

The guard shook his head. He grinned. "Never thought I'd have this chance," he said. He extended his hand. "I'm gonna tell my kids about this. I met Henry Briggs."

"Of course they won't know who the hell you're talking about," Briggs said, rising from the chair. "But I appreciate it."

"Hey," the guard said, "some of us remember."

The guards left the office. Calley smiled. "Leon knows everything there is to know about dealing with the public," he said. "Except how to do it."

"And Henry knows nothing about dealing with the public," Cobb said. "Except exactly how to do it. Ever cross your mind with all your polls and shit that you waste money on, might be a good idea to factor in a little thing like that?"

"Our approach, Mr. Cobb," Calley said, "is empirical. Strictly, completely, empirical. Have you got a point, if it's the point I think you're making? That some things about politics aren't empirical? Sure. Of course you do. And no, we don't factor those in, the guy's looks or how he smiles. Because so far at least, so far's we know, no one's figured out a way to calibrate how one guy's looks, his manner, or his charm affects voters. If we could do that, and be sure, be absolutely sure, that we'd identified a way of shaking hands and smiling that makes people love your ass, and also had it nailed down what makes them hate your guts, every office like this one'd have an in-house plastic surgeon and a weight room with a trainer, and every politician that's showed up here since November nineteen sixty'd've left this place the spitting image, JFK, maybe fake bullet holes and all. They sure, the big majority this country sure liked him a whole lot better, good and dead, 'n they did when he was breathing.

"Thing of it is," Calley said, "somewhere there's a line you wouldn't cross to get that vote, even if you'd win. Stopping breathing's probably on the other side of it. I don't rule it out, mind you; I've seen politicians that would at least consider it, if they thought it guaranteed a nice plurality. And suppose you did discover things've changed: Now average Joes love rich kids; pretty hard to take a guy like Mister Briggs and make him filthy rich, even though I doubt he'd really mind. And even though he's young enough, for a politician, he's just now getting started. So by the time he gets somewhere, by then he won't be young.

"So, that's the thing I'm driving at," Calley said. "That's what I'm telling you. You, Mr. Cobb, are sitting there and getting ready, tell me you are a known Democrat, and you got yourself elected from a district that'd never done a thing like that before. But you happen to come from an Assembly district, 'bout five percent the geographical size of the Second, where flukes and chance and changes in land use've concentrated a whole bunch of immigrants. In a region that already happened to've bred an unusual number of native-born mavericks. You live in a pocket of Dems.

"You were, in other words, lucky, another factor we don't weigh when we map out advice. Not because we don't respect it as a very potent force, but because we have no way of quantifying who's got luck and who has not. And, if we did have such a way, what we'd tell the

206

lucky ones would not be: 'Run for office.' We would tell them: 'Play the market, with as much margin's you can get. That will make you major rich, and you won't need the office—you can buy the guy who's in it. Hire him to do your donkey work, and take all the abuse. As long's he does what you tell him, you're green and golden, chum.'

"Your situation," Calley said, "was the same as the olive's in the gin. The blindfolded guy who just eats the olive says: 'This is a glass full of olives, that somebody dumped in the gin.' Because that's what he got out of it. But the blindfolded guy who drank all the gin, after the olive was gone, he says: 'That was a glass full of gin.' The Democrats in Vermont are scattered olives here and there, absolutely drowning in Republican gin lakes. The guy who tells me your election, or the governor's, proves that a good Demmie beats the odds now is a guy who's fooling himself, because that just did not happen. What happened in your two cases may be the start of a new trend—I doubt it, but it could be—but that trend if it is one hasn't changed things enough yet to transform the Wainwright district.

"So," Calley said, "if Mr. Briggs runs now, as I expect he will— I'm not under the impression what I say will change his plans—the best that he can hope for is that it really is a trend, and that the trend will spread. So that and maybe if he runs again, in 'seventy, and then runs again some more, sometime before the century ends he may get elected. All depending on the trend, if that is what it is, and how fast it spreads, making him the heir apparent, just reward for all his pain.

"For you, gentlemen," Calley said, "that may be enough. Some people like to play cards and gamble, but they don't make their living from it. Me, I do. I'm not after fun. It's purely the living I want. So I stick to poker, and win."

Cobb's face had become progressively redder. He started to speak and Briggs stopped him. "Just a second, okay, Ed?" he said. Cobb glanced at him and subsided. "I got a couple questions, if it's all right," Briggs said. Cobb made a brushing gesture with his right hand. "Mr. Calley," Briggs said, "I understand your position. I played for some bad teams and got tagged as a loser, and I didn't like it a lot. Then I played for some good clubs, and, all of a sudden, I was a winner, you know? It was a lot more fun, and I made more money, too. Would've done it sooner, I had your option here. You get to choose who you play

207

for. And you gave us good reasons, the choice that you made, even though Ed here doesn't like it."

"I don't like it either," Beale said. "I don't like a man who takes money from me, and then says I get nothing for it. Except maybe the horselaugh for letting him take me. I don't go for that stuff at all."

"Don," Briggs said, "the man didn't say that. What he said was that we got what you paid for, you and Caroline Cooke and the other people that gave. You and me, and maybe even Ed, a little bit anyways, we thought we were buying a miracle. A secret that nobody else knows, but he does, and he's going to tell it to us. So we win. Well, he's telling us that he looked for the secret, and that was all that he said he'd do. And what he can tell, there just isn't one, and he won't blow smoke up our ass. And that we should respect him for that. Realize that we got our money's worth."

"That's exactly right," Calley said. "You put the point well, Mr. Briggs. Better'n I did, I think."

"I hope so, Mr. Calley," Briggs said, "because I haven't finished yet and I got a couple more things to say here. In the first place, I think you did a truly shitty job of trying to get that fact across. At least a couple times there, you as much as told us that you called up all those people and asked them if they liked Wainwright, and when they said, the most of them, that they liked him okay, then you went and asked them if they might like someone else better. That about the gist of it?"

"About," Calley said. "Someone else who took positions on the issues that didn't really contradict Wainwright's record but at least varied significantly from it. What we did basically was tell them how he'd come down on things like the war, price supports, health insurance, inflation—all that stuff. And then tell them what most Democrats— not identifying them—thought about those issues, and ask them which they preferred."

"But not: 'Who,' " Briggs said.

"No," Calley said. "Our orders were to ascertain whether there are any issues on which the majority of voters in the Second District, regardless of whether they know it, hold opinions that differ significantly from those of their congressman, and if we found any, whether those philosophical differences would be enough to cause them to switch parties a year from November. Very seldom did we get the kind of responses to the first set of questions that would have warranted going on to the second. Wainwright's district's secure."

"Okay," Briggs said. "I want a list of both sets of questions. And a complete chart of the answers that you got."

"Why?" Calley said. "Why do you want all that stuff? I've told you the results."

"Well," Briggs said, "I suppose I could say: ' 'Cause we paid for it, so we own it, so give us our property.' But we're all high-toned gents here, and we don't talk like that. So I'll just say: 'Because I'm a rookie at this, and I don't know much about it, and you're an experienced player—maybe I'll learn from you.' Like I did from the veterans who charted my pitches, told me what was getting hit and what was fooling hitters, so that I'd know what to throw, and what not to throw."

Calley nodded. "You're a reasonable man, Hank," he said. "I'll have Esterly get you the stuff."

" 'Mr. Briggs,' to you, Mr. Calley," Briggs said. "Let's keep things professional here."

In Park Square the wind came down Stuart Street sharp-edged, and all three men hunched themselves into their coats. "Great," Cobb said, "now we get to freeze our asses off, traipsing back to the Common."

"Hail a cab, Ed," Beale said. "I'll pay for it, all right? Cheaper'n a fender job, we'd parked where you wanted."

They started east across Arlington Street as the traffic paused at the light on Boylston, and Cobb said: "Nice fuckin' guy that Calley is. Caroline got clipped. And therefore so did we. Drive down here to hear we're fools."

"Forget it," Briggs said, the printouts of the poll under his arm. "Don't kid yourself and don't kid me. This changes nothing. You asked me to run, and I said I'd think about it. I thought about it and decided I would do what you proposed. I didn't think then I was golden, and I don't think so now. Never mind what that guy said. I said I would; I will."

"You'll run anyway?" Cobb said.

"I'll announce when the deer season's over," Briggs said. "I do what I say I will do."

20

Russ Wixton at 7:15 on the evening of November 14th kept his appointment with Ed Cobb in the Montpelier Tavern. They agreed that it was cold outside. "I came out of the State House tonight," Cobb said, "old Ethan Allen coughed up there on his pedestal and asked me if there's any way he could spend the night inside. Said he never got so cold when he was Italian marble, 'maybe some of that nice, warm Mediterranean sunlight gets trapped in the rock over there.' But since they rebuilt him out of Danby stone back in 'forty-one, he's been freezing his balls off every year."

"And knowing you," Wixton said, hanging up his coat, "you told him that there wasn't; kindness goes against your grain." He took the stool next to Cobb's. "As, I assume you agree, Ed, simple fairness does not. Unless you think it'd be fair to haul a man out in this cold after sunset, without planning to tell him something worthwhile." He ordered a Johnny Walker Red and water.

Cobb showed half a smile. "Such as what, Russ?"

"Such as," Wixton said, "a word that finally lets me go with an exclusive that I've had for six, eight weeks, as you damned well know, that I haven't gone with because I gave a man my word."

Cobb expanded the partial smile into a sly grin. "Well, you see, Russ," he said, "that should teach you a useful lesson, a reminder why you newspaper guys should never give your word. You don't have enough practice at it, keeping it, I mean, and then when you really have to, it really bothers you."

"Oh," Wixton said, "no more'n a chunk of a Smokehouse Almond you got stuck in your teeth after takeoff from Boston on a nonstop to the West Coast and not a toothpick in sight. But I did it. I let Henry paint me right into a nice corner, and not a day's gone by since I didn't open up opposition or watch the magic box at night, that I didn't dread seeing someone beat me to it. Now, you gonna set me free, Massa Lincoln, please?"

"Look," Cobb said, "you can't use this on my say-so, all right? You've got to corral the horse for yourself now, and get it out of his mouth. How you do that's your problem. But I can tell you, I'm telling you now, the 'let's-think-about-this-crackpot-idea' is over—he's gone beyond that. Hank Briggs is running for Congress. I don't think he's got a snowball's chance, but he wants to and there's no one else."

Wixton stared at him. After a few moments he said: "You know, Ed, I've got to admire you. I don't want to—it's against my religion. Or would be if I had one. But I have to respect a man who can do that. Do what you've just done. Sit there and pretend you didn't dragoon Henry into this, very much against his will, telling him you really think he can knock Bob Wainwright off when you and I both know that you think no such damned thing, and tell me without cracking one smile that it's all his own idea. You're a piece of work, my friend. You're a real piece of work."

Cobb pulled a small bowl of mixed nuts closer to him and selected a cashew. He put it into his mouth. He pushed the bowl toward Wixton. "Thanks, Russ," he said. "No almonds here, but would you like a nut?"

Shortly before midnight on the Tuesday before Thanksgiving, Wixton reached Briggs by telephone at home. "You're a hard man to locate, Henry," he said. "I know it's late, but spare me a minute?"

"Hey, Russ," Briggs said, "the nimrods're out. You know me, I'm just doing my job."

"I do know you," Wixton said, "and I also know Ed Cobb, and he tells me you're gonna do what you told me quite a while ago you were thinking about doing. Now this is on the record, Hank: Are you going against Wainwright?"

Briggs said: "Yep."

"*Okay,*" Wixton said. "I'm gonna go with it. Going the holiday morning."

"Okay by me," Briggs said. "Appreciate you sitting tight on it long's you have already."

"Well, glad to hear you say that, Henry," Wixton said. "How about you show me your appreciation, by not leaking it to anyone who might jump me on it?"

"Happy to oblige, Russ," Briggs said. "We've known each other a long time. Anybody else calls up, well, I won't be here."

Russ Wixton's Thanksgiving column in the *Valley Press* read as follows:

"This is the time of the year when all natural human instincts in this part of the world call for imitation of the bear's. The light comes late, shines thin and dwindles fast, and the snow soon piles around the eaves to meet the icicles descending. Politicians say that even Ethan Allen shivers on his State House pedestal, as this time of year comes 'round. This is no time to venture out of doors, where the only sounds are those of the ice cracking and reforming on the ponds, the soft rush and then the thud of snow falling from the overladen branches of the evergreens, the keening edge of the wind that comes down sharpened by its journey across the barrens of Canada. This is the time, these days and nights, to hunker down beside a low fire, fingering the remaining coins of the holidays, conserving our strength for the dark cold brunt of the season ahead, considering what has happened in the year so far, meditating on what is to come.

"This sort of inward-turning tendency contradicts the newsman's basic plan of occupation. The very dailiness of our jobs conditions us to covet what is freshest of events and makes us impatient for what will make them obsolete. The quotidian dominates our working hours, and, sooner or later, one way or the other, we tend to lose sight of the destination in our close attention to the journey, and of whether progress can be measured.

"If there has ever been an American Thanksgiving morn inappropriate for that habit (and there probably has been, come to think of it; nearly 200 years ago, George Washington and his frozen remnant gathering at Valley Forge had ample leisure to reflect on whether their chosen mission—and that of Ethan Allen, too, that habitual thief, scarcely more comfortable in Dorset—had been such a good idea), this is surely it. Stepping back from a summer that left our cities torn by riots and many people dead at the hands of hostile men (not since the Civil War more than 100 years ago have we Americans been so ready to commit wholesale violence on one another); taking still another long and painful look at whether a long-promised victory is any closer to achievement over there in Vietnam; taking inventory of the blood and treasure that we have expended thusfar to repair injustice here at home, and prevent its continuation overseas, it is almost impossible to see much to celebrate as this old year winds down and a new year rolls around.

"But it is necessary, all the same. And there are some indications, faint right now but growing stronger, that if we are not yet through with political convulsions—and no informed observer I have talked to thinks we are; most think they've just begun—the ones that seem to be in store may leave us stronger and more peaceful, and somewhat better off.

"We Vermonters have the reputation, south of Brattleboro, north of Newport, east of White River Junction and west of St. Albans, of preferring a marching cadence different from that set by most drummers. Some call us 'conservative'; others call us 'cussed,' but none of them convinces us that we don't see pretty clearly in the purer air we have, in these Green Mountains where we live. And this Vermonter, at least, sees or thinks he sees in recent developments some substantial reason to be cautiously encouraged.

"The crucial event of the coming Presidential Year, after the election's over and the acrimony spent, may very well turn out to be one that's already happened: the appearance of Sen. Eugene McCarthy, Democrat of Minnesota, as a challenger of Lyndon Johnson for his Party's nomination at the annual convention set for next summer in Chicago.

"This nation is not used to selecting presidents from among its ranks of poets—and a good thing, too, the man says, if you've read some of their stuff. Neither is this nation accustomed anymore to assessing candidates for high office purely by referring to what they say about the issues. The foreigners who surround us in this clamorous Republic

213

share at least one of our traits: In neighboring New Hampshire and New York and in Wisconsin, all the way to sometimes-baffling California, they too stress the practical. One seasoned fellow that I talked to in Montpelier looked at the McCarthy story from a thoughtful angle:

" 'I don't think there's any question,' he said, 'but that if you asked them, and they really thought about it, most of the people in this country could find at least one real good reason why they think McCarthy's right. Most of them probably wouldn't choose the same one he did. I don't know if "this is wrong, and therefore we shouldn't do it" is an argument for getting out that would appeal to most. But getting out's the issue, and there's lots of reasons for it. It costs too much, in lives alone. We haven't got the money, if we're also really serious about this Great Society. You could go on and on.

" 'So the question maybe isn't whether this McCarthy guy sees something that the other pols've missed. The question may be whether, in this day and age, a man can be elected just on what he says he believes. Think about it. Have we ever had a president elected on that ground alone?

" 'Don't tell me "Lincoln." That's not true. He didn't win because he said that slavery was so awful he would go to war to end it. His campaign speech was that if we didn't end it, or at least stop it from spreading, we'd have to go to war about it and he didn't feature that.

" 'Grant and Eisenhower: elected to reward them for their military triumphs. FDR: elected because everyone who blamed Hoover for getting us in trouble just wanted someone else. If FDR'd done in office what he said he'd do, to get it, he would've been another Hoover, and he would've been thrown out.

" 'Maybe, just maybe,' this man said, 'you could say "Woodrow Wilson." That he got himself elected because he sounded like a pacifist and that's what people voted for. But of course he turned out different, which might mean he was a hypocrite or could mean he changed his mind. No, the only presidential candidate that had an actual chance he got by offering ideas, I think, was William Jennings Bryan. I remind you: Bryan lost.'

"Well, to that man it may be that the best response is: Change. This summer's convention in Chicago will be called to order 60 years after Bryan accepted the last of his three nominations to lead the national

214

ticket. Two declared wars and one so-called police action began and ended in the 42 years that passed between Bryan's last hurrah and John F. Kennedy's first (which tragically proved to be his last, as well), and with each of those conflicts came accelerating change in the way that the majority at home came to view armed conflict in particular and international affairs in general. Not until the *Lusitania* was torpedoed, and American lives were lost, did the nation pivot on its ideology toward intervention in Europe's war. There was still sufficient isolationism in the country to keep us at least formally disengaged from World War II until the Japanese descended on Pearl Harbor.

"But in each case, and later in Korea, the critical turning point for public opinion came only when the nation as a whole received irrefutable evidence that interests vital to us had come under vicious attack.

"Technology has speeded up that process of chain reaction. The consensus that America Came First didn't last as long when the Germans began bombing Britain in World War II as it had when the Germans started World War I. The nativist preference for staying at home under our spacious skies, surrounded by our fruited plains and staying out of foreign quarrels, remains powerful, but it yields far more quickly to calls to Battle Stations than it ever did before.

"That is because, at least vicariously, television puts us all, not just our fighting men and women, in the thick of combat. And that same explanation accounts for the swifter deterioration of the consensus that we ought to fight, or should continue to fight, once we have begun. One wonders whether the American determination to vanquish Germany would have survived direct, televised observation of the wasteful slaughter of our troops under the capricious command of British Gen. Bernard Law Montgomery during the invasion of Sicily in 1943. One doubts also whether today's Ban-the-Bombers would be quite so vehement in their opposition to atomic weapons if they had, by viewing nightly what was happening to American soldiers retaking Tarawa, Kwajelein and Iwo Jima, known before Hiroshima and Nagasaki what lay in store for those men when they attacked the Japs at home.

"So the short of it is probably as the man in Montpelier sees it: Eugene McCarthy is certainly attempting something never done within our lifetimes, perhaps never in the country's history. But he is attempting it in a country that is different from the one that others faced, and at very least he has a better chance than his forerunners had. He says he is a different man. Well, this is a different time. Maybe he's suited to it, and it could be that other unconventional candidates for public office are waiting in the wings.

"There is some evidence of that gradual shift right here, and voters in our Second Congressional District if they haven't seen it yet don't have long to wait. As *New York Times* political commentator James Reston once observed, reflecting on his early career as a sportswriter covering the Cincinnati Reds, it is not a bad thing for a young reporter to prepare for a career of writing politics by first covering sports. He said something to the effect that the advantage to be gained stems from the fact that in sports you never know in advance how the game—or the season—will turn out, for good or ill, and when you shift over to politics, that remains a good thing to keep in mind so you don't get too sure of yourself.

"So, stating right here that I don't know how this contest will turn out, I can still report for the first time that it's definitely underway: When you wake up in the Second District tomorrow morning, either with your well-earned headache or your virtuously clear mind, you will have the prospect of something that the District hasn't seen since right after the war years, a fight for the congressional seat occupied since 1939 by Bob Wainwright. It's not official yet, but what's been rumored since the leaves turned is in fact going to happen, and happen pretty soon. Out in the bullpen of our memories, Henry Briggs of Occident is warming up, tuning his arm, for a new kind of pitching. You read it here first, folks: Hank Briggs is running for Congress.

"More on this Sunday."

21

Late on Sunday afternoon, when the sky was purple gray over Canterbury, Jane Wainwright called Emily Poitrast at her apartment in Alexandria. "I'm sorry to bother you at home, Emily," she said. "I tried to reach Andy at home, but nobody answered. And I know he was home earlier because Bob talked to him."

"That's surprising," Emily said. "All those football games to watch. He told me when he left for lunch on Friday, never did come back, of course, how when he saw me Tuesday he'd probably be divorced. I guess Helene just can't stand him sitting there and watching all those games all day. Maybe he's gotten drunk at home for once, or else Helene's taken the kids out, and he's taken the phone off the hook."

"Well, I got no answer," Jane said. "That's why I'm calling you."

"Oh, I don't mind," Emily said. "I was just sitting here all by myself and reading. With my little glass of sherry. It's been such a lovely, restful day. Not even many planes coming in and out right over my bathroom sink. Have you read John O'Hara's stories? I used to see them in *The New Yorker*. Only reason I subscribed. But then something happened there, I guess, and they weren't in it anymore. So I stopped. Now I just get the books when they come out. Wonderful, wonderful stories. That man has a dirty mind."

"Yes," Jane said. "Well, no, can't say I have. My taste runs more along the line of Willa Cather, I think. It's been so long though, since I've read anything except the newspaper, I'm not even sure she is. My taste, I mean. But that's why I was trying to reach Andy, and why I'm calling you."

"For Willa Cather?" Emily said. "I'm afraid I don't have any of her books around. I did have *Death of the Archbishop* . . . was that what it was called?"

"*Death Comes for the Archbishop,* I think," Jane said. "I was calling because of the newspaper."

"That's right," Emily said. "*Death for the Archbishop.* I knew it was something like that. I did used to have it, I think, but I believe I left it at home when I first packed to come down here. With Mr. Wainwright. He is such a lovely man, Jane. So was his father, in case you haven't thought of that good man lately. A wonderful, kind, wonderful man. I see so much of him in Rob. I remember when Rob's grandfather first brought him in to visit the bank. In his shorts and jacket. And I thought then: 'Just like his dad. He looks just like his dad.' And he did, too. And now, after all these years that I've been with him, and his father before him, well, there are days, I can tell you, when I scarcely know which one is which. They're both so alike. Except of course his father's dead. But God knows where that book's gone now. The minute that I left, I swear, that brother of mine just went pell-mell through my parents' house like a regular cyclone. Well, not the minute that I left, but as soon as Mother died. He didn't want it? Throw it out. 'Now of course you don't want this, Emily. You've got no place for it in your tiny apartment. We'll just throw it out right here. All it does is catch the dust.' A lot of valuable antiques went galley-west in that affair, I can tell you that. Oh, very valuable things too, I bet. They were worth some money."

"Emily," Jane said, "I'm calling, I called Andy because of the newspapers. The holiday's and then today's. I just read today's myself. Bob got up first this morning and so he got it ahead of me, and he wouldn't let me see it. He took it with him on the train. So I had to get another copy after I dropped him off. Of course he'd been on the lookout for it, after the one on Thanksgiving."

"Yes, I know," Emily said. "He does like his paper. I've often wondered how he manages to wait to read it until he gets to the office.

Should think he'd have one delivered at home. His father was like that, too. Very careful with a dollar." She hesitated. "As a matter of fact," she said, "the two of them are exactly the same in that respect. Cheap."

"Emily," Jane said, "have you been home all weekend?"

"Why yes," Emily said. "Haven't left the house. Why would I? Where would I go? Everyone goes home, you know. Always, over the holidays. Have since I've been coming here. I just have no reason, you know. To go anywhere. This is my home. Not to see my brother, certainly. He's in a rest home now. Not much good that wife of his was, after he got sick. Quick enough to take the house, make it over to suit her. But the minute Leonard got sick, I tell you, he was out the door."

Jane sighed. "Emily," she said, "can you think of any place where I might possibly reach Andy? This is very important. I need to talk to him today. At least before tomorrow morning. I *need* to talk to him."

"I don't know where he went, Mrs. Wainwright," Emily said. "I know where he usually goes, when he disappears like this, but that's when he's working. Supposed to be working. Do they show football games in bars? Maybe that's where he went. But I wouldn't know which one."

"Emily," Jane said, "please let this sink in. Bob is terribly upset. I've never seen him so upset, in all the years we're married."

"Yes," Emily said. "He's ordinarily very easygoing. Was the turkey bad or something?"

"What?" Jane said.

"The turkey, Mrs. Wainwright," Emily said. "I told him when he told me about it, how the bank was giving them away if you put in a thousand dollars, I said: 'Mr. Wainwright, those are frozen turkeys. And it's all the way out almost to Baltimore. Even if you do take the early train and get off and open the account and then get on the next train, that turkey will be thawed by the time that you get home. You could get food poisoning or something. You could get real sick.' And he said: 'No,' that nothing like that would happen. Did he get sick from the turkey? I was afraid he would."

"Emily," Jane said, "the turkey was fine. Absolutely fine. I don't think it was anywhere near as good as the ones we ordinarily get from Mr. Whipple for Thanksgiving and from the butcher store in town here for Christmas, it was tough and kind of stringy. But it was free, and nothing free Bob ever ate ever disagreed with him."

"Yes," Emily said. "He's a very careful man. As I say, he's cheap, and so was his father before him."

"Now, Emily," Jane said, "you have to remember this in case I can't reach Andy before Bob's train pulls in tomorrow. Can you do that for me?"

"Of course I can, Mrs. Wainwright," Emily said. "It's very quiet here today, without all the planes and so forth. I suppose it'll be a real bastard for noise tonight, though, all those happy people coming back from their weekends at home."

"Do you think you should write it down?" Jane said.

"Why?" Emily said. "Why would I do that? I always remember things. Remember everything."

Jane sighed. "All right," she said, "I hope you're right. You have to remember this and be sure to tell Andy what's happened, in case I don't get him first. Bob was furious about what Russ Wixton wrote in the paper, first Thanksgiving Day, and then again today. He was positively boiling."

"What did it say?" Emily said. "Andrew won't get it 'til tomorrow. That's when we get the paper."

"Well," Jane said, "tomorrow, then, you'll have two copies, because he took ours down with him. I've never seen him so angry. For once I wished I'd given in, one of those times he's ordered me to cancel our subscription. Wished it hadn't come today. But anyway, I didn't get to see the second one, today's, until I dropped him off. But I heard him on the phone to Andy this morning. That's how I know he was home then. And Bob was yelling his head off. So all I got was pieces. I asked him to let me read it, and he utterly refused. And then after I did finally get to read it, well, I could understand how he felt. It was real brass knuckles stuff, Emily. Very, very tough.

"I don't like to see him like this, Emily," she said. "He's not a young man anymore. I know he's sensible. I know his habits are good. But he's not a young man anymore. So I worry about him, and it really is important that I get ahold of Andy. He has to meet that train. Should I call him again at home, do you think?"

Emily laughed. "It won't do any good, Mrs. Wainwright," she said.

"I think you'll just have to count on me. Just like you always have, all those years you've stayed up there, in your lovely home."

"*Damn,*" Jane said.

The conductor came through the train as it approached White River Junction in the dusk and announced that dinner service would be commencing in the dining car in forty-five minutes. The other eight passengers stirred in their seats and began rearranging their possessions, but Wainwright remained huddled in his, the dim reading lamp throwing scant light on his sparse hair and blue suit and his folded copy of Wixton's column in the morning paper. He rested his left elbow on the valise on the aisle seat next to him.

The headline read: ACCIDENT MAY HAPPEN TO CONG. WAINWRIGHT SOMETIME SOON. The text, now smudged by his fingers, read: "Sixteen years ago, baseball fans across the nation were notably impressed by the hard-throwing debut of the Green Mountain apple chucker, Henry Briggs, the Accident from Occident, whose 12–3 record in relief that year enlivened a dreary season. Now, on a different playing field, Briggs is warming up for another kind of contest, one that could turn Second District politics into an extra-inning struggle voters there have not seen since the end of World War II.

"Because what knowledgeable political observers—maybe we should call them 'scouts'—have been taking seriously for months has been confirmed by the man in the best position to know: Henry Briggs himself. Running as a Democrat, he will challenge 14-term GOP Rep. Bob Wainwright in this fall's elections.

"Wainwright's record is well known, as is he, to Second District voters. All together, initially with his late father's strong backing, he has delivered nearly 30 years of unwaveringly conservative—Speaker Ed Cobb says 'miserly'—views on the floor of Congress.

" 'Fortunately,' Cobb goes on, 'at least for the little guy, most of the time he and his pals've had their hats blocked for them. But father and son, those two've been in the forefront of every backward movement in this country since the war.'

"Cobb openly admits that he and Gov. Randolph were determined to recruit opposition to Wainwright this year. 'And I don't mean some patsy that stands up and gets knocked down,' Cobb said. 'John and I're serious about this. Let's face the facts. We know it's an uphill struggle, for anyone who runs. Bob Wainwright's an institution. He's a leading citizen, he's dead honest, and the day there's a scandal about Wainwright is the day Gabriel's trumpet blows and the end of the world is announced.'

" 'But he's also a throwback, a Neanderthal, and one of the big reasons this country's in the blazing mess it's in is because people like Bob Wainwright, nicer people you can't find, don't understand that we're all in this together. They won't work toward compromise and therefore make things worse.'

"It's true that Ed Cobb's never been known for his reticent approach to politics. My dictionary has a drawing of him, next to the definition of 'flamboyant politician.' But Cobb has a response to that (as usual): 'The governor and I're looking for a lively candidate. Someone who can go up against Bob Wainwright and put it to him, all right? Say: "Is this the way you want it? Do you really want it so our dairy people are operating at a disadvantage, compared to other farmers? If we're going to take care of city people, and the South, who can't take care themselves, do you really want us to neglect the people in Vermont?" And I'm interested in what Bob'll have to say. If we find a candidate, we think can do the job.'

"So this column last fall repeatedly asked Cobb if he had any names on his list. And he said then that he and the governor, until now not known as the best of bosom buddies, 'have a few names we're considering. We haven't picked one yet.' Not even one that went up against the best hitters in both major leagues, and when he couldn't strike them out, put them in the dirt? 'No comment,' said Ed Cobb. And then he grinned. Two nights ago, at Cobb's favorite haunt, Hunter's Tap on the lake, that grin was ear-to-ear.

" 'Had to talk him into it,' Cobb said, looking at Briggs. 'Only way that he'd agree was if Don Beale's wife, Julie, and my wife, Gwendolyn, 'd hold him by the hand and help him through this thing. But he's aboard now—that's for sure. I think we've got a winner.'

"Memo to Congressman Wainwright: Cobb may have something. Hank Briggs in his 14 years in the big leagues played for underdog teams that fulfilled all gloomy expectations. The Red Sox '53 through '57 and '62 through '65 were punchless teams with no defense. The Pirates in his four years in Pittsburgh struggled mightily. Cleveland did not field a good team while he was an Indian. And yet somehow he toted up 122 victories against 68 losses, with a 3.93 ERA.

"Relief pitchers are called in either when the game is out of reach or when it's in jeopardy. They only pitch hard games. Hank Briggs's record in such situations shows that he won nearly twice as many tough games as he ever lost."

The conductor returned through the car. He paused at Wainwright's seat. Wainwright looked up. "Ah, Congressman," the conductor said, "don't know if you heard me: Coming up, the dinner hour. Dining car'll open in about a half an hour."

Wainwright sat up straight. "Thank you," he said. "I'll keep it in mind." The conductor left the car.

Wainwright opened his valise and rummaged in it. He brought out a turkey-and-cheese sandwich wrapped in waxed paper and set it on his lap. There was a small paper napkin inside the wrapper; he tucked that into his collar. He took out a one-pint Thermos, unscrewed the cap, and poured tea into it. He rested the cup of tea on the windowsill, the motion of the train jiggling its surface, and began to eat the sandwich.

The early morning sunlight added a rose tone to the Capitol dome but did not dispel the chill in the air on the walkways of the tracks outside Union Station. Prior braved it for a while, but retreated behind the Plexiglas doors of the waiting room at Track Six and waited for the Montrealer to arrive. The train came in about forty minutes late, steam venting around the wheels, but Prior remained inside until he saw Wainwright climb clumsily down from the fourth car into the cloud of steam, emerging with his hat somewhat askew and the second button of his overcoat buttoned into the first buttonhole. Prior pushed the door open and hurried down the walkway, dodging the few other passengers disembarking from the train. A faint odor of urine lingered where the steam had floated.

"What the hell're you doing here?" Wainwright said. He had a growth of white stubble on his face. His eyes were red and watery. Prior reached for the valise. Wainwright pulled it back and held it with both hands against his middle. "I said: What the hell're you doing here?"

"It's a cold morning, Congressman," Prior said. "You've had a tough weekend. Mrs. Wainwright called, and she said I should meet you."

"She did," Wainwright said. "Damn that woman. I'm perfectly capable of finding my way home."

"Mr. Wainwright," Prior said, "may I take your bag? At least while you fix your coat?"

"My coat," Wainwright said.

"You've got it buttoned wrong," Prior said.

"Oh," Wainwright said. He looked down. "So I have," he said. He handed the bag to Prior. He used both hands to button the coat correctly. He squared his hat on his head. He stood up straighter. "Well, come along," he said, and started down the walkway.

Prior shifted the valise from his left hand to his right. "Mr. Wainwright," he said, the valise bumping against his leg with each step, "I still haven't seen it. The papers. But I gather from what Mrs. Wainwright told me—she called me late last night, I'd been out with the family to dinner and a movie—you think there's more behind this than we talked about, the phone."

"Devilment's what's behind it," Wainwright said. His face was set. "This Wixton fellow: What's got into him? I scarcely know the young man. Loaned him some money once—well, loaned his family money. And met him once or twice since then, I 'spose, meetings, that sort of thing. Never had a cross word with him, not that I recall. It's not him that's after me, and it's not that fellow Briggs. It's Cobb, Ed Cobb, that's doing this. He's got the devil in him. He's put them up to this."

"Well," Prior said, "but what I mean is: What's the result of this? Because I've thought it over, since we talked yesterday, and while I still don't like it, I don't see how it hurts you much. It's not as though Ed Cobb's insults, no matter who prints them, can knock you out of office. Your people've been loyal now, for years and years and years. This won't change how they think."

"This won't?" Wainwright said. "No, of course it won't. But what's coming after this, what I can see coming, may change how people think. It certainly won't help me. I don't understand that young man Wixton, why he'd lend himself to this."

"Didn't he used to be a sportswriter?" Prior said.

"Don't really know," Wainwright said. "Never paid much attention to him. Didn't call for it."

"Well, he was," Prior said. "I wonder if it isn't, if his motive isn't simply that he knows this Briggs from then. Maybe they're old drinking partners, something along that line."

"Huh," Wainwright said. "Well, that could be, I 'spose. Drinkers tend to stick together, my experience."

"Well," Prior said, "wouldn't it be worthwhile to see if the committee has got anything on him? I mean, he has been doing this, this political column thing, for more than a little while. Usually they keep tabs on those guys."

"I'm aware of those things," Wainwright said. "Our noble President has a card at Hoover's little library. 'Dirty files,' they're called?"

"By some," Prior said.

"Not interested," Wainwright said. "That stuff doesn't interest me."

"Mr. Wainwright," Prior said, "I'm just trying to think of things, that might give us some help."

Wainwright seized his valise. "I assume you've got your car," he said. "Drive me home. We'll have some breakfast. Then we'll go to work. Real work. Not this foolishness. This man Wixton's got it in for me. That's what we have to deal with: what Wixton thinks up next."

22

Wixton had been relaxed but firm at the end of 1967 when he prodded the editor-in-chief, Ramsey Mortimer, to let him add new staff. "I know the situation you're in, Ram," he said, "and I think you've got to admit that I've busted my ass proving that I do. When Jim retired and you people asked me to start spending half my time here at his desk, and half my time reporting from Montpelier, and the other half of my time doing the column and so forth, I didn't let on that my arithmetic was good enough to add up those three halves.

"And when Perkins died on us, well, I know he didn't plan it just to make my life harder, but that left my department short two guys. Not just one. Seasoned guys, Ram, not replaced. Perk may've only had the one good eye, and most grocery clerks're better writers, but there was nothing wrong with his hearing, and nothing wrong with his prose that an hour or so of blood and sweat couldn't turn into readable English. And Jim, well, I thought I saw him move once, wasn't anything major, just a sort of involuntary twitch or something, a vagrant rictus perhaps, but he did pencil up the copy, and one way or the other it did get from one side of his desk to the other.

"Now I'm both of them, and me as well," Wixton said, "and I've got to say it's kind of humiliating, after all those years of bitching about them, but I have to admit one guy doing all three jobs isn't quite as good as three guys were, even if one of them seemed to be dead and the other one couldn't write. I'm getting older. I've got forty-four years on me, and there's every indication that unless I think of something fast, I'll have another birthday this year that'll make me forty-five. I'm staring down the barrel of tuitions, a few years, and I can't duck the fact I'd better spend some time now with the kids, before they hit the road. Plus which, I'm getting tired."

"Of course we could talk about that," Mortimer said. "Could be one of the reasons you're so beat all the time is that management gave you permission, take that part-time teaching job at UVM. Maybe you should cut back on that."

"We could," Wixton said. "Sure, we could do that. But you know how I am, Ram. That'd just get me off on that other tedious discussion about how come the benevolent management doesn't pay the help enough. Especially its political editor, chief state house correspondent, and political columnist. Especially even more when you consider that all three of those guys sleep in the same bed every night, wear the same suit every day, and only eat three meals—not nine—a day when all three of me's on the road."

"For the price of the meals you eat," Mortimer said, "never mind how much all the booze you drink costs, for that kind of money, though, three guys could eat nine meals and have some change left over, too."

"And that's what I mean, Ram," Wixton said. "There's no reason getting into that because those sob stories bore us both, and that's not what I'm after. We've got elections coming up this coming year. The Briggs-Wainwright story is big. I've got to have more staff."

"That brings up another point," Mortimer said. "Have you got a grudge against Wainwright? Those two columns you fed him with his turkey dinner, that was pretty rough stuff. I've heard suggestions you might be biased, something involving a mortgage."

"Look, Ram," Wixton said, "there's hardly anybody whose family lived in the Second District since the turn of the century who hasn't gotten a mortgage from Bob Wainwright's granddad's bank. And hardly one of them that didn't have some trouble with it, when the Depression hit. My father was no luckier'n most of his neighbors were, and he lost the farm, and it soured him. But it soured him on the banks in general, not just Wainwright's, and I heard him talk. It wasn't pleasant for him, Ram, and it wasn't fun for me. But I play it down the middle, Bob Wainwright or Jesus Christ, and if you're suggesting otherwise, I think I've been insulted."

"Take it easy, Russ," Mortimer said. "You do know, I have to ask."

"And if there's still any doubt in your mind," Wixton said, "well, maybe that's the best argument I could make for letting me have some more staff. Some kids that wake up to a new world each morning, and haven't got any history. I need to have backup on this one, and the moneybags have to provide it."

"They're aware of that," Mortimer said. "Had a conversation with Olympia a month, three weeks ago, and she said to me then that the Tallower family understand we'll probably have to do some hiring. And I'm sure, and I've said this, that when the time starts getting closer, they will authorize."

"I'm sure they will," Wixton said. "When it's plain enough so that the guys down at the lunchroom spilling coffee on themselves can see just by reading us that we're badly understaffed, I'm sure then I'll get a memo of royal generosity telling me to hire two people. Which will mean they will've saved Jim's salary and Perk's salary, for two-plus years or so. And will they be grateful? Sure, of course they will, and I will be Cinderella in my beautiful new gown, riding in a fucking coach behind six elegant gray horses. Furthermore, when they do that, very grudgingly, they will also peg the slots at entry-level pay. Which will mean that instead of replacing two guys with a total of about sixty years' experience, they'll be bringing in two people who have absolutely none, but come cheap. I'll be recruiting rookies.

"Well," he said, "that's fine. No gripe from me on that. We could use some young legs on this old team anyway. And frankly, I'd like to bring some people in here a little closer to the age group, that unless I'm wrong on this, we're gonna wind up covering. No guy our age is ever going to get a handle on what these kids're thinking. Sure, once we were kids ourselves, and for us it isn't a new world every day, but just the same they won't know that, any more'n we did, and they won't open up with us.

"But if that's what I'm gonna have to do, and I don't doubt it is, I need to get the kids in soon, so I can get them trained. It's not gonna help me if the ownership stalls me off for another year, and then relents about the time the conventions're coming up, and says: 'Okay, okay then, Wixton, go and snatch a couple bodies.' They're gonna need some seasoning before I turn them loose.

"So," Wixton said, "you approach Mount Olympus, and Ben, and tell them: 'Look on the bright side.' Remind them about all the dough that they've saved, one guy retired and one dead, and tell them that unless they want to wind up paying top dollar to raid other papers, trained people, real old farts, sometime in the coming year, they've got to spring for the small beers right now, so we have the bodies in place."

"It might work," Mortimer said. "Jesus God, though, but I hate to go up against that damned Olympia. The man in the family's scrimy enough, but when that woman hears something that she smells might cost her money, she hits full boil in a second. She makes her descendants look like patsies—she bowls overhand."

"Ram," Wixton said, "I know it. But it really is important. Give it your best shot, will you? I really need these people right now, and the situation will be critical if we wait until next year."

"I will," Mortimer said. "You got anybody in mind?"

"Well," Wixton said, "I checked around. Walter Lippmann didn't return my calls. Reston was tied up, but his secretary said she didn't think he'd be interested. David Broder says he's happy down in Washington, and I guess Arthur Krock is working on a book. So, no, I haven't got any ideas. I've surveyed my classes for vital signs of such things as intelligence and learning potential, plus at least some indication that on even-numbered Wednesdays they might take some direction, but so far I've come up dry.

"The ones that look as though they do have brains enough to learn 're almost always also the same ones that will not listen. They're so smart, you see, they already know it all. The ones that pay attention, try to do what they are told, well, the reason is because they're low on wattage and don't know how to tie their shoes. There's one kid who looks like he might have the stuff, but he's a cocky bastard, and besides, he's draftable. So we bring him in here, and we train him, and the draft board draws his number, and poof, away he goes, like the down of a goddamned thistle. And I'm back where I started from. Oh, and there's a girl that thinks she's a photographer, or wants to be at least, but I've seen some of her work and Margaret Bourke White shouldn't worry. What she does have, if she works, are some real prospects as a writer. She's never really thought about it, so she's got a nice, plain style. So I'll see what I can do, soon's you give me the go-ahead."

In December of 1967, when Scott Pokaski and Donna Taunton completed their six weeks of probationary service, Ramsey Mortimer refused to listen to any further complaints from Wixton about their behavior. "It's very simple, Russ," he said, "it's either up or down. What are the pluses? What are the minuses? How do they compare? Is it just possible these kids, being young and all, will correct the things that you don't like, and improve the things you do?"

"Well," Wixton said, "I would rate the chances in his case at fifty-fifty. In her case not so optimistic—forty-sixty'd be my guess."

"And the next two questions," Mortimer said, "are whether you want to take the chance, given that you've already got some investment in them, or can you locate someone better in the time that you've got left? Seems to me, comes down to that. Never mind if they're not perfect. You've got some flaws yourself. The question is: Can we do better? What's your answer, huh?"

"If we can," Wixton said, "I for one do not know where. I'm not happy with these kids. They drive me nuts sometimes. I don't know where this notion got started, that an employee is someone who deserves an explanation when the boss tells him to do something. I thought what bosses got to do was tell people what they wanted done, and then the people did it. That's how bosses treated me, and how I treated bosses. 'S the only reason I wanted to be one—be a boss, I mean. So I could order people around, wait for something disagreeable to come up and then make someone else handle it. Time I finally reach that station, they repealed the rule. Now the boss has to cajole, wheedle, beg, and plead.

"But I guess I'm happier to have them'n I was before they got here. As *fucking* difficult as they can be, they do get the work done. Not when I want it done, and not the way I want it, but usually it does get done if I beat them 'til their ears bleed and then massage their egos for them. If there were only some way to make them check their goddamned attitudes at the door. Like Marshal Dillon taking guns away from people coming into Dodge. But so far I haven't found one. Maybe age'll do it."

"Then it's settled," Mortimer said. "They're on permanent. They are on staff now."

Wixton sighed. "Yeah," he said. "I think I'll make a few calls this afternoon, see whether there's a bed open at some nice quiet nursing home where the help plays canasta with you, and only lets your family see you on your better days."

When Wixton emerged from Mortimer's office he went into his own and sat down at his desk and rubbed his face. At the other end of the city room, to his right, Pokaski put his paper down and walked slowly toward Wixton. He passed the entrance to the library, stopped, looked in, cleared his throat and said: "Donna? Big doings, I think. Time to go stroker the man." She was at the file drawers. "Be right out," she said. Pokaski continued on to Wixton's desk. He took the chair on the left.

Wixton nodded at him. He stretched in his chair, arching his back against it. "*Ahhh*," he said, "sun's barely up and I've already been chewed out. Some days this job sucks."

"Just get a ration of shit?" Pokaski asked.

Wixton nodded. "Uh-huh," he said, "Olympia's not happy. I guess she got the paper Sunday after Thanksgiving, and if I made her mad on the big holiday, what I did on the Sabbath was worse. Had herself a small tantrum. Not a Richter-scale tantrum, but a pretty good one all the same. Called Ram at home and told him to get ahold of someone, and whatever I was doing yesterday, to kill it. And he said he wouldn't do that. And she said: 'Well, then what is it?' And he said he didn't know, and she called him several names, and she threatened him with death or at least mutilation if it turned out bad for Wainwright, and slammed the phone down in his ear. Then Sunday she got the paper and she did not like what she saw. So she called Ram up again and had another chat. During which, Ram listened, and she did all the chatting."

"Well, what the fuck, right? If she can't take a joke? The old bat's got to get it through her silver-blue-dyed skull that she's the one who loves Bob's ass, not her goddamned paper. So she's been pals with old Bob ever since Eden got boarded up? Well, that's the way it was sometimes, movin' west."

"Mortimer pissed?" Pokaski said.

"He's not happy," Wixton said. Donna came out of the library and took the chair next to Pokaski's. "What the hell, he's normal. I don't know a single soul, likes getting his ass reamed out."

"So what do we do now?" Donna said.

"You mean: 'Do we ease up?' " Wixton said. "In a pig's ass we do. Stick to what you're doing. Run down every piece of legislation that Bob Wainwright's voted on. Don't know why this wasn't done a hundred years ago. Should be a running chron, a complete chronology, on everyone in public office, every issue that they deal with, cross-referenced by date. We've finally got something going on in that damned district, and we're going to play it like it was our own zither."

"This, ah," Pokaski said, "this isn't personal?"

"Look," Wixton said, "you got two questions there. The first one's whether we show bias. Answer is: We don't. We play it right straight down the middle. Second's whether Bob and his friends will believe we're doing that. Answer is: They won't. This will be the first time that he's ever had the treatment. Ever had the scrutiny that guys in real contests get. He doesn't like what he got so far, and he won't like the rest.

"But we are gonna give it to him. With his morning tea and toast. Lying low and keeping quiet aren't gonna work for Bob this time. When Briggs takes a position, on the war or public health, or any other goddamned thing that comes into his head, we'll report what he says, and we'll ask Bob to respond. And then when Bob won't comment we'll run sidebars with the story that report Bob said 'No comment.' And then list what Bob has done, when that subject has come up in the hallowed halls down there.

"There's nothing dirty, underhanded, sneaky, or tricky to it, although he will claim all those things. It's just a matter of doing our job when a guy gets an opponent, of showing where he stands. Maybe he's been right every time. Maybe he's been wrong. But either way, he did exist, and wants to exist some more. The question's whether we want that—'we' being the voters. And he has to answer that question. Like it or not, and he won't, I know that, but that's what the man has to do. And we have to make sure he does."

23

Congressman Parker Hoess, R., Oklahoma, had the gout again. Andrew J. Prior was silently grateful. It was cold in Washington late Friday afternoon, with a bitter wind rolling off the Tidal Basin among the buildings on the Hill. But that would not have diverted Wainwright from his usual route back to the Longworth Building from the Capitol. Carrying his overcoat and hat, he would have made his way on foot via the subway passage to the northeast corner of the first floor of the Old Senate Office Building, pausing at the revolving door to dress for the weather, then setting out briskly on foot along Constitution Avenue down to the bottom of Capitol Hill before crossing the mall and starting the long climb up Independence, past the Cannon House Office Building to Longworth.

Prior dreaded those progresses. Wainwright in his later years had somewhat reduced the marching pace he had learned as a young man at the Great Lakes Naval Training Station—Prior used his own experience in ROTC to estimate his boss's tempo at somewhere around eighty-eight steps a minute—but neither the oppressive heat and humidity of summer nor the worst cold of the winter—"nor," as Prior told Helene at home, "rain, nor snow, nor dark of night"—deterred the Congressman from his appointed daily round.

"And you know why?" Prior said. "You know why the old bastard does it? Why he'd rather march down the Hill, and then march around the Hill, and then march up again? Instead of working out in the fucking goddamned gym? Which is also free, goddamnit? It's because he thinks it's all right to wear the same shirt three days, if you sweat into it from walking, but it's not all right to put it back on tomorrow, if you've been working out today. Because then the other people in the gym will know you're cheap.

"As though they didn't. And the son of a bitch, it's not the laundry bill, you know. He doesn't have a laundry bill. He doesn't send his shirts out. He rinses out the goddamned things, right in his apartment. In the bathroom sink. No going down to the basement, putting quarters in machines—those quarters can add up. And then hangs them on wooden hangers, on the shower rod, to dry. He's still wearing those drip-dry shirts that my father used to buy. From the New Process Company. Thirty of them for ten bucks—something along that line. The nylon ones that look all gray? Blue ones, yellow, white ones? All of them look gray? I bet he's got a clause in his will, that when he dies that he gets buried standing up. No box. Which will save a few dollars right there, because he won't be lying down. So instead of hiring gravediggers, Jane just borrows a posthole digger, from one the neighbors, reams out the grave and drops him in."

"I still don't see why you have to go with him," she said.

"Well," Prior said, "neither do I. But you can depend on it: I do. Every day of every week, while Congress is in session, Vermont's senior congressman stops at my desk on his way to where he's going, and tells me, meet him at the cloakroom when the day's business is over. 'Got a few things on my mind, we ought to talk about.' So I keep in touch with what's in progress on the floor, and then when everybody else's ducking out to some nice quiet bar, I go down into the basement and get on a subway car. And I meet him at the cloakroom and we walk around the building. And we get back to the office—*and he never says a word.*"

"Maybe he's afraid he'll get mugged," she said. "He wants you there for protection."

"Mugged?" Prior said. "Who the hell'd mug him? Just by looking at him, I don't care how dumb you are, if you can read and write, you can tell by looking at him if you kill the old bastard, most you'll get's thirty-five cents. Fifty if he was planning to stop the drugstore, on his way home, and buy a new Q-tip. 'Don't make these things like they used to, you know—only got six months out the last one.' And a watch that's no good after sundown because it's a damned sundial. Maybe an hourglass. He could walk through meanest Harlem, and he would not get mugged. The thugs would give *him* their money, without being asked.

"And he would take it, too. Put it in his Christmas Club. He's still pissed off, since we got married and we get the paper here. He used to grab mine, the minute I came in, 'fore I had a chance to read it. Emily came back from lunch the other day with a copy of Manchester's book about Kennedy—treated herself to a paperback. And he tried to take it. 'Been meanin' to read this,' he said. 'So've I,' she said, and grabbed it back from him. 'After you're finished then,' he says. Well, she sent over to the library, had them bring him one. 'So he won't swipe mine,' she said. Wished I'd worked for his father too—then I could face him down."

Congressman Hoess ran for election on agricultural issues, but depended on oil money to intimidate prospective rivals and pick up his restaurant tabs. He was a large man with a florid complexion, a great mass of unruly gray hair, and an active understanding that he carried some importance and could make others do things that they did not want to do. When his illness flared up, he used a cane, and not only appreciated but commandeered the car and driver dispatched at once for his convenience by the Department of Agriculture, often keeping the driver idling until after midnight outside the 1776 House in Georgetown, while he contemplated rich food, fine wines, and government matters.

"Well," Prior said, when he got home that night, "I got saved by Parker Hoess. God bless the fat old shit. I didn't get a T.G.I.F. drink, but I didn't have to walk. Here's the old walrus in full plumage, big as life, I got to the cloakroom, and when Brother Wainwright came out, Parker waylaid him. 'Bob, ah, Bob,' he says, 'have a word with you.' And of course old Bob looked like he just had a check bounce.

"I am standing there, my trenchcoat, for our constitutional, and the first thing that old Bob does is look over at the coat rack and make sure that nobody's stolen his blue overcoat. Grandpa'd be real pissed off, someone stole that coat. Been in the family, generations now. Barely broken in. I wonder where it goes, when Bob dies, him without a son. Probably to the Smithsonian. 'This coat came over with Leif Eriksson, at least—maybe with Saint Brendan. Long before Columbus, anyway, and it outlasted lots of guys. This coat is made of iron. Discovered America. Somebody that was President must've had it on. Everybody up. Let's have a big hand for the coat. It's a fuckin' artifact.'

"But no, the coat's still there, all right. And so's the goddamned hat. But Bob isn't going to wear it, the hat or the coat, either one of them, because Hoess would like a word, and Hoess has got the gout. This has got nothing to do with the fact that Parker Hoess never ate a fucking lobster unless it was up to its jockstrap in butter and crumbs. It has got nothing to do with the fact that Parker Hoess, the last time Parker Hoess drank water, and the time before that, and the time before that as well, was when the water was brown because of all the Wild Turkey in it. The last time Parker walked was when Japan surrendered. They didn't have a limo then, for junior officers, when the emperor signed the treaty on the battleship *Missouri*. Or maybe it was when he got tied-up in committee and missed his only dinner meeting.

"So Bob gets this look on his face. After all, what can he do? If Parker wants something from Bob, well, chances are Bob has to give it. And one of the things Parker wants is a ride back to his office. So we take the subway car.

"He *hates* it when I get on the same car with him," Prior said. "I know he hates it. It shows on his face. It's the same thing with the elevators. Every other congressman I know, one of his staff's briefing him and it's elevator time, they all get on the 'Members' car and just keep right on talking. Perfectly natural. Not our Bob. I'm not a 'Member.' What I am is 'Staff,' and even though it says that 'Staff' rides on them too, Bob does not approve of that. Staff is not elected. Therefore we're not members. We're not equal. He had to kiss *every*-body's ass. I only have to kiss his. Well, if you can't get a completely private ride for kissing all that ass, what the hell's the point of it? This is how he thinks.

"But I figure: 'What the fuck? He's not gonna make a scene with Hoess riding up front.' See, that's what makes him such a bastard, how you know he is. If it was him, just him and me, and something just'd happened so he hadda take the subway, he would glare, and I would

236

know: 'Wait for a staff car.' But when someone like Hoess's there, well, then Bob doesn't dare. He doesn't want the world to know, just what a prick he is.

"Well," Prior said, "we're on the car. Those two are in front. Bob is carrying his coat. And his hat, of course. I have also got my coat, and I am saying nothing, sitting back in the cheap seats. Bob's about as comfortable as a man with piles. He knows the only reason that Hoess ever collars you is when he's in trouble, and his memory is sharp. He will never ask you to do anything if he doesn't really need it. But if he does ask, then he does, and he really means it. You don't deliver? You have fucked him. You fucked Hoess? Then Hoess fucks you. It may take a while, but the bastard will do it. And you will remember it.

" 'Bob, ah Bob,' Hoess says, 'just want to check with you.' When Hoess says he wants to 'check with you,' that means he wants to make sure you've still got both your kneecaps, and you still like your knee-caps, and you still realize your kneecaps're just about the most comfortable height for him to hit with his baseball bat, and you won't mind if he just takes a couple practice swings, to make sure everything's right where he wants it, 'case he has to take you out.

"So, all I can see of Bob's the back of his neck, and some of his left jaw, and you know how he clenches that muscle? The one in the lower part his jaw? Well, that muscle bunches up, and I can see the back his neck get red, and I know he's getting madder'n a hornet. And I also know that Hoess's got him, right where the hairs're short. Because what Hoess's got in mind's this goddamned oil depletion thing that Hoess is in the tank for, seven ways to Sunday. And it's not what you'd call real popular now, not around the House, and what Hoess is angling for's to make sure our Bob's there.

"Bob's about as eager to vote on that bill as Bob is to reconsider whether we oughta restore diplomatic relations with China. He's coming up on twenty-eight years, and he's missed fourteen roll calls, and he's very proud of that. But when it comes to standing up for something that looks to him a lot like it'll raise the heating bills, his district, Bob's idea of a principled stand, is a 'present' vote. Or maybe a courageous 'paired,' with some coward from Texas. Who also isn't there. Bob does not like confrontation.

"So we're bouncing along there, with me in the back like the footman with the luggage, the two of them up front managing democracy, and Parker's using his cane, making sure Bob understands. 'Very important, Bob,' he says. 'This is most important. Really need you here on Thursday. Most important vote. I don't need to tell you, this one goes the wrong way, kind of damage it could do, agricultural subsidy. These people all remember, Bob. You know how they are.'

"I'm choking," Prior said. "I am absolutely choking. I'm choking because Bob is dodging and ducking, doing everything else, trying to think of a reason that he can't back Parker up, and in the meantime I have got one, 'cept he doesn't know about it. And the reason that he doesn't is because he won't talk to me.

"So, I got a moral dilemma, right?" he said to Helene.

"I don't see it," she said.

"Well, *listen* to me, all right?" Prior said. "Jesus Christ, if you're not gonna listen to me, why the hell'm I talking to you?"

"I had a hard day myself, mister," she said. "I'm really sorry you got to deal with this old fart you hate, but if you don't like it so much, whyn't you do something else?"

"Is this gonna be a fight?" he said.

"Can be if you want," she said. "I'm certainly in the mood."

"You know what I think?" Prior said. "I think I'll put my coat on, and go back out the door, and get back in the goddamned car, and drive back up the Hill, and see if maybe I can find a place where someone listens."

"Go to it," she said. "Glad to see the back of you. And don't hurry back, neither."

He took a deep breath. "Look," he said, "all right? What I'm trying to tell you is this: Our Bob cannot be anywhere except in his home state on Thursday, because one of his constituents got wiped out in Vietnam."

"What does that mean?" she said. "Does that mean you have to go?"

"It means: 'Anthony French,'" Prior said. "Whether, what it means for me, I don't know. I do know what it means for him. Curtains. He got killed at Phu Bai last week. Defense can't tell me anything. How it happened, what he did, how come he'll be home so fast. But there's no way, you know, that the boss, that he can miss this funeral. Which is certainly next week, but not much before Tuesday. Maybe not until

Thursday. So there isn't any way that Bob can say he'll be there. To do what Parker Hoess wants done. While slitting his own throat."

"I don't follow you," she said.

"Helene," Prior said, "listen to me. This is the whole point. Anthony French is coming home in a box. Anthony lives in the district. Anthony French has a certain amount of notoriety there. He killed another kid in an accidental shooting. The judge let him off on the condition that he volunteer for the army. He met it. He went to Vietnam. He got killed. So it's expiation. He was sentenced to death for making a mistake that killed a friend of his. This is a story that tugs at the heartstrings. It'll play nationally, all the elements of the brutal ironies of this war we're in.

"Bob Wainwright's his congressman. Wainwright has to be there. To pay his respects. Now he's got what I was hearing he had, before Halloween. He's got opposition. Well, if he didn't have to go before, which he did, *that* means that now he's got to go. He may have to take *a plane*. And you know how he hates to spend the money on that. I tap him on the shoulder and the bastard hits me with a glare. Can't I see he's talking to the great Congressman Hoess? So I shut up, and Hoess keeps talking, and with every word he utters, Bob goes deeper in the shit. Doesn't say he will not do it, 'cause he can't say that. Doesn't say he doesn't want to, because that is just as bad. But also doesn't tell the truth: A pair's all he can do. He's got to go back to Vermont, and admire the body there. And even Hoess will understand this, asshole that he is. Even Hoess will realize: Bob Wainwright cannot do it, what he wants him to do."

"So what?" she said.

"It gets him off the fucking hook," Prior said. "*It gets him off the hook*. Don't you understand me? All the waffling he's doing's all unnecessary. But the damned fool doesn't know it, and he will not let me tell him. And then Hoess limps off and gets his car, and we go to Bob's office, and on the way I'm telling him, and you know what he says? 'If you were any good at all, you would've told me this.' When that's what I was trying, do, all the train ride over.

"He complains all the time, I don't help him enough, and I agree with the bastard. But the reason is, that I of course can't make him see, the reason's because he won't let me. I never should've left HEW, even though the money stunk. I should've stayed there and done the press releases about how we're flooding money into goddamned pilot programs, see if fish can learn to read, and put my pay into the credit union so that some day I could retire."

Helene looked thoughtful.

"What's the matter now?" he said.

She shook her head. "I don't know," she said. "It's just, he must know how you feel. He must sense it."

"He doesn't 'sense' it," he said. "He knows it. He expects it. I feel the same way about him everybody else feels. His constituents feel the same way. You can hear it in their voices, when they call up for something. Which isn't very often—only real emergencies, like war or the black plague. Otherwise, stamp's good enough, waste on a congressman.

"They look at politicians up there just like we do garbagemen. You got to have them. They cost too much and they smell bad, but you got to have them. Look, any group of people that knows cowshit's valuable, and actually stores it up, saves it for next spring, well, they'll put up with anything, if they're convinced it's useful. They vote the way they save string. They don't really know right now how what they're doing can be worth much, but maybe it'll come in handy. God only knows what for. They don't trust him, and he knows it, and he never would admit it but the fact is, he agrees with them.

"He used to be a respectable person. He was a damned banker. Had the power of life and death. Now what the hell is he? Nothing but a damned expense. Might's well be on the welfare, all the good he does.

"I tell you, a guy like Hoess is a pompous old windbag, and if he came to dinner I would count the goddamned spoons. But Hoess at least's got some notion, what he does is *worth* it. Old Bob doesn't have that. He's ashamed of himself. And that is why he's such a prick. And why he acts like one. The man is logical, Helene. I've got to give him that. Ruthlessly logical. If he's just horseshit, in his job, what are we, that help him?"

"No wonder you don't get along," she said.

"I give up," he said.

240

24

"Why now?" Pokaski said, the first Friday in December, "I don't see why now. We didn't do it before. Why should we do it now?" Donna Taunton sat to his left and nodded in agreement.

"Because I just thought of it," Wixton said. "Should I've thought of it sooner? Absolutely. Should have. Did I think of it sooner? No in fact, I didn't. You read *The Commoner* today? *The Boston Commoner?*" Both of them shook their heads.

"Uh-huh," he said, "well, I did. And you should've read it too. Because they had a story in it that was well worth reading. The story was about a kid that none of us've heard of. His name is, or his name was, Timothy Gaffney. *The Commoner* milked his story. Absolutely milked it. Brought the Tet truce agreement home.

"Here is this kid that grew up in West goddamned Roxbury. He graduates from high school, and he joins the damned marines. His mother and his sister're very proud of him. And what's he get his first assignment when he gets to Vietnam? He gets the rear-echelon detail, 'cause he's a model soldier, and the marines don't want those guys killed. And what does that mean to his lifespan? Means that he lives forever.

"Except for one minor thing, which is today's big story. They will give us Christmas off, from fighting, and therefore we give them Tet.

And then they say: 'Aha, we fooled you.' And they attack. And this kid from West Roxbury gets himself fucking killed. And then some *Commoner* reporter with more brains'n we have got—I include myself in that—says: 'Well, shit. Here's a local angle. This here war's not getting won, and our guys're dying. And here's a chance to show it's true. That our guys're the ones that're dying.'

"Well, one of our guys died too," he said. "Kid from down the Notch. His name is French. Anthony French. What do we know about him?"

"Same thing that we know, boss," Pokaski said, "about the other guys that died. Nothing, in other words. I can tell you right now, before you even ask me, there is nothing in our files, says a thing about this kid. We don't care about those kids. It's the country's attitude, and it's the same as ours."

"Thank you, Senator Fulbright," Wixton said. "Now, if we can just get back to our occupation for a moment? Thank you very much. We do know something about the late French lad. A judge sent him over to 'Nam, less'n two short years ago here. To die, as it turns out. Now he's coming home, with an escort, no less. The body will be escorted by four men from his unit. Let's get on it."

"That's unusual," Pokaski said. "When one my high school friends got it, he was fighting there, they just sent a couple guys up from the local Reserve unit. Plus a firing squad, of course, and a guy to play the taps. The guys that had the rifles didn't know what they were doing. Sounded like about five volleys, time they all got through. And the trumpeter was cold or something. Maybe forgot his teeth. It was more like blatting he did. It was terrible."

"You see?" Wixton said. "You're catching on. That's what I'm telling you. The North Koreans take the boat. Just a week ago. We got over eighty guys there, eating rice and being tortured, and the meantime there's our leader, saying everything's all right. Well, it *isn't* 'all right,' all right? It's all going down the drain. And nobody's telling us.

"Well, that's our goddamned job," he said. "We're the people who do that. We're supposed to be, at least. The French kid got it three days before his year was up. Apparently these four other guys, they were friends of his. And they were rotating home, and so they volunteered."

"Okay," Pokaski said, "might be a story there. For once get some of the real stuff that's going on. From some people that were there. 'Stead of all the horseshit that the Pentagon hands out."

"I faint. I swoon," Wixton said. "Oddly enough, that's exactly what I thought myself. And I also thought it'd be nice if you yourself personally did that story. So, tomorrow morning, as you're driving down to Lancaster Notch, on your way to interview as many people's you can find, you'll have the consolation of knowing that I'm with you too. In spirit."

"Hey," Pokaski said, "tomorrow's Saturday. And besides, it snowed last night. And it's supposed to snow tomorrow."

"I know that," Wixton said. "There's a window in my house. More'n one of them in fact. I looked out of one of them last night, and another one this morning. And I said: 'Unless mine eyes deceive me, it is snowing out.' Very perceptive of you, Scott. I can throw my radio away. When I want to know the weather, I'll just call you up."

"Well, I mean," he said, "Lancaster's way the hell up in the hills."

"And geography too," Wixton said. "As I live and breathe, the wonders never cease. What other skills've you been hiding? You any good on the stock market? Horse races and stuff like that?"

"Boss," Pokaski said, "if I drive down to Lancaster tomorrow, well, first of all I miss the mayor's press conference here. And then I'm liable to get stuck. I don't have four-wheel drive."

"First thing," Wixton said, "the conference. That was my thought, too. My thought was that there are several things my little heart desires, and like any other spoiled brat, I want them all today. The conference has to be covered. Hizzoner isn't likely to say anything of any importance whatsoever to any normal person, which is why he's having it on Saturday and not a day when he'd have to compete for space. But there's always the possibility that he'll fall down on his face, right in the middle of it, and start gobbling up the carpet, while he's foaming at the mouth. And that would be real news. So, it's got to be staffed.

"Second thing," Wixton said. "The trip to Lancaster. I want that done tomorrow because when next week comes I want a full-court press on. As you've already observed, you should tag along with French's honor guard and suck their brains right out. But to do that, you are going to need to know something about French. Which you will not learn here, and you will not get from his pals that are flying in with him. They didn't meet him until Vietnam, and they don't know shit about him, and that's what you need to know. You cannot do that while the body is arriving, because in my experience, dead bodies don't talk much. So Donna does the blow-by-blow of where the corpse goes, and also how, and you find out all about how our dead hero grew up. And both of you get the clips about how he got to 'Nam."

"How do you know where these escorts come from?" Taunton said.

"I know it from the goddamned Department of Defense," Wixton said. "See, I've been keeping something from you. I used to be a real reporter. Honest Injun, really was. I get a call from Washington that a boy from up here kicked it, I thought I smelled a story. Maybe one I'd like to read. So I said: 'About these escorts—where do they come from?' And none of them's from our zip code. So that is how I know."

"I didn't know they had that information," she said. "Available, I mean."

"Well," Wixton said, "have you ever seen the pictures in the paper, all those cleancut young men that just finished basic training? Or got their first promotion?"

"Sure," she said. "I just never paid much attention to them's all."

"Well, lemme ask you," Wixton said, "skipping over how attention's how you make it, in this line of work: If I told you those dispatches from Fort Dix and places like that, Benning, Bragg, and Miramar, come in here like windblown trash, why would you think that was? Because AP services that stuff to us? Or we have stringers sitting there, at every goddamned base, waiting for Mrs. Dodder's only son to show everyone in Newfane he knows how to shoot a gun and he got his Marksman's medal? Or would you maybe think instead: 'Army must collect this stuff and mail it up to us. And include a photograph. And we must print it because we know that our readers like it. Not because we think it's news. Just because they like it.' "

"You don't have to get sarcastic," she said.

"No, I don't," Wixton said. "And I'm not getting sarcastic. I've always been sarcastic. I do it on a volunteer basis. I enjoy it. Any other questions?"

"Yeah," Pokaski said. "Why can't I go down there on Monday? That way I could cover the conference tomorrow and still have plenty of time. We've had plenty of bodies come back before. Never put a push on one like this. Starting four or five days ahead."

"Well," Wixton said, "two answers to that one. I'm in a charitable mood, so I'll give you both. The first one is that when the other bodies've come back, the war was sort of background music. Like in elevators? Nobody liked it very much, and if you had asked them, and they thought you really meant it, they would've looked at you and said: 'Yeah. Turn it off.'

"This Tet thing makes it different," Wixton said. "I think it does, at least. Up 'til now you've had this poet from the Midwest, and the guy has slipped his leash, so now he's in the Senate and he's making lots of noise. But he doesn't really fit in there, and no wonder, I suppose, if he thinks he's Jesus Christ. Or maybe the Pied Piper—that might be closer to it. And in the meantime you've had Bobby, chewing on his rope. Remembering his brother while he looks at Lyndon there.

"My guess is that the rules're changing. Who gives a shit if Lyndon gets mad today? Everybody's mad at Lyndon. Safety here's in numbers. You're going to have the electronics on this story like a blanket. I don't want us to be left out, all right? I want us to be better.

"So," he said, "what I want to do with this French kid's take sort of a snapshot of how folks're thinking now. What's the reaction to his death? Was it worth something, in their minds? Or was it just a joke?"

Pokaski snorted. "In other words," he said, "what you're telling us right now is that all the stuff we did, back when it was summer, you were doing all along, treating all these deaths as routine, that was just the way it was? Then it was ordinary, and it wouldn't sell the paper? And now it isn't anymore, so now we're getting busy?"

"Does selling the paper offend you, my child?" Wixton said. "Does it annoy you when people pay good money to read your work? Do you think it's dishonorable to stay one jump ahead of their changes of heart, so that when they wake up craving some new information, they find it in your paper? Have you sought spiritual counseling? Or do you plan to get the clips out now, and read what we have got, and then drive down to Lancaster, and do what I have said?"

"I still don't see why I have to go tomorrow," Pokaski said. "I could go on Monday, still cover the mayor today."

"Or I could go to Lancaster," Taunton said. "I could go down there and start on the research, and Scott could still cover the mayor."

"Which brings me to the second part of my answer," Wixton said. "The reason for Scott driving down to Lancaster tomorrow is that one of us must do it, and we must get started now before all the folks up in the Notch get all confused by the bright lights in their faces. The reason you won't do it, Donna, is because I don't want you to. The reason I don't want you to is because I have other chores for you.

"I am covering the mayor because I do a column about politics for this rag, as you may or may not've noticed, and I haven't given that clown a good going-over for a while. Which means he hasn't gotten one in this newspaper for a while because Scott is screwing his reception-ist. And making nice about the mayor so he can play games with her. Any rebuttal on that point, Scott?"

Pokaski did not say anything. "I have failed you as your editor," Wixton said. "I apologize. It didn't occur to me to tell you, when I hired you, that when I sent you to cover the circus, you were not supposed to fuck the elephant.

"But that's just by the way. She's a very good-looking lady, and I can well understand your behavior. Understand; *not* approve of it. The rest of my second reason, Donna, for sending Scott to Lancaster, is that going to the press conference is the cushier assignment, and when you are the boss, and you get to call the plays, you call your own number when there is a comfort difference.

"So, Donna," Wixton said, "the reason you are not going to Lancas-ter is not so I can beat Scott's time with the beauteous Miss Sarah. It's because you are going to be very busy in the morgue, familiarizing yourself with everything that Wainwright's done since the glacier went back. We were not prepared to deal with this French thing, or any-thing else along that line. But now we're gonna be, all right? Places everybody—curtain going up."

25

Scott Pokaski drove into Charlotte on Monday morning and found St. Mary's Church without any trouble. It was small and white and locked in the early afternoon, and it made him feel lonesome. He took note of the small wooden sign that directed visitors to the rectory on Willow Street, two blocks down. He parked his red Triumph TR4 in the sloping driveway of the low gray house in the hollow off the road and got out and rang the doorbell. A short man in a shabby gray sweater and brown corduroy pants answered the door. His skin was chapped under the eyes, and his gray hair was sparse. He stared at Pokaski through the screened door. He said: "Yes?"

Pokaski shifted his weight from his right foot to his left and jammed his hands deeper into the pockets of his blue nylon parka. "I'm uh, I'm a reporter," he said. "My name's Scott Pokaski. From the *Valley Press,* you know?"

"I've heard of it," the small man said. "I read it every day."

"My editor'll be glad to hear it," Pokaski said. He shivered.

The small man smiled. "Would you like to come in?" he said.

"Yeah," Pokaski said. "Matter of fact, I would."

The small man opened the door. "I should think so," he said, looking past Pokaski toward the car. "You need something sturdier'n that, in this part the country. Mind your head now." He extended his right arm and placed his right hand in the air between the frame of the door and Pokaski's lowered head.

"I know," Pokaski said, stamping his feet in the hallway. "I came up here in the first place, I was under the impression winter didn't last all year around. Now I been here, five years, I know a little better. Only now it's too late."

The small man laughed. He shut the wooden inside door. "Two kinds of people live in Vermont," he said. "Those who're too cussed to live anywhere else, and those who've lived here long enough so that they're getting the same. You're just in-between. You'll get over it, or you'll get out. That will be your choice. In the meantime, come into the sitting room."

The room was dim. The ceiling was low. There was a tall, fat, brown iron stove sitting on a quilted asbestos mat near the center of the room, its aluminum stack making two right angles on its way to the blocked-off fireplace. Two cushioned Boston rockers flanked the stove. "It's nice and warm in here now," the small man said. "I just got back, few minutes ago, and stoked the thing." He pointed toward a thread-bare, overstuffed mauve couch, three antimacassars arranged along the back. "Take your coat off and sit down. Would you like some tea? I was just about to have some."

Pokaski hesitated. He turned to face the small man. "I'm looking," he said, "for Father Morrissette. Reverend Gerard Morrissette."

"You don't need to be so formal," the small man said. "Most people call me 'Bunny,' and that's all right with me. The question's whether you want tea."

"All right," Pokaski said.

"Good," Morrissette said. "Just sit down, and I'll be right back. I won't be a minute."

Pokaski removed his parka and sat down on the couch. He could feel the spring coils under his buttocks. The priest was right about the warmth. It was sedative. The priest returned carrying two U.S. Navy mugs. He handed one to Pokaski and retreated to the rocker to the left of the stove. "It gets so cold out there," the priest said. He blew across the surface of the liquid in the mug and then sucked at the fluid. "I do enjoy my tea." He chuckled. "I had a mentor in the sem, name of Father Shaughnessey. His expression for good tea was: 'You could throt a mouse on it.' And that's how I like it."

248

Expecting a jolt of caffeine, Pokaski drank from his mug and choked. The priest looked up and chuckled. "Oh," he said, "I should have asked you. I like some rum in mine. Although brandy's also nice, but terribly expensive. I guess I just assume, when I get back here in the morning and it's cold, that everyone knows about my treat, and would like it, too."

"No, no, it's fine," Pokaski said, sipping from the mug. "I just wasn't expecting it."

"Our churches are so small," the priest said. "Well, what we *call* our churches. Saint Mary's is really the only one that really is a church. But it's cold, too. It seems to get into your bones. I was up in the Notch this morning? This is my day to offer morning Mass at the Notch. I suppose it's silly. Only six or seven people. This time of year especially. So hard to get around. And the ones who come, you know, have nothing else to do. Older people." He laughed. "Some of them have ten or twenty years on me. I'm surprised each time they come. But devoted people, really. Truly followers of Christ. And at their age, getting pretty close on His heels, too. It's just that cold seems to come right through the walls. It actually *hurts*."

Pokaski set his mug down on the floor. "Oh, you can put your tea on the doily on the table," the priest said. There was a wooden pole lamp to Pokaski's left; it had an oval table mounted halfway up. "It won't do any harm," the priest said. "Won't do any harm at all. And you might turn the lamp on, if you like. These old houses are so dark."

Pokaski located the doily principally by touch and set the mug down on it. "I noticed that," he said, groping until he found the chain that turned on one forty-watt bulb. "What is it? The mountains cutting off the light? Or because we're further north, and there's just less of it?"

"It's both of those things, partly," the priest said, inhaling the vapor rising from his tea. "But mostly it's the heat."

"The heat," Pokaski said. "I hadn't noticed that."

"Where do you come from?" the priest said. "If you don't mind my asking, I mean."

"Oh," Pokaski said. "Well, Long Island, I guess. I grew up there, I mean. As much as anyplace else. Bethpage. We moved around a lot. My father's a design engineer. Grumman Aircraft. It's kind of a funny job. I wouldn't want it."

"Did you live in a house?" the priest said.

249

"Oh, yeah," Pokaski said. "Yeah, we always lived in a house. The one we had the last three years, it was really pretty nice. Wasn't on the beach, but we could see the water."

"And it was light inside," the priest said. "Comparatively, I mean."

Pokaski thought. "Yeah," he said, "I guess it was. Now I think of it."

"And you had big windows," the priest said.

"Well," Pokaski said, "everybody did. Picture windows, you know? Everyone had one of those. And the sliding doors. You're out on Long Island, even if there's no way you can possibly see water, the houses're all built the same, just as though you could."

"Well, that's the reason, then," the priest said. "That's what I mean. Your houses were heated with oil, were they? You had an oil burner?"

"Sure," Pokaski said.

"So, you had heat," the priest said. "Lots of heat. As much as you wanted. The people who built these houses had no heat, except what they got for themselves. Heat was expensive. Not something that they bought with money. Anything they bought with money was something that they couldn't make. Because they didn't have much money. And they could make heat. They made it by chopping down trees, and cutting them up, and splitting them. After the haying was over. And the season didn't allow them, really, to do much of anything else.

"Well, that's hard work. An ax and a bucksaw. No gasoline chain saws in those days. And a wedge and a maul. And then getting the wood back up to the house, and stacking the wood near the door. They got their heat from the wood that they cut. So, when it came to building houses, they made the rooms small, less to heat, and the windows small as well. Because glass loses heat much faster'n wood, and in the fall the difference between laying up eight cords of wood, and laying up, oh, twelve, is something you appreciate. When your back gets sore."

"I see," Pokaski said. He drank some more of his tea. "You've lived here all your life, then?"

The priest shook his head. "My, no," he said. "I've only been here since nineteen forty. I'm a newcomer. And by rights what we get in this neck of the woods should seem like the tropics to me. I grew up in Colebrook."

"The Northeast Kingdom," Pokaski said.

"Yes," the priest said. "Of course I say: 'I grew up there.' But I didn't, really. Only 'til I was fourteen. Then the seminary. But I still remember how very cold it was. I suppose I'm getting old and soft now, my teeth chattering down here. But they still do. The reason doesn't matter."

"You became a priest when you were fourteen?" Pokaski said.

"Oh, no," the priest said. "That was just when I went into the seminary. It was really just a high school the priests ran in Burlington. But the only way you could get in was if God had called you. I was blessed. God had called me. And so I went, and stayed. I was there ten years."

"And then you came here," Pokaski said.

"Not at first," the priest said. "When I was first a curate, I was down in Rutland. But then this parish opened up, and no one wanted it. There was no place to live. So I got it. My aunt was still alive then, so I could live here with her. It pleased her to have this little house become the rectory. Her pride, and also the fact that she didn't have to pay any more taxes on it. So I made the sign and put it up. At the church, I mean. And when she died, well, people were used to it. And it didn't do any harm. So I left it up." He paused.

"I didn't get very good grades in the seminary," he said. "It was a blessing that this happened. I see God's hand in it. I wasn't fit for much. 'What on earth am I going to do with Bunny Morrissette,' He thought. And then He had this idea. And I've been here ever since. And I've loved every moment. I know, well, every night we priests pray that we've tried to serve Him that day, and look forward eagerly to the day when we'll see Him, face-to-face.

"I do it. But I don't really mean the second part, you know? Oh, I mean it, but when it finally happens, that my Saviour calls me home, I'm afraid I may be tempted to say: 'Please, Lord, a few more years?' It's the perfect place for me."

"So you know it pretty well then," Pokaski said.

"I think so," the priest said. "After twenty-seven years. And not that there's much to know. But I've known the Frenches all that time. I can't claim that I'm as close to them as some other families. They keep to themselves. But a nice family, a good one. Hardworking, and devout."

251

"Father Morrissette," Pokaski said, "that's what I came here to ask you about."

"Of course," the priest said.

"Has somebody else been here first?" Pokaski said.

"Goodness, no," the priest said. "Why would they come to see me?"

"Same reason I did," Pokaski said. "To talk about Anthony French."

"I'd've been very surprised if they did," the priest said.

"But you knew that's why I was here," Pokaski said.

"And I was very surprised," the priest said. "So while I was making the tea, I asked myself why you were here. And the only reason I could think of was young Anthony French. You were up at the Notch Saturday. So that had to be the reason. I did know him, a little bit. I thought he had promise. And as I thought about it, I thought: 'Well, perhaps God has some plan, and this young man's His angel.' "

Pokaski grinned. "Would you mind calling my editor, Father?" he said. "He's called me lots of things, and so've other people, but that's one he's never heard. It might help me a lot."

The priest laughed. "I'm afraid I've never been much help," he said. "Not by saying what I thought. I'd like to be, though, so I'll call him if you like."

"I'll keep that in reserve," Pokaski said. He pulled his spiral pad and pen out of his parka pocket. "Let me ask you about Anthony French. You said you did know him."

"I knew him all his life," the priest said. "I knew him before his life. I officiated at the marriage of his mother and his father. I baptized him when he was born. I heard his catechism. I heard his first confession, and gave him his First Communion. I prepared him for Confirmation, and presented him at Burlington as ready for that sacrament. Each Lent I at least assume I heard his confession, among others."

He smiled. "In villages where you do well to find twelve Catholics, it's pretty hard not to know how many have come in, to be forgiven for their sins. And sometimes, God forgive us, it is pretty hard as well, not to recognize the voices, and know who wasn't there. So now and then the devil whispers: 'Twelve received, but eight confessed. You've got four ringers in there, Father, sacrilegious bastards.'

"But I'm too much for the devil, you know. I'm too smart for him: 'Get thee behind me, Satan,' I say. 'They went up in Burlington.

Or they had some business in Charlotte, when I was hearing there.'
The devil is a tricky one. Have to stay one step ahead. And I think
that's what Tony did. Until this business happened. I hope he did, at
least."

"So now you'll be presiding at his funeral Mass," Pokaski said,
scribbling in the low light. "You've brought him the complete
circle."

"I assume so," the priest said. "Robert and Janet, those're his
parents, were at Mass this morning. They've been coming since it
happened. Since they heard about it. In addition to Sundays, of
course. They're very faithful people. If the Sunday Mass is here,
they're here. If it's in Canterbury, they are there. In Occident. In
Springs. But he's a working man, and she has two children at home, so
it's a real stretch for them to make a weekday Mass." He sighed.

"I've been offering each of my Masses, except the two funerals and
one nuptial that I've had since the news came, privately for Tony. The
repose of his soul. It's all I know how to do."

"Have you told the family this?" Pokaski said, his pen poised.

The priest sounded as though he had gotten some gravel in his
throat. "No," he rasped, "and I shouldn't have told you, either. So
don't write that down, and don't put it in the paper. Is that clear, young
man?"

Pokaski dropped the ballpoint on the couch. "Father," he said, "I
didn't come here to make you mad. Honestly, I didn't. If you don't
want me to print something, I won't."

The priest cleared his throat and drank from his mug. "Thank you,"
he said. "I suddenly felt stupid. And I deserved to, too.

"You see, the Frenches're like most people. They have their dignity.
And if they knew what I was doing, celebrating Masses for the repose
of his soul, they'd think themselves obliged. To make offerings. Well,
in the first place, I don't need them. And in the second place, they
can't."

He shook his head. "I spoke to them after Mass this morning," he
said. "The other kids were with them. And they all looked so forlorn.
And I tried, as I did last week, to say something that would help them.
And failed. Again. Of course. It's an awful, awful thing. I know it's
God's work that I'm doing. But sometimes He makes it hard."

"You said you 'assume' you'll be saying the funeral Mass," Pokaski said.

"Well," the priest said, "yes, I do. After all, I am their pastor. I was Tony's, too. So normally I would expect that I would celebrate the Mass. But I gather from what they say that there's been some pressure on them. Someone's been asking them what they wanted done. Someone they don't know. And that troubles them, you know? What is going on. That's if something is, but it clearly seems to be."

"Like what?" Pokaski said. He picked up his pen and pad again.

"I really don't know," the priest said. "Bob told me this morning that the congressman'd called him. Or, rather, his office had. Now I may be exaggerating this. But Bob was, I don't know, *concerned*. So was Janet, too. You have to understand that they are quiet people. I know them. I've been with them before in times of sorrow. When her parents died, within two weeks of each other. When that terrible accident happened at the gorge.

"So I know them. They know me. I've shared their sadnesses. And when Tony graduated from junior high school, well, I gave the benediction that day—Ev Glennon gave the invocation, and talked much too long, altogether too conscious of being the Protestant minister using a Catholic pulpit—and they invited me back to the Notch, for their family party.

"Mine's a small parish. I could tell you the same story about most of my parishioners. I suppose what I'm saying is that after all these years of dealing with our lives, we know how each other acts, when something bad happens.

"Well," he said, "today was different. Today was very different. Bob and Janet were upset. They did not know what to do. I'm sure Congressman Wainwright, or the fellow in his office, I'm sure what they had in mind was to show their sympathy.

" 'But we don't know these people,' Bob said. 'He's no friend of ours. I've met him, sure. Shaken his hand. We've both voted for him. But what the hell's he want with us? Why's he *calling* us? Don't make any sense to us.' He was really quite upset."

"Well," Pokaski said, "did he say what Wainwright said? Give you any details?"

"No," the priest said, "he didn't, really. I was tempted to ask questions, but I decided not to. He was already confused, and my asking would've bothered him more'n he was already. 'We didn't ask this Wainwright to do anything for us. We never asked a single thing, and now we got this trouble. Why's this happening? What's going on?' I just tried to calm him down."

"Well," Pokaski said, "if you want a guess: My guess is that Wainwright's coming up here for the funeral."

"That was mine, too," the priest said. "And then Janet said to me: 'Who's officiating? They also asked Bob that. What did they mean by that, Bunny? What did they mean by that? Anthony was our son. He did not belong to them.' I did not know what to say."

"Father," Pokaski said, flipping back through his pad, "you said you were with the family after the accident at the gorge. What was that accident?"

The priest shook his head. "Accidents are accidents. Some are good and some are bad. That's all back in the past now, 'specially since Tony's dead. And that's where we will leave it. Back where it belongs. The dead to bury the dead."

Pokaski made a check mark next to his note. He flipped farther back through the pad. "You said you thought he showed a lot of promise. What did you mean by that?"

The priest slumped in his chair. "Oh, I don't know," he said. He waved his left hand feebly. "It's so hard to know. These young men that grow up here, they don't have many choices. You try to teach them, to persuade them, of God's love for them, but then they look around and they don't see anything except more hopelessness. It's hard. It's hard for them.

"I've known so many, all these years. Not just my parishioners. Young people from all the towns. Of whatever faith. Young Paul Whipple, for example—his father is my friend. And a brilliant, brilliant kid. He is going to make it. But so many of them don't. Never have a chance. Young boys grown into men, that I've known all their lives. Boys I've fished with, boys I've hunted with, boys I've talked to, man to man, about how they should live their lives.

"And the girls, the same way. Growing into women. With the same damned hopelessness. Anthony had that. I know he suffered with it. He had no choice, the army, but he welcomed it, you know? *Welcomed* it. A way to get it over with. Or else to get out. And all I can tell them is that they serve God by living their lives purely.

"And it's not enough."

"You don't care to say what made you think he had promise?" Pokaski said.

The priest shook his head. "Maybe I was wrong," he said. "Maybe I was wrong. Or what would be much worse, maybe I was right."

26

just before noon, Pokaski parked the Triumph and went inside the two-story regional junior high school south of Carmichael's gas station in Occident. The door to the administration office was the first on his right. He entered and stood at the counter to introduce himself to a pretty girl, about sixteen, who was typing something. She picked up the telephone on her desk and prepared to dial, but a man, about thirty-five, in a tan corduroy jacket and gray slacks, emerged from an office inside the enclosure and smiled at him. "Come right in," he said.

Pokaski went to the swinging gate at the far end of the counter. The man opened it and showed him into the office. He extended his right hand. "Walt Crosley."

Pokaski shook it. "Scott Pokaski," he said. "*Valley Press*. I'm working a story about Anthony French."

Crosley directed Pokaski to the gray metal armchair facing the desk and took the chair behind it. He clasped his hands behind his head and tilted back in his chair. "Yes," he said. "How can I help you?"

"Well," Pokaski said, taking his pad out, "I was going to start by asking you if Father Morrissette has a telephone, but I guess that won't be necessary."

Crosley grinned. "Before I became a headmaster," he said, "I taught chemistry and physics."

"Yeah?" Pokaski said.

"I taught them in Springfield, Massachusetts," Crosley said, "and I was pretty good. But I wanted to be an administrator, young, and I wasn't going to be, there. So I came up here. And besides, the skiing's better—Mount Tom's nice, but Mount Tom's low. So I came up here. And I've learned a lot. But I didn't forget what I knew, part of which is the Heisenberg Principle: When you measure a system, you disrupt it. When you put the thermometer into the water, it's either colder than the water, so it makes the water colder, or warmer than the water, so it makes the water warmer. So you cannot measure the system—you can only measure the system that you happen to be measuring at the time."

"Sort of a Zeno's paradox," Pokaski said.

"Sort of," Crosley said. "Well, that's what you're doing here. It's what I was doing, I came here. You've intruded yourself into a closed system. A very small, closed system. It didn't have you in it yesterday, so it was different, then, from what it is right now. Today all the molecules, the Morrissette molecule, the Crosley molecule, and God knows how many other molecules with different names, are vibrating at different pitches than they were yesterday."

"I don't want to seem callous," Pokaski said, "but what's the excitement about? The kid is dead. D, E, A, D. He died in Vietnam. There's going to be a funeral, and they're going to bury him. Everybody knew that before I drove into town. All I'm trying to do is get some background on him. How does that disrupt?"

"It disrupts because you are a stranger, and you want to get the background to publish in the paper," Crosley said. "A lot—not all, not as many as used to, before television, but a lot, just the same—of the people in this region read the paper. They don't read it all, and they don't believe it all, but they get it and they look it over. And they know what to expect. They do not expect to see their names in it, except when they get married, or someone in their family dies. And even then they're a little surprised, despite the fact that they themselves supplied the information.

"Nothing *happens* here—you see what I mean? Things *happen* in other places, down the road from here. Things happen down in Washington. Things happen overseas. In Occident, Lancaster Notch, Springs, and places like that, the events the paper reports are mere

258

reality. Someone gets born? We knew that, hour afterward. Someone died? Expected. 'He'd been ailing for some time.' Two someones get married? No surprise in that. 'Knocked her up in June, probably the night of the senior prom. Here it is September—'bout time that they did something.'

"The only thing the paper does for events here is confirm our certain knowledge. Satisfy our expectations. Make a record of the history that we throw away tomorrow. Or stuff in the stove tonight.

"You being here unsettles us. It means we missed something. We knew Tony French, a long time. He was in the army, went to Vietnam. We knew he got killed. Hey, tough break, but not the first one. Won't be the last one, either. His body will come back here, and we'll bury it.

"So why is this reporter here? What is it he wants? What's the story here? You're after news? You *are* news, just because of that.

"So," Crosley said, "you've heard of the jungle telegraph? We've got our own version. No drums involved, just telephones, and also Whipple's store. If Bunny hasn't called Paul Whipple, and I'd bet ten cents he has, then Bunny has called Wilse Carmichael, and Carmichael's been to Paul's, and he calls his wife up at the Notch, just like she calls him down here, when you go to see the Frenches. And everybody on those lines picks up the phone, their ring or not, so they all know you're here."

"So I'm not going to get anything," Pokaski said.

"Sure you are," Crosley said. "The question is: What? And that's what everybody that you're likely to interview is discussing now. 'What do we say to this reporter fella? How much do we tell him?' Nobody's going to *lie* to you. That is not the style. It's more like censorship than lying. Just keeping things back."

"And that includes you," Pokaski said.

"It does and it doesn't," Crosley said. "I'm describing a system that I know from observation. Not from membership. And only three years' observation. So I sympathize with your predicament at the same time I describe it, and I'm therefore disrupting it. You're a figure of suspicion. So am I, and always will be, because I wasn't born here. Not with as intense suspicion as you're under here today, but suspicion nonetheless. If I stay here for twenty more years, which I certainly will not, every single day of those years, when I come in to work, people who were born here will watch me carefully—to see if I'm buck-naked when I get out of my car. There's nothing in my past to suggest that I'd take off all my clothes and go terrorize the town. And it's not part of my ambition. But they're not convinced they really know all of what's my past. And, therefore, where they're concerned, well, I will bear some watching. And, unlike you, they can fix me, if I step out of line."

" 'Fix' you," Pokaski said.

"Sure," Crosley said. "They can fire my ass. And they can destroy my résumé, so I can't find a job elsewhere. You're bulletproof, as far as they're concerned. Unless they use real bullets. Which they won't resort to, matter of this magnitude."

"There's encouraging news," Pokaski said.

"You should think of it that way," Crosley said. "You really should, you know. What I'm saying's I can tell you what is on the public record, and therefore what you should look for, the back issues of your paper. But I can't tell you what is not—not that much isn't—because if I do that, they will know, and know too where you got it."

"And then they will use bullets," Pokaski said.

"No," Crosley said. "Then they will use gossip, which is even deadlier. Because it never misses. Even the wild shots."

Pokaski sighed. "Tell me what you can," he said. "I'd appreciate it."

Crosley pulled a manila folder across his desk and opened it. "Anthony French entered the Iroquois Regional School in September nineteen sixty. He graduated in June nineteen sixty-seven."

"He was in high school seven years?" Pokaski said. "Was the kid retarded?"

Crosley shook his head. "This is a combined junior-senior high school," he said. "Anthony French entered the seventh grade in September of nineteen sixty. He had completed the primary grades at Lancaster Notch. He did not attend Iroquois Regional during the first half of his last year. But he did manage to graduate with his class in June. He transferred credits back here."

"Where was he?" Pokaski said. "What the hell was he doing?"

"That's not in this record," Crosley said. He closed the folder.

"But you know," Pokaski said.

Crosley shrugged. "A lot of people know," he said. "It was not a secret. It was in the paper, even. But it's not in this folder."

"Are you going to tell me?" Pokaski said.

"Nope," Crosley said. "I believe in Jesus. I am glad he saved me. But Jesus had more balls'n I do. Cross, crown of thorns, and scourging—doesn't interest me. I will leave this town someday, and I hope it's someday soon. But I am driving out, all right? Don't bother, pluck the chickens. Never mind the boiling tar; leave the fence rail where it is. Crosley will go quietly, under his own power."

"Not even where to look?" Pokaski said.

"I already did," Crosley said.

Shortly before 7:00 that evening, Wixton entered the *Valley Press* morgue in search of clips of stories about George Romney. He found what he needed in the green file cabinets and took the drawer of small brown envelopes to the row of tables at the rear of the library. Taunton sat to his left, a drawer of envelopes to her right, a collection of clippings spread in front of her, gnawing her lower lip and making notes on a pad of pulp. Pokaski sat to his right, a drawer of envelopes to his left, a collection of clippings spread before him, making notes on his spiral pad and scowling.

"Well," Wixton said, "gracious goodness me. As I live and breathe. The governor of Michigan does the dry-dive on the presidential race, although he may not know it yet, and I come in here like a tattooed serf to do his public-life obituary. And here I find my staff. Two whole hours after the quitting whistle blows, and both my crack reporters're still bent over the anvil. Son of a bitch."

"Blow it out your barracks bag, Russ," Taunton said, without looking up. "If Wainwright's not the dumbest guy God ever put on earth, he's sure the carefullest." Pokaski said nothing.

"And you, Scott," Wixton said, "what pleasantries have you? And what is it you're doing here, instead of in the Notch?"

Pokaski looked up. "I am doing the same damned thing that the CIA should've done and didn't do in Vietnam," he said. "I was down in Occident today, and what I principally learned was that I didn't know anything. And no one was going to tell me. So now I'm here to find out what it is that they know and I don't, and tomorrow I am going back down there and kick them in the nuts."

"Well, well, well," Wixton said. He grinned. "As God is my witness,

I believe I see before me two genuine reporters. What I got will take two hours. Thereabouts or so. Anyone for chops, then? And perhaps some cheap red wine? At the Hunter's Tap?"

"Can't afford it," Taunton said. "Blackjack charges too much, on the pay I make." Pokaski only grunted.

Wixton dropped his tray on a table and sat down. "Donna, Scottie," he said, "what I mean is: I'm buying."

Taunton looked up and stuck her pen in her mouth. Pokaski lifted his eyes and looked at Taunton. They nodded at each other. "We did it, Scott," she said. "We finally snowed the bastard."

27

Wilson Carmichael in soiled blue coveralls over an insulated vest, with a dirty Red Sox cap on his head, was pumping gas into a Ford pickup truck when Pokaski arrived at his Amoco station in the morning. Pokaski parked the TR4 on the other side of the island and shut the engine off. He rolled the window down and waited. Carmichael shut off the pump and collected six dollars from the driver of the pickup. He put the money in his pocket and approached Pokaski's car. He said: "Yeah?"

"Fill it with the high-test?" Pokaski said.

Carmichael stood up and surveyed the car. He shook his head. "Ain't leaded, you know," he said. He wheezed.

"I know that," Pokaski said.

Carmichael nodded. "You got dual Strombergs on this," he said. "I don't know much about Strombergs, but I know one important thing: They're a bitch to balance."

"Sure are," Pokaski said.

"You got her runnin' right," Carmichael said, "you don't want to mess with her."

"Nope," Pokaski said.

"You had 'em balanced, leaded gas?" Carmichael said.

"Yeah," Pokaski said.

" 'N you should stick to leaded," Carmichael said. "Get it up at

Whipple's. Don't want you coming back here, claiming I screwed up your car. Hate these little puddle-jumpers anyway. Don't work on 'em. Don't even like, see them around. Nothing but cheap junk."

Pokaski nodded. He turned the key in the ignition. "All right if I park on the street?"

" 'S all right by me," Carmichael said. "Don't own the thing myself."

"Because I'd like to talk to you," Pokaski said.

Carmichael nodded. "Figured," he said. "Don't have to buy gas to do that."

Pokaski parked the Triumph at the curb on the street beside the station. He braced himself against the cold wind and entered the sales room. The bell above the door jangled when he opened it, and again as he shut it. Carmichael sat behind his oak desk. He had his hands behind his head. There was a cigarette smoldering in the black metal ashtray. "Take a load off your feet," he said.

Pokaski sat down in the oak armchair facing the desk. He unzipped his parka.

"Anthony French," he said. He took the spiral pad and the pen out of his parka.

"Knew him," Carmichael said.

"Well?" Pokaski said.

"Moderate," Carmichael said.

"Because the reason that I'm asking," Pokaski said.

"I know why you're asking," Carmichael said. "You're that reporter. From the paper. No need, tell me that."

"Name's Pokaski," he said. "My name is Scott Pokaski."

"Yeah," Carmichael said. "That's all right with me."

Pokaski drew a breath. "Okay," he said. "You had a son name of Harold."

Carmichael shifted his position. "Nope," he said.

"No?" Pokaski said. "That's what our files show. The files at the paper, I mean."

"Paper's wrong," Carmichael said. "Harry's name was 'Harry.' Named him for my father. Father's name was Harry. Don't know where the 'Harold' came from. Wasn't my idea."

"Anyway," Pokaski said, "your son died. Back in the summer, 'sixty-six."

264

"Yeah," Carmichael said. "Got killed is what he did."

"At Huntington Gorge," Pokaski said.

"That's right," Carmichael said.

"He was shot," Pokaski said.

Carmichael nodded.

"Mr. Carmichael," Pokaski said, "I know this is painful for you."

Carmichael shook his head. "Year ago," he said. "Painful when it happened. But now's just something, did. Used to it now."

"Anthony French was accused of firing the shot that killed him," Pokaski said.

"Yeah," Carmichael said. "Convicted of it, too."

"Of manslaughter," Pokaski said. "Involuntary manslaughter."

"That's right," Carmichael said. "They didn't think he meant to."

"Did you?" Pokaski said.

Carmichael hunched his shoulders and raised his eyebrows. "Didn't really know," he said. "Still don't. Wasn't there. Didn't see it. Didn't matter at the time. Hasn't mattered since." He paused. "Tough on his mother, though. Still mentions him a lot."

"Do you know what happened?" Pokaski said.

"Know what they said happened," Carmichael said. "The boys went up fishing. Did that a lot. I was expecting Harry, come down here and help me out, he got out of bed that day. But he didn't. I guess French come by, with a couple other boys, and he decided that he'd rather fish with them 'n work with me. Harry wasn't strong on work. He liked the fishing and the hunting, doing what he pleased. Harry was a good boy, never gave a minute's trouble, but he didn't like to work."

"How old was he?" Pokaski said.

"Fifteen, when he died," Carmichael said. "Him and his other friend. French was sixteen, though, close to seventeen. Harry would've turned sixteen in the fall. Except Harry didn't make it, but the others were all right."

"The clippings at the paper make it look like an accident," Pokaski said.

Carmichael nodded. "That's what I thought," he said. "I thought that at the time. Stupid accident, but still an accident. The French boy, hell, the lot of them, they should've known guns. But they didn't. You been up the gorge?"

"No," Pokaski said.

"No," Carmichael said. "Well, if you'd've been up there, you'd know. The walls're sheer—rock sheer. Black. And the water comes over the top and out the bottom of the dam at the electric plant. The river bottom's marble. It isn't regular. You got your boulders sticking up, all across the thing. And, it's only natural, snakes crawl out on them. So what the boys did, when they went there, looking to catch trout, they'd take their pistols with them. Case the fishing wasn't good. What I heard was: It wasn't. Day that Harry died. So they're using their Hi-Standards, to plink snakes, you know?

"Now you've got to be a young kid, or else you've got to have no brains, to be shooting twenty-twos off in a place that's full of rocks. Damned thing's nowhere near as dangerous to the thing you're shooting at as it is to what's around you when the damned thing ricochets. I guess what Tony French did was, he missed the snake he saw.

"But he never should've shot at it, with Harry fishing from the next rock, twenty feet away. Caught him right under the right ear. Poor kid never felt a thing."

"The clips said that he died of drowning," Pokaski said.

"Don't doubt it," Carmichael said. "Didn't then and I don't now. You take a bullet in the head, and fall into that white water, see how good you are at swimming. Course he drowned. I would."

"Did you think that Tony French was adequately punished?" Pokaski said.

"Don't follow you," Carmichael said. "The hell does that all mean?"

"Did you think," Pokaski said, "or: Do you think now? That Tony French was punished enough? For killing your son."

Carmichael stared at him. "I never did like Tony French. I wished Harry didn't. Couldn't figure that one out. Harry was a lazy kid, but he was a good one. Tony French was lazy, too, but he had a mean streak." He hesitated. "Thing he did, Paul Whipple's daughter, well, that shows what I mean. What that boy really was. But that don't mean that he was different. They were all alike. They went up there, to fish the gorge? Had no business doing that. Bob French told me, Harry's funeral, Tony didn't have permission. I said: 'For Christ sake, Bob, you left the damned keys in your car. He didn't need permission, he could start the thing.'

"Was he punished enough? I guess so. He was in the School for Boys for the best part of a year. I didn't really see the point then. And I don't see it now. He did a stupid thing, and Harry died because of it. Now he's dead. Like Harry. Someone else's stupid thing."

"Our files show," Pokaski said, "at least they seem to show, that the crucial evidence in that case came from Henry Briggs."

" 'S what most seemed to think," Carmichael said. "He was the game warden then. Had to do his job."

"Now he's running for Congress," Pokaski said.

"Heard that, too," Carmichael said. "Told me so himself."

"Do you plan to vote for him?" Pokaski said. "After his testimony?"

Carmichael shook his head. "Nope. Didn't before this, neither."

"Because of the French case?" Pokaski said.

"Nope," Carmichael said. "Just don't believe in it."

"Mr. Carmichael," Pokaski said, "what did Tony French do, to Paul Whipple's daughter?"

Carmichael shook his head once more. "Nope," he said. "Anybody tells you that, have to be Paul Whipple. Not going to come from me."

"Does anybody else know about it?" Pokaski said.

Carmichael nodded. "Couple people," he said. "I know of, at least."

"And will they talk to me?" Pokaski said.

"Don't know," Carmichael said. "Have to ask them. Yourself."

"Who are they?" Pokaski said.

Carmichael shook his head. "Nope," he said. "You come in here and ask questions, about how Harry died. Well, I'm Harry's father, and if anybody's going to talk about him I would say I'm it. Anybody wants to talk about Paul Whipple's daughter, that's Paul Whipple's business. Not mine."

"And, if I go around and ask," Pokaski said, "everyone besides Paul Whipple will tell me the same thing. He's the man I have to see."

Carmichael nodded. "Most likely," he said. He stubbed out the cigarette and lighted another from a pack of Viceroys. He put it into the ashtray and sat back again. He coughed.

Pokaski gazed at Carmichael. What seemed like a long time went by in silence. The smoke from the cigarette curled upward from the ashtray. Carmichael sat almost perfectly still, his eyes expressionless, his face in repose. Pokaski began to fidget. He closed the spiral pad and put it back into his parka, along with the ballpoint pen. "Well," he said, standing up, "guess I'd best be shoving off."

Carmichael nodded. "Nice talking to you," he said.

"Lemme ask you something," Pokaski said, gesturing toward the ashtray. "You light those things, but you don't smoke them. Why is that, you do that?"

"Bad for the lungs," Carmichael said. He wheezed again, and coughed. "Also not a good idea, smoke while you're pumping gas."

"Then why light them at all?" Pokaski said.

"Been smoking all my life," Carmichael said. "Ever since I was a boy. Habit that I got. Tried to quit. Can't."

"But isn't it kind of a waste?" Pokaski said.

Carmichael raised his eyebrows. "Some might think so," he said. "I feel comfortable. And that's all I ask."

28

Pokaski sat slumped in his chair in the *Valley Press* library, brown envelopes arrayed in front of him. Taunton came in, her cheeks flushed from the cold, and took the seat opposite him. She slapped her notebook down on the table and used her knuckles to rub her eyes. "Andrew J. Prior is an asshole," she said. "A major league fucking asshole. How a guy like that can work for a congressman—and he's Wainwright's top assistant, keep in mind—is something I will never understand."

Pokaski considered. He nodded. "Martha Glennon's not," he said. "What she is, is one mean woman."

"I'll bite," Taunton said, "but I'm biting second. I get to do my bitching first." Pokaski nodded. "I called this son of a bitch, all right? I called him yesterday, and he didn't return my call, and I called him again today. And he was out. Gone to lunch. At eleven-fifteen in the morning? I call back at three. He isn't back yet. 'Where's he eat lunch?' I say. 'Somewhere in North Dakota?'"

"Gets me nowhere. Wainwright's got this secretary that when you talk to her it's like being back in the second grade."

Taunton made her voice nasal. " 'This is Miss Poitrast.' She knows everything. You know nothing. And she's not telling you anything until you're sitting up straight, with your hands neatly folded on the desk in front of you. I say: 'Look, all I'm trying to do's a story about the

269

congressman's career. And I'd like to get it right. I'm going to want to interview him, but in order to do that right, and take up as little, his time, as possible, I need a summary of his committees. What he considers his most important accomplishments. Things like that, you know? Ordinary things that every politician's office has at their fingertips.'

"She says Mr. Wainwright is not an ordinary congressman but a very special one. Anytime one of his constituents has a specific question about how Mr. Wainwright stands on some particular matter, 'they know all they need to do is ask him a specific question, and he answers it right off. Your question's not specific.'

"I tell her I can't ask her a specific question until I get some background. Some facts about his background, and that's why I'm calling him. For a background sheet. She doesn't think Mr. Prior has, that they have, such a thing. You'd've thought I was asking her to send me a list of Wainwright's favorite dirty books.

"So I call back again at four," Taunton said. "Now Prior is back. And he actually takes my call. As Russell says: I faint. I swoon. Be still, my beating heart. I tell him what I want. The gargoyle at the desk was right. No such thing exists. 'Well, look,' I say, 'I mean I hate to impose or anything, but could you possibly put one together?' I mean, after all, we are paying taxes, are we not? Isn't this guy working for us?

" 'I could,' Prior said, 'but not this week. We're very busy here this week. It's a very busy week.' And then he tells me the congressman's coming up here, and he's got to leave early on Thursday so he can take the train. So it's a short week, too. 'What for?' I said.

" 'Why?' he said. 'Because I need to talk to him,' I say. 'If he's coming home this weekend, maybe I can do it then.' He doubts it. Wainwright will be very busy. He's coming up for your damned funeral. Going to be in attendance for your hero's burial."

"Huh," Pokaski said, "he may be disappointed."

"The kid's not dead?" she said.

"Far's I know, he is," Pokaski said. "Dead is not the problem. Problem's making him a hero. I haven't found too many—hell, I haven't found a one—who'd describe him as a stalwart youth. Even a good one." He summarized what the priest and Carmichael had told him. "I mean," he said, "the best you could say about the kid at that point was that he was a trigger-happy little bastard who had also done a bad thing to one the girls in town."

"What was that?" Taunton said.

"Just about what you'd expect," Pokaski said. "Common act, I understand. Thing of it was, the girl he picked was a sitting duck. She's a mute." He shifted his voice into a harsh falsetto. 'Marie Whipple's a lovely little creature, but she has a handicap. And her family means well, I'm sure, but they've been sadly mistaken in the way they've handled it.' That's Martha Glennon for you. 'We try to be charitable,' she said. 'After all, Everett is the minister, and we do have to be forebearing. But it's been hard, I can assure you, to sit idly by and watch while her father ignores her.' This is a lady," he said, "this is a lady who is going to do good works for you—regardless of whether you like it or not."

" 'Whether' includes 'or not,' " Taunton said.

"Shut up, Russ," Pokaski said. "If I want Wixton teaching me grammar, I'll put it on copy paper and leave it on his desk. And then, after she performs her good works on you, over your objections, then she is going to brag about it, to everyone she meets. 'I had hopes, I really did. There's this most unfortunate young woman, staying here with us. She has a little baby, and we took her in. To stay under this roof with us. And I hoped, I had this hope that if she could get to know Marie, and Marie's father saw them together, well, the two girls might have a friendship, and his heart might be softened. Hasn't done a bit of good.' "

"So what'd the hero do, rape her?" Taunton said.

"No," Pokaski said. "He just spotted a weakness, and took advantage of it. The kid was so grateful, someone paying attention to her, that she did anything he wanted."

"And she got pregnant, of course," Taunton said.

"No," Pokaski said. "He just told about it, all over town, and pretty soon some of his pals thought they'd give her a try, and she was even more flattered. And finally her father caught on and beat the shit out of her. And that was all that happened. But it doesn't make a nice story, as dead-hero stories go. What the hell do I write? 'Tony French came home today from Vietnam to join in death the boy he killed, and the living girl that he as much as raped'?

"The priest got it right. He wasn't a really bad kid. But he was not a really good kid, either. 'It's sometimes hard to find God here. Like the mountain lion. God isn't seen too much around here. Just the traces of Him. The same thing with the catamounts—all we ever see are traces, but that doesn't mean, because they don't show themselves to us, that they're gone. And the fact that we don't see God very much around these hills doesn't mean that He is, either.'

"So," Pokaski said, "if going in the service was the best thing Tony French did, and you can bet it was, well, he didn't do it because he was a patriot, or anything like that. And he didn't do it because he was some kind of victim. When Tony French enlisted it wasn't only because the judge made him do it—it was also the best thing that probably could've happened, and not just for him, either—for the people that he knew. If he hadn't gone where he went, God knows what happened next."

"So what do you do?" she said.

"Wait for his buddies to bring him back up here," Pokaski said. "Interview those guys tomorrow. Try to talk to his mother and father. Again. Maybe one of them'll've thought of something good by then to say."

The bar in the Carroll Arms in Washington was quiet in the evening, a few harassed-looking middle-aged men sitting by themselves at separate tables with *Washington Stars* propped on salt shakers across their plates of salisbury steak or pot roast, now and then lifting their glasses of beer. Prior sat in a corner booth in the back with Ferdie Norman, turning his martini glass in his hand. "I don't know," he said. "If he'll go for it. I just wish that we'd been sure, 'fore he got on the train. It's pretty hard anyway, talking him into things, but the few times that I've done it, it was always in his office. On the phone he is a bitch."

"When'll he be back?" Norman said.

"Tuesday," Prior said. "The body comes back tomorrow. Then two days of visiting hours, and the funeral's on Monday, and he gets his butt back on the train, and I'll see him Tuesday morning. In a lousy mood. What exactly did Jerry say?"

"Jerry's known Neil Cooke for a long time," Norman said. "Much longer'n I have. And Jerry's told me, many times, he can't push Neil too far. Neil's the kind of guy that you don't want to push much anyway. I dunno—it's like he's innocent. Not stupid—innocent. Which naturally he can't be, since he's been around so long. But Neil likes to talk, which he knows can be a weakness. So if you don't alert him that you're interested in something, he will probably tell you, just to show how tight he's wired. But if you give him even a hint, then you'll never get it. What Neil wants is: You admire him, because he's got the inside stuff. Well, if you admire him *before* he shows you what he's got, there's no reason. You take away his reason for showing it. Therefore he doesn't. But if you treat him, say, indifferent, then he has to impress you. And that is when you find stuff out."

"Yeah," Prior said, "but that means he picks the stuff. Which may not be the actual stuff that you want to know."

Norman nodded. "Sort of like a yard sale," he said. "It's possible you're wasting your time. Likely you are, in fact. But you keep stopping off at them, and poking around on the card tables, because every now and then, in the midst of all the junk, there's something you can use, and the price is really right. Jerry says you can always go to the bank on what he tells you. It's maybe not what you had in mind, but it's true, and you can count on it."

"The ball player I got no trouble with," Prior said. "It figures Cobb'd go looking for someone who's already kind of known. And there isn't anybody else, the district, that's already sort of famous. And also dumb enough to challenge. So I got no problem with that. And, what you've been telling me, and I found out myself, I figure he's no problem. Unless our man makes him one."

"Which of course is the problem," Norman said.

"Yup," Prior said. "Our Bob is really mad. He's got a tendency to clam up on me. Sit and fucking sulk. And he does it, to me, whenever something else pisses him off. Which this trip home does.

"Now I get this call, all right? Perfectly reasonable call from the paper up in Burlington. What they want's an interview. But before that, a summary, of what *he* thinks he's accomplished in this town.

"I tell him. I say: 'Mr. Wainwright, okay? They can do it themselves. They can go through their clips, and stay up all night, and decide the most important thing you ever did was get the road paved in Vergennes. But maybe you think, or I think, that we want the emphasis on what you've done, say, for the dairy industry. Now, we've got a chance to make a friend there. Wixton's not doing the story himself, but Wixton's the boss on the story. And they're *asking* us, all right? To tell them what the story is. So I think we should do it. Give them a big box of marshmallows. So when you get up there, that is what they throw at you.'

"I got a sermon," Prior said. " 'We've got more important things to do here than spoon-feed the newspapers.' Well, I'm not sure we do have more important things, now that this ball player's going to run, and that's what I become rash enough to tell the man. I got another sermon. 'If that's what I have to do to keep my job against some tinplate like that, well, I don't want the damned job, then. They can have it, for all I care.' "

"Think he means it?" Norman said.

"Course he does," Prior said. "That's what frightens me. Look, Bob Wainwright's crowding eighty. He has got his service, and he's got twenty-eight years in here. Plus which he's got his bank stock, and he never did have kids. So he's got his pension locked up, and what he's put in the bank, and he can afford being nasty. Which he prefers to do.

"I can't. I'm at the other end of the tunnel, and I've got a longer train. If he stands up and takes a leak on his goddamned job, well, he can zip his pants up, go home, and snap at his wife. But I don't have that option. And I don't have others, either."

"I dunno what to tell you," Norman said.

"Look," Prior said, "there is no doubt, at least in my mind, that Cobb's the force behind Briggs. And there's no doubt in my mind that sometime or other Ed Cobb did something he wouldn't like people to find out about. Every politician has. It's an occupational hazard—it goes with the trade. Well, if we can find out what Cobb did that was even slightly smelly, and hit him good and hard with it, well then, we've clobbered Briggs. And my source says that if we give money to this guy, this guy will do that for us. Dig up that kind of stuff."

"How much money does he want?" Norman said. "That's the bottom line."

"He'll do it for two thousand," Prior said. "He says that he wants five, but he'll go cheaper'n that."

"And Wainwright won't pay it," Norman said.

"*Pay* it?" Prior said. "He won't even listen. 'No,' he says, 'that's wrong.' "

29

Wainwright in the front seat of Ralph
Carlisle's Cadillac sedan watched the Allegheny 727 spew black ex-
haust against the clear sky on its descent into Burlington Airport. In
line on the tarmac behind the sedan were a Cadillac hearse and two
Cadillac seven-passenger limousines. Two gray Chevrolet sedans idled
side by side in front of the sedan. Pokaski in his parka stood with the
group of reporters and cameramen huddled in the wind two hundred
yards beyond.

"Think he'll show up here, then?" Carlisle said.

"Doubt it," Wainwright said. "He'll make an appearance sometime,
'fore this whole thing gets over. But everything I've heard, this Calley
fellow's foxy. Andy says Cobb got him to advise him, with some Jewess's
money. Shrewd man would tell him not to. So I don't think he'll show
up here."

"Worried, Bob?" Carlisle said.

"No," Wainwright said. "I was worried when I had to face off
against your dad. Dick was a damned good man. But I managed to beat
him. Lucky for me. I guess. I haven't been worried since then. Pissed
off'd be more like it. This is a damned nuisance. There's no damned
need, me being here, I should be down in Washington, taking care of
business. Henry Briggs's the only reason I'm here. The only reason. I
don't know Henry Briggs. Oh, I know who he is, and who his family

was. But I didn't know him or his father. Never did a thing to them. Nothing for them, either. So it's no grudge he's working out. And no ingratitude, either. Just that I'm not used to this. Having an opponent. Haven't had a real one since I faced your dad. Not the kind of thing I need. My age, anyway. Makes you wonder if it's worth it. Least it makes you stop and think."

"Well," Carlisle said, "he's got a right."

"I know he's got a right," Wainwright said. The plane touched down, bounced once, came down again, and decelerated into the middle distance, throwing more black smoke. "You had a right. Your dad had one. I had a right, myself. I just don't think there's any need of this. If people were fed up, wanted somebody else, well, I think I would know that. And I would say: 'All right. I guess I'm stepping down.' And that would be the end of it. The same's you would've done, folks're tired of you. But I don't get that notion, and I talk to lots of people. Not the way to handle this. Not the way at all."

The plane rounded up at the end of the runway and started back toward the terminal. A white pickup truck fitted with a flight of metal stairs moved out on the apron, followed by another white pickup equipped with a rubberized conveyor ramp and a ladder with a catwalk over the cab, and two blue tractors towing baggage carts. The plane pulled up about three hundred yards from the Cadillac. The trucks moved out at once, the one with the stairs wheeling and pulling up under the fuselage, so that the stairs matched up with the door aft of the cockpit. The truck with the conveyor matched the maneuver at the first luggage bay aft of the wing. The tractors with their trains of carts pulled up at the foot of the conveyor. The driver of the stair truck emerged from the cab and sprinted up the stairs. He rapped on the cabin door. It opened slowly. The driver of the conveyor truck climbed the ladder and stood on the catwalk to unlock the baggage door. He climbed down and reentered the cab of his truck. The conveyor began to roll. The driver of the first tractor dismounted and climbed the ladder to the catwalk, disappearing into the baggage bay. The driver of the second tractor got down and stood at the foot of the conveyor. Baggage began to emerge from the hold as the first passengers came out of the plane, wrapped their coats more tightly, and tentatively descended the stairs.

"Shouldn't we get up there?" Wainwright said.

"No," Carlisle said. "It's always the last item. They put it on first. It comes off last."

Four men in army dress uniforms were the last passengers off the plane. They paused near the foot of the stairs. The other passengers straggled into the terminal. The first baggage train moved away from the conveyor. The second took its place. The two Chevrolets moved forward toward the plane. Four large duffel bags came out of the cargo bay. The Chevrolets pulled up about thirty feet from the plane. All their doors opened. Eight men in army dress uniforms and overcoats got out, six of them pulling on gloves, the other two opening the trunks of the cars. The four soldiers from the plane went to the foot of the conveyor belt and claimed their duffels from the second tractor operator. They carried them to the cars and stowed them, joining the men who had ridden to the plane. One of the Chevrolet drivers bent into the trunk of his car and removed a folded American flag. He shut the trunk.

"I guess it's about time now," Carlisle said. He put the Cadillac in gear and drove slowly toward the soldiers. The second baggage train moved away from the plane. Carlisle parked the Cadillac behind the Chevrolets. The hearse approached the plane and made a U-turn, so that its loading door was about fifteen feet from the conveyor. The two limousines stopped near the hearse. A man in a black suit, wearing a white shirt and white socks, assisted a veiled woman in an emerald green coat from the first limousine. A girl with pale blond hair got out of the car after the woman. Another woman remained in the car. The girl's hair blew in the wind, and she brushed it away from her face. The four soldiers from the plane came to attention. They marched to the foot of the conveyor and flanked it. The man with the flag stepped between them. The other seven soldiers formed an honor guard. The man in the black suit put his arm around the waist of the veiled woman. The front of a large aluminum box came out of the cargo bay and stopped for a moment.

"Best get out now, I think, Bob," Carlisle said. "I was you, I'd stand with the honor guard. Go to all this bother, least might's well get your picture in the paper for it."

Wainwright shivered. "Wouldn't think one man could move that thing in there, all by himself."

"They've got rollers in the bays," Carlisle said. "All he has to do's kick the thing along. Long's he don't get too carried away, so she drops off the ramp. Had that happen, once. Tough on the family."

"Think it would be," Wainwright said. He buttoned his coat and put on his hat. He got out of the car. Carlisle shut off the engine and got out. He pointed his finger at the driver of the hearse. The driver got out of the hearse and went to the rear. Carlisle joined him as he opened the loading door. The aluminum box emerged halfway into the light. The men with the cameras began taking pictures, stepping apart to get different angles. The woman put her right hand under her veil for a moment. Wainwright walked up to the honor guard and stood at the end nearest the hearse. The front of the aluminum box dropped slowly onto the conveyor, so that the back pointed skyward for a moment before the box started to descend.

The driver of the hearse shook his head. "Remember that Hoskins kid, Dick?"

Carlisle shuddered. "Hope they don't do that again," he said.

The box reached the foot of the conveyor. The soldier with the flag stepped forward, flanked by two of the escort soldiers. They grasped the handles at the front of the box. He unfolded the flag and began to drape the box. The other two escort soldiers flanked the rear of the box. Between them Wainwright could see stenciled red lettering— HUMAN REMAINS—on its sides, disappearing under the flag. The four escort soldiers carried the box to the hearse and the eight other soldiers stood at attention. Wainwright saw the veiled woman shake her head. The girl took a deep breath and brushed the hair away from her eyes again. The man lowered his head. Wainwright stood stiffly as the escort soldiers slid the box into the hearse. The driver shut the door. One of the eight local soldiers said: "Ease."

The driver of the hearse reentered it. Carlisle spoke to one of the officers, nodding toward the second limousine. The officer nodded in reply. He pointed toward the car. "That second one's your transport, gentlemen," he said.

Scott Pokaski delivered his story to Wixton at 7:50 P.M. "Took you long enough," Wixton said.

"Hey," Pokaski said, "first I freeze my ass off at the airport. Then I drive all the way down to Canterbury in the damned parade. Then I freeze my ass off again at Carlisle's funeral home while they haul the corpse inside. 'Now,' I figure, 'now's the time I get to see his buddies.' But I don't get to see them. Not then. There's this wiseass lieutenant from Fort Ethan Allen, and he won't let them talk. He's going to pile them all into this car they got waiting at the funeral home, and take them back up to the base. 'Hey,' I say, ' 'least I can talk to them first.' Nope. Says they're tired. Says they're hungry. Says they got to have a chance to eat and rest up some, they start standing guard tomorrow. No interviews today.

"Okay," Pokaski said, "I can't fight the army. I'm no Vietcong. So maybe I can get some nice heartrending quotes, the family. Nice fuckin' try."

"They're not sorry?" Wixton said. "Or they just won't talk?"

"Oh, they're sorry," Pokaski said. "The mother's all beat to shit, and the sister's just a kid hardly knows what's going on. The old man doesn't know what hit him, either. Hell I don't know if they *can* talk, even when they're feeling good. But they weren't worth shit today."

Wixton leafed through the copy paper. "Eight takes?" he said.

"You told me, Russ," Pokaski said, " 'leave it run 'til it's cold.' "

"Yeah, I know," Wixton said, "but how'd you get eight takes out of a story where no one talks?"

"It wasn't easy," Pokaski said.

"And you got Wainwright in the lead?" Wixton said.

"Well, at least he showed up," Pokaski said. "I think that's part of the story, a congressman shows up."

"And six more grafs farther down?" Wixton said.

"He's the only one," Pokaski said, "had really anything to say."

Wixton picked up his grease pencil and began marking up the story. He drew a line through Wainwright's name in the first paragraph. "Hey," Pokaski said, "guy's got to be in there, you know."

Wixton nodded. He drew diagonal lines through four of the six remaining paragraphs dealing with Wainwright's appearance. "I know he's got to be in it," he said. "No question about that. But I also know why he came up here today. Old Bob has got opposition this time. Guy should worry him, and this shows he does."

"So what?" Pokaski said. "How's he get into this?"

Wixton shrugged. "Who knows?" he said. "Guys do funny things. I don't like Bob Wainwright."

"So what again?" Pokaski said. "What difference does that make?"

Wixton looked up at Pokaski. "Have a seat," he said. Pokaski sat down. "I got back from the service," he said, "this's 'forty-six we're talking now, and I'm twenty-two years old, and I sort of know what it is, that I want to do with my life. I'm gonna be a reporter. But for that a college degree, even back in those days, is a real advantage in this crummy business. Well, I got no worries. I got the GI Bill. And no one said I couldn't work. All I've got to do is go.

"Except for one thing. My two sisters're getting married, and they got no place to live. One of them is all right—my parents like her husband. They've got room for the two of them. He can take my place on the farm. The other one has a problem. Her husband's an electrician and a pretty good one, too, but he's setting himself up in business and he doesn't have a dime. So my father and my mother sit down with the bunch of us, and they say: 'Well, if Lucy and her husband're taken care of here, and Russ is off to school, then we've got to do something for Ruth. Because that's only fair.' On which we all agreed. And what they decide is that they'll take out a mortgage on the property, and give Ruth and her husband a stake. And then Lucy and her husband'll help them pay it back.

"My father went to see Wainwright's father, that son of a bitch," Wixton said. "Wouldn't give him the money. We all had to go in there and sign all kinds of notes. He made us grovel like a bunch of goddamned beggars, even though he knew damned well that he'd get the money back.

"I never forgot that," Wixton said. "For the next ten years, when I wanted to get married, buy a car, get some furniture on the installment plan? For the next ten years I had trouble every time I went to do something. Because I didn't have much money myself, and I already owed almost five grand.

"So," he said, "Wainwright's in the story, sure, but not up at the top. And you tell Photo if he's in any of the pictures, I want that bastard's face cropped out, or I'll do it myself."

"I thought you were friendly with him," Pokaski said. "I thought you talked to him."

"I do my job, and he does his," Wixton said. "What he thinks of me, I don't know. I just know where he came from, and therefore what I think of him. I don't take it out on him. I won't stab him in the back. But he gets the same treatment I'd give anybody else. Same we're going to do for Briggs. Straight down the fucking middle. TV boys did everything but suck Bob's dick for him tonight, but that's TV for you, and this is print. For me. No free passes, this performance. Not while I run the show."

30

briggs arrived in his Jeep at Carlisle's funeral home in Canterbury after 6:30 in the evening and had his choice of spaces in the asphalt parking lot overlooking the pond in the back. He shut the engine off. He sat staring down the incline at the black water and gray ice of the small pond behind the lot and spent a moment gathering himself. Then he got out of the car, buttoning his trenchcoat.

Ralph Carlisle was in his office just inside the rear door, murmuring into the telephone. Briggs shut the door and entered the office, unbuttoning his coat. Carlisle looked up and nodded at him. "I think that would be all right, Paul," he said. "Yes, I really do. I'm sure the family will appreciate that." He replaced the handset in its cradle. He stood up and offered his hand. "Henry," he said. "Glad to see you. Have a chair." He gestured toward the phone. "Paul Whipple," he said. "Wondered if the family'd like it, the Legion Hall had everyone back there, after services. Said I thought they would. Christ, they don't have a pot to piss in, even with insurance. And the father's death on drinking. So Paul's idea's much better."

Briggs sat down. "Thought I'd better come bit early," he said. "I don't really know this kid—all I know's that he caused an accident, and a friend of his got killed. Don't know his family, for that matter. Thought maybe you could fill me in. You'd be kind enough."

Carlisle nodded. "Not much to say," he said. "Mother's name is Janet. She grew up in Springs. Father's name is Robert. That boy I've got lying out there, what's left of him, 's their oldest. There's a sister, thirteen, fourteen. Name's Elizabeth."

"The casket's closed?" Briggs said.

Carlisle sighed. "You bet," he said. "My father, I remember him, when the bodies came back from Korea. And he was used to it by then. When he was starting out, my grandfather had this place, it was nineteen forty-four. Never got over that. There were maybe ninety families that'd call on us in those days, and he had over twenty funerals. Can you believe that? And there were three or four more, I guess, that either left their boys in Europe, the Pacific, or took Arlington. If you took four families from around here in those days, any four, you know? At least one of them'd lost a man. Some of them lost two. And Korea. Not as bad, of course, but the same kind of thing. I think we had eleven.

"And my father told me then, you know, do the best you can. Try to talk them out of opening it up. I don't mean for the viewing. It's, there's a lot of people that don't want to believe it, you know? That it really is their boy in there. They want to see him. Make sure. And it's really not a good idea. Because lots of times there isn't much left of him. By the time he gets back here. Especially from one of those warm climates. It's not, they think they're going to see something like they saw when grandpa died in his sleep. Only thing was different was he had a suit on in the box, his teeth in, and his hair combed.

"I never saw a pretty corpse. I don't expect to, either. But there's a world of difference between one that died at home, and you went right there and got him. And one that got shot in the face out there in the jungle, and a couple days went by before they could pick him up and stick him in a bag.

"Well," he said, "now this's only the third one that we had from Vietnam, but so far I've been lucky. No one's made me open up. I tell them: 'Put the flag over it. And give me the best picture you got of him, and we'll put that on the top, and that'll be the way we'll all remember him. The way we saw him last.' And the Frenches did that. They took my advice." He hesitated.

"They're not the kind of people," he said, "understand a lot of things. It's like they expect bad things to happen to them all the time, and they're usually right, and they have to go to someone that can help them get through it. They don't expect him to change it.

"Tom McLeod told me, he'd been on his rounds, up the hospital, the day we got the news here that the kid was killed. He said: 'When Bill Cooke was putting up some fence at the old Lawton place, had a saw kick back on him? And it wasn't fatal, you know—lots of blood, but he would live. So I told him, I went over there right off, soon's Dean Lawton called, and I stopped the bleeding there so we could take him up to Burlington without him dying on us. Gave him some morphine, of course, and he said: "What's the damage?"

" 'And I said: "Well, no promises, but I think we'll save the leg. Thing of it is though, Bill, and I got to tell you this, you won't have the full use of it, unless I miss my guess. You've got tendon damage there, ligaments and so forth. We'll put you back together, but you're going to have a limp."

" 'And you know what he did? He actually grinned at me, like he'd of course expected worse. Could've been the morphine, I guess, but I doubt it was. Here's this poor bastard on the ground, covered with his own blood, and I'm telling him that he'll be lame, and it made him feel all right.'

"Well, that's the same sort of thing I run into when I went to talk to them, about planning Tony's send-off. It kind of throws a man, you know? You're surprised, and you feel bad, even if it is your trade and you're used to it. But they don't seem to feel that way. They expected it."

Briggs expelled breath loudly. "How old you say this kid was?" he said. "I call him 'Tony,' do I?"

" 'Tony,' " Carlisle said. " 'Anthony' on all the papers, but 'Tony' to his parents. Twenty. Turned it just last fall."

"Ye gods," Briggs said. "Know the circumstances?"

"If you're looking for the stuff that they give medals for," Carlisle said, "got to say you're out of luck. He was on a patrol, broad daylight, and he stepped into a clearing and got damned near cut in half. Phu Bai, some place like that. 'Bout two weeks before he was supposed to rotate out. Four kids from his old unit're the honor guard. One of them told me, you should've see his eyes, the only thing that Tony did was walk out standing up instead of going on his belly. 'And that wasn't brave, just stupid,' he said. No, I can't help you there."

"Then it's just: 'Gave his life for his country, and you should be proud of that,' " Briggs said.

" 'Fraid so," Carlisle said. "And, you know what's really sad? They will probably believe you. They will thank you for it."

"It wouldn't've hurt you, you know," Briggs said to Lillian in the morning. "It's not like I was asking you, fly to Washington with me. It was just a matter, going to the funeral home, paying your respects. That was all it was."

"In the first place," she said, "you know how I feel about those things."

"Of course I do," he said. "You didn't even go the Liggett funeral, Christ sake. You didn't even tell me. And here I get back, and one the people you knew in school dropped dead? And you didn't even go? What the hell makes you so goddamned special, you get not to go? You think anybody actually likes, going those things?"

"Martha Glennon does," she said. "Her face gets all rosy and everything. Of course Everett gets a fee, and she gets to show off."

"Oh for crying out loud, Lil," he said. "That's her job, doing that. She doesn't actually like it. I bet not even Ralph Carlisle likes going to funerals, and that's how he makes his damned living."

"I don't like looking at dead people," she said.

"There wasn't any dead person to look at," Briggs said. "They had the casket shut, and there was a flag on it, and next to it they had a picture of the kid when he joined up. That was all."

"And the smell," she said, "the smell of the flowers makes me just about sick, my stomach. Carnations. I can't stand the smell of carnations."

"You still should've been there," he said.

"Look," she said, "you're the one running for office. Not me. I didn't get you into this. I told you not to do it. You didn't listen to me? Fine. You never do. But don't come around and tell me now I have to help you do it. Because I said I wouldn't. And I meant it."

"That's not the damned point," he said.

"And besides," she said, "I knew what you'd do. I knew you wouldn't just go there and pay your respects, as you call them. I knew damned well you'd find someone to go drinking. And you did."

"I was not drunk," he said. "Paul collared me and said that he was going back, the hall. And Winston Thomas was there too, and he said the same thing. And they both had me, you know. Paul said to me a while back, been a while since I was there. Well, I am running for office. And so now, I'd better go."

"What baloney," she said. "What cheap damned baloney. You should be ashamed of yourself."

"Why?" he said. "I do know these guys. I grew up with most of them. I got nothing, be ashamed of. I care what they think."

She snorted. "That's not what I mean," she said. "You never paid the slightest bit, attention to the war. Until now all of a sudden, you're convinced it's wrong. You're turning into a phony. I hate that, Henry. You've got your faults. I've got mine. But you never faked it before, and now I see you doing that."

He sighed. "Lil," he said, "my whole life I've been the kind of guy that people tell him, what to do. The only thing I ever did, my own, because *I* wanted to, was throw the ball. And then when I found out I really could do that, well, I never said to anyone that paid me: 'I wanna start.' Or: 'I don't like it in the bullpen.' Now, maybe I should've. I'd've been a starter, would've made more money, probably. Maybe played a few more years. But I didn't. I knew I could do what it was that they wanted, and that was for them to decide.

"Well," he said, "now I can't throw the ball anymore. Okay, what else can I do? Well, I can enforce the laws, I guess. Looks like, anyways. I dunno how good I am at it, and I dunno if they ask me back next year, and it sure isn't making us rich. So, is there anything else I can do? Well, Ed says I can win this thing, and that if I don't, I'll get something else. So what have I got to lose? I tell them what I think. I'll let them decide."

"What you think," she said. "You don't think at all, all right? That is a big joke. It's what Ed Cobb thinks, you tell them. You aren't Edgar Bergen—he is. You're Charlie McCarthy. And it's probably not even what he thinks, really. It's just what he thinks might get people to vote for you instead of Mr. Wainwright."

"I thought about the stuff he told me I should say," Briggs said. "And

I don't see anything wrong with it. It's not like he said to me: 'Go out and tell them all their daughters should be whores.' Or: 'We should invade Canada,' or something. What he said sounds reasonable to me. The war thing? Well, we're losing kids, and we are spending a hell of a lot of money. And as a matter of damned fact, we also are not winning. So then we should negotiate, so we can get out. That seems sensible.

"And the race thing, and the student riots? Well, we should do something about both those things, and maybe beating people up, and shooting at them, maybe we should not do that. The stuff I read about farming? Goddamnit, every other kind of farming gets some kind of help. Price supports and stuff. But dairymen don't get it, and that's important here. Then I read the other stuff, and I thought about it some.

"This is a rich country. I don't know how many there are, but there must be quite a few kids like Whip's daughter there, that could use some help. And that crazy woman with the kid that I met down at his store. And I know we've got people going hungry around here because they had some bad luck. But you look at Wainwright's record, and every time somebody wants to do something like that, Wainwright is against it. The only thing he ever thinks about is whether it costs money. If it does, he doesn't like it, and that's the end of it. And I think he could be wrong.

"So that's the kind of thing I'm saying. 'Let's just think about these things, all right? Maybe we're on the wrong track, and the guy we send to Washington should be working to set us straight, 'stead of always saying no, so everything gets worse.' And I believe that."

"You believe it *now*," she said. "Let me ask you something: What did you say to that boy's family? What exactly did you say?"

"Well," he said, "I introduced myself, they didn't recognize me, and I said I was sorry their boy died, and they thanked me. And his sister there, that's just a kid, she sort of did, in fact I know she did, she said her brother had my picture in his room, when I was playing ball. And that he was grateful that I testified for him. Which got him killed, of course, but she didn't mention that. And she knew if he knew I was there, he would appreciate it. And the mother just stood there, kind of silent, and his father shook my hand again and thanked me for stopping by."

"And then what did you do?" she said.

"Well," he said, "I went out in the back, see if Ralph Carlisle was still around, and he was. Him and Paul and Winston, like I said, they're all in the smoking room. So I sat down for a minute, shot the breeze with them, and Ralph asked me if it's true what he hears that I am doing. And I asked him what he hears. And he says: 'Congress. That's it, right?' And I said that it was. And Winston says he figured that was it, when he saw me show up. And I said that's one of the ways I go about it, when I'm thinking something over. Go out and look around and see if it looks like a good idea.

"And Ralph says: 'Well,' he says, 'I doubt it. Doubt it's such a good idea. Bob's pretty strong around here, you know. You're pretty sure to lose. Found that out, myself, when my father lost. Seat's been in his hands now, damned near thirty years. Might find it kind of tough, you know, get people toss him out.' And I said that was one the biggest questions in my mind. Whether I would have a chance, if I did decide to run. And that was about all."

"And then you went over the hall and got yourself all beered up," she said. "That's a stupid thing to do, think you can get people, vote for you, they see you getting drunk."

"We've been all through that," he said. "We've been all through that. I had four beers with Winston and Paul, and Carter Boyd was there, and Mike LaFreniere, and then Bunny Morrissette came in, and he joined us for a beer. I grant you, Winston got himself about three sheets to the wind, but he never could drink much. Any more'n he can fix much. And we just sat around and talked some. Bunny'd just been over to Carlisle's, paid his respects too, even though they're dries, which is not Bunny's religion, and we got to talking about the war and so forth, and Paul told Bunny what I'm up to, so we talked some about that.

"Bunny was actually very encouraging. Said from what he saw, sending someone besides Bob'd be a good idea. And he went on about what he's seen, just in his own parish, and we should be doing more for people besides getting their boys killed and letting people like that Garner girl just fall through the cracks. And then Winston got pissed off at Bunny and said lots of people had hard luck, and he'd had some himself. But nobody bailed him out, or gave Lida money either, and he was damned if he could see why he should pay more taxes now, to help somebody else. And Carter and Mike agreed with him, you know? None of the government's damned business.

"But then I asked them, you know, how they would feel themselves? I mean here're all these guys out in Iowa, growing corn, and the government helps them, and we have to help pay for that. Doesn't look like much we're going to stop, so why shouldn't the government, if it's going to help the people raising hogs and selling bacon, why shouldn't it help the people who're raising herds for milk? Well, they didn't come right out and just agree with me, you know, but I could see it made them think.

"And it was that sort of thing," he said. "And then I just came home."

"Drunk," she said.

"You know," he said, "I didn't think of doing that. Maybe I should've done it. Would've enjoyed it more."

She stared at him. "All right," she said, "that should do it. From now on you get home at night, you sleep in Ted's room, by yourself. And I hope you like it just as much as Teddy did."

31

$\mathbf{O}$n the morning of the first Monday in February, Emily Poitrast entered Andrew Prior's space in the office of Representative Robert Wainwright with hesitant determination. "I know you don't like to be bothered on Mondays," she said, "but I think you have to talk to this man."

Prior was reading documents, and he did not look up. "Impossible today," he said. "I've got a lunch and then the congressman to brief. There was nothing in my book this morning, and I know because I checked it. I don't want things in my book for Mondays anyway, and that's why there's nothing in it."

"I think you'd better talk to him," she said. "He's really quite insistent."

"I don't care how insistent he is," Prior said. "He has not got an appointment. This is not a barbershop, you just come in the mood strikes. The congressman has got to go back to Vermont some time this week. I'm waiting for the call to come in, from the Pentagon, so I can get the information and tell him what is up."

"This man isn't here," she said. "He's on the phone, from New Hampshire, and he's in jail, and he says he can't wait on the phone long because the other prisoners want to use it too. He says his name's Earl Beale."

"Emily," Prior said, "I know what his name is. And that's enough to

290

know. He has called before. Mr. Wainwright wants no part of him, all right? I've got to figure out some other way to help the congressman. 'Cause if I don't, and he sure won't, we both're out of work. Do you understand me now?"

"Andrew," she said, "that's what I'm saying. What I'm trying to tell you. This man says that he's the brother, that his brother's helping Cobb. And that he knows something that will finish this guy Briggs."

Prior put the papers down. He pushed his chair back. "Emily, it's the same guy, I'm telling you," he said.

"He sounds very serious," she said. "I think you should talk to him."

"All right, all right," Prior said. "I'll talk to him again."

Prior sat rigidly in Wainwright's office. Wainwright said: "No I won't."

"You have to think about this again," Prior said. "This could be important. This could mean your career."

Wainwright scowled at him. "Andy," he said, "I don't have one. I have no career. My name is Wainwright. Robert Wainwright. 'S what it's always been. I don't, and I never have, thought about much else. I am who I am. Do what I do. And I've told you before, and I'll tell you again: I just will not do that. That's not something that I'd do."

"Ed Cobb, Mr. Wainwright," Prior said. "Ed Cobb's the man behind this. Ed Cobb wiped out the record. Ed Cobb had a reason. Ed Cobb was protecting Briggs. This guy Earl knows everything. He can sink these people.

"Ed Cobb is crooked, Congressman," Prior said.

"Uh-huh," Wainwright said. "Well, I've got some faults myself. Man did a friend a favor once, well, I'd do that myself."

32

The afternoon in August 1989 was benign on Lake Champlain, and the small boats swung at their moorings at the Basin Harbor Club.

"Monster shown up since I've been gone?" Briggs said to Wixton, taking another forkful of lobster salad.

"How would I know?" Wixton said. "Mortimer retired me two years ago. Newspapers aren't like Congress. You hit sixty-five, when the Tallowers sell out to a big chain, and Bay Cities owns your ass, you're there on sufferance after that, and after I made the mistake of having that birthday, he decided that they'd suffered me—well, my paycheck—long enough, and he fired me. 'Retired me' was the phrase he used. 'Fired' was what he meant."

"Well, you still get the paper, right?" Briggs said. "You still read the thing."

Wixton laughed. "Now and then," he said. "I get it now and then. I guess I'm old and bitter. Didn't mean to be. I liked that life. I liked my job. I had a lot of fun. I look at guys like you and Ed, people that I knew, and you're still hard at it, every day, and I envy you. If you're not old at sixty-two, why'm I at five years older? If Ed Cobb can be a judge until he's seventy, and then get recalled, senior status, be a judge some more, why can't I stay in harness too? Why dump me just when the time comes that I finally know something?" He picked at chicken à la king on his plate.

292

Briggs picked up his wine glass and washed the lobster down with Chardonnay. "Mmm," he said, "good lunch here."

"Always has been," Wixton said, "ever since I recall. Which is not that long ago. I could not afford it until recently."

Briggs nodded. "There's that to be said about campaign funds," he said. "Those PAC funds are damned nourishing. They'll buy a good lunch or two."

Wixton frowned. "You, ah," he said, "you don't have, I hope, a small problem with that coming up."

Briggs put the glass down. He grinned. "Nope," he said, "I've got no problem at all." He sat back in his chair. "Want a scoop for yourself, former newspaperman? I'm not running again." He removed his napkin and put it on the table.

Wixton stared. He did not say anything for almost a minute. Then he said: "You're not in danger, I know of. You probably won't have an opponent. You're sixty-two years old, young for the Congress. You sit on some prime committees. What you can do, with the power you've got, can be important to this state. Why the hell do you want to quit?"

Briggs laughed. "You hit it, pal—that's exactly the reason. The reason I get all those campaign donations is that I'm on all those committees. If I quit this year, I can keep those donations. If I don't, and I stay, then I can't. So what do I want? Another ten years? Or twenty-eight, like Bob Wainwright had? Or would I rather become a rich man, with my own million dollars? Actually, more than twice that.

"Well," Briggs said, "that's an easy question. I know the answer right off. Caroline's got cash—what she had of her own, plus what she got when her first husband cracked up his birthday Mercedes and got caught romancing his honey—and she loves me a lot, but I'd like to have my own, too. I quit now? I've got it. I don't? Then it's forfeit, into the Treasury coffers, to disappear into the deficit. Tell me, what would you do?"

Russ Wixton did a guest column in the *Valley Press* for the third Sunday in August 1989. It read: "I did my swan song in this paper back on March eleventh. This is a kind of reprise.

"Henry Briggs went to Congress 20 years ago. We were all much younger then. There had been unprecedented convulsions in the country for two years. Conventional and unquestioned shared assumptions of all varieties—political, religious, racial, economic: you name it—were first shivered and then shattered by events most of us found difficult if not impossible to comprehend.

"The murders of the Rev. Martin Luther King and Robert F. Kennedy shook us terribly, perhaps more devastatingly than had the assassination of John F. Kennedy a mere five years before. In 1963, at least, those of us with no personal experience of homicidal anarchy had the option of believing that killing was an act aberrant in our peaceable kingdom. But as violence on the campuses and the streets of our cities—especially those in Chicago during the Democratic National Convention—erupted in the aftermath of those fresh deaths, many began to wonder if our society had not reached something close to what scientists describe as 'entropy'—the point at which a system overheats and degenerates.

"It was hard for many Second District voters in that year to regard Briggs's candidacy with much more than idle curiosity. Robert Wainwright had taken the seat twenty-eight years before. He was popular in the only sense Vermonters actually approve: self-effacing, prudent, unexcitable, sure of himself, seeming to be precisely what he was.

"Andy Prior, Wainwright's chief aide for several years, now special assistant to the GOP National Committee, summarized it nicely: 'He was reliable,' Prior said, 'and his people knew it. If you scratched the surface of Bob Wainwright, what you got was more Bob Wainwright. He said he was for fiscal restraint, and he was. Bob Wainwright was consistent, and he looked unbeatable.'

"Especially up against a retired ball player, forced to concede at his official announcement of candidacy in March of '68 that he had had to check with the town clerk to make sure he was registered to vote in Occident. 'And when I did,' he said, 'I found out they had me down as an independent. So I'm standing here,' at the Legion Hall in Charlotte on a blustery day that gave little hint of imminent spring, 'and telling you that I've been a Democrat for two days, and I'm going after the party's nomination in the Second District. I figure if you get that down, you'll swallow anything.'

"Former Gov. Ed Cobb, approaching mandatory age-70 retirement from the Second Circuit Court of Appeals, remembers the first

Briggs campaign with more than a trace of nostalgia. 'There's no harm in admitting it now,' he said, 'although none of us would've then, but if you'd strapped any one of us to a polygraph and asked us if he had a chance, we would've either said he didn't, or sent the needle off the meter. I don't think Henry, even, thought he had a chance. He didn't know Bob Wainwright, really, but what he knew he kind of liked. The only reason that he ran was because a friend asked him to, and talked him into it.

" 'It cost him,' Judge Cobb said. 'It cost him a heck of a lot. In personal terms, I mean. Politics is rough on a man's family life. There are sacrifices, and he made them, and I know that those things hurt. But he also gained a lot. I think until Hank ran he never really understood his own potential. And if that sounds like a funny thing to say about a man with his career before that—really, with a national reputation he made for himself in baseball—I still think it's true. Hank found out he could move people, strike a common chord with a total stranger who had only seen him pitch, and get that stranger's vote. You don't hear the word used a lot, but that *exhilarated* him.

" 'I'd known him since we were boys, and I'd seen him many times, when he had every reason to be excited, and he was. But I never saw him quite as excited as he started to get when the first campaign heated up. And I couldn't understand it. Everything said that Wainwright would win, was going to win in November. Hell, people turned out in the primary, to give Bob a confidence vote. Hank for all his effort only pulled about 8,000 or so Democrats into his line. Bob had more than twice as many, on the other side.'

"Briggs, after his retirement announcement yesterday in Charlotte, winter in the richness of the summer seeming as far off this year as it did twenty-two years ago, was as candid as he's always been throughout both of his careers.

" 'I don't kid myself,' he said. 'I've never kidded myself. Or other people, either. The people in the Second District didn't want me to replace Bob. The majority, at least. They didn't want anybody to replace Bob. I told Andy Prior, when I met him the first time: "There's no way I could've whipped him. Your boss had me licked. I think most likely Lyndon Johnson would've beaten him, or else Nguyen Cao Ky, but he didn't live to have that happen, just as he didn't live to beat me, and maybe that was just as well." Bob Wainwright, of course, died on Election Eve; Henry Briggs won by surviving.

" 'I got to like the man myself, once I got to know him,' Briggs said of Wainwright last week, as he reminisced. 'There was many a time that summer, we'd both be at some celebration or another, he'd give his speech and I'd give mine, and then we'd talk awhile. He certainly didn't agree with most of the things I was saying, and most of the things he was saying were the opposite of mine. But I'd buy him a beer or two—Bob was awful close with a dollar—and we'd grab a couple chairs and wipe the sweat off of our faces, and we got to like each other. I never heard him make a crack about me, and he could have done that, if he'd wanted to. "Broken-down baseball player? Running for Congress? The Congress of the United States? We talking about the same thing here?" But he never did that. Bob Wainwright had a lot of class. I think he taught me some.'

"Emily Poitrast seemed to endorse that point of view. 'Well,' she said yesterday, from her home in Washington, 'I think, and I was surprised, I have to say, but I think the one thing that stands out in my mind about the years I worked for Mr. Briggs was that he was the kindest man. Mr. Wainwright had his own style. He was very austere. A nice man, a very nice man, and he'd never do anything in the world to hurt you. But right after he died, well, it wasn't necessary for Mr. Briggs to come down here, talk to us, and tell us he was going to keep us on. If we wanted to, I mean.

" 'And naturally we did. Because he didn't have to keep us on. He could have hired his own people, started over fresh. But he made a special trip down here just to tell us not to worry, that he'd gotten to know Mr. Wainwright, and he'd decided if he liked the man that much he'd probably like his people.

" 'And that made a lot of difference. Most people who've never been here think this is a big snakepit, people fighting all the time. And it's not like that at all. We could have found some other jobs. But here was this man we didn't know, who didn't know the Hill, and he thought we might be worried that we would be out of jobs. So he did a decent thing. I tell you, after that first meeting, I would've killed for him. Even if he did bring his dog in all the time, shedding over everything.'

"Briggs had 'his' dog with him yesterday. Gus is a boxer of majestic demeanor, and he admires his master. But most onlookers thought that Gus preferred his mistress, Caroline Briggs. Forthright as usual, Mrs. Briggs confirmed this. 'Of course he does,' she said. 'I feed him. All males are alike. They'll hang around with the people who pat them, but the ones they really like are the ones who give them food.'

"Briggs was also reinforced by his daughter, Sally, and his son, Ted—'my bullpen,' as he calls them. Ted manages the Briggs farm in Occident, where he lives with his wife and his mother, and Sally is noncommittal about whether her plans for the future include a move from her post as her father's principal assistant to the chair he's relinquishing now. 'I'll tell you in about three weeks,' she said, and smiled.

"I have known Henry Briggs since 1953, when he broke in with the Red Sox. Our paths crossed often in his later baseball years, and then again when he entered politics. He toiled in the bullpens of a number of bad ball clubs, and I floundered in a number of tedious jobs. Many of the games he won in those days, he also won by surviving. We both came home because we had to—I think it was Robert Frost who described home as the place where when you have to go there, they have to take you in—and we both started new careers. Had Wainwright lived, Hank would not have gotten a shot at a political career; he actually lost that first election to Bob Wainwright, by nearly 11,000 votes.

" 'And you know what my ERA was, when I was playing ball: it was 3.93. Know why it wasn't 3.45, like it was in my good years? Because I threw the ball hard, but when I lost a yard or two, and they got around on me, they put the thing over the fence. I hung around too long. I will not do that again.'

"And I, for my part, prefer not to dwell upon the times that I too have succeeded just by managing to survive. Tony Conigliaro was a certain star back then, but he was hit on the temple by a pitch in 1967, and later had a stroke. Tony died this year. Scott Pokaski, who covered Hank's first campaign, is still missing in action. Somewhere in Vietnam, after all these years.

"But we are still here, and so is the country. And now it is time to cede, as Henry Briggs has decided to do, control of matters to the next generation. He put it well himself:

" 'My first political victory wasn't much different than most of the ones I picked up in ballparks. I did some pitching after someone else'd done some pitching, but things worked out so that while I was putting in my share, someone else chipped in with some offense, so that when it was over, *I* got the credit for the victory in the record book. Okay, that's the way the systems work: Someone has to get the credit, someone has to take the blame. But the reality's different: The other guys on the team had just as much or more to do with getting us a win as I had more or less to do with us taking a loss in the games where the other team won. So how many victories are there in a game or an election? Probably, I think, as many as there are people who took part. So who knows what victories really are, then? What they mean, if they mean anything? The only thing that matters is that we were all there when it happened, and now when we look back at it, it seems like it was probably worth the try. It must have been, or we wouldn't all've done it.'

"Twice a week since last March I've enjoyed Donna Taunton's column in this space, a pleasure that I hope continues for many, many more. *Ave, atque vale.*"